HUNTRESS

LIFE AFTER

BOOK ONE

HUNTRESS

LIFE AFTER

BOOK ONE

JULIE HALL

Julie Hall

www.JulieHallAuthor.com

Cover design by Amalia Chitulescu. Interior artwork by Kalynne Pratt.

CONTENTS

AWARDS

Finalist, Speculative Fiction
Huntress
2018 ACFW Carol Awards

Young Adult Book of the Year
Huntress
2018 Christian Indie Awards

Gold Medal Winner
Huntress
2018 Illumination Awards

First Place Winner, Religion
Huntress
2018 IndieReader Discovery Awards

Christian Fiction Finalist

Huntress
2018 Next Generation Indie Book Awards

Alliance Award (Reader's Choice)
Warfare
2018 Realm Makers Awards

Parable Award Finalist
Logan
2018 Realm Makers Awards

Gold Medal Winner
Huntress
2017 The Wishing Shelf Book Awards

Best Inspirational Novel / Best Debut Author
Huntress / Julie Hall
2017 Ozarks Indie Book Festival

Second Place Winner
Huntress
2017 ReadFree.ly Indie Book of the Year

First Place Winner
Huntress
2012 Women of Faith Writing Contest

USA TODAY Bestselling Author
August 17, 2017 & June 21, 2018

PRAISE AND REVIEWS

The romance is sweet, mysterious, frustrating, and perfect. With fantastic world-building, Julie Hall has created an interesting and desirable afterlife. I love the unique take on angels, demons, and the life after death. Characters are relatable: Audrey, flawed and confused, but also filled with untapped strength; Logan, strong and swoon-worthy. Enough action and mystery to keep me flipping the pages.

Jaymin Eve
USA Today bestselling author
of *The Walker Saga* and
Supernatural Prison series

Julie Hall is destined to be one of the great fiction writers of our time. Not since Frank Peretti has an author had the writing genius to weave together spiritual and physical worlds into a believable epic journey.

Rebecca Hagelin
columnist with *The Washington Times*;
author of *30 Ways in 30 Days to Save Your Family*

Huntress will have you holding your breath and falling in love. Beautifully creative! Julie Hall expertly weaves an action-packed plot and swoon-worthy romance with powerful, heartfelt themes of love, family, forgiveness, and redemption.

Kelly Oram
author of *The Supernaturals* series
and the *Jamie Baker Trilogy*

Julie has created a world so imaginative and exciting that I can't help but want to be there. In Audrey, Julie Hall has given readers a heroine who is strong, vulnerable, and relatable. This book creates a safe place to ask questions, but also shows us we will not always get the answers we want. The adventure is in moving ahead, in faith, even without them.

Catherine Parks
author of *A Christ-Centered Wedding*

Huntress is absolutely charming, imaginative, and sweet. It is a fast-paced, original, and intriguing story.

Susan Elllingburg
senior writer for Women Of Faith

PROLOGUE

The chains rattled when he changed positions, grinding against both flesh and floor. Chains so familiar you'd think he'd be used to them by now. He wasn't. Whether standing in his tower, as he was now, or roaming grasslands and streets, his illusion of freedom was always only that—an illusion.

He ground his teeth in anger.

The misshapen messenger who'd interrupted his musings did not even bear looking at. His contempt for it and its companions was almost as strong as his contempt for *them*. The chosen ones. Those inferior beings created with limited sight and innumerable weaknesses. He was sick of watching them fumble around in the dark with the freedom he deserved.

"What is it?"

"We think we have something. Something new our spies have discovered." The creature's voice was thick and oily, with barely a wisp of its former cadence.

"What exactly would that be?"

"We think it may be what you've been waiting for."

His interest was piqued, if only marginally. Numerous false reports over time had dulled his curiosity.

"Go on."

"An ancient weapon has awakened—a double-edged sword that blazes to life at a touch. It's been witnessed to penetrate even to the division of the soul and spirit."

"The cherubim sword?"

"We believe so."

The creature had his full attention now. His shackles marred the ground as he walked briskly to look down over his domain.

"Who wields the weapon?"

"A mere girl."

He was surprised. Then his eyes narrowed. Why give that much power to someone so feeble? He would have to verify the findings himself. If the news was correct, this could be it— what he'd been searching for. Something this important couldn't be trusted to his slaves.

"Where is she now?"

The creature had the sense to look nervous. It shuffled its feet and brought its body lower. As if groveling could assure protection from his master's wrath.

"Sh—she's no longer here. She's been taken back up."

Red anger flashed in his eyes. Fools, all of them! The messenger scurried out of reach. He turned back to look over the expanse. The pathetic being wasn't worth the energy it would take to destroy it.

"You will tell me the moment she returns."

"Yes, of course."

The creature hadn't been dismissed, but it took the opportunity to quietly back away. He didn't notice or care. After all this time, could it be that a mere girl would be the key to his freedom? Oh, the irony.

He smiled to himself. Deceiving a girl had been the start of his imprisonment. Perhaps it would also be the end.

1

IN THE
BEGINNING

"*O*of!"

Air exploded from my lungs as I hit the ground and rolled. I wish I could say I saw my life flash before my eyes, but I didn't. In fact, my eyes were squeezed shut. My body jostled painfully with each lumpy impact. Through the noise I heard a name being yelled. A desperate sound. I wanted to respond, but I couldn't find my voice. My nostrils stung, and there was a metallic taste in my mouth. I tried to spit it out. Something warm dripped down my chin.

And as suddenly as it began, everything stopped. My body was no longer moving. The silence was deafening.

After forcing my eyes open, I immediately wished I hadn't. I stood in nothing. Startling white all around. Brilliant and soundless.

Without a sense of up or down I stumbled as I tried to take a step forward. Turning in a shaky circle, the breath in my chest hitched. I dropped to my knees, patting the space before me, and my hands began to sink—down and down until I pitched forward and my down was up. My arms stretched to their limits and I found myself reaching into the space above my head rather than below my feet.

Where was I? How had I gotten here? I was about to grasp something important, but with a sudden whoosh the memories were yanked from my mind. Tendrils of my consciousness reached out to haul them back, but returned with emptiness . . . a mirror of my surroundings.

One memory remained, standing out like a lone star in a black night. A jar of pickles on a black granite countertop. A memory that made something inside me prickle with anger even as I wondered why. But everything else was simply gone. Every other memory gone, as if it had never been there. As if *I had never been.*

I was about to lose it. Hysterics bubbling up inside, but before they broke free something caught my eye.

Squinting, I saw something, a dot. It was either very far away or extremely tiny. Without the luxury of surroundings to give it perspective, I wasn't sure which. I blinked—it was barely, but perceptibly, larger. I squeezed my eyes shut and opened them again. Suddenly, not only was there a dot, but the expanse around me had a line.

A horizon.

Relief washed over me. The dot continued to grow in size and began to take shape—a man, I realized. A man with his back to me and partially bent over, moving his arms and hands as if conducting a silent symphony. The more intently I stared, the closer he appeared to be.

His arm arched down in a curve and then back up, and a great crash came from behind me. Spinning around, I gasped.

A mighty sea had appeared, waves smashing against the break. I stood on a cliff, the sea churned below me in a kaleidoscope of blues, and the smell of salty water wafted up, tickling my nostrils until I sneezed.

As I took a step back, something brushed at my ankles. Glancing around my eyes widened. More splendor had sprung out of the nothing. Bright green grass—so lush I could feel its suppleness beneath my feet—covered the ground. I was filled with a sudden yearning to slip off my shoes and sink my toes into its cool softness.

But then the man was inexplicably closer. Close enough to see the color of his brown hair and the medium build of his body. His arms had stopped their quick pace and were instead swaying back and forth to a slower, unheard melody. Stretched out before him was a landscape with trees, fields, and rolling hills dotted with flowers, a pinwheel of colors displayed before my eyes. The salty air mingled with the sweet tang of fresh summer blooms.

My breath caught when I flicked my eyes up and a vivid blue sky burst from horizon to horizon. A magnificent red bird shot through the air with a sweet song, followed by a flock of brightly colored birds echoing the melody. They danced in the air before soaring away and disappearing from view. No sooner had they vanished than a brown streak shot through my peripheral vision. I glanced around in time to see a doe dart out from a cluster of trees and lope, carefree, through the pasture.

Twisting my neck, I peered over my shoulder at the man, who was now standing only an arm's length in front of me. He was focused on something hidden from my view, nodding to himself and humming a tune I couldn't place. I remained where I stood, uncertain; wanting to get his attention but unable to bring myself to move. The strangeness of the whole experience was too overwhelming. Unsure of what to do, I waited, convinced for some unknown reason that the man was also waiting for me.

At last, he straightened and turned to face me. He was just a man. A man with skin darkened from either birth or sun, dressed in dark washed jeans and a smudged white T-shirt. His fingers were tinged with what looked like powder or paint. He brushed one hand over the other and then rubbed them on his jeans. They came up clean. A soft smile of contentment lit his lips.

And then he spoke.

"We've been waiting for you." His baritone was as deep as it was soft.

"You have?" I replied, not even trying to hide my confusion.

He nodded.

"Do I know you or something?"

He shoved his hands in his pocks, smiled pleasantly, and nodded again. "I'm here to welcome you and to show you the way."

"Welcome me where?"

"Welcome you home." It was said simply and without irony. "So welcome home. You can call me Joe."

There was a familiarity in the man's voice that distracted me, but what he was trying to explain was more important. Concentrating hard, I pulled as much of my attention back as possible to reconcile the word 'home' with where I was now. I rolled the word around in my mind, slowly, deliberately. And strangely, I discovered a deep-rooted sense of truth buried inside of me.

"Home." I tested the weight of the word in my mouth. "And . . . you're Joe?"

He just nodded, affording me the time I needed to process what he'd said. His eyes, so dark brown it was hard to see the pupils, appeared young and sharp, even with the faint age lines that sprayed from the corners like rays of sunlight. As with his voice, there was something distracting about his eyes. Something familiar that danced on the edge of my subconscious. I desperately grabbed for it, but it slipped by like water through cracks.

I shook my head to clear my thoughts. Something wasn't clicking. I was unable to shake the feeling that there was truth to what he said, but this place felt completely alien.

"Have I been here before?" I asked.

"No, but this place has been prepared and waiting for you for a long time. From before you even learned the true meaning of home."

How could that be right? I had just watched this place be created from nothing.

"I'm not where I used to be?"

He smiled. "No, you're not," he said gently. "How about I show you around?"

"I suppose . . ." but I paused in apprehension. "But shouldn't I be somewhere else?"

Another gentle smile. "No, I promise you are exactly where you are supposed to be. Not a moment too soon, not a moment too late." He gestured forward. The air sweetened as we retreated from the ocean and through the lush greenery of the world he had just orchestrated.

The grass tickled my ankles as I stole glances at Joe. I had trouble concentrating on his features. I'd look at his hair to memorize the exact shade of brown only to look away a moment later and forget. His build seemed average at first, but with each new look I was convinced he'd grown taller or shrunk to a smaller size. Even his skin seemed to lighten or darken with each glimpse.

Most disorienting of all was the burning familiarity at the edge of my consciousness. Without a memory to search through, it was impossible to place him. Everything about him was so utterly nondescript—even racially ambiguous—it was possible I was trying to remember an entirely different person.

We walked over fields of grass freckled with delicate flowers and through forests of trees that reached impossible heights. We traveled for what might have been hours, or mere minutes, until we stood on the banks of a tranquil river.

"I thought you might be thirsty," he said.

Now that he said the words, I found I was parched. So much so I couldn't get a response out, only nod in agreement.

"Then drink as much as you please." He sat down on the ground and crossed his legs, keeping a watchful eye on me.

I dropped to my knees on the soft bank and cupped my hands to dip them into the water. My insatiable thirst was quenched in a moment. The water was so crisp and fresh I had the wild thought that I'd never be thirsty again—as if the river was flowing inside me. But what felt possible at the time seemed ridiculous when the moment passed.

After drinking my fill, the water calmed, turning into a glassy mirror. I leaned forward eagerly—but the face that rippled on the surface was utterly unfamiliar to me.

I brought a hand to my cheek, and the image in the water did the same. Large, dark brown eyes set in a petite, heart-shaped face, stared back wide-eyed. Equally dark straight hair poured over my shoulder as I leaned closer. It grazed the water's surface and mingled with the reflection, creating an artificial curl in the mirror image. Who was this girl looking back at me? I touched a finger lightly to the surface, and her face distorted from view.

"Would you like to tell me what you are wondering?"

I looked back at the stranger sitting next to me with that unwavering smile on his lips. Now that we weren't moving, his image was once again static. His hair, which hung almost to his shoulders, was a shade darker than my own. Stubble across his face aged what might have been a younger complexion. He appeared to be in his late twenties or thirties, but small physical contradictions prevented a more accurate guess. He was so normal, yet completely atypical at the same time.

"Joe," I once again tested his name on my tongue, "why don't I remember anything? Why don't I remember you if we've met before? Where am I? What happened?"

"Good questions, but perhaps not the right ones. You will remember your life again in time, but for now, you're meant to focus only on this new existence. It would be a distraction to have your memories before you settle into life in the ever after."

He leaned back, resting his weight on his arms. "You now have an eternity to experience."

It was then that I knew—I had died.

It was strange the way my mind and body accepted the fact peacefully, even as I knew I should be feeling something else. Frightened, perhaps? Sad? Angry even? Emotions I told myself to have, yet was incapable of feeling.

"Shall we continue?" Joe asked. He stood, never taking his eyes off me. "There is so much more waiting to be discovered."

I pushed to my feet and we continued along the river's edge. I split my attention between the man and the scenery until a mountain range cut a jagged path through the landscape in the distance. The mountains, with whitened tips, grew before my eyes at a much faster pace than they should have. I looked down to see the land speeding along underneath me with each step. The details of the ground blurred, as if we were traveling too fast for eyes to focus.

Giving up my attempts to make sense of it, I lifted my eyes to a radiant city that had suddenly come into view. Structures nestled snugly within a mass of piney trees at the feet of the mountains. Giant spiraling towers wove their way into the air. Glistening monuments reflected the light in every direction like crystals. Smaller buildings stood proudly at the feet of the others, refusing to be overshadowed, some with milky smooth façades and others with intricately carved corners and trim, all shining brightly.

Both awed and repelled I fumbled a step. Was this where we were headed, and if so, how was I supposed to find a home in a place so splendid, so perfect? Would my own imperfections corrupt its purity?

A chill ran down my spine as a breath caught in my throat. There was movement in the city. People dotted the ground around the magnificent buildings. That changed everything. Maybe someone there could help me understand. The beating in my chest picked up a notch, hammering in my ears. I knew the city was where I was supposed to be.

Below, the river had swelled to a powerful rush, and it stood in my way. I looked to the left and right but couldn't find a bridge in either direction. The water was too ferocious to cross without one.

I glanced at Joe, who was studying me silently.

"Can you help? I don't see a way across."

"And you're sure you want to go forward?"

"Yes, please. I want to see it up close."

He nodded. "Then that is where you shall go."

No sooner were the words out of his mouth than the water split in front of him, and a dry path formed on the riverbed. Not even a droplet of water remained.

He turned to motion me forward.

"Are you scared?" he asked, seeing my hesitation.

"Yes," I admitted. Afraid of not just walking through the waters, but also of what was ahead. The future I was taking a step toward, and the past I was leaving behind.

"You needn't be."

I believed him.

An unexpected thrill of excitement suddenly propelled me to act, curiosity alongside apprehension. Striding forward, I marveled at the dryness of the ground below my feet. The walls of water shot well above my head, yet stood as still as glass as we passed. I stopped to take note of a brightly colored fish, at least the size of my forearm, the O shape of his mouth opening and closing as he watched us in return.

Reaching a finger out, I touched the wall of water. The spooked fish vanished. The tip of my finger started a series of small ripples that caused the wall to undulate wildly.

I looked back at Joe in alarm.

"Not to worry, it'll hold," he said.

Joe stayed next to me during the short walk between waters but stopped just before the river's edge.

"We've traveled together as long as needed. You'll take the next steps on your own."

"But wait!" I was suddenly desperate to stay with the one person I knew. I couldn't navigate the city before me alone. "What will happen to me? Will I see you again?"

He stepped forward and wrapped me in his arms. He quietly said something in my hair—was it "I missed you"?—before he stepped back once again. It was the first time he'd touched me.

"Yes, most certainly you will, Little One. But now you have other things to do."

"But isn't this it? Is this how it ends?"

An easy smile crossed his face, almost as if I'd said something he found amusing. "No, Audrey, this is how it begins."

He reached down to me, touched a hand to my cheek, and in a blink was gone. But he'd left me with something I hadn't had before.

A name.

2

PROCESSED

"*A*udrey?"

I was shaken out of my reverie by that one simple word. The only thing I knew belonged to me.

I fixed my eyes where I thought the voice had come from, but there wasn't anyone there. Instead, across from me and to the right, an open doorway appeared where a smooth white wall had been a moment before.

When I'd taken my first step out of the dry riverbed, it hadn't been onto the soft green grass of the opposite bank as I expected. Instead, I stood alone in a room with four white walls and a glossy, unremarkable plastic chair. The first thing I did was tap the floor with my foot to ensure I was still on solid ground. As I moved the chair across the room, it scraped against the floor with a nails-on-the-chalkboard screech. The normalcy of the sound comforted me. A quick turn confirmed that the room didn't have any doors or windows

Glancing back down at the chair, a note on thick white

parchment paper appeared. The marks on the paper were elegantly written in gold strokes. At first, the large swirls were illegible, but when I tilted the paper, my mind made sense of the characters.

Please take a seat.
We shall be with you shortly for processing.

"Processing," I mumbled under my breath. "What am I? A sheep?"

Without any other options, I folded the paper and put it in the pocket of my pants, before obediently taking a seat. I'd lost awareness of time while trying to get past the jar of pickles and the confusion in my memory, until someone had called my name and the doorway had appeared on the wall across from me.

"Okay, off to processing I go," I said under my breath with a false sense of bravado.

I pushed myself out of the chair and took a few tentative steps forward, just far enough to peer through the opening.

A pretty blonde woman sat behind an oversized mahogany desk with a boxy-looking gray machine mounted on top. Carvings on the panels and legs of the desk depicted battle scenes.

My eyes scanned the carvings as I hesitantly made my way through the doorway. Unfamiliar creatures were frozen in combat. Long and powerful wings spread behind some of them. Many brandished large swords, their faces oddly peaceful even in the midst of such turmoil. Others, with misshapen bodies bent over and twisted at impossible angles, extra appendages that often came to a sharp point, and faces utterly malformed, were sure to give me nightmares for days. That is, if I dreamed anymore. Did dead people dream?

I was still studying the images when the blonde woman cleared her throat. My head snapped up, and I found myself staring at her. She couldn't have been older than mid-thirties, with skin as luminous as porcelain. Her hair was carefully swept back into a loose bun at the nape of her neck. What appeared to be a forgotten pencil stuck out of it.

Blondie made another sound with her throat, and I realized I had missed something.

"Oh, I'm sorry," I said, forcing myself to pay attention to the words coming out of her mouth. Was she glowing?

"Don't worry about it, sugar. It happens all the time," she drawled with a Southern accent as smooth and sweet as honey. She smiled at me. "It's a big adjustment. Why don't you come all the way in and sit down for a moment while we get your assignment figured out?"

I didn't know what she was talking about, but I smiled and nodded anyway as I pulled out the only chair in front of her— an underwhelming black plastic one. "Um, I'm sorry. My assignment?"

"Yes, of course. What you learned about in orientation, dear." She smiled patiently back at me.

"Orientation?"

"Yes, orientation." A wrinkle of concern appeared between her brows. "You did come here from orientation, didn't you?"

I didn't like that she sounded so unsure. "No, I mean, I don't think so. I've been in the white room ever since I crossed the river."

Blondie's eyebrows shot up, and I could swear she glowed

even brighter. I twisted my head up to see if a spotlight or something was adding to the effect.

"Really? Well, that is rather . . . unusual."

Her reaction gave me the urge to hop up on the desk and start demanding answers, but instead I sat rooted in place, patiently waiting to be herded to the next thing. Everything was so surreal.

Whatever was so "unusual," she recovered from it quicker than I did. The soothing tone returned to her voice. "We'll get this all figured out in a snap. But to give you the abridged version, this is where you come to get your working assignment for eternity."

One heartbeat, then another.

"I'm going to have the same job, like, forever? And I get *assigned* . . . as in, I don't get a choice?"

"Yes, of course you'll have the same job for eternity, but it's nothing to worry about. Everyone gets the right one." She said that as if it would make everything all better, and then continued without giving me the opportunity to respond.

"Let's move forward, shall we? Can I ask you your name, sugar?"

"Audrey."

"Can you tell me how old you were?"

I didn't know. I looked across the gleaming desk at the woman. She stared back at me patiently. Then suddenly there was a sound in my head like a cork being released from a bottle, and my brain supplied the information.

"Eighteen." That surprised me. I thought the reflection in the river had looked younger than that.

"And Audrey, dear, can you tell me how you died?"

Finally, the words struck me with emotion. I bit back tears, making a mental note that you could still cry when you're dead.

"I'm not sure," I whispered.

I didn't miss the softening of her eyes. "That's okay, sugar bear. Sometimes it takes some extra time to get caught up."

I nodded numbly, not knowing how to respond.

She reached forward to give my hand a reassuring squeeze. Her touch was more than just warm; it spread a feeling of goodwill throughout my body. It was both soothing and disconcerting at the same time. I pulled my hand back. I didn't want to feel either of those emotions.

Blondie gave me a small smile as if to say she understood before focusing her attention on the boxy object in front of her, which looked almost like a large, very outdated computer monitor. She worked for a few moments without looking up at me, her raised fingers moving quickly and silently over the screen. But that was the side I couldn't see, so I really didn't know what she was doing.

Finally she said, "Oh, here we go, it's coming up now."

Even though I had no idea what was going on, I held my breath in anticipation.

"Oh dear," she murmured.

I let the breath I had been holding escape in a loud rush. She looked more flustered than when she'd found out I'd skipped orientation. The nervous itch returned. What I read on her face was a mixture of concern and confusion. That couldn't be good.

She suddenly remembered I was still there and tried to wipe the look from her face, replacing it with a mask of calm assurance.

"Well, if you'll excuse me a moment, dear. I need to go get someone. I'll be back in no time."

I nodded since my throat had gone dry. Blondie gracefully lifted her willow frame from her chair and pressed her hand to the white wall behind her. A door swung open, one I hadn't even realized was there. It shut soundlessly behind her.

The slight nervousness that had started in the pit of my stomach spread and grew into a near panic as I waited for her. I looked around the room to get my mind off what was happening, but it was empty. All white walls, no pictures hung. Besides the desk, which stood like a monolith in the white drenched room, there was a gray table behind me and black chairs lining the walls. Ordinary office furniture. After a few minutes I gave up trying to distract myself and started gnawing on one of my fingernails. This was crazy. I mean, after you're dead, what kind of administrative mix-ups could there really be? Was I not supposed to have died? Could I have been sent to the wrong place somehow? If so, was I going to be sent back? And what was up with skipping orientation?

I was torturing myself with ideas of where I was *really* supposed to be when the door in the wall magically appeared again, admitting another woman, tall, with raven hair swept up in a high, tight bun and a no-nonsense look on her face. She moved briskly toward the desk. Blondie was on her heels, talking quickly as if I wasn't even there.

"It's just so *unusual* that I thought I should check with someone else before processing her."

The words "unusual" and "processing" stuck like knots in my stomach.

"I mean, I know mistakes in the assignments don't happen, but look at her."

Blondie gave me an apologetic smile. I couldn't help but feel a little offended even though I had no idea what she was talking about.

The second woman had her eyes glued to the machine and gave no indication she was listening to Blondie whatsoever.

She finally spoke. "I understand you wanting to verify, but He doesn't make mistakes. She's been assigned." She looked up from the machine to fix me squarely with a grim stare. Whatever the screen said, she wasn't too happy about it. "I'll take her from here, Celeste."

Blondie looked relieved. "Oh well, yes, that would probably be for the best." She glanced at me with worried eyes. "Don't worry, Audrey, you'll be in very good hands with Shannon."

Shannon smoothly rose from the chair. "Audrey, you can come with me now."

Her words might have made it sound as if I had a choice, but her tone confirmed that I did not. I took a deep breath and rose from the chair. I gave Celeste one last look before following Shannon out the door. I think she mouthed, "Good luck," but I couldn't be sure. My spirit fell even further when the door clicked shut behind me.

3

THE JOB ETERNAL

Ten minutes later, Shannon held a door open for me as I stepped past her and into a room jammed full of people—and not just anyone. The room was packed wall-to-wall with huge, well-muscled guys! My stomach dropped. I'd been mistakenly drafted by the afterlife division of the NFL. This had to be a mistake.

Shannon placed a firm hand on my back and nudged me further into the room. I tried in vain not to gawk at the scene around me. Beefed-up guys sat conversing around twenty-five round tables. The atmosphere felt relaxed, almost like a break room. I couldn't pick up full conversations as we wove our way through the room, so my mind worked overtime inventing some of my own.

Hey man, what did you do today? the guy in the skintight purple T-shirt that said "I ROCK" on the front would say. And the dude on his left would answer in a deep, Schwarzenegger-esque accent, *I picked things up and put them down.*

We reached the other side without stopping to talk to anyone. Shannon placed her palm on the wall and produced another hidden door.

From my limited view behind Shannon's head, it appeared to be a gym of some kind. Not even the high-decibel manly noises coming from behind me drowned out the unmistakable sound of metal on metal. Shannon stepped to the side. That's when I saw, on the far end of the gym, two fighters locked in a death match. They were bearing down on each other so quickly I could hardly distinguish the movements. The source of the sound was the thick, heavy swords they were fighting with.

One of the fighters jumped high into the air and landed at least two body lengths from where he'd been standing, narrowly escaping a blow aimed at his shins. I gasped. A move like that wasn't humanly possible!

The fighters, wearing silvery, sleek body armor, didn't miss a beat as they bore down on each other with a series of quick blows. The movements blurred with their speed, the sound of the swords meeting deafening.

I gasped again when one of the opponents swung his sword in an arc and nearly took off the head of the other, who ducked and rolled just quickly enough to avoid decapitation. If this was a sparring session of some sort, it must have gotten out of hand. I looked up at Shannon anxiously. Surely someone should stop this!

Her face was a mask of calm, mixed perhaps with a bit of impatience. One of the fighters took advantage of an unsteady moment to get his opponent to one knee. He was just about to deliver a final blow when Shannon loudly cleared her throat. Both fighters froze. Shannon smiled coolly at them and said, "Logan, may I have a word with you?"

The fighter who had the advantage took a step back and lowered his sword.

"Sure, Shannon, just give me a sec," he said, not sounding nearly as out of breath as I thought he should. He reached an armored hand down to give his opponent a hand up. Not a bit of malice remained in their movements.

Logan shook the hand of his opponent, who was quite a bit bigger in both height and girth, and gave him a friendly pat on the back. They said something to each other I couldn't make out and chuckled before parting. The other guy gave Shannon a wave and a nod before pushing through a different set of doors.

As Logan moved toward us, his armor began to evaporate. First, his shin and shoe guards melted into the air, revealing brown sandals and dark-washed jeans. Then the metal covering his arms and hands disappeared, followed by his breastplate, uncovering a T-shirt that read "Hunters Rule, Demons Drool." He was leaner than the guys back in the break room, but still muscular. Last, his helmet evaporated. He looked younger than I expected . . . perhaps only a few years older than me. But who knew if age really meant anything here.

Shifting my weight I craned my neck to the left, trying to make sense of where his armor had just gone, peering around him as if it might magically appear somewhere behind him.

I was still gaping when he stopped a few feet short of Shannon and me. "Hey Shannon, what's up?"

He glanced my way with only a mildly curious look. I wasn't certain if I should be offended or relieved.

"Actually, I've brought you a new trainee."

Logan tilted his chin up to scan the area behind us. I turned my head as well to see who he was looking at.

"Oh yeah, that's great! Where is he?"

Shannon gave me a firm prod. Unprepared for the push and still gaping at Logan, I stumbled forward.

"Here *she* is," Shannon said with a smile.

Logan's eyes opened wider, and this time he *really* looked at me. He had dark blond hair, on the longer side and tousled, with wild highlights throughout, the type you get from too much time spent in the water and sun. His eyes started at my feet and slowly moved up my body until they locked with mine. Under the scrutiny, I registered that his eyes were a deep cobalt blue. It reminded me of the color of the ocean on a sunny day. The intensity of his stare embarrassed me. Heat rose to my face but was trapped in his gaze. I felt judged.

Without releasing my eyes, he addressed Shannon. His words came out deliberately, with an icy edge.

"You have got to be kidding me."

His tone sent a chill down my spine, which actually helped combat the warming of my cheeks. That was the final straw.

I broke his stare and pivoted on my heel. I'd had enough of all of this. Muttering to myself about how crazy this all was, I marched purposefully toward the door. I didn't care if there were a zillion muscle dudes on the other side, I just wanted out.

Before my fourth step, Shannon was in front of me. In fact, she appeared so quickly I walked right into her, bounced off, and landed on my butt. Dang, how'd she get there so fast? She appeared to be glowing but was no longer smiling. She looked over my head at Logan.

"You know we don't make mistakes about these things. There is a reason for this."

"She'll be eaten alive out there. Just look at her, Shannon."

Shannon glanced at me, sitting there on my butt, before looking back up at Logan. A shadow of doubt crossed her face but was gone almost as quickly as it had appeared. Eaten alive. How was that even possible when you were already dead?

"Logan, it is what it is. You've been chosen as her mentor. You need to train her as you would anyone else."

Neither of them spoke. I looked back and forth between the two. Then Logan asked with slightly narrowed eyes, "Is this because of what happened?"

Shannon's features softened perceptibly.

"No, Logan, this isn't some sort of punishment. You know things don't work like that here." Her voice was quiet but still strong when she continued, "What do you think they said about Romona when she first joined?"

Logan let out a deep sigh. There seemed to be some silent communication, a faceoff, going on between those two. Shannon must have won, because after a few minutes her calm, cool smile returned.

"Thank you, Logan. I'll leave her with you now. You know what to do." The words sunk in fast as she turned to go.

"Wh-what?" My speech was stuttered as I scrambled up to stop her. In my rush I lost my footing again and ended up half-running, half-crawling after her. When the door shut behind her, it occurred to me how pathetic I must look. I struggled to my feet and stared at the door.

Indecision about whether to run after her or turn around and face my fate, kept me rooted in place. I was equally torn between wanting to shout at someone or break down crying.

What in the world was going on? Whatever I might have thought the afterlife would look like, it surely wasn't this.

I inhaled a deep breath to steady myself. There was no use getting too upset until I found out what sort of job I had been assigned to anyway. Could it really be that bad?

So far, Logan hadn't made any attempt to talk to me. For all I knew, he wasn't even still there. I squeezed my eyes shut and let the air escape my lungs. When I opened them and turned, Logan was exactly where he had been when I attempted to make my grand exit. He was either giving me time or didn't know what to say, so I took control of the moment. At the very least, I needed to try to pull back some of the dignity I'd already lost.

I plopped my hands on my hips and let out a breath. "Okay, so will you at least tell me what exactly it is that we do?"

Logan looked me straight in the eyes and said, "We kill demons."

I saw his eyes, heard the words, and then everything went black.

I had never fainted before in my whole life. At least, I was pretty sure I hadn't. But when I came to, I knew exactly what had happened—it wasn't like the movies when someone slowly wakes up, looks around, and asks "What happened?" in a calm and sleepy voice. Nope, I woke up into full awareness and total embarrassment. And it hurt! My left shoulder was throbbing, my arm was crossed in front of my chest at a weird angle, and my face was squished into the floor but didn't hurt. If I stayed like that much longer, my arm and face were likely to fall asleep.

I considered pretending I was still out cold. Maybe if I stayed on the floor long enough Logan would just go away, or better yet, I'd magically be back in the real world.

Deciding I couldn't just stay there, I rolled onto my back with a groan. Logan was standing directly above me looking down. He had a look on his face that might possibly be concern. And then he opened his mouth to speak, and I learned what really worried him.

"Do you do that often?"

Irritated, I sat up, ignoring the question. That was as much of a dignified stance as I could muster considering the circumstances. I needed a little more time before getting to my feet.

I took a moment to scrutinize the gym more closely. Logan's fight had completely monopolized my attention earlier, and I was beginning to notice all the details I'd missed. It was a small gym with high ceilings. Three of the walls were nondescript and gray. The left wall stood out, as it was lined floor to ceiling and end to end with more hand weapons than I had ever imagined even existed. Some I had never seen before. They had odd angles and sharp edges and looked menacing enough that I hoped to never touch them.

I didn't want to think about the weapons. I didn't want to think about what they were supposed to wound.

The floor beneath me was black and slightly squishy. I reached down to poke it with my index finger, which left an indentation for a moment before smoothing over. I spent a few more moments than was necessary poking at the spongy ground. It was time to stand and face the music, or in this case, Logan.

He was silent while I mentally and physically pulled myself together. I didn't have to wonder if he was still there; I felt his stare boring into my back. He didn't offer to help me up.

Stumbling at first, I managed to get to my feet and turned to face him. He was leaning against the wall with one foot crossed over the other, arms folded over his chest like he had all the time in the world. His hair was still tousled, but in just the right way to make you wonder if it was styled or just messy. His eyes were slightly narrowed, sizing me up, but the rest of his expression was closed off.

"Okay." He pushed himself off the wall, apparently having made up his mind about something. "I guess we should at least get you settled."

He walked straight toward me and then straight past me. He didn't say so, but I assumed I was supposed to follow him, so I did. Heading down a long gray hallway, we passed a number of doors with strange sounds emanating from most—swords clashing, maybe somebody practicing martial arts or just listening to a Bruce Lee movie really loudly. I scurried past one door that vibrated with the roaring noises coming from within. None of this fazed Logan, who forged ahead as if I wasn't there.

Logan stopped suddenly in front of a door and pushed it open. The light from the other side was so bright it stung my eyes. I blinked a few times. We were outside. It was beautiful.

We'd exited a building on the edge of the glistening city, but it was the mountain range before us that completely captured my attention. Tipped with white snow and rising from a base of lush green forest, the sight truly took my breath away. Moments passed before my gaze dipped lower. Laid out before me were streets and sidewalks to the left and green space to the right. There were people everywhere! Briskly zigzagging around each other to my left and relaxing, playing, and running in the fields and courts on my right. There were young people and old people and every age, shape, size, and nationality.

I followed Logan as he walked straight into the masses and headed for a sidewalk that appeared to skirt the city. At his brisk pace I had to pick up my own to keep up.

To the right was a small field with people playing a game I didn't recognize. A few shouted greetings to Logan. He nodded or gave short waves in response. Straight above us was a crystalline blue sky, free of any clouds or imperfections. It was so clear, in fact, that I noticed the absence of the sun, despite the overwhelming amount of light all around.

Apparently I stared up too long, because when my eyes lowered, I wasn't following Logan anymore. I turned in a quick circle and spotted him to the left. *Whoops! No time for sight seeing I guess. Time for a quick jog.* When I caught back up, he either didn't notice I had been missing or didn't care. Both possibilities irked me. It wouldn't kill him to be a little sensitive to my situation. But instead of saying anything, we walked along in silence. Him leading and me following behind like a little duckling.

"Quack."

"What's that?" Logan turned his head.

"Nothing." I hadn't meant to say that out loud. Logan didn't press it, just rolled his eyes and refocused his attention forward.

There was too much to take in to be annoyed at Logan for long. Leaving the sidewalk, we veered off on a stone pathway that led us toward the mountains and trees and past small meadows of brilliantly colored flowers, winding brooks with water as clear as glass, and familiar yet oddly misplaced things like ice skating rinks and sledding hills next to swimming pools and skateboard parks. As we walked, the tall spirals and buildings became smaller, and the forest before us captured my full attention.

Trees soared hundreds of feet in the air, wider than small skyscrapers. It was only when we reached the wooded edge that I realized just how enormous they really were. We were like grasshoppers standing next to them.

Logan put his hand to the trunk of a tree, and for a moment, it looked like the bark was melting off. Reds and browns merged together and streamed down to pool at Logan's feet. With a poof, the melting bark evaporated, and a shiny brown door appeared on the side of the tree.

Logan reached for the doorknob without hesitation. It registered with me that this should be completely insane, but after what had happened in only the past few hours, it wasn't the strangest thing by far. I considered staying outside longer just to see if he'd notice but decided against it. He most likely didn't care, and I was too curious about what was inside that massive tree to wait.

We entered a corridor. The walls were uneven and dark brown like dirt. It was slightly musty inside, and the humidity made the air feel sticky. Whatever they used for lighting wasn't working very well, because I had to wait for my eyes to adjust before I could see much.

About ten feet in front of me, Logan moved gracefully and quickly through the corridor. I reached my fingers out to lightly touch one of the walls. It felt soft and mossy. I held the fingers up to inspect them, but the tree wall had left no residue.

Still examining my fingers, I walked right into Logan's back. He barely budged, but I bounced off of him like a basketball and rebounded into the wall. Luckily the mossy texture had some cushion, so it didn't hurt as much as it could have. No words of concern from Logan, of course. He simply glanced over his shoulder and then held his hand up to the wall much the same way he'd done to the tree trunk. This time a white door materialized out of the brown. He stepped back and finally looked at me.

"Here it is," he said.

"Here *what* is?"

Logan shrugged. "You know, your room."

I stared at him incredulously. "You mean I live in a tree?"

One corner of his mouth quirked up in amusement. "Don't worry, it's not forever. And you'll get used to it after a while."

And with that, he turned and headed back the way we'd just come. No good-bye, no see ya later, no instructions or explanations. He just left. And despite the million questions I should have asked him, my mind had gone completely blank. I was too overwhelmed for a quick retort. I mean, was someone coming back to get me? Was I supposed to know what to do next? How long was I going to have to stay in this tree?

When I couldn't see Logan's retreating figure anymore, my body finally unfroze. I peered at the white door. It was so smooth. Could it be plastic rather than wood? How stupid would it be to live in a tree and have the door be made out of something other than wood? I gave myself a mental shake. *Pull it together girl!* Gripping the white handle I slowly opened the door.

The room was white. Utterly and completely white. So white it caused a bout of déjà vu, as if I stood in the nothingness once more. The walls were the same color as the floor, and it didn't look like there was anything else to the room. I was alone in a big white room . . . again. What the heck?

Taking slow and steady steps forward I hesitantly reached for one of the walls, afraid it might be padded like at an insane asylum. Something mechanical clicked at my touch. My feet tangled from my hasty retreat as a bed slid out from the wall. It was white too.

At least I now knew the dead still slept. Judging by the serene whiteness of the room, it must be true they even rested in peace. A little giggle escaped my lips. Okay, that wasn't an appropriate or even a good joke, but I was a little slaphappy at this point. I sat on the bed, unsure whether I wanted to touch another wall to see if anything else would pop out. The bed felt soft and luxurious, but how was anyone supposed to sleep with all this light?

The moment I thought it, the room went pitch black.

Okay, that was creepy, I thought. *I think I preferred the lights on.*

They came back on.

My brows furrowed. *Hmmm, let's try that again.*

I thought lights off, and the room darkened. I thought lights on, and they came on again. *Well, that is definitely cooler than The Clapper,* I thought with another chuckle.

I lay back on the bed, staring straight up at the white ceiling. How was it I could remember The Clapper but not anything about my life? I tried to catalog what I did know: The Clapper. That Logan's highlights came from time in the sun. I knew facts and details of things on Earth, I just couldn't pull up any personal memories. I remembered peanut butter but didn't know if I liked it, hated it, or was allergic to it. I remembered actors and movies and TV shows, but I didn't remember when I had seen them or whom I was with. I couldn't make sense of any of it.

Lying on the bed made me realize I was beyond exhausted. When had that come on? I curled up into the fetal position with my eyes still open. I tried in vain to feel bad about what I had left behind, but instead, I found myself aggravated that I couldn't remember what exactly that was. Exhaustion pulled at me, and I wasn't able to hold onto my frustration for long.

Just before I nodded off, I remembered to think *lights off,* and everything went dark.

4

TRACKING

I was awakened by a knock at the door. On the second knock, I sat up so hastily I almost tumbled out of bed. *Lights on*, I thought quickly, and the room was drenched in white. I shut my eyes against the sudden change. Another knock sounded at the door.

I rolled out of bed, free of bedding because I hadn't bothered to get under any. Was it Shannon or Logan? I hesitated a moment before reaching for the knob. I couldn't decide which option I preferred.

When I opened the door, a girl around my age but taller, with warm brown eyes and a wide, friendly smile stood on the other side. Some of my tension eased.

"Hi, I'm Romona." She waved, then reached out for a handshake.

When our hands met, I sucked in a sharp breath and immediately snatched mine back, protectively holding it to my chest as if injured. It had happened so quickly it was difficult to make sense of—as if a feeling of warmth, salted with pity and concern, had spread from our connected hands and through my body. I glared accusingly at Romona. Her dark brows furrowed, then smoothed a moment later.

"Oh, right, the empathy link. You must not know about that yet. Whenever our skin touches, we get an impression of the other person's emotions." She brought her hands together to demonstrate. "I know it's a little odd at first, but you'll get used to it after a while. Well, most people do at least."

I regarded her warily. "And what if you don't get used to it?"

She gave a slight shrug. "Then you just get used to not touching anyone, I suppose."

Ha, I thought, *just like that, huh?*

"Anyway," she went on, "I wanted to come introduce myself and see if you wanted any company on the way back to the training center today. I know it takes some time to get used to things around here, especially with all those guys." She rolled her eyes with a lopsided grin. "Logan was supposed to get you, but when I heard you were here, I asked if I could instead. I'm a little excited to have another girl in the ranks. And . . ." she swiftly bent to retrieve a small white bag at her feet and held it proudly out in front of her, "I brought you some breakfast!"

I was still trying to figure her out. "Are you a . . . um . . . you know, one of them?"

"A hunter? That's right! We few girls need to stick together!"

I released a breath I hadn't intended to hold. "I'm *so* glad I'm not the only girl."

"I'm getting the feeling they didn't explain much to you, did they?"

I could have cried with relief at being understood. "Everything has been pretty vague so far. I didn't even know what I was supposed to do when I woke up today. So I guess I should say thanks for coming to get me. And for breakfast too."

"Of course! Can I come in?"

"Oh yeah, sorry." I stepped aside to let her through the doorway.

She glided into the room, making a quick turn to take in all the whiteness. I wondered if the floor made her dizzy too. Within seconds the room filled with the pleasant aroma of whatever she had in her bag.

Romona sat on the end of the white bed. Her skin, the color of a light latte, stood out in contrast to the starkness of the room. Her hair, a shade of brown-black, was braided in a plait that fell over her shoulder and almost down to her waist. Her brown eyes sparkled with excitement. She was trying hard to keep herself in check as her folded hands, resting on her knees, bounced up and down with the jiggling of her legs.

Finally, she couldn't wait any longer. "So how long have you been here?"

"Oh, just a day. I got, uh, here yesterday. I think. Are there still days here?"

"Yep. And they already have you training? Gee whiz, that's fast."

"Really? How does it usually work?"

"There's not really a 'usually' about it. Everyone is different. But most of the time they give people time to adjust. I suppose there is a reason to throw you right in."

That wasn't reassuring. Sensing she'd said something wrong, her face fell. She continued quickly. "But that's *better*, because it means you get to acclimate yourself to being a hunter that much faster. And you'll get to meet people and train right away."

The smile on her face looked plastered on. It was obvious she was trying hard to make me feel better. I plastered on my own smile in return.

"Well, I guess that's a good thing then. So what am I supposed to be doing this morning?"

"Oh right!" She jumped up from the bed. "I'm supposed to be taking you to your first day of training. Would you like to change into your training clothes?"

I looked down at myself. I was wearing camel-colored flats, dark-washed skinny jeans, and a couple layers of purple-hued tank tops. I didn't know what was appropriate for training, but it was safe to assume this wasn't it. Romona, in tight-fitting Spandex and sporty shoes, looked ready for a five-mile run. I did not.

"Um, I guess so?"

Her eyes sparkled. "Let's get you ready for your first day of training!" She put her hands on one of the white walls, which split apart to reveal a wardrobe.

Only a few other people were at the training center early. I was pleased—I wanted a moment to get my bearings. I was grateful for Romona. Not only had she fed me and shown me the secret closet, but she'd given me a brief tour of the facility.

The training center was even larger than I had imagined. There were four main gyms for general use. Each was almost as large as a football field, with a wide array of machines, weights, and weapons. Never-ending hallways led to smaller individual training gyms.

Romona explained that a hunter is always either in training or training someone else. She was working with another new recruit, as she called him. I briefly wondered how he was handling being trained by a girl. Although the way Logan had shut up after the mention of her name yesterday, I imagined Romona had a reputation for holding her own.

Apparently, the first few weeks of training for a newbie were the most intense, something about shocking the body into becoming a fighting machine. Nothing about that appealed to me.

I now sat alone in the middle of the training gym waiting for Logan. Even with my workout clothes on, I felt incredibly out of place. My mind wandered to what I must have done to be assigned this type of occupation in the afterlife. Was it possible I was in a gang or something? If so, I would bet I had some crazy street moves buried somewhere in my memory. I glanced over at the weapons wall. Was I a championship fencer or archer? There had to be *some* special skill I possessed or they wouldn't have let me in here, right?

I chewed a fingernail as I let my eyes browse the room. Weights and punching bags. Slightly padded floor; no windows unless you counted the small ones at the top of the doors that let out into the hallway. Everything looked pretty normal, that is, except for that massive wall of weapons.

Wanting a closer look I pushed myself off the mat. The wall was without a doubt the most interesting part of the gym. There were swords and knives of all different shapes and sizes, bows and funny-looking arrows, and ninja-type weapons like nunchakus and fighting sticks. It was obvious all these weapons were fashioned for men. Most of them looked extremely heavy and sharp, and were larger than the width of my arm. I tried to visualize wielding one with confidence, but I couldn't imagine using them with any sort of ease. I was fascinated, but I didn't feel a stirring familiarity that would suggest I had been into any of this stuff when I was alive.

I stopped in front of the collection of swords. Unable to restrain myself, I tentatively picked up one of the heavier-looking blades, holding the handle in both hands. The sharp blade on this sword was slightly curved and wider than most of the others—wide enough to see my reflection.

Dark eyes stared back at me—eyes that should have been familiar but weren't. Brows slightly raised in surprise. They were delicate and evenly shaped, a few shades deeper than the dark brown hair pulled back in a ponytail. The eyes were a rich brown color. Not dark enough to look black but not light enough to be hazel. More like a deep walnut. The nose was small with a slight slope and sat in the middle of a heart-shaped face that was completely nonthreatening. I tried to memorize the contours of the stranger's face in the reflection.

The sound of the gym door being thrown open made me jump. I dropped the sword and let out a short, high-pitched scream. I immediately clamped a hand to my mouth to stop the painfully girlie sound. The sword narrowly missed my foot, embedding itself in the soft floor of the gym.

Two sets of eyes watched me from the gym's entrance. Their faces telling. One friendly if not mildly curious, and the other annoyed.

Logan, the annoyed one, spoke first. "You shouldn't be touching those. You could hurt yourself."

In contrast, the guy standing next to him wore a wide grin.

Tall, broad-shouldered, and Viking-like in appearance, he stuck out his hand. I extended mine and was slightly unnerved as his emotions rushed in. At least now I knew why he was grinning—it wasn't so much out of friendliness as amusement. He gave my hand a good shake and then let go. His hand was so large it was like shaking hands with a bear. I had to crane my neck to look up at his face.

"Hi there, my name is Alrik. I didn't get the pleasure of introducing myself yesterday."

Yesterday? He must have been the one training with Logan. I took Alrik in again as he pulled the sword out of the mat and returned it to its place. Sandy blond hair fell to his shoulders. With a jolt, I realized that with a name like Alrik he might actually *be* a Viking. When he straightened, he turned toward Logan, who was tall but didn't come close to Alrik's semi-giant stature.

"See, no problem here, Logan. You don't have to pout over there like a baby."

Alrik turned back to me with a grin large enough to say he knew exactly which of Logan's buttons he was pushing. He bent closer to me and whispered, "Don't worry, Aud, Logan's really a big softy at heart. Don't let him push you around too much."

He straightened and gave me a wink before leaving. After a moment his voice boomed from down the hall. "Now try not to kill each other, you two. You know the expression is make love, not war." He was laughing at his own lame joke as the door swung shut.

I willed my face not to turn pink. Logan didn't say anything, but he was shaking his head as he walked over to a bench to set down his bag. Without a word, he pulled out a pair of shoes to replace the ones he was wearing. Self-conscious and itchy in my own skin, I shifted my weight from one leg to the other. Even though he had been pretty rude so far, it hadn't dampened my curiosity about him.

Some hair fell over Logan's face as he finished tying his laces, so I lost the opportunity to study it. So far, I'd only seen his moods range from stoic to annoyed and slightly angry. I hoped he had a broader range than that.

He looked up and caught my blatant stare. I turned in a futile attempt to cover my gawking and pretended to be extremely interested in a particularly menacing-looking weapon with multiple spikes attached to a large wooden handle.

"Okay, let's get started with some warm-ups. We'll see what kind of shape you were in when you died."

Another pit formed over the seemingly permanent one in my stomach. I was willing to bet that working out could be added to the list of things that weren't familiar to me in life.

Forty-five minutes later, I was throwing up into a garbage can in the corner of the gym. Logan had apparently been using the term "warm-up" loosely. He started by running me through twenty-five minutes of calisthenics, which left me struggling for breath. He followed that up with what he called a light run around the gym. When we finally stopped, I started dry heaving and gagging. Logan rolled his eyes and pointed to a trash can in the corner of the room. I barely made it there before my breakfast came back up. There was no way I was ever eating eggs with cheese again. When it finally felt as if my entire meal was out and my breathing and heartbeat had slowed, I straightened.

Logan was standing just a few feet away with a paper cup in his hand.

"Here," he said, extending the cup toward me. I was careful not to touch his fingers when I took it. I didn't want to know what he was feeling.

"You'll want to swish and spit. Then fill it up over there." He jerked his head to the left to indicate a drinking fountain. "You can get dehydrated fast when you throw up." His mouth turned down at the corners. "You're more out of shape than I thought."

I took a gulp of the water, swished, and spit it into the can. *So disgusting.*

"You're going to have to work on building up your endurance outside of training," Logan went on. "I won't be able to do much with you if you're throwing up before we even get to skills training."

My blood boiled at the flippant insults. Before I realized it, my mouth was moving again. "Well, I'm really sorry I didn't get in better shape before I *died.* Had I known I'd be working with a bunch of meatheads for eternity, I'm sure I would have prepared a little better."

Shaken, I pitched the empty cup and turned to get fresh water from the drinking fountain without waiting for Logan to respond. He was silent as I took a few glorious gulps of cold water.

When I finished and turned back to the gym, Logan threw something at me. I was so caught off guard that one smacked me in the shoulder and the other bounced off my stomach.

"Put those on."

"Huh?" I looked down. Boxing gloves. He had thrown boxing gloves at me. He had to be kidding.

"Don't I get a break?"

"You just did." He moved a large punching bag into position.

I grudgingly pulled the gloves on. I fiddled with the Velcro straps, trying to figure out how to tighten them with so little mobility in my thumbs, until Logan finally came over to adjust them for me. He pulled the straps around my wrists tight enough to cut off circulation.

Suddenly, I had the worst itch on my nose, impossible to scratch with these oversized oven mitts on my hands. I lifted my arm to try to scratch it on my sleeve when I noticed Logan staring at me. He waited by the punching bag with his arms crossed over his chest.

"Are you done?" His voice was even as usual.

I slowly lowered my arm and willed myself to ignore the itch as I shuffled over to him.

Logan didn't wear gloves as he demonstrated a few basic punches for me. He moved slowly to demonstrate the correct stance and form, but the bag still swung violently when he connected.

When he felt satisfied with his instruction, he let me take my turn. I wound up for my first punch and put as much power as possible into the hit. The bag barely groaned. My hand started to throb.

"Oww! You didn't tell me that was going to hurt!" I shook my hand out to alleviate the pain.

His brows furrowed. "It's not supposed to. That's why you have the gloves on."

"Well, it totally did."

"That means you're not doing it right."

I didn't have a comeback. He was probably right.

"Okay, then what am I doing wrong?"

"Hmmm." He took a moment to think about it. "Pretty much everything."

"Well, that was extremely helpful."

"It's obvious you didn't listen to anything I was saying."

"That's so not true. I did exactly what you told me to."

He rolled his eyes. "Well, let's see. Your stance was off, your arm was in the wrong position, and you didn't have any follow-through."

"Wow, is that all?"

"No." Logan didn't elaborate, but it looked as if he wanted to. His blue eyes blazed.

We stared at each other in silence. I knew it was stupid, but something about him made me bristle.

We were interrupted by another loud bang of the doors.

"Oh, isn't this cute? Staring deeply into each other's eyes."

I flushed a few shades darker. Alrik was leaning one shoulder against the doorframe, grinning.

"That is so not—" I sputtered.

"Not a good time, Alrik," Logan spoke up behind me.

"Yeah, I can tell." He barked out a laugh. "So, did she?"

Logan was silent for a moment. "Yeah, right after the run."

"Ha!" Alrik looked extremely pleased with himself. "You can settle up with me later."

I gasped. "Excuse me? Am I hearing you right? Did you actually bet on whether I would throw up today?"

Logan wouldn't quite meet my gaze, but Alrik appeared to be having a dandy day. "Not quite *if*, hon, but *when*."

My blood pressure spiked. "Seriously?"

Logan still refused to look me in the face—suddenly, repositioning the punching bag was really important to him. "I thought you'd last until at least after kickboxing."

Using my teeth to tug off my oven mitt of a boxing glove I chucked it at Logan's head. To my utter annoyance, he caught it easily before it smashed into his face. I ripped the other one off and threw it at him too. He caught it just as effortlessly.

"Oh, hey there, hon, don't be so upset. We all do on our first day. It's nothing personal," Alrik said from the doorway.

"Do you guys even care that I died, like, literally yesterday?"

Finally Alrik, with shoulders hunched and downcast eyes, had the decency to look a little convicted.

"We're just trying to make you feel like part of the team." He pushed himself away from the door frame. "Okay, okay, I can tell when I'm not wanted. I'll let you guys finish whatever it was that I walked in on and get back to work. Don't worry, Aud, the first day's always the worst."

Then he looked over my head to address Logan. "Good luck with this one. She's got some spunk!"

When the doors shut behind him, I was determined to do a better job. I couldn't be *that* bad at all of this.

"Okay, give me the gloves back."

Logan gently handed them to me. I flinched away when he tried to help me and stubbornly tightened them with my teeth instead, way past caring how I looked. I was going to get the bag to swing or die trying.

5

CELESTIAL HEIGHTS

"Is this a joke?"

I stood next to Romona inside her favorite restaurant, staring straight up. Giant cotton balls floated aimlessly through the air in twenty stories of open space above our heads. The white puffs, which reminded me of clouds, were about the size of small cars. People lounged on them as if sitting on oversized floating bean bags.

Romona had insisted on bringing me here to celebrate my first day of training. I couldn't stop staring. The waitstaff buzzed around the cavernous room with small bronze wings fastened to their backs. They flitted through the air with the grace of ballet dancers, trays brimming with all sorts of foods and drinks.

"Pretty neat, huh?"

I tore my eyes from the scene above. Romona was grinning from ear to ear.

"Yeah, I guess. I mean, is this for real? Do we really eat on those?" The height was making my stomach flutter in nervousness.

"Yes, it's a lot of fun."

"How do we even get up there?"

"Using those." She pointed to the right where a row of bronze wings hung on pegs.

"You're not kidding, are you?"

"Nope. You're going to love it. Flying is amazing!"

She tugged me over to the wings. The hostess appeared and demonstrated how to fasten and operate them properly. We were assigned a cloud—that's actually what they called them—toward the top of the room. Romona took off and glided through the air with ease. I was told flying was like swimming, but without having to kick to be propelled forward. Taking a deep breath, I bent my knees and pushed off the ground.

She was right: flying was amazing. I enjoyed it for all of five seconds before smacking my shoulder on the floating crystal chandelier. I dipped hard to the right and plummet down, then bounced off the side of a cloud. The people seated on it gasped as they were shoved into a wall. Fortunately the clouds were as soft as they looked, so it didn't hurt much to ricochet off one. Unfortunately, the hit literally dumped me in the middle of someone's dinner.

The couple in front of me was covered in food. I'd hit their table at an angle, causing everything that wasn't on me to cata-pult onto them. The man and woman stared at me with matching looks of shock as I tried to get right side up. In an instant Romona gracefully landed on the edge of their cloud.

"Oh my goodness! Are you okay?"

I didn't know if she was asking me or the couple I'd just baptized in aqua-colored gravy.

Alrik's familiar voice boomed from somewhere above. "Hey, Aud, that was amazing! I'm giving it a 9.5! Would have been a 10 if the landing had been a little cleaner, but extra points for dramatics!"

I looked up and instantly regretted it. Not only was Alrik beaming down at me from twenty feet above, but he wasn't alone. Logan and a boy named Kevin who I'd met at lunch were leaning over the edge of their cloud as well. What were the chances they'd be at this same restaurant? I looked at Romona with the question on my face.

She cringed. "Sorry, I may have mentioned to Alrik that we were headed here tonight."

I ignored the boys to deal with the problem at hand. The couple I'd crashed into were mopping food off of themselves and their seats.

"I am *so* sorry! I can't believe I did that. I've never tried this flying thing before. That chandelier just popped out of nowhere." I laughed nervously.

"Is there anything we can do to help?" Romona asked.

The woman stopped cleaning and looked up. An unexpected smile blossomed on her lips. I was startled by the agelessness of her face. If I had to guess, I would say she was frozen in the age between motherhood and her golden years. Her beautiful silver hair refracted the light when she moved, and the slender wrinkle lines on her face didn't make her appear old but rather accentuated the interest of her appearance. Her eyes of blended browns and greens sparked with life.

"Oh please, this is nothing to fret about. It was a simple

accident." Her smile reached her eyes. "And besides, we welcome unplanned interruptions in our lives. Don't we?"

She playfully poked her companion in the side to get his attention. He was handing a batch of soiled napkins to the server and receiving clean ones in return.

"Pardon?" With a head of thick salt-and-pepper hair and dark brown eyes, the man possessed the same ageless splendor as the woman. "Oh yes, no harm done. You just took us by surprise, that's all. Things like this keep us sharp in our old age. My name is Lapidoth, but please, you call me LD. Most people find Lapidoth quite a mouthful."

"Are you injured?" The woman's slight frown did nothing to diminish her timeless beauty.

I did a quick assessment of all my appendages. Everything seemed to be working properly. Only a few sore spots, but those could have been from training. "I don't think so. Thanks for being so gracious. I feel so bad."

"It is a small price to pay to meet new friends. Would the two of you care to join us?"

"Oh, ah," I looked to Romona for guidance. She smiled at the pair.

"Yes, thank you. That would be nice. My name is Romona, and this is Audrey."

"My name is Deborah, and LD is my husband. Please do take a seat."

She indicated a hand toward the soft bench on the other side of the table. "Now, I hope I'm not being too presumptuous, but by any chance are you new, Audrey?"

I smiled at her. "Not presumptuous, just insightful. I've only been here a short while. This is my second day, in fact."

I snuck a glance up at the guys' table, but they'd gone back to eating their dinner.

"Should we order some more food to replace what we ruined for you two?" Romona offered.

"You read my mind!" LD said.

Romona's smile broadened. "We'll let you order then. I like most things." She left out the part about me not knowing what I liked.

"That is most kind," LD said and then waved over one of the servers.

I took the opportunity to sneak glances around the restaurant while he ordered. Mercifully, no one appeared to be watching us anymore. Maybe crashes were a regular occurrence.

After taking our order, the server politely cleared what was left of the mess on the table. I watched as he expertly zipped through the air.

"So, Romona, Audrey, what brings you out to Celestial Heights tonight?"

"This is one of my favorite places." Romona answered. "I wanted to show it to Audrey. Although I'm afraid she's no longer going to trust my picks."

Romona glanced my way for confirmation. I lifted my eyebrows at her as if to say, "You've got that right." Romona laughed back good-naturedly.

"Oh no, you mustn't be turned off to things so easily. Some things just need practice and perhaps a little bit of patience," Deborah said.

"I suppose you're right." I conceded.

"So Audrey," LD interrupted. "What has been your favorite

thing so far? Or perhaps the most surprising? I love to hear from the new arrivals what they think."

I thought about it for a moment but couldn't come up with much. Everything had been a surprise, and I hadn't been here long enough for favorites.

"I'm not really sure. I haven't actually seen very much yet. I think I'd love to go hiking and explore the mountain range, though. Are we allowed to do that?"

"Of course! I would suggest going with someone who knows the lay of the land before venturing out on your own," LD said.

"I'd love to take you sometime if you'd like," Romona quickly offered.

"That would be amazing! There just seems to be something out there calling to me." No one spoke. "Sorry, that probably sounded kind of weird."

"Not at all. It's completely understandable." Deborah leaned forward to pat my hand. I got a wave of good intentions from her. It felt like being wrapped in a warm fuzzy blanket on a chilly night.

She, on the other hand, quietly gasped and jerked her hand back a few inches. Her clear eyes widened, and her gaze seemed far away. The next moment she leaned back, and the smile returned to her face. I looked over to check if Romona had caught what had just happened. From the look on her face, she had.

Deborah changed the subject without addressing her odd behavior. "So do you two know each other well?"

"We just met, actually. We're kind of the only girls in our jobs."

"Ah! You must be huntresses, then?" LD's eyes lit up with interest.

"That must be extremely exciting."

I looked at Deborah doubtfully. She laughed. "I have a feeling you are in for quite a ride." I didn't miss the pointed look she gave her husband.

LD took Deborah's hand. "My wife is usually right about these things."

That's when our dinner arrived. The food was a beautiful array of colors and smells that effectively distracted me from our new friends' strange comments. It took three servers to bring it all. It couldn't be possible for us to eat everything. Some of the dishes were so perfect they could be mini works of art. The smells were equally captivating. My stomach rumbled loudly in expectation.

LD picked up a plate of something purple, about the size of a small potato, and encouraged me to try one. I tried not to appear skeptical.

"Sometimes looks can be deceiving," he said with mischief in his eyes.

With a forced smile I reached for the object. It had a soft texture and felt like it would pop if I squeezed hard enough. That thought almost turned me off. I took a small bite, which broke off easily like a soft roll. My eyes widen as I chewed. It reminded me of a dense cake doughnut with fresh fruit inside. *Mmmm, delicious.* It was just the right amount of sweetness without being overpowering. The second bite was even better than the first.

"Wow, this is great," I said between chews.

LD sat back proudly.

Deborah pointed to a pureed dish, red with green seeds

throughout. Christmas colors. I spooned some on my plate and added a few other suggested dishes. Everything was incredibly tasty.

Deborah and LD were wonderful dinner companions. LD shared about the first time he came to Celestial Heights and how, after forgetting to put the wings back on, he almost fell off the cloud after the meal. We all laughed. I appreciated his sincere attempt to put me at ease. Before I knew it, we had finished everything in front of us. I stared at the empty serving dishes in amazement. My stomach was full beyond belief.

"This was so much fun! I'm glad I crashed into you two," I admitted.

"We would welcome the intrusion anytime." Deborah said with a smile.

As if on cue, a familiar voice boomed to the right of our table. "Hey, you girls want to join us for dessert?" The guys' table had drifted down next to ours.

Even if I weren't utterly stuffed, I wouldn't have wanted to join them.

"Thanks for the invite, but we're not done here, Alrik."

"Oh don't be silly, of course you can join your friends. We've already taken up enough of your time," Deborah jumped in.

"No, no really—"

"Great, and Aud, look, you can just walk over nice and easy so you don't cover us in food too." He wore a wicked grin. He was having way too much fun with this.

Romona turned to our dinner partners. "It was truly wonderful to meet you."

"Oh I assure you, the pleasure was all ours. We wish you both nothing but the best." LD waved good-bye. He was already standing and adjusting the wing's straps on his shoulders. He picked up Deborah's once his were in place to assist her.

She rewarded him with a smile and accepted the wings. "Why don't I meet you at the door? I'd like a moment with Audrey if you don't mind."

There was a knowing look in LD's eyes. "Of course, I'll see you shortly." He turned and gave Romona and me a small bow of respect before rising and disappearing below the cloud.

Romona stepped easily over to the guys' table, taking both of our wings with her. She immediately launched into a story, purposefully capturing their attention.

I turned to face Deborah, curious and a little apprehensive. What could she possibly want?

She didn't bother to ease into her topic. "Audrey, it's important for you to know that you do have a purpose."

"Oh, okay." I didn't know how to respond.

"When things look the darkest, I hope you remember that. There is always a plan, a bigger picture, even if you don't understand at first. Despite how it might appear, how you might even feel, you are never alone, not for one single moment."

Okay, that sounded creepy. A chill ran down my spine like someone had just walked over my grave, but even so, her words resonated within me, causing my heartbeat to pick up its pace. Something inside was telling me to pay attention.

"Thanks. I'll try to keep that in mind."

"I hope you will. I realize this may not make much sense now, but I believe that someday it will." She hesitated, pursing her lips as if considering whether she should continue. "Also, be careful to trust the right people. Learning to correctly discern motives is going to be important for you."

Without warning, she hugged me tightly. I was wooden in her embrace. Her words stirred something inside that equally scared and thrilled me. For a wild moment it felt as if she spoke a deep wisdom that my soul recognized. But mostly, I was weirded out.

Over her shoulder, Logan considered us carefully. When she pulled back, she gave my arms a final squeeze, shooting a bolt of fearlessness through me before releasing them to gracefully slip on her wings.

She turned to the table across from us before leaving. "Enjoy your evening." She waved and then addressed Logan: "It's nice to see you again."

Logan smiled and inclined his head in a friendly gesture.

"I take it you are still figuring things out?"

"That I am," he answered.

"There's nothing wrong with that. I have faith you will work it out."

"I appreciate the confidence."

"I think you know I have more than that."

Logan smiled. "That I do. Please pass my respects along to Lapidoth."

"I will." And with that, she rose into the air and descended to her husband.

What was all that about? My mind reeled with what she'd said. Was there something she knew that I didn't? Could Logan help make sense of it? I was hesitant to share her words with him. What if I sounded silly or even arrogant? I was frozen in place while I considered it all.

"Audrey!" Romona shouted. The sharp tone in her voice shook me out of my musings. "You need to come over now."

The clouds had drifted further apart. I groaned. I'd have to make a jump for it. Romona had taken my wings with her. Alrik was moving the table out of the way for me.

"It's now or never, Princess."

I took a deep breath and jumped. I landed without taking anyone, or anything, out.

"Ha!" I shouted in glee.

Alrik looked disappointed as he moved down so I could take the seat next to him.

"Expecting another show, huh?"

"Well, you have to admit, it was a pretty safe bet."

"Don't listen to him, Audrey, it was a very graceful leap," Kevin came to my defense.

"Thank you, Kevin, that's very nice of you to say."

I gave Alrik another smug look before turning my attention to the desserts on the table. They looked delicious. I was still full, but I started calculating how many of the brightly displayed treats I could stuff down before having to be literally rolled back to my room.

The remainder of the evening was unexpectedly enjoyable and blessedly incident free. Kevin and Romona went out of their way to bring me into the conversation, especially since most of their talk went far over my head. Alrik kept us entertained with outrageous stories of his adventures in the afterlife, most of which I had a hard time believing. I insisted on meeting his pet polar bear if he truly had one.

Logan was pleasant enough. He did a decent job giving off an air of relaxation, participating in the conversation, laughing, or chiming in at the appropriate times—but more than once I caught a remote look in his eyes. That seemed to be the trick with Logan. He could expertly mask the rest of his face, but the eyes were his tell. I couldn't stop myself from casting curious glances his way when I thought no one was paying attention. He was too deep in his own mind to notice, although I think Alrik might have caught me once.

After that I only turned Logan's way if he was addressing everyone, but my mind wandered to him and Deborah. It wasn't long before I caved.

"So Logan," I began when the other three were preoccupied, "you know Deborah and LD?"

"Not well," he answered, barely looking in my direction.

"That's odd," I said, "you sounded pretty acquainted. You must have made an impression?"

Logan causally turned toward me. He sounded blasé but took the opportunity to capture my gaze with his steely blue eyes. "I would guess she remembers all of her prophecies."

There was a pause the span of exactly three heartbeats before I could answer.

"Her what?"

"Prophecies," he repeated. "Deborah is a prophetess."

I was stunned into silence as my brain raced to digest the news and jogged over her words again. Purpose . . . plans . . . things looking the darkest . . . trusting the right people. Could her words have carried more importance than just friendly advice?

Logan's eyes were clear and intense as he waited for my response.

"Prophetess—like a fortune-teller?" I squeaked out.

He shook his head. "Not even close, although I can see why you might think that. The title has gotten distorted over time.

Prophetess was more of a title for a leader in her time. But she's gifted to see some of our destinies as well."

"So she *is* like a fortune-teller."

It was disturbing how conversational Logan was being about this subject. Almost flippant.

"No, she's not. The fortune-tellers like you are thinking of are either frauds or getting their information from a dangerous source. If the latter, whether they've spoken truth or not, I can promise you their words are not for our benefit. It's extremely unwise to mess with fortune-tellers. The things pulling their strings are motivated only to mislead."

"What 'things' are pulling their strings?"

"Demons."

"Why would they want to do that?" My throat was suddenly dry.

He answered with a level gaze and deliberate words. "Because they're looking to destroy humans. They hate us."

His words hung in the air for a time.

"We're the recipients of God's unconditional love, not them. It's part of what happened to turn them into demons in the first place. With how flawed we are, they didn't think we deserved that love. They became angry and bitter at God for giving His love to such unworthy beings. So to get back at Him, they've devoted their existence to destroying as many of us as possible."

I swallowed past the dryness coating my throat. "How could what happens to ordinary people get back at God?"

"Destroyed lives, denying His existence, hurting each other, all that pain people endure yet still refuse to turn to Him for help—it all hurts Him. He cares. It was never intended to be like that. And someday it won't be anymore, but this is what we deal with now. That's the small part that we hunters play. We go back to Earth to protect people from the demon's influence. There's a battle raging that most aren't even aware of. A battle for souls."

"But what about free will? Aren't people just going to do what they want anyway?"

"Of course, but by keeping demons away from people, we're protecting their minds from influence. Anyone hell-bent on doing wrong is going to find a way to do it." Some dark emotion flashed across Logan's eyes. "Demons don't have the power to force anyone to do anything."

"If they don't have the power to force anyone to do what they want, then why are we interfering at all?"

"You're underestimating the power of suggestion. Just because they can't force someone to do what they want doesn't mean they aren't *very* effective at manipulation and deception. And I'm not even talking about the people who purposefully invite them in." Logan let out a strong, low whistle. "Those demons are buried in so deep it's like trying to dig out a tick."

The idea was repulsive. "Why would anyone ever do that willingly?"

Logan held up his hand and started to count reasons off with his fingers. "Power, greed, selfishness, loneliness, acceptance, or because they simply don't realize what they've opened themselves to. Pick one. It happens all the time for many different foolish and selfish reasons." There was a bitter bite to Logan's words. They chilled me. I wanted to get back on topic.

"So Deborah told me my destiny?"

Logan shrugged a shoulder like he was done with this

conversation. "How should I know? I don't know what she said to you."

"Hey lovebirds!" Alrik shouted. "What ya chirpin' about over there?"

Logan rolled his eyes. "Nothing interesting."

Ouch.

The conversation digressed from there, and I pretended to listen to the others as I wondered about the repercussions of tonight's revelations. Demons, angels, prophetesses. I didn't think the afterlife could get any weirder, but I was wrong.

6

OVER THE RIVER AND
THROUGH THE WOODS

"Wow, he's out for blood today," Romona said as I joined her outside the gym. Inside, Logan glared at me. I ignored him. He'd called it quits for the afternoon in exasperation after I spent a good portion of the time picking myself off the padded floor.

"You've been here a while?" I guessed.

"Not too long. Hard day today?"

"Ha, you don't know the half of it. I'm starved. Want to grab something to eat? We skipped lunch."

"You skipped a meal?" Romona's brows furrowed in concern, and she cast a dark look at the gym door. Logan was throwing knives at the wall for target practice. He needed to get a life. Or at least an afterlife. He spent too much time in that gym.

"Yeah. I accidentally slept in this morning, and a grueling workout paired with no lunch was Logan's way of getting back at me. At least, that was the second half of his evil master plan. The first involved getting woken up by a pitcher of water. I thought I was drowning."

"What? Logan went to your room and poured water on you?" She seemed genuinely appalled.

"Yep. Speaking of, is there any way I can get a lock put on my door?"

In the three last weeks, I'd gotten a little stronger and gained a bit more endurance. I had to—Logan was making every day a meat grinder. Our relationship had a few ups and downs but generally hadn't gotten any friendlier, and my skills were nowhere close to what he wanted. The other hunters and trainees weren't too bad, and I had made a few friends. But I still hated it here. The feeling that I didn't belong with this group hadn't dissipated. Whenever I mentioned it to Logan he would bark platitudes about everyone's assigned jobs, sometimes even while complaining about my progress.

Romona was still fixated on the water incident. "I can't believe he did that. Logan's too disciplined to pull something like that."

A snort escaped me.

"And there's really no excuse for not letting you eat lunch. That's not safe." She glanced back at the gym door, her face a mix of concern and calculation.

"Hey, well, I'm okay now. Let's just go get something to eat." I grabbed her arm and tugged her down the hallway. I didn't need Romona fighting my battles. Especially not with Logan, who I expected would be twice as hard on me for it. I considered heading to the locker room to clean up but was too famished to bother. Romona would just have to put up with my stink.

Romona and I were practically inseparable by now. I couldn't pinpoint exactly how it had happened. She simply seemed to be there all the time, and I certainly didn't mind the company. She had a quiet strength about her. And as an added perk, she knew everyone. I'd probably met half the other hunters during our lunch breaks alone. She had a way about her that made you feel she truly cared. That was a deeper comfort to me than I would admit.

There were times when I felt a black hole of bitterness welling up deep inside me. I wasn't even sure where it came from, but its intensity scared me. Romona always seemed to be able to sense it, and she would offer wise and calming words. Perhaps it should have been intimidating to be around someone who always appeared so peaceful and put together, but it was a soothing balm to my soul.

To see her agitated over something as small as a skipped meal was new.

"So what's up?" I prodded to regain her attention.

"Oh." She gave herself a visible shake and offered an apologetic smile. "Sorry about that. I was waiting to ask you about your day off tomorrow."

"Huh?" My plate was already loaded with food, its aroma teasing me. Now I was the one having difficulty paying attention.

"You know, our day off training."

"We get days off?"

She laughed. "Of course we do. We get them off whenever we need them, and usually one every seven days. I noticed how hard Logan's been training you." She let out a huff. "Let me guess. That's something else he forgot to mention?"

"I think he was more focused on the retribution he was

going to dish up today. That's great, though. I could use a day off."

"That's what I was thinking. I wondered if you might want to go hiking? You've mentioned that before."

I looked up. Windows ran from floor to ceiling in the cafeteria where most hunters ate, letting in a plethora of light and a view of the distant mountains. She was right. The need to explore was strong. An innate part of me knew there was something out there worth searching for.

"Yeah, that'd be great," I said around mouthfuls of food.

"Perfect! Leave everything up to me. I know just the spot."

I woke the next morning thrilled to be going somewhere other than the training center. I'd been dead for weeks now and had hardly seen anything past the bland walls of the training center and gym. Romona had said it was good to ease into some things, but that obviously didn't include training. Logan had pitched me in the deep end immediately.

This morning was different. Today I wasn't going to get bumped and bruised by my own mentor. Today I wasn't going to throw on ugly workout clothes and sweat through them within the first hour. Today I wasn't going to feel like the task I was undertaking was too big, too hard, and too impossible to handle. Today the black hole wasn't going to get me. Something bubbled inside my chest that said today anything was possible.

I started my morning routine with a bounce in my step. My only moment of hesitancy was when I stood in front of my closet, unsure of what to wear. I finally pulled out some jean shorts and a light blue T-shirt, plus a pair of brown and blue sneakers. My first instinct was to pull my hair up in a ponytail, but I decided against it since I was always forced to wear it back in training. I left it cascading down my back and shoulders instead. It was likely to make me hot if the hike was strenuous, so I stretched a ponytail holder over my wrist just in case. With that I was out the door.

I was supposed to meet Romona near the ice skating rink. I watched as snowflakes appeared about twenty feet above the skaters and floated lazily down to the icy surface. People materialized hats, gloves, coats, and scarves as they stepped on the ice. A group of kids skated together in a swarm with their heads tilted up and mouths open as they tried to capture snowflakes on their tongues.

"I'll bet you loved skating." I hadn't heard Romona join me.

"How do you figure?"

"By the look on your face. I think this is the most peaceful I've seen you."

"Hmmm." It was something to consider, but until I got my memories back there was no way to truly know. "So what do you have there?" I asked, pointing to the two bulging backpacks placed at her feet. She handed one to me with a smile.

"I'm making you work for your food today!"

"I wouldn't want it any other way. Which way are we headed?"

"That way." Romona lifted a hand and pointed toward the mountain range. My smile grew. I'd wanted a closer look at those mountains since the first time I laid eyes on them.

"I thought you might like that. They're even more beautiful up close."

"I'm looking forward to seeing that for myself."

Romona motioned with her head. "Great, let's go!"

We left the rink and headed toward the forest in the other direction from where I lived. Here the trees were denser, but not nearly as large. I imagined Hansel and Gretel picking their way over the vine-and-moss-covered ground, leaving bread-crumbs to find their way home. With no clear path to follow, I had the urge to start dropping markers ourselves. I was glad for Romona's experienced company. I could easily have become lost for lifetimes in those trees.

The deeper we traveled, the heavier my feet felt as they stuck to the soggy forest floor, making suctioning sounds with every step. The smell of rotting leaves and dank mushrooms permeated the air. On a few occasions I heard scampering in the thick canopy above our heads, but there was never anything there when I looked up. I followed close behind Romona, not wanting to lose her in the low light.

"Man, this is intense." We hadn't spoken much since entering the tight foliage.

"Yes, I know. It's what's on the other side that makes it worth picking through this mess."

I cast a weary glance up at the tangle upon tangle of branches above us. "It's going to have to be pretty amazing to warrant enduring this."

"Well, I guess you can tell me for yourself . . . I think we're finally through."

I'd missed the growing brightness in front of us while I concentrated on the underbrush that constantly snagged my feet. As if on cue, my foot caught on a root and my body jostled forward the moment I tried to make out what lay beyond the tree line. I braced myself on a moist trunk to keep from falling. My hands came away with brown and green mossy residue. *Yuck.* I scrubbed them against my shorts before moving forward.

It was a few more slow-moving minutes before we broke free from the forest to stand on the edge of a rolling meadow of vibrant red and yellow flowers. I blinked against the sudden brilliance, and the sweet fragrance of the flowers swept away the smell of decay behind us.

"Wow."

"That was pretty much my first reaction as well. It is beautiful, isn't it? They're tulips. They bloom all the time here. They aren't the most fragrant of flowers, but where there are so many of them like this, the smell is lovely. We're not stopping, though, just headed through to the foothills beyond."

From where we stood, the slight undulation of the meadow cut off whatever lay beyond and made it appear that the tulips continued indefinitely.

Free of the narrow forest path, we could finally walk side by side. I cautiously treaded through the radiant plants. Romona giggled beside me.

"What exactly are you doing?" she asked. "Trying out a new walking technique?"

"No, the flowers are so pretty I'm trying not to step on any of them," I answered with a knee in the air and arms spread out for balance. "But it's hard because they're so close together."

She laughed again. "It's really okay. Look." She stepped in front of me and crushed a few soft tulips under her foot.

"Oh, come on, I was trying really hard not to do that!"

"No, wait, watch this." She lifted her foot, and the flowers sprang proudly back up. "You can step on them. It won't hurt them at all."

"Oh, I see." I felt a bit foolish for my high-stepping. "I just didn't want to ruin them or anything. They seem so perfect."

"I shouldn't have laughed. You just reminded me of a little kid playing hopscotch or something."

Still hesitant, I forced myself to take a step forward without looking down. The tulips made a soft ground covering, but I snuck a quick look behind us as we moved on to make sure Romona was right. Satisfied that I wasn't leaving trampled flowers in my wake, I focused ahead just as we crested the first hill.

From here, we saw a glassy stream cutting a natural barrier between the two-toned meadow and the mountain's foothills beyond. The water was full of blue and green river rocks and tiny purple creatures that darted through the water like aquatic hummingbirds.

We walked along the bank until the water was low enough for us to jump on protruding rocks to the other side. The purple creatures, which at a closer look appeared to be starfish with large, flat tails, followed along with us until we set our feet on the opposite bank. Then they splashed away in a blink.

"Those don't look familiar. What are they called?"

"I'm not sure. Perhaps they haven't been named yet."

"Is that even possible?"

"Sure. There are lots of different species of plants and animals here that didn't exist on Earth. God's always creating new things for us to see and experience. Whoever sees them first gets to name them."

This wasn't the first time someone had mentioned the big "G" by name. There were also lots of mysterious, "Hims" and "Hes" thrown around that I assumed meant God, but not a lot of elaboration. I didn't remember going to church, conversations about God, or ever praying, but as I dug internally I found facts about God embedded in my mind. Much like the knowledge I had of things like the process of osmosis and how to do long division by hand. I must have been taught about it all at some point, but I didn't remember anything that gave me a personal connection to such a powerful being.

I turned my attention back to the starfish. "How do we know if we're the first to see them?"

"Give them a name; then we'll check the living museum when we get back. There's a record of every named plant and animal there. If you're the first to name them, we'll be able to look them up under the name you've given them."

"This is weird. You want me to name a new type of fish?"

"Sure, why not?"

I didn't really know—naming just seemed like a big deal. "Don't you have to have credentials to do that? And what would I even name them?"

"Well, what did they look like to you?"

"Star shooter . . . thingies." I was instantly embarrassed. "That's totally lame, right?"

"No, no, not at all. I think it's a cute name. Star shooters. We'll have to check out the museum when we get back. Let's keep going. I want to get a little further before we have lunch."

The foothills in front of us were frost covered but also dotted with plants in full summer bloom. I could hardly comprehend how so many diverse terrains and climates could exist in one place. The breeze that blew my hair was kissed with warmth even as icy grass crunched beneath my shoes.

My feet had just started to protest when we reached the top of the third foothill and Romona suggested we stop and enjoy the picnic. My stomach growled its approval as we bent down to fish the contents out of our backpacks. The frozen water on the patch of grass in a ten-foot circle around us began to melt and then evaporated into the air, leaving us a warm, dry place to set out our picnic.

"That's incredible! Did you do that?"

"Nope, it happened because we stopped. Neat, right? The ground was only frosted because no one has been here for a while. It'll frost back over sometime after we leave."

My pack contained several large loaves of bread. Romona's contained the heavier bounty. After materializing a blanket, she removed a feast of meats, cheeses, breads, fruits, and even delicately decorated desserts. I'd learned food was one of the few things you couldn't just materialize here. It had to be grown in order to be digested; something materialized would just dematerialize again as soon as you started chewing.

One of the contents of her pack caught my attention. I picked up a red cylindrical roll and gave her a questioning look.

"Just thought you might like that," she said.

"A fruit roll-up? Seriously?"

She shrugged and went back to emptying her pack. Romona had probably packed too much food, but I was famished.

I settled on the blanket, and my gaze turned toward the mountains. I'd been so preoccupied with all the wonders at, or below, eye level that I hadn't looked that high during our hike.

The mighty cliffs appeared to emerge from the ground in front of us, even though we were still some distance away. Green vegetation and snowy peaks dotted the mountain face, bare patches beneath them exposing rich mineral veins. But everything paled in comparison to the structure perched on the highest peak of the tallest mountain. My jaw dropped.

There above us, stretched so high it reached into the clouds, sat a blazing fortress of gold.

The golden light was blinding, like trying to look directly at the sun. My eyes teared as I tried to make out the form of the fortress. Little by little, I picked out more of the details. It was made out of translucent material: rather than simply reflecting the light, the blazing golden radiance flowed in undulating waves from the structure itself. It literally took my breath away.

I tore my gaze away to question Romona. Her back was to me as she arranged food on the blanket.

"Romona, what is that?" I asked, awed. "Oh my gosh! Are those angels flying around it?"

The great winged beings suspended in air were humanoid in their features. Their white-garbed bodies glowed like the moon next to the radiance of the structure. I took an unsteady step back as understanding blossomed. Celeste and Shannon must be angels—they emanated the same white luster as these creatures. Brightness from the fortress sparkled off their wings. Romona looked over her shoulder, then turned to give me a perplexed look. She seemed uncomfortable.

"You can see that?"

"Of course! It's so bright I can't believe it took me so long to notice!"

"It's just that most people can't see it until after their

memories return. So I assumed you couldn't." She tilted her head. "It's a little odd that you can."

Well, that was nothing new. "Chalk it up to the oddity that is me. But hey, at least I'm overachieving in one area. So what is it?"

"Well, technically it's the tabernacle. But in layman's terms it's God's home. That light is what gives us our daylight."

Questions flooded through my mind so fast I tried spitting them out all at once. "Really? God has a home? Like a normal person? He's just hanging around here like the rest of us? Have you ever seen Him?"

"Whoa there!" Romona floundered for a moment before regaining her composure. "First of all, God is not a normal person, but yes, He does have a home. But not like what I think you are imagining. More like a holy dwelling, but that's completely confusing. Yes, of course He's here, and yes, I have seen Him. I think that covers all the questions, right?"

"So I may just randomly bump into Him one day?"

"No, it doesn't *exactly* work that way. I'm sure you'll meet Him, but it won't be until after you remember. You have to remember *Him,* remember your relationship with Him first. When you do, He'll reveal himself to you. It's part of the process we all have to go through."

What in the world was that supposed to mean? Relationship with God? Was that like having an imaginary friend or something? Wasn't God just there to *be God?* To set things in motion and then watch everything play out?

I peeled through the layers in my mind for what I knew about God: Creator of the universe, been around forever, angels do His bidding. I hit a wall, though, whenever I tried to make a personal connection. Just like what happened anytime I tried to pull up a memory.

Romona squeezed my forearm and offered an apologetic look. Her uneasiness rushed through the empathy link as strongly as her encouragement. She knew I didn't like her explanation.

"Don't look so worried. It's different for everyone. It'll come back when the timing's right."

My frustration suddenly threatened to come out in tears. "I don't think I understand what that means. Romona, why can't I remember my life? No one seems able to really explain that to me."

She paused. "I can't tell you. And I mean that. Not that I *won't*, but that I truly *can't*. It's different for everyone. It has something to do with dealing with the grief of losing your former life, but it's also a lot about learning what your new life, your eternal life, will be like. It's a fresh start, but the memories always do come back. Who you are today is still about who you were on Earth. There are just some things you need to take in without the distractions for a while. You have to have faith that there's a purpose."

"Faith in what, though?" I blinked away the new tears.

"Faith that the Creator of the universe knows what He's doing."

I looked back up at the gleaming fortress. Angels circled the structure as if in continuous orbit around the sun. Romona wanted me to believe God cared. But what if that was exactly what I doubted? When I searched my heart, I wasn't sure I truly believed He cared about me. So far, my life in the ever after felt like one giant mistake, not like a celestial fairy godfather was taking care of me. How could things be going according to His plan when I felt so alone?

Romona brushed her fingertips on my elbow and gave me an encouraging smile. "Maybe you can see the tabernacle because He wanted you to know He's actually here?" There was a hopeful note to her voice.

"Just like the great and powerful Oz. The man behind the curtain."

"No, Audrey, he's nothing like that. A man didn't become a wizard to deceive us. Instead the wizard became a man to save us."

I was less enchanted by the scenery on the hike back and even quieter than before. Romona, cognizant of the fact that I needed to process, gave me time alone with my thoughts.

I couldn't stop wondering about the life I no longer remembered. Everything led back to that. My gratefulness for Romona caused me to wonder about my pre-death friendships. What if there were people who depended on me but I wasn't there for them anymore? It was sad to think that I couldn't remember the people who were mourning me. It seemed unfair that they had to go through that pain when my slate was wiped clean. I simply didn't understand the point of it all.

I turned my head to get another glimpse of the fiery sanctuary high up on the mountaintop before we ducked into the shadowed forest. It was just a speck sparkling in the distance.

Who was this God who ran the realms in this way? If He couldn't even bother to see me right now, how important could I really be to Him? Why couldn't He just explain all of this to me Himself rather than force me to bumble around in the dark?

I struggled to feel anything other than anger and frustration toward Him. The heavy darkness and mucky topography of the forest appropriately reflected my mood for the rest of the hike.

7

DUMPED

*a*gain," Logan barked from across the room.

I kept my eyes squeezed shut and concentrated on making sure all my limbs still moved properly. There was a dull ache on the left side of my head where a golf-ball-sized bump was growing. Since my arms were, in fact, still working, I lifted a hand to gingerly probe the spot. *So not fair that you can still get hurt after you die.*

"Audrey, get up. We're going at this again."

Logan was clearly annoyed, but I had no interest in jumping up for another beating. He had thrown me across the room and into the padded wall for probably the fifth time that day. I was supposed to be practicing defensive techniques, but like everything else so far, I was failing miserably. And my body hurt everywhere.

I lay corpse-still and prayed Logan would believe I was dead—if it was even possible to die after you'd died—and leave me alone. Logan stomped over as I calculated the severity of the injury I'd have to sustain for him to ease up. I stubbornly refused to open my eyes. Stubborn was one thing I had probably been fairly good at in life.

"Audrey, you can stop faking it. I know you didn't faint, and you certainly aren't dead."

I let what I hoped sounded like a pitiful moan out of my throat. The next instant, Logan hauled me sharply to my feet. But I wasn't done making my point. As soon as he dragged me up, I simply let my legs go limp and landed on my butt in a heap on the ground. At that moment, maturity seemed highly overrated.

"Audrey, this isn't a joke."

I looked up and stuck my tongue out. I suspected it was the only muscle in my body that wasn't going to be screaming in pain later. Logan's eyes narrowed, and his facial muscles hardened.

"Fine, if that's the way you want to play this."

In a blur of motion, he bent down and heaved me up and over his shoulder.

"Hey wait, what the heck are you doing?"

I used the remainder of my strength to pound his back while attempting to squirm off his shoulder. I twisted to the left and felt myself slip, but he simply compensated. I found myself hanging upside down even further, with his hold tightened to steel. The blood rush to my head was beginning to make me dizzy.

I craned my head to the side to see where he was taking me. With a small shock, I realized we were already out of our gym and walking through the training center, past startled bodybuilders giving us weird looks. I thought I spotted Romona practicing on a punching bag, but Logan moved so quickly I couldn't be sure it was her. We were swiftly past before I thought to call out for help. Some part of me was probably too mulish to ask for it anyway.

"Okay, Logan, you had your fun, you can let me down now. If I knew most of these people, this would be pretty embarrassing." I was breathless. It was hard to talk while dangling upside down.

No answer from Logan as he continued parading me through the training center.

"Logan, come on, I'm starting to get really lightheaded."

No answer.

"Logan!"

This time I balled my hand into a fist and tried a reverse punch on his back. He didn't even flinch. *Man, I really do stink at this hand-to-hand combat stuff.*

Logan pushed through the front doors of the training center and carried me into the light of day like a sack of potatoes. Shocked faces seeped into my peripheral vision. This was definitely getting embarrassing. I was almost happy the blood was already pooled in my head, or else the blush of humiliation would have shown through.

I was gearing up to launch a verbal assault when Logan halted. *Finally!* But my relief was premature, for the next instant I was flying through the air, arms and legs flailing. I let out a huge scream that was muffled by a frozen blanket and a big lung full of water. It took a moment to figure out which way was up, but I eventually came sputtering to the surface coughing and hacking.

Logan had thrown me into a lake. Or rather, a fishing pond. Surprised strangers all around weren't even hiding their stares. Logan had managed to toss me at least sixty feet. It was too deep for me to touch bottom, so I noisily struggled to the shoreline and then hacked up a couple lungfuls of nasty fish water. I looked up to see Logan push through the training center doors without glancing back.

By the time I'd reached land, most of the people had resumed fishing and were politely pretending not to stare. A few were not very discreetly covering smiles, and those closest to me came over to make sure I was okay. I should have been happy that at least someone cared, but at that moment I was beyond furious. I couldn't imagine I'd ever been so mad in my entire life. Who did he think he was? He hadn't even stuck around to make sure I could swim! He'd tossed and left! I choked down my anger long enough to assure the small crowd around me that I was in fact okay, even as I sporadically coughed up water.

As the crowd dissipated, Romona burst out of the training center. She surveyed the shore of the pond before spotting me and sprinting over, her face radiating concern. Fully dressed in workout gear, she didn't appear the least bit winded.

"Audrey, oh my goodness, are you okay?"

I was not okay; I was furious. I took another moment to empty my lungs and shakily rose to my feet, setting my sights on the training center doors. If the murderous look on my face didn't give away my intentions, Romona was assuredly tipped off when she grasped my arm to help steady me.

"Whoa, Audrey, you shouldn't go back in there just yet. Logan's not in the best mood. I know you must be angry, but trust me, you don't want to get into it with him right now."

I was already purposefully striding toward the door by the time she finished her last sentence.

Oh yeah? Not get into it with him? He doesn't want to get into it with me right now!

I shoved the front door open with enough force to draw attention. The puddle at my feet grew as I searched for the first muscle-built guy who would look me in the eye.

"Where is he?" I ground out.

His eyebrows shot up, but he gave a quick jerk of his head, indicating a set of doors behind him. I stalked across the room and busted through both doors. My anger had tripled since I'd entered the center, and I was ready to do some serious damage.

Logan was alone in the room. He'd done his own serious damage to a practice dummy, which was now slumped over with multiple broken appendages. The startled look on his face was short-lived. After a quick sweep of me from head to toe, a corner of his mouth quirked up in amusement.

With that, something in me broke free. I snatched the closest weapon I could find and ran straight toward Logan with a banshee scream. Romona yelled a warning behind me, but I wasn't sure if it was meant for Logan or me. I was both out of control and completely focused. Time seemed to slow, and I was able to calculate things I'd never thought possible—such as the weight of the object in my hand, which I finally recognized as a fighting staff, and how far until I was in striking range.

I took a premeditated swing at Logan, which he narrowly deflected with a staff that instantly appeared in his hands. Using his surprise to my advantage, I twisted fast enough to catch him in the stomach with a back kick that sent him stumbling a few feet. I followed up with a roundhouse kick straight to his shoulder, swinging my staff around and then immediately up, disarming him.

Before I could savor my victory, Logan dropped low to swipe my feet out from under me, and I landed hard on my back. Even disarmed, Logan was faster, stronger, and more skilled than me. Before I could regroup, he kicked my rod out of my hands and held the blunt end of my own weapon to my throat. He stood above me, breathing as heavily as I. Whether from exertion or anger, I didn't know.

Everything happened over a short few seconds, but it felt as if we were locked in that stance for ages. Eventually the rest of the world leaked into my consciousness and I realized we were being watched, but I couldn't break from Logan's blue gaze. Our breathing slowed, but neither of us moved an inch.

"Looks like you have your hands full with that one, Logan," someone laughed from the newly gathered crowd.

The laughter broke the tension, and chuckles, followed by a few jokes, were thrown our way. The atmosphere felt noticeably lighter. Logan looked away as he lowered the weapon. He turned to head across the room, picking up his staff on the way. I propped myself up on my elbows to see we'd managed to attract a few dozen people—filing out of the room since the show was clearly over. I was surprised to find that my anger had dissolved. It must have burned off in the fight, and now that it was over, I was exhausted to the bone.

Romona hunched down to my level, a slight frown on her face.

"You okay?" she quietly asked.

"Yeah." I rolled my right shoulder and instantly regretted it. "I just feel like I've been through a cement mixer today."

Her features softened, and she gave me a small, comforting smile. I guessed she still didn't approve of what I'd done. Logan might have dumped me in a pond, but I wasn't exactly blameless. "It will get better."

I looked at her skeptically.

"I promise," she continued. "Let me help you up."

She stood up and reached a hand down. I grasped it. Even with her help, I struggled to stand.

"Wow, you are tired, aren't you?"

I gave her a half-smile since it was all I could muster. Her brows furrowed in heightened concern.

"Seriously, can you even make it back to your room?"

I shrugged a shoulder and turned toward the door. "I'm fine."

"Romona, can you give us a minute?"

The sound of Logan's voice jolted me. After my fury burned itself out, I'd actually forgotten he was still there.

Romona only paused for a moment before she nodded. I watched her go. She sent me an encouraging smile before closing the door firmly behind her, blocking out prying eyes. The small burst of energy from hearing Logan speak evaporated, and I was left incredibly weary, so much so that I had a hard time staying on my feet as I turned to face him.

Standing at a distance, Logan looked somewhat weary himself. Of course, he'd hardly broken a sweat, but his eyes betrayed him. If he wanted to talk, fine, I would let him start.

He took a big breath of air and ran a hand through his hair before saying anything. "Can we at least call a truce?"

I gave him what I intended to be a skeptical look. He laughed. A true, genuine, hearty laugh—something I'd not heard from him before now. It was a rich sound that actually eased some of the tension from my shoulders. Man, I was tired.

"Here." He materialized a metal folding chair behind me. "Sit down; it looks like you are going to fall over . . . or maybe faint for real?"

I was a little jealous he could do that so easily.

"I told you I don't faint," I grumbled under my breath, but I didn't argue as I slid into the metal chair. I was convinced I might fall over at any moment. Part of me was already fantasizing about my bed. If we were going to have this talk, I wanted to channel as much energy as possible into talking rather than staying upright.

Logan materialized a chair for himself and sat down about an arm's length away. His motions were deliberate, like someone approaching a spooked animal. He waited a second before speaking. When he'd chosen his first words, his eyes focused and locked with mine. "It seems you retained at least a little of what I've been trying to teach you."

A pause. I didn't know how I wanted to respond to that.

"I mean, your form was sloppy, but you did get in a few solid hits before I disarmed you."

I was too tired to be offended and more than a little surprised at being given any sort of praise, even if it was weak. It must have shown on my face.

"Audrey, I'm not here to antagonize you, you know." The weariness in his eyes returned as he lifted a hand to run through his hair. "I think we made our points today, probably the wrong way on both sides, but we do need to find a way to work with each other."

I was struggling to comprehend. This was the first time Logan had initiated a conversation with me that wasn't tactical or related directly to a new fighting skill or technique. I could only nod in agreement. No argument from me. What we'd been doing wasn't working.

He continued, "You know it's my job, my responsibility, to make you a fighter. You can't imagine what you will face out there. You need to be able to defend yourself as well as others. This is only a small fraction of what you will need to ultimately learn. You have no idea the amount of things I need to teach you in a short time."

Rather than his usual threats, this sounded more like a plea.

"Is there going to be a test on this stuff that I don't know about?" The question may have come out flippant, but I was at least half-serious.

"There's no test, Audrey. You go straight from training to the field, where you won't have the luxury of making mistakes. Any errors or miscalculations will directly affect those you are trying to protect."

"What exactly does that mean?"

"That means that if you screw up, if you forget how to use a weapon or where to deliver the most effective punches, or you run out of energy on a chase, then someone on Earth gets hurt. That could mean yourself or someone on your team as well."

This was the most information I'd gotten about being a demon hunter so far. I was intrigued. I wondered if I'd be able to contact anyone I knew on Earth, my family perhaps, if I even had one.

"We need to find a way for you to tap into your fighting instinct and skills when you aren't angry."

Against my will, I smiled. And because I couldn't help myself, I said, "Oh, you noticed that, huh?"

His mouth turned into a smile that didn't quite reach his eyes.

"Yeah, you're a mean fighter when you're mad."

We sat in a comfortable silence for a moment as we contemplated our options. For once, Logan was treating me like an equal. I wanted to be careful with my next words.

"I think," I finally began, "that I might do better if it wasn't so serious all the time."

I went on quickly because I imagined he was already starting to reject the idea. "I mean, if it didn't feel so much like a class all the time or if we were friendlier with each other, I would enjoy training a little more, and maybe I'd start to do better."

I shrugged and looked to my left, unsure of myself. When I looked back at Logan, he was staring at the wall above my head with what appeared to be a thoughtful look on his face. He didn't say anything for a while. Finally, he gave himself a small nod and looked me in the eyes. The full effect of his blue stare was always somewhat startling. Despite myself, my stomach did a little flip before settling again.

"Okay, Audrey, I hear what you're saying. I have a few ideas. Will you give me another chance to try this out?"

His face had taken on an intensity that was overwhelming. I was still slightly leery of his methods, but that he was *asking* me for anything, rather than demanding, was a change. And right now I was so tired, I probably would have agreed to anything. It felt a little like defeat, but I slowly nodded.

"But only if you agree not to dump me in any more ponds."

His face lightened, and he barked out a short laugh. "Well, I can agree to that. I'm sure I can think of more creative ways to get you motivated in the future. And if not, there are always pools and lakes around here as well."

I frowned. He laughed even louder.

"Don't look so worried!"

I wasn't so sure, but I was beginning to get tunnel vision, so I only nodded and focused on the floor in front of me.

"Audrey, are you okay?" Logan asked.

I nodded again without answering. If I could just get to my room, I'd be fine. I shook my head to clear my vision. Logan put a hand on my shoulder, careful not to make any contact with my skin. He may have said my name again, before giving me a little shake. I tried to shrug off his hand. I'd been manhandled enough that day.

"I just need to get some sleep," I mumbled and attempted to stand.

I'd spoken the truth, but my body demanded sleep sooner than I had intended. My legs gave out on the first step, and my tunnel vision narrowed to near blackness. Logan lunged forward to catch me before I hit the ground.

I must have caught him unawares, because he forgot to materialize protection between our skin. There was a moment of contact when I could almost grasp what he was feeling, but it was swept away with blackness.

8

CHANGES

"Oh no!" I sat up with a start. I was back in my room. Romona perched comfortably on the corner of my bed, her darker complexion striking against the monochrome white of the room. The last thing I remembered was talking with Logan in the training center.

"Is Logan here?" My words rushed out in a breathless huff.

"Nope. He brought you around the back of the training center. I don't think anyone saw you guys. He asked me to check in on you. We both think it was a case of over-exhaustion."

I rolled my eyes. She ducked her head to hide her expression. My eyes narrowed.

"You think this is funny!"

She coughed and stood up, turning her back on me to walk across the room. "Would Sleeping Beauty like some water?" Even with her face obscured from view I heard the smile in her voice.

Traitor.

Romona knelt down and pushed some points on the white wall as I mulled over the fact that Logan had seen me faint . . . again. How badly was he going to hold that over my head?

A small door swung open in front of Romona, catching my attention. *Where did that come from?* Craning my neck, I glimpsed a few bottles of something before she grabbed two clear ones and shut the door, which instantly blended back in with the wall.

"What in the world?"

I popped out of bed far too quickly and wobbled my first step. I took another step and a half before regaining my footing. Dropping to the floor in front of Romona, I ran my fingers over the flat white surface. Smooth like seamless plastic. "It's gotta be here somewhere," I mumbled. I barely registered Romona's bemusement.

"Um, Audrey, what exactly are you doing?"

I lifted my gaze. Romona stood with a bottle in each hand and a look that said I'd grown an extra head. I was on all fours with my face only inches from the wall.

"How'd you do that with the door? Where did those bottles come from?" I rocked back on my heels.

"Here, drink this. It's only water."

After I reached up to accept the gift, she motioned toward the wall.

"It's your room fridge," she said. "You just need to push here and here." She indicated two invisible spots on the wall, then deftly punched them with her fingers. Two spots glowed red momentarily, then a panel swung open and gently bumped into my knee.

I peered inside at the treasure. Nestled within were five

rows and six columns of different colored bottles. I bent my head to look deeper; the bottles appeared to go on infinitely. Already, the clear bottles Romona had taken had been replenished. I giggled. This room was amazing!

"Shut up!"

"What? I didn't say anything."

With my head still in the fridge, I said, "Oh no, not you . . . I was just making an exclamation."

"Oh, well, I know the variety isn't that extensive, but once you move out of here, you'll have a wider selection."

I gawked. I couldn't even name as many different types of cold drinks as were in that fridge.

Romona startled me out of my musing with an irritated snort. "No one's told you much about your room, have they?"

I shook my head. "What 'they'? Logan just dumped me here the first night, and that was it. There hasn't been any other 'they' to tell me anything. Just you about the closet."

Romona let out another perturbed burst of air as I scrambled to my feet and said "boys" under her breath.

"That explains why this place still looks like a padded cell in an insane asylum." She crinkled her nose. "Come over here. I'm going to give you a real lesson. This room is a blank canvas. It's up to you to paint the picture. I think we need to begin with something simple."

She drummed her fingers on her bottom lip, considering. "How about we start with the wall color? What color would you like your room to be?"

Logan's distinct blue eyes popped into my head.

"Maybe blue?" I answered hesitantly, turning my face to cover a slight blush.

"Okay. Can you think of the shade of blue? Exactly what it looks like?"

"I think so."

"Close your eyes and really imagine the color. Feel the shade of it. If you can imagine where you've seen that shade before, get a mental picture in your head. Then imagine the color splashed on these walls."

She gave me a moment to produce the image in my head. Rather than cobalt eyes, I imagined a bright blue sky with big, fluffy clouds floating in it. We sat in silence for a few minutes until Romona started to laugh lightly.

"What?" I asked, lids still pressed together to concentrate on keeping the picture.

"Let me guess—you're picturing a sky?"

I took in a quick breath of surprise. "Hey, how'd you . . ." My lips stayed puckered on the word "you" because I opened my eyes and my room *was* the sky. Not just any sky, but the exact sky I had pictured! The precise shade of startling blue dotted with fluffy marshmallow clouds. And the two-dimensional picture was more than just a mural—the clouds drifted slowly as if a slight breeze nudged them lazily through a summer sky. Staring at the floor, which was also moving sky, had a slightly dizzying effect. I gave my head a good shake to free myself from the vertigo.

"How in the world did I do that?" I whispered in amazement.

"I still can't believe he didn't tell you *anything*. I would have done this ages ago if I'd known." She rolled her eyes and crossed her legs as she settled herself on the bed, launching into teaching mode. "This room is attached to you. Specifically to your imagination. This should be the spot where you feel most comfortable. In many ways it can be whatever you want it to be, whatever you can imagine it to be . . . within some limitations, of course."

Throughout the next hour, Romona showed me wonder upon wonder hidden in my four walls. In fact, I learned my room didn't have to have four walls. It could be almost any shape I wanted. In addition to the mini fridge, I also had a built-in snack bar with everything from potato chips to fresh fruit and even fruit roll-ups. She said the room knew what my favorites were and automatically stocked the selection. I was both grateful and jealous that the room knew my favorites when I didn't.

We tweaked the color of my room a bit because the movement of the clouds was disorienting, and I settled on a lighter and more muted shade of motionless silvery-blue. Romona also helped me materialize some furniture, since I still wasn't very good at that. I tried and only managed to bring up some loose stuffing. She thought materializing would get easier for me when my memories returned.

When we were done, I was extremely pleased with the result. My bed had been changed into a four-poster bed of dark mahogany wood, delicately carved with damask designs and scrolling. The bed covers and pillows had been transformed into a pretty shade of lavender with a light damask pattern to match the posts. With just a push of a thought, the bed was still able to magically fold up and disappear into the wall. We created a seating area as well, with comfortable sofa chairs and a low coffee table. I was envisioning a coffeehouse feel, where people could come in and chat and enjoy a few of my super delicious snacks. That is, when I finally made a few more friends.

I shook my head. What a big bad huntress I was going to make with tea parties in my room. I wondered again what in the world they were thinking, making me a hunter. I couldn't brush off the suspicion that one day someone would admit a huge mistake had been made and assign me to something more appropriate. Maybe party planning or dress designing?

Perhaps that was wishful thinking.

Romona interrupted my thoughts. "What are you thinking about? You have a strange look on your face."

I shook my head and smiled ruefully. "Oh, just that it's obvious someone made a colossal mistake. Look at this place. It's definitely more pretty-pretty princess than bloodthirsty demon hunter."

Romona frowned. She looked hurt, which puzzled me. I hoped I hadn't offended her. She was the only person who had truly taken the time to get to know me, and I would hate to have said something to make her unhappy.

"No, Audrey. Mistakes like that don't happen here. Ever," she said. Her eyes avoided mine. "Being a huntress doesn't mean you're not feminine anymore. It does mean, however, that you have something valuable to bring to the table. It means you were specifically created for the job. You might not see it now, but I believe you will eventually. Not everything about being a hunter relies on brute strength and agility."

"But it sure doesn't hurt."

One side on her mouth turned up in a smile that didn't quite reach her eyes. "I'll give you that one."

Romona gave herself a visible shake. "Let's get out tonight. It's not good for you to spend all of your time in this room or the training center. The afterlife is so much more than that. I think you need a little fun after the day you've had."

"That is the best idea I've heard all day." I headed toward my magic closet, determined to end the day well. It was time to change more than just my room.

Romona knew exactly what to do to get my mind off of training, fights with Logan, and my ongoing string of embarrassments. We had dinner with a couple of her friends at a place that resembled a 1950s diner. We sat in red vinyl booths and were served by waitresses on roller skates with foot-high beehive hairdos. But far more interesting than the venue were Romona's friends.

One was a petite, redheaded girl with a great sense of humor, named Sarah. She looked even younger than me, but she said she had been here a while. She didn't elaborate, but the way she said "a while," I assumed she was older than me despite her appearance. She worked as a historian in the great library, which I didn't even know existed. That alone proved I needed to get out more.

The great library not only housed all the books of the world but also the accurate histories of the ages. Sarah explained that she spent time making sure all the events on Earth were cataloged and recorded properly so everyone here could keep up with what was going on there. Most of the information was relayed to the historians through the angels, who frequently traveled between the two realms, but she also admitted there was another source she wasn't allowed to talk about. She remained pretty tight-lipped about it, laughing good-naturedly at my unveiled attempts to pry more details from her. I made it my secret mission to get more information out of her the next time we met.

The other of Romona's friends, Gary, was an equally interesting character in a completely different way. Gary was a black man who grew up in Georgia and actually lived through the American Civil War. He looked about forty years old. Gary's Southern accent was thick, and he was quick to laugh at my "Yankee" accent, immediately making me feel comfortable. His work here had something to do with agriculture. He said it wasn't exactly farming, but close. The next time I had a day off, he'd show me where he worked.

I stayed up late talking and laughing with Romona and her friends and woke up regretting it. Lethargy weighted my limbs as I dragged my feet through the training center hallways. But it wasn't only the lack of sleep that had me moving slowly this morning. Logan had left a note on my door with special instructions for the day. Included was a list of needed items. Considering he'd chucked me in the pond the day before, I thought it was a joke—a bad one. Towel, swimsuit, sandals, and bag lunch. Luckily for Logan, Romona had stopped me from hunting him down to tell him exactly where he could put his list. She somehow even managed to convince me to bring everything he requested.

Logan was doing pull-ups with his back to me when I entered the gym. I didn't bother to stop the door from banging shut behind me. The sound echoed loudly through the room, but it didn't interrupt the rhythm of his reps. I waited for him to acknowledge me. The muscles in his shoulders and arms flexed as he smoothly pulled himself up and down. I was both jealous and impressed at the ease of his movements. I had struggled with just a few pull-ups the day before. He made it look effortless.

Logan finished his set before hopping down and bending over to grab his water bottle. From the state of the room, he must have been there for a while. The practice dummy was once again missing a limb that lay about seven feet away from the rest of the body. A pair of boxing wraps were unraveled next to the punching bag, and the room smelled. *Eww.*

Logan put down his water bottle, wiped his forehead with a towel, and finally jogged over to me. Apparently he did sweat. Kicking my butt must not be much of a workout for him. That prickled my already heightened annoyance. I was prepared to walk straight out of the gym if he said one word about my fainting episode.

"You know, if you've already had your workout, I'm happy to call it a day and come back tomorrow."

"Ha, you should be so lucky. This was just my warm-up"

"Lovely."

"Glad to see you're in another one of your good moods, Sunshine." He eyed my bag. "Did you bring all the things on the list?"

"Yes."

"Good," was all he said.

I let the shoulder strap slide, and the stuffed bag thumped to the floor. "So, speaking of, what do you have planned today?"

"It's a fun surprise. I can tell you one thing, though."

"What's that?"

"We're going down today."

"Down? Down where?" He'd lost me. There was only one

floor to the training center. Maybe there was a basement I didn't know about.

"Down down . . . down to Earth down." He motioned and said the words slowly, as if he were speaking to a child. That was annoying, but I was too caught off guard to care much.

"Really? I mean, we can do that?"

"Of course. Where do you think we fight demons, anyway?"

Holy cow! "We're going to fight demons today? That's what you consider *fun?*" This guy was certifiably crazy.

"Nope, something better." He read concern on my face, and his mouth split into a grin. "Oh come on, don't you trust me?"

"No," I answered flatly.

"Well, fair enough. I did dump you in a pond yesterday."

"Yes, you did."

"But didn't we have a good conversation afterward? Didn't you say that you would trust me?" He took a step closer, and I had to tilt my head back to look at his face. He was trying to manipulate me.

"Yes, but . . ."

"And didn't we agree that you needed to be trained properly?"

I glared at him. I had serious reservations about going back to Earth, even if I wasn't sure why.

"So we can go back, just like that?"

"Yep, just like that."

"We don't need a permission slip or something?"

"Nope."

I met his eyes and tried to look serious. "Are you sure this isn't your evil plot to get rid of me once and for all? Go to Earth and leave me there to wander for the rest of eternity?"

"No, Audrey. I promise." He had the serious face down better than I did. All the earlier teasing was put aside now.

I chewed on my lower lip. Thinking of going back to Earth caused a knot to lodge in my stomach. And maybe I did know why. Going back would mean I would have to admit to myself that this was all real. Was I really ready to start moving forward? So far everything had been new and weird and different, but it certainly didn't feel like *real* life—or rather, *real* death. More like a really long and weird dream.

"Oh, come on, Audrey." He was close enough there was no need to speak loudly. It felt like a whispered dare. "What are you so afraid of?"

His stare was so intense I wanted to squirm. I suppressed the urge and swallowed my remaining reservations.

"Okay, then. How does this work?"

The words escaped my lips as a chill slid down my spine. I didn't have to be a prophetess to see change coming. It encircled and tugged me forward like a rope tied at my waist. The way I saw it, my only options were to either concede to the change and walk upright toward it or plant my feet and be dragged. Either way, change was coming.

9

RIDING THE WAVES

*L*ogan led me across the training center to a room that must have been based on stolen blueprints for the *Star Trek* transporter room. Focused technicians stood behind counter-height panels punching buttons, barely sparing us a glance. In front of them and to our right was a raised, rounded platform with lighted pads just large enough for a human to stand on. I swallowed a giggle.

Logan told me to hang tight while he spoke with the technicians. When he returned, he gave me a few short instructions. After stepping onto one of the pads, I simply had to close my eyes and empty my thoughts.

I stepped up. Clearing my thoughts was harder than expected. Nervous fingers of apprehension skimmed over my body. I'd been told not to talk, so I was left in the blackness to silently wonder what was next.

"She's a little worked up, but it shouldn't be a problem. You're a go for transportation whenever you are ready,

Logan." Suddenly a blast of warm air hit me from all sides, then began to swirl like a tornado, blowing my hair in all directions and muffling my surroundings. I experienced a moment of weightlessness right before the whirlwind stopped.

I squinted against the sudden brightness behind my lids. Tears welled in the corners of my eyes as I forced them open and the world slowly came back into focus. I smelled the salt in the air and heard the rhythmic sounds of the tide flowing in and out before my eyes adjusted enough to see a strip of beach stretched out on either side of me.

Seagulls were calling above, and I smiled. In that moment I discovered something else about myself. I *loved* the beach. I loved the feel of the sand beneath my feet and between my toes, the warmth of the sun on my skin, and the coolness of the water. I loved the weightless feeling of the tide sweeping the sand from beneath your feet as the waters recede back into the ocean.

With a laugh, I stripped off my shoes and ran into the surf. It was as cool and refreshing as I had hoped it would be. I waited with my toes buried in the wet sand to feel the pull of the tide and lifted my face to the sky to soak in the warmth. Inhaling a deep breath I absorbed the peace of my surroundings. There was nowhere else I wanted to be.

And then I was attacked.

I shrieked in surprise when a large, wet, and furry being jumped on me. I lost my balance and landed butt-first in the sand with the creature on top of me. My hands came up in defense as the thing goobered me with its tongue. The sun was so bright and I was so startled that it took me a moment to recognize that a very large dog was on top of me, licking my face as if his life depended on it. Some demon fighter I was! Rendered useless by a family pet.

Realizing I wasn't in any immediate danger, I started to laugh again. The dog licked me with increased fervor. In my defense, the thing must have weighed at least a ton. I struggled to get him off me between mouthfuls of laughter. Why is it always harder to move when you're laughing?

Mercifully, someone yelled, "Peanut! Come here, baby, what are you digging at over there?" The girl calling from down the beach was a petite brunette who didn't look at all as if she could handle an animal his size. "Come here, boy, I've got a treat."

At the word "treat," the dog lifted and turned his head toward the voice, his overgrown apricot coat blowing in the breeze. He sniffed the air as if it testing the validity of his owner's promises.

"Come on, boy, let's go home."

With that, the dog stepped on my throat before bounding off after his owner. I was left on the ground covered in sand, seawater, and dog saliva, but it was the happiest I'd been since I'd woken up dead.

"Some animals can see us, but the people here won't."

Logan's voice jerked me out of the moment. I bent my head back to see him standing a few feet behind me with a relaxed smile on his face, looking off in the direction of my furry friend. "His owner probably just saw him pawing at the sand."

"Yeah, well, I appreciate the chivalrous rescue." I couldn't sound too serious with the big grin on my face.

Logan certainly didn't look offended. "And stop the love fest that dog was giving you? Never!"

He gracefully seated himself on the sand next to me. I was

intrigued by the information he'd just given. "So none of them can see us, huh?"

"Nope. They just see currents in the water or wind blowing the sand."

"So will they, like, just go through us like ghosts? Because I'm going to say right now that I think that would be a major violation of my personal space."

"Well, first of all, there's no such thing as ghosts, but to answer your question, no. When we're on Earth, the people living here have a sixth sense to avoid running into us. Watch this."

He pointed off to the right, where a family of six was walking along the beach with arms full of beach gear. Mom and Dad were trying to corral three young boys and a girl right toward us. When they got within about five feet, the mom pointed at a spot on the beach near the water, and the whole lot of them veered off before stepping right on Logan.

"So what happens if we bump into them?" I asked.

"They trip."

The family was busy setting up their beach chairs and cooler. "So what else should I know about being back on Earth? To actually hunt and fight demons, this is where we need to be, right?"

"Yep, this is the battleground. We usually come down in rotations. We do most of our training back in our realm and then spend time down here protecting, patrolling, and some-times following up on leads. But we don't stay down here for too long. The longer we're on Earth, the weaker we get—both mentally and physically. We're not made for this realm anymore, so it takes a toll on us. It can be pretty dangerous if we're here for too long."

"How long is too long?" I asked.

Logan shrugged his shoulders. "Don't know exactly. We usually try not to stay for more than a few days at a time. Even that is hard. You'll see what I mean."

He picked up a shell in the sand and threw it side-handed into the ocean. I watched it skip across the water before pressing him.

"But what happens if we stay longer?"

Logan's silence was telling. Apparently he wasn't ready to have that conversation yet.

"There are other interesting things about being back on Earth," he told me. Without warning, he picked my hand up from the sand and held it between both of his. I was so taken aback that he was holding my hand that I didn't notice the point he was trying to make. Logan was always so careful to avoid touching my skin.

My hand was so small between both of his. His fingers were long and graceful, more like a painter's than a fighter's. They were a lot softer than I would have imagined them to be as well. Not that I'd ever imagined them to be anything! With that thought, my cheeks started to heat up. Thank goodness for the warmth of the sun.

"Pretty cool, huh?"

Was he talking about holding my hand being pretty cool?

It was only after he dropped mine and went on talking that it registered that I hadn't felt anything from the empathy link. I had been feeling too much of my own stuff to realize I wasn't getting anything from him. That thought made me shift uncomfortably on the sand, putting a few extra inches between us.

"None of us have the empathy link with each other here. It

feels the same as when we were alive. But more importantly, you need to know that we can link with the demons." The muscles in his shoulders tightened, and he sat up straighter. The talk was getting serious.

I finally found my voice. "The demons?"

Logan nodded gravely.

"But why would we want an empathy link with a demon?"

"Exactly. We don't. But *they* do."

As usual, I wasn't following. My brows came together in confusion. "You see, the demons are filled with everything dark in the world—all the hate, wrath, lust, greed, jealousy, and just plain blackness out there. If they get hold of one of us, it's as if we absorb what they are feeling, and it's incapacitating. Not only that, they feed off our emotions. It's similar to the myths of vampires sucking blood from their victims."

I jerked another inch away, creeped out by the thought. "Eww, you have got to be kidding me. That is nasty!"

"Afraid not. Of course, they can't ever *really* suck what's good in us away unless we let them, but it's something I hope you never have to experience."

It was on the tip of my tongue to ask him if *he'd* ever experienced it, but the way he talked about it, it felt too personal a question to ask.

"Demons grow stronger by destroying the people here on Earth. They latch onto people and encourage them to do all sorts of things that ultimately hurt them in the end. The more lives the demons ruin, the greater they grow, but their hunger doesn't stop with the living. If the lives of the living are food to them, then we're a drug. Sometimes they even seek us out because of it . . . like an addict looking for his next fix. It makes some demons very unpredictable and even more dangerous."

That sent a chill down my spine. "I hadn't heard that before."

"There's a lot you still don't know." Logan stared at the waves. A faraway look had captured his eyes. I felt comfortable studying his silhouette because he was so focused on the unseen. "That's why it's so important for you to get all you can out of this training. We try to work in units as much as possible, but you need to be able to defend yourself alone if it ever comes to that. What we do is important to the people we are protecting, but it's also dangerous to ourselves—perhaps even more so for you because they might see you as weak."

I would have been offended by that last comment if he hadn't said it so matter-of-factly. And it wasn't like I could disagree. I'd already admitted more than once that I was a pretty pathetic hunter.

We were both quiet for a few more minutes. I couldn't feel the sun warming me anymore. It felt as if a ball of ice had lodged itself in my throat, preventing me from swallowing. I had to break the tension somehow.

"So did you bring me out here to teach me to swim or something? Because you know, I already figured out that I can swim thanks to the pond you dumped me in yesterday."

The corner of his mouth went up. Now that we weren't in the heat of the moment anymore, even I acknowledged the humor of our fight.

"No, as a matter of fact, I brought you here to teach you to do that."

He pointed. I brought a hand up to my brow to block the sun and spotted a person on a bright blue-and-green board gracefully riding a wave. He agilely cut the board to the left and right to stay on the wave and rode it back to shallower waters.

Immediately, anything demon related was forgotten as I jumped to my feet in excitement.

"Now *that's* what I'm talking about! Where do we start?"

Logan took his time getting to his feet, brushing the loose sand off.

"I'm glad I found something you can be enthusiastic about."

He reached down to the duffel bag he'd brought with him and fished out two wetsuits. I eyed them skeptically. They didn't look particularly comfortable or fashionable. He tossed one at me. I managed to grab the suit before getting slapped in the face with it.

"First, you need to get your bathing suit and that on." He nodded at the black bundle in my hand.

"Why aren't you just materializing yours?"

"Ah, that's another thing about Earth. It takes a *lot* of skill and time to learn to do that here. It's a handy trick to have back home, but it probably won't do you very much good here. You have to bring all your supplies with you. Only what you bring with you will remain invisible to the people here. We can't just pick up a weapon off the ground. We need to use one we've brought with us so people don't see a crowbar or base- ball bat floating in the air. But don't worry; we stash weapons from home around so that anyone who needs them can find them in a pinch."

I picked up on probably the most unimportant part of the explanation.

"So you're telling me other people can do something you can't."

Logan, smart enough to realize I was trying to bait him, just rolled his eyes and pointed a finger behind me.

"Girls' bathroom is that way."

I rolled my eyes back at him and headed in the direction he'd pointed.

After getting changed, I rushed back to the beach. The wetsuit, a rather thick unitard, was not as uncomfortable as I'd imagined. Unfortunately, it was twice as unattractive. I shouldn't have worried since Logan was the only one who could see me, but I was still pretty self-conscious about how ridiculous I looked.

Logan was down the beach a little way waxing up one of the boards. The other lay flat in the sand. I was slightly disappointed that he didn't look half as silly as I felt wearing a wetsuit. But his didn't cover everything from his wrists to his ankles like mine. It was T-shirt style and only went down to his knees. It clung to him like a second skin and showed off all of his lean muscles. More than that, for once he truly looked relaxed.

He stopped working on the board when I walked up.

"Great, you're ready. Have you ever been surfing before?"

I gave him what I hoped was a scolding look.

He winced. "Whoops, sorry about that. I forgot you wouldn't remember. I think we should assume we're starting from square one. The most important thing about surfing is balance. That's why I think this will be a great training exercise for you: if you can learn better balance on a surfboard, it'll help with your balance when fighting."

"Hey, what's wrong with my balance?" I put my hands on my hips in mock annoyance.

Logan shot me a bland look before continuing. "So as I was

saying, balance is the first building block you need to become a good fighter. You need to be in control of your body at all times. Surfing will help you get a feel for your core so that, when there are variables on the outside that are changing, you are still in control."

"All right, I'm ready. Let's go." I grabbed the board he wasn't working on, hefted it under my arm, and turned toward the surf. Before I could get two steps, Logan grabbed my arm to stop me.

"Hold on there. The lesson starts on land."

The water called to me. I stuck my lower lip out in a pout and set the board back down as I gave the ocean a longing look.

Logan laughed. "Oh come on, don't look like that. You look like a puppy that just got his favorite toy taken away."

I put a hand on my hip. "You know it's an incredible tease to be this close and not be able to enjoy it. You just had to find a way to torture me, didn't you?"

Logan laughed harder. "Yes, that's it, Audrey. I'm here solely to make you miserable."

I had to laugh too, despite my annoyance. "Just as I thought. At least you've finally admitted it. And I don't really appreciate being compared to a dog."

He got in another short laugh. "Duly noted. Now let's get started. The faster you catch on, the quicker we can get in the water."

That was motivation enough for me.

10

THE GREAT
ESCAPE

When Logan finally gave me the okay to pick up the board and paddle out into the surf, the water felt as amazing as I'd thought it would. We had spent an hour on the beach as he proceeded to teach me every idiosyncrasy of surfing—including its history. The lengthy wait in my black wetsuit made getting in the water as refreshing as a long drink of iced lemonade on a hot summer's day. I used my arms to paddle out past the breakwater. Although breathing heavily when I finally made the distance, the peaceful surroundings engulfed me. Sitting upright on the board and letting my feet dangle on either side in the water, I took in the vastness of the ocean in front of me.

Logan paddled up beside me.

"It's beautiful, isn't it?"

I just nodded. With all the wonders in the afterlife, seeing the ocean sparkling in the sunlight still took my breath away.

"It's hard to imagine that people would deny a Creator with

all the beauty around them. This doesn't just happen by chance. His fingerprints are all over this world."

I took a deep breath to process his words. There was a lot of wisdom in what he said. "Did you enjoy the ocean this much when you were alive?"

It was the first time I'd ever asked Logan anything about his life on Earth. It was the first time I'd ever cared enough to ask. I turned my head to study him while I waited for a response.

His eyes stayed on the horizon, his expression unreadable. His stoic face safely locked in place. "Yeah, I used to come here a lot. My family owned a home not too far down the beach. This used to be one of my favorite spots."

Here? Logan used to live *here?* I was equally surprised that he was comfortable bringing me to this spot. I looked toward the shore and tried to imagine Logan as a kid running along the beach. It was difficult to envision him so carefree.

"Let's get started," he said, interrupting my thoughts. And with that, Teacher Logan was back. He launched into another lecture on surfing that I was forced to wait out until trying the real thing.

Three hours later, I lay in the sand exhausted. I didn't even care that my hair was covered in sand or that there was a beach crab getting dangerously close to my foot. I was wet, tired, and happy. The surfing had been harder than I anticipated, but I thought I'd done okay. There were times when it felt as if I was flying along the surface like a bird. Eventually my body just gave out on me, and I started making stupid mistakes. Logan picked up on it and called it a day. We both rode a wave toward the shore. I'd pulled my board up onto the sand and collapsed. Logan had taken a moment to look out at the water before setting his board carefully in the sand and taking a seat next to me. As usual, he hardly looked winded. I was too content to care.

"That was fun! Definitely my kind of workout!"

"I'm glad you enjoyed it. It's good to see that when you're properly motivated you're not so much of a klutz."

The backhanded compliment warmed something inside me, and I smiled.

Logan reached up and unzipped the back of his wetsuit, peeling it off to his waist. I almost gasped in surprise at the angry scar that ran diagonally from his left shoulder blade down to his ribs on the right. It looked as if the flesh had been torn from his back. What could make a wound that large? It was the first scar or deformity of any kind I'd seen since entering the afterlife.

I resisted the urge to reach out a hand and trace the scar. Logan looked back at me. If he guessed at what I had been staring at, he didn't let on.

"You ready to get back? I think it's probably about time we got going."

I let out a deep sigh. "If we have to."

The beach was almost deserted. From the position of the sun, I guessed we had an hour of daylight left, if that. I pushed myself up to a sitting position and tried not to stare at Logan's bare chest. I had to admit it was pretty distracting. *My gosh, the boy probably doesn't even realize what effect he could have on girls because he's cooped up in the gym all day.*

I tore my eyes from Logan to stand. Now that we were out of the water, I was equally eager to get my wetsuit off. I reached up to pull the zipper down my back and started to peel the wetsuit from my upper body.

"What are you doing?" Logan sounded startled.

I stopped in the middle of peeling off the right arm. "What?" I looked down at myself and then around at the beach. What was the big deal?

"Don't you want to go to the bathroom or something to do that?"

Huh? "I'm just taking off the wetsuit. I've got my bathing suit on underneath." I didn't know why, but I became a little defensive. "I'll get all my clean stuff nasty if I don't take it off here. It's not as if you've never seen anyone in a bathing suit before." And because I couldn't keep my mouth shut yet again, I added, "Besides, you look practically naked in that thing yourself."

I gestured to his upper torso as I continued to peel the wet material from my skin. Geez, I was even wearing a one-piece. Would his head have exploded if I'd worn a bikini? The thought made me chuckle and lightened my mood.

Although he tried to hide it, Logan looked anything but relaxed. He sat rigidly in the sand with his face trained on the ocean. He might have been a shade or two redder than normal. I was enjoying the idea of making him uncomfortable. Served him right.

All of a sudden he made a huffing sound and pushed himself gruffly to his feet. "Whatever. I'm going to put these boards back. I'll see you back here when you finish getting changed."

Logan grabbed my board as I struggled to get the suit off my legs and stomped up the beach. Seriously, what was his problem?

In a moment I was free of the wetsuit and feeling very sandy and salty. I'd seen showers in the bathroom and decided I deserved the extra time to wash off the grit. I didn't see

Logan anywhere. *Oh well*, I thought, and made my way to the bathrooms.

The shower felt heavenly. I wasn't sure what the people there were seeing—probably just a broken shower steaming up the bathroom—but at that moment, there was nothing nicer than the feeling of clean water washing away the sand and salt from my body.

When I got out, I pulled the towel from my bag, dried off, and quickly put my clothes back on. I sent a silent thanks to Romona for convincing me to bring the bag of extra things. She must have known what we were going to do. I spent a few extra moments working knots out of my long hair, especially happy I'd thought to put a brush in my bag. With my hair down so it could air-dry, I exited the bathroom carrying my bathing and wet suits in my hand.

More time had passed than I realized. The sun was already setting over the water as I traversed the cooling sand. *Huh, guess that means we must be on the west coast somewhere. My money's on California.*

The sky was a mixture of purples and pinks that faded to orange and gold toward the horizon where the sun made its final farewell for the day. As breathtaking as it was, I didn't take too much time to admire it. Logan was likely impatient for my return. In my mind's eye I saw him leaning up against a post with his arms crossed against his chest in frustration. I swiveled my head to find him, but the beach was almost empty. I couldn't see him anywhere.

Suddenly, a bad feeling clenched my chest. It was as if I smelled something wrong in the air. But it wasn't a smell at all. It was something icky trying to burrow its way into my brain. I looked around frantically to locate the source. I could have sworn there was a pressure against my head, but when I turned there was no one there. My breathing picked up as my mind went wild with possible explanations.

Out of nowhere Logan appeared, grabbed my hand, and jerked me into a run. It was difficult to sprint across the sand, especially carrying a bundle of wet things and a pack, but I somehow managed to keep up. When we reached the road and rounded a corner, I was finally able to yank my hand free.

"What in the world was that all about?"

Logan looked at me with the familiar annoyed look. "Keep walking."

"Logan, what's going on?"

He refused to look at me as his eyes scanned the area. He spoke more to himself than me. "I know there's a boardwalk around here, not too far away. We just need to get there."

"Logan!" I shouted this time. "What was that back there?"

I slowed down, forcing him to look back at me. He finally did.

"It was a demon. We have to keep moving."

I stumbled on nothing when he said "demon" and took a few quick steps to steady myself. This wasn't the time for questions, but I had a million of them. A cord of dread grew thicker in my gut. Logan looked concerned, and if he was concerned, I was sure there was cause to be.

"Did it see us? Does it know we're here?" I took a quick look around us, suddenly convinced we were going to be attacked at any minute. My imagination was running ahead of me, but I didn't know how to stop it.

"I'm not sure. If we get to a group of people, we should be able to blend in. Usually, the only way they can distinguish us —when we aren't in body armor—is that we can see them. If we blend in naturally, there's a chance the demon won't realize we're here."

We were still walking at a fast clip. Logan continued, "Getting back isn't as easy as getting down to Earth. We have to get a lift back from an angel. One was scheduled to get us on the beach, but we can't wait for her there anymore. We'll have to go to the backup location after we've lost the demon."

My mind was spinning. There was so much I didn't know.

"Don't you want to, maybe, stay and fight it or something?"

Although that was the last thing *I* wanted to do, I wondered why we were running. Weren't we supposed to be fighting? Wasn't that what we were, demon hunters?

Logan's eyes flicked toward me for a moment before scanning the area.

"We aren't prepared, Audrey. We don't have any weapons, we have no armor. You're almost completely untrained. This isn't a time we want to meet a demon."

He suddenly grabbed my hand again. "Quick, it's this way, I'm sure."

We made a sharp turn to the left around a small dune, and sure enough, there was a bustling little boardwalk up ahead. The lights were just coming on with the darkening sky, and it was filled with people. It was exactly what we needed to blend in. I started to get giddy with renewed hope, but a moment later, I sensed the demon again: the smell that wasn't a smell, the dark pressure on me. It pushed against me from behind.

"Logan . . ." Something in the tone of my voice made him turn to me. "I can feel it coming."

Logan looked less worried and more determined and gave my hand a quick squeeze as he pulled me forward.

"We're almost there." It was all he said, as if getting somewhere would mean we were safe.

And he was right. We stepped onto the planks of the boardwalk and were swallowed into the crowd. I was relieved for about two seconds until I realized the crowd was parting around us, just like Logan had said they would. There was something wrong with this. We were still too conspicuous to hide, and I felt the demon behind, stalking us from the beach. We needed to go somewhere more private but still busy, somewhere where it wouldn't look weird to have people avoiding us.

Logan must have been thinking the same thing, because he quickly pulled us toward the opposite side of the boardwalk where it was slightly less crowded. It took all my willpower not to look behind us. The fine hairs on the back of my neck stood up, and the non-smell was getting worse.

We walked by some of the less popular stands on the boardwalk. Logan kept me moving at a quick pace. I dug in my heels all of a sudden and tugged on Logan's hand to get him to look at me.

"Logan, we have to stop running. It just makes us look more obvious."

It went against every instinct I had not to break out at a full run in the opposite direction of the demon, but I knew I was right. Logan looked at me doubtfully but stopped, and together, we started again at a slower pace. What could we possibly do to blend in with normal living humans? And then a thought came to me.

To our left there was a space between two stands that was slightly dark but still partially lit by the boardwalk's bright lights. Impulse took over, and I went for it. I caught Logan by surprise enough to drag him in after me.

"What the . . ." was all Logan was able to get out before I crushed his mouth with my lips. My face heated with embarrassment, but I willed him to understand what I was doing. No such luck. He was an unmovable statue, with his arms tense to his sides and his feet rooted to the ground. He obviously wasn't catching on. This wasn't going to work if he couldn't play along.

I pulled back enough from the fake kiss to urgently whisper, "Put your arms around me." When he didn't immediately comply, I whispered the command more forcefully, "NOW!" and stomped on his foot for emphasis.

Something finally roused in him. His arms obediently slid around my waist, and he pulled me closer. I reached a hand around the back of his neck to bring his mouth back down toward mine and kissed him like my life depended on it.

As Logan suppressed his surprise and regained control of himself, he also captured control of the kiss and softened it. As his lips molded to mine, I tried hard not to think about how soft they were. When he tilted his head to change the pressure, I tried hard not to notice that he tasted like peppermint and that my lips were now tingling a little. With a mind of its own, my hand moved up the back of his neck to bury in his thick hair. One of Logan's hands slid up my arm to cup the side of my face, leaving goosebumps in its wake. His other tightened around my waist to pull me even closer. He tilted his mouth to deepen the kiss as his thumb slid under my chin to stroke the sensitive skin there.

With a sigh, my body melted into his hard chest. The quickening of my pulse now had nothing to do with the demon stalking us, and I forgot why we were kissing. A moment later, when Logan pulled back slightly, I found myself stunned, and a small sound of protest slipped out of my throat. He looked down at me with lidded eyes. Like always, his steel-blue gaze held me prisoner. We were both breathing far too quickly.

"I think it worked," he said huskily. I was close enough to feel the words vibrate in his chest.

The sound of his voice snapped me out of my daze. Right! The demon! The kiss was to throw the demon off us, and it had been my idea. My earlier embarrassment flooded back. One of my hands rested on his chest and the other was still buried in his thick, soft hair. I felt his heart beating through his shirt, almost as fast as mine.

With a small gasp, I yanked my hand out of his hair and pushed against his chest to free myself. But his hold on me tightened, and I found I couldn't move. He tilted his head down to bring his mouth close to my ear. His breath caressed my neck, and his thumb was now making lazy circles on my cheek.

"Hold still. It's still out there."

My body immediately tensed, and he felt it. "It's okay. I just want to get a little more distance between us."

Logan held me close, trapped between his arms and chest, for what seemed to be a few more minutes. My heart beat wildly, and my whole body remained tense. What had just happened?

Finally, Logan used the hand under my chin to force me to look up at him.

"Are you all right?"

His blue stare captured me. He should not be allowed to be dead with those eyes.

It took me a second to find my voice. "Yeah," was all I could squeak out.

"That was pretty quick thinking."

I did not want to talk about that kiss, especially since we were still in a "fake" embrace. I put pressure on Logan's chest again, and this time he released me. I took a few shaky steps back and looked anywhere but at him. The air felt hotter than it had under the midday sun. My mind grasped for a way to escape the discomfort.

"So where do we go from here?"

Logan took a moment before answering. When he did, there was a change in his voice. He was all business again. "We have to find the backup extraction point. I don't want to go back to the beach tonight. I think I know of another one in the area, though."

"How do we know we won't be followed?"

"I'll be more careful this time. I should have seen the last one coming from a mile away. I was distracted."

I snuck a look at Logan. He wasn't looking at me. He had a shoulder leaned against the wall of the stand and was scanning the crowd behind me. He looked both casual and alert.

Where *had* Logan been when I got to the beach? I was about to ask when he straightened and quickly brushed past me.

"Come on," he said as he passed.

He stopped at the boardwalk to wait for me. Serious Logan was back, and for once, I was glad of it. I bent over to grab my discarded items. I must have dumped them on the ground when I attacked Logan. He didn't grab my hand this time when he stepped out into the crowd. I was glad about that too.

We walked along the boardwalk in silence. Not close enough to touch, but close enough to still make it appear that we were together. It was probably the most awkward moment of my life. Or so I would guess, since I couldn't remember any of the other moments.

Shaking my head in chagrin, I realized I had been right about one thing: change had definitely arrived.

11

THE DAY AFTER

*I*s there a word stronger than "awkward"? If so, multiplying that by twenty would describe what it was like to be in the training gym with Logan the day after our trip to Earth.

We'd returned the evening before and were immediately directed to fill out a report on "the incident." I'd mumbled through some answers before finally claiming a headache, hiding from Logan as much as from the questions. Logan stayed to finish the report while I fled. I cringed to think of what he'd revealed.

I lay awake half the night thinking of other ways we could have escaped the demon. We could have hidden behind a building, pretended to be in line for cotton candy, taken an empty seat on one of the rides, or jumped off a high bridge into shallow water. *So* many attractive options. Why couldn't I have thought of one of those?

Hunters swarmed our training gym in the morning, wanting to know all the details. I wished we'd come up with something clever to tell people other than that we'd made out. And that it was my idea.

"Hey Audrey, I hear you *knew* the demon was coming or something? That you could feel it? What's the deal with that?"

The curious question came from someone to my right. This was a safe topic. Some of the murmur died down.

"Yeah, well, it's hard to explain, but I just kind of knew it was gaining on us and generally where it was. It felt like a pressure. Or maybe a smell, but it was a smell that wasn't a smell, ya know?"

Apparently the articulate part of my brain was in the off position.

The guy, most likely trying to help by changing the subject, veered to a topic that caused my stomach to jump to my throat.

"Well, what did you guys do to shake it? I'd love to hear how you gave it the slip when it was already on to you."

Heavy silence hung in the air as they waited for an answer, hoping to discover a secret for bluffing a demon. A sea of faces full of anticipation. My cheeks heated and my mind buzzed. My "technique" could not be duplicated—not by this bunch of meatheads, anyway. I couldn't think of what to say.

An unexpected rescue came from across the room. "Audrey pulled us between two of the stands."

"And it didn't see you guys? That didn't look suspicious?"

"We tried very hard to look inconspicuous."

The way Logan said it gave finality to the answer. There was a disappointed murmur throughout the crowd, evidence that the muscle-bound hunters didn't understand the logic. "Sorry it's not more exciting. We were lucky to have gotten out of there unscathed. And if you guys don't mind, we've got to get back to training so the next time we won't have to do so much hiding."

There were a few chuckles from the crowd at the not-too-subtle dismissal, but they got the point and dispersed.

My feeling of relief was short-lived. It was only after the last person left and the doors slammed shut that I reluctantly turned in Logan's direction. Taking a deep breath, I looked him in the eyes. His clear gaze stared back, and his familiar stoic expression was in place. That, in a way, was oddly comforting.

"Do we need to talk about this?" His voice was flat and to the point.

"Nope," I answered just as directly.

"You sure?

"Yep."

"Okay then, let's get back to work."

And with that, the matter appeared to be closed. But I couldn't shake the awkwardness of simply being around him.

Before yesterday, I'd spent a good amount of time imagining Logan getting his butt kicked by one of the other hunters or losing his balance and falling on his face. I'd be lying if I didn't admit he'd always had unquestionable good looks going for him, but he drove me so crazy I never cared. He yelled at me, pushed me past my limits, made me train when I didn't want to, and remained a constant reminder of every strength I didn't possess.

Now, what I thought of Logan was all jumbled up, and I didn't like that. I'd even arrived a few minutes late this morning because I couldn't decide what to wear.

The change in my behavior was not welcome. How could

one stupid fake kiss change so much so quickly? I was resolved to get back to where we'd been before, even if that meant being at each other's throats. At least that made sense to me.

Only I wasn't sure how to make that happen.

Logan was characteristically quiet as he went across the room. I tracked his movements as he bent over and pulled something metallic out of his bag. He brought it to me, stopping with a gulf of space between us. He tossed the object. I snatched it from the air before it collided with my face. Perhaps my reflexes were improving.

Pinching a section, I rubbed it back and forth between my fingers. It was some sort of fabric or bendable metal, incredibly smooth and slick, almost like reptile skin. I held one end up and let the rest drop to the floor—a garment. It made a faint clinking noise as it fell.

"It's your body armor."

Oh.

"It's what we wear for hunting. It creates a barrier so the demons can't create an empathy link with us, and it protects us from getting physically hurt. It's very difficult to cut through."

I took my eyes from the material and looked up at him.

"You were wearing this the first day we met, weren't you? When you sparred with Alrik?"

That had been the first time I'd seen anyone dematerialize anything. The sight of the armor melting off Logan had been shocking. That day seemed lifetimes ago.

"I was. Sometimes we wear it when sparring—it's good to be accustomed to it. It's incredibly strong. You know chain mail, right?"

"Huh? Like a spam e-mail you're supposed to pass on to

everyone you know?" I couldn't see how that had anything to do with the bundle in my hands.

A small smile snuck its way onto Logan's lips before they flat-lined again. "I believe you are thinking of chain letters. Chain *mail* is a type of armor. They used it in the Middle Ages. It's made from metal linked together." He linked his fingers together to demonstrate.

"Oh right, that." I ducked my head in embarrassment.

"Well, this material is similar except the links are unimaginably small. And it's made from a metal that's not found on Earth. That's what makes it so light but still strong and protective."

"That's pretty cool, actually." I brought the material up to my eyes. Despite closing one eye and squinting at the armor, I couldn't discern the weave. It looked completely smooth, like a flat sheet of metal.

"Anyway," Logan continued, "I figured since our adventure yesterday, it's time for you to start learning about our fighting gear. It's what you'll be wearing the next time you face a demon. So you need to go and get that on."

"It goes right over my clothes?"

"Yes. It will form to whatever you're wearing and create shields for extra protection on vulnerable areas of your body."

Logan materialized his own armor covering. Shadows clung to his form, and an instant later solidified into a full body covering.

As I remembered it, his suit was made of closely fitting metal armor. His shins and thighs were covered with extra plates, the ones on his shins stretching low enough to cover his ankles as well. A belt encircled his hips, complete with a scabbard encasing his sword. A breastplate protected his chest, and similar plates of metal shielded his arms. From the neck down, whatever parts of him weren't fortified by a metal plate were covered with metallic material, including his hands and feet.

The armor made him look like a cross between a medieval warrior and Batman. Logan wore it as if he were born to do so.

I really did need to learn how to materialize things better. It was going to save me tons of time. I looked down, doubtful that what I had in my hands was the same thing Logan had just materialized. I grimaced at my mental picture of myself in the armor.

"Okay, Show-Off," I said lightly enough so he would know I was kidding, "I'll go put mine on."

Logan didn't crack a smile, but his jaw twitched—as if he was clenching his teeth to keep his mouth shut. He really was in rare form; as if he couldn't decide what his mood should be.

I pushed through the training gym's doors, forcing Logan and his moods out of my mind, and walked toward the girl's locker room. Empty. I turned the fabric over in my hands, trying to find an opening to insert a limb. I was baffled. The armor rolled through my fingers like slippery seaweed as I searched for a seam or some kind of shape.

"It's easier to put on if you hold it right-side up."

Startled, I dropped the material. It landed on the ground with hardly a sound. I spun.

Resting a shoulder against one of the lockers was a girl dressed in black-and-pink workout clothes. She was tall and lean with honey-tanned skin. Her long blonde hair was pulled back into a high ponytail that brushed her right shoulder. My hair never looked that good in the sporty do, but it both fit and complimented her features perfectly. She reminded me of a beach volleyball player—not overly muscled like the guys, but well-toned.

And gorgeous.

I gaped as she continued talking, repeating herself as if I hadn't understood the first time. "You know, the armor." She gestured toward the heap on the floor. "You need to hold it the right way to get it on." She was smiling, but I wondered if it was really a smirk.

"Oh, well, that's news to me," I answered with bite to my words. Why hadn't Logan explained that?

"Whoa there." She pushed her shoulder off the locker and put her hands up in front of her in an "I mean no harm" manner. Two perfect eyebrows rose. "Listen, it just looked like you needed some help."

"Sorry." I blew out a frustrated breath and forced a smile. "I've just been a little stressed lately. I didn't mean to be rude. It's one of those days, you know?" I looked down at the material at my feet and bent to pick it up.

She nodded as if she understood, her smile still in place. I couldn't shake the suspicion she was laughing at me.

"So, ah, could you tell me which side is right-side up?"

"Here, do you mind?" She plucked it from my hands. "You see this?" She showed me an almost indistinguishable bulge in the material. "You need to hold it there."

When she demonstrated, the armor magically took form. There was clear definition between the top and the bottom as well as where your limbs were supposed to go.

She continued, "Then you see there's a seam here that acts kind of like a zipper. You slide it down in order to step into it."

She handed the bundle back to me right side up. I quickly found the seam she was talking about. I lifted my head to say "thanks" only to catch a glimpse of her back as she exited the locker room.

Now that was weird. Who was she? Another hunter? There were other female hunters, but besides Romona, I hadn't seen any, and frankly, I'd hardly given them much thought.

But if I had done so, that girl was what I would have imagined. Nothing like me. Whereas her limbs were long and toned, mine felt short and weak. Her posture oozed confidence; mine usually radiated clumsiness.

The new feelings bubbling up inside were ugly. I shoved them down.

Giving my head a shake, I forced my mind back to the task at hand, which was getting into this ridiculous outfit. Twenty minutes later, I achieved victory.

I was taken aback when I faced the mirror. Mine was obviously a girl version of the suit. The metal plates that covered my legs, chest, and arms were less pronounced and more delicate. The armor fit like a second skin, as much as it did Logan. I looked like some sort of futuristic, comic-book warrior queen. All I needed now was dark, smudgy makeup and a few purple highlights. Perhaps looking the part would help with my training?

I threw a few practice kicks and punches at the air in front of the mirror. The suit still felt slightly cumbersome despite its sleekness. It was going to take some getting used to . . . but I was willing to put the work in. I definitely looked more hard-core now.

I was in a decisively good mood as I marched down the hallway back to the training gym. I received some curious stares and someone even whistled at me, which in a weird way helped increase my confidence as much as it tinted my face. I was giving myself a silent pep talk when light, singsong laughter wafted out from our training gym. I stood on tiptoes to peer through one of the door's high windows. It was a precarious position to say the least, but it offered a view of the whole gym.

Logan was standing in the middle with the girl from the locker room, facing her with an easy smile on his face. He said something, and the girl tilted her head back to laugh, flipping her ponytail over her shoulder at the same time. She leaned in closer and put a hand on his armored bicep, whispering something in his ear. Logan smiled and nodded at her when she pulled back.

That same ugliness gurgled in my chest once again. It nettled me immensely that she had touched him so familiarly, and even more so that he didn't seem to mind.

A hand on my back scared me so much I yelped and pitched forward, smashing through the gym doors with a crash and landing sunny-side down on the floor. I somehow managed to elbow myself in the stomach on impact, knocking the wind from my lungs. I gasped for breath on the ground, my face squished to the padded floor. I *seriously* needed to get better at reacting to the unexpected.

Logan and the girl looked up from their conversation with matching expressions. My attacker quickly stepped forward and offered me a hand up.

"Oh man, sorry about that, Audrey. I didn't mean to scare you."

I craned my neck to look up. It was Kevin. Tall and lankier than most of the warriors, Kevin was nevertheless imposing. He glanced down at me and then at Logan and the girl, and then back at me again. The look on his face said he realized what an awkward situation this was.

"Ah, yeah, it's no problem," I mumbled hastily and accepted his offered hand. He practically dislocated my shoulder jerking me to my feet.

"Whoa there, sorry! You're a lot lighter than you look." His face turned from his normal latte color to a deeper coffee hue when he caught his mistake. "I mean, just that, you know, you ah . . . I mean, it's not that you look heavy or anything. Really, you're super short and all; it's just that you're really light."

He was digging himself into a deeper hole with every word and finally gave up. There was a moment of uncomfortable silence. Logan and the girl continued to stare at us as I rubbed the feeling back into my left shoulder.

Kevin broke the silence first. "Well, anyway, I'll let you get back to it." He backpedaled out of the gym. "Your armor looks great, by the way, Aud. Fits you really well. Not that I was noticing how it fit you or anything, but ah, yeah. Well, ah, I'll see you around then."

With a quick wave, Kevin turned and fled. The doors swung shut behind him.

It was painfully quiet after he left. Logan and the girl remained rooted in the same spot, their faces turned toward me. The silence stretched for a few heartbeats.

The girl let out a nervous laugh. "Well, I helped you figure out how to get the armor on, but I'm afraid I can't help much with your coordination."

To my extreme embarrassment, Logan laughed with her. My face turned colors, but there wasn't much I could do. I'd just been caught eavesdropping and proved to be the biggest klutz alive. I still didn't appreciate the jab at my expense.

"Kaitlin, as you've probably already guessed, this is Audrey."

The girl, Kaitlin, stepped forward and extended her hand, practically daring me with the empathy link. I was prepared to step up to the challenge but remembered as she grasped my hand that my armor prevented me from getting an emotional read. I was covered from fingertips to toes. I twisted my mouth in disappointment. I really wanted to know if she was purposefully trying to make me look stupid or not.

"We met a little while ago in the locker room," Kaitlin told Logan. "Audrey needed some help getting her armor on."

I felt like the third wheel in the gym even though, technically, *she* was the intruder. This training time was supposed to be for me.

"I guess that was fortunate," Logan answered. He finally addressed me. "Kaitlin and I go way back. She's stationed with another group of hunters in a different part of the realm, but she's over here helping out with a special project. We were just talking about her training with us sometime while she's here to give you some pointers. She's got some great moves."

My eyes narrowed. "Sure."

Kaitlin laid her hand on Logan's arm again. Could she stop touching him already?

"Well, I should probably get going. It was great to get a minute to catch up, Logan. I'm sure I'll see you soon."

"Yeah, definitely." Logan offered her one of the easy smiles I so rarely received.

She walked past me as she left. "It was nice to meet you, Audrey. I'm hoping to see you around too. It's always nice to have another female hunter in the mix."

The smile she gave me seemed genuine enough, but I couldn't muster the emotion to return it. She looked unsure for a moment and her smile slipped fractionally, but she stepped gracefully through the door without another word.

I waited for the door to shut fully before turning back to Logan. He was watching me rather than the door. I felt myself go hot, then cold. His face quickly changed, and he turned toward the weapons wall.

That was odd.

Logan came back toward me with a sword in his hands, his training face back on. "We'll train without the helmet at first until you get used to the rest of the armor."

He extended the hilt of the sword to me. As always, it seemed a little too heavy.

"All right, let's get started."

We barely said two words to each other the rest of the day. Mostly just Logan's short commands to correct my form or tell me to try harder. There was none of the warmth or carefree spirit I'd seen a day earlier. There was no light banter. Logan kept his distance, and I trained on practice dummies the entire day. It was as if, with that one kiss, we'd erased any positive progress we'd made—even taken a step back. There was a cold tension that hadn't been there.

I was exhausted when I left the training center later that day. I didn't notice that I was mumbling to myself until someone answered me.

"What was awkward?"

Romona's voice made me jump, and I put a hand to my chest to calm my beating heart. Why was everyone startling me today?

"Oh my gosh, sneak up on people much?" I snapped.

Romona didn't deserve my sarcasm, but I was in a testy mood. The look on her face said I'd hurt her feelings.

"Oh geez, I'm really sorry, Romona. I'm just kind of out of sorts today." I smiled meekly at her. "Yesterday shook me up a bit."

Always quick to forgive and comfort, she moved to put a sympathetic hand on my arm. I quickly jerked out of reach, not sure which of my jumbled emotions the empathy link would reveal. Her eyes widened as she regarded me suspiciously.

We stood in silence. Without a plausible excuse for pulling away, I froze.

"All right then, when you want to talk about it, let me know." She briskly turned and walked away.

I felt incredibly alone watching her retreating figure, but I didn't have the nerve to chase after her. I wasn't ready to talk about it. Besides, it was just a kiss—a fake kiss at that—so things would surely go back to normal in a few days. I hoped.

With a resigned sigh and an overwhelmed heart, I headed toward my tree, feeling as if I missed a best friend I'd never had. Or perhaps I had, but I'd forgotten her along with the rest of my life. The thought depressed me further.

Once back in my room, I flopped onto my bed, curling my knees and hugging them to my chest. Something warm and wet rolled down my cheek and absorbed into the pillow under my head. I squeezed my eyes shut to stop feeling so much. Fresh tears leaked out of the corners anyway. A flood I couldn't dam crashed down on me. And as the salty water continued to flow, it revealed a cavern inside. An emptiness I had ignored that had been growing steadily every day since I arrived, fed by hopelessness I didn't know how to overcome. Unchecked, I feared it would leave me as a hollow shell—only a husk of a person.

I was suddenly very angry at the God I hadn't met and

didn't remember. I sat up and punched the pillow that collected my tears. I'd forgotten my past, and my future was uncertain at best. I didn't have a family to mourn or even a God to turn to. I was utterly alone and completely abandoned. What kind of God would plan for this? Would take away everything only to replace it with nothing? Giving me a task that was so beyond my abilities was an extra punch in the gut.

I held my breath and waited for something catastrophic to happen. Wasn't being angry with God cause for expulsion from this place? Wasn't that why I hadn't been honest with myself until now—hadn't been willing to admit how angry I really was?

I continued to wait as the tears dried on my face and nothing happened. The longer I sat in silence, the better I felt. I hadn't thought I'd be allowed to be mad at Him without repercussions.

An unexpected emotion stirred in the empty hole of my heart. God was giving me the freedom to be angry without turning His back on me. It didn't make sense, but in that moment, alone in my room, without saying a word, I experienced something that felt an awful lot like comfort.

More tears welled in my eyes, but these were born of a different emotion. One strong enough to soften my hardened heart.

I jumped up off my bed, wanting immediately to share the revelation with Romona, but then I remembered our parting. I deflated a little.

With my hand on the doorknob, I considered my options. I did need to apologize, but I wasn't ready to tell her what had happened between Logan and me.

My feet were moving before I realized the decision was made. I at least needed to make things right with her.

Finding her, though, might be somewhat tricky. I chastised myself for never taking the time to find out where she lived as I hurried though the damp hallways and then out into the dwindling light of early evening.

12

APOLOGIES

"Hey, Audrey, wait up!"

After exiting the forest I skirted the city on the sidewalk, heading back to the training center to look for Romona. I was so buried in thoughts I hadn't noticed the familiar face I passed. I jerked my head to the left to see Kevin jogging to catch up.

I wasn't angry at Kevin for today's embarrassment, but his wasn't the friendly face for which I was searching. I stopped anyway. Someone just knowing me well enough to want to talk made me feel better.

"Hey, Kevin, what's up?"

He wore his easy smile. "Nothing much. I was just hanging out with some guys." He waved his hand over to a group playing basketball on the court I'd walked right by. The players not currently in the game nodded their heads or waved back. I looked back up at Kevin. His height and lanky limbs made me wonder—I could imagine him effortlessly finding a home on an NBA court or some other professional sport. Someday when I knew him better, I'd ask about that.

"You kicking any non-hunter butt over there?" I asked instead, returning the smile he'd offered.

"Ha, more like learning from the best. Some of those guys were all-stars down on Earth." He leaned a little closer and lowered his voice a little. "Although I did win a wicked game of HORSE a few minutes ago. Hunter jumping skills may have given me an advantage." He looked so proud of himself I couldn't help but laugh with him.

"So where are you off to anyway? You look like a girl on a mission. Had to yell your name a few times to get your attention."

Man, was I that dense sometimes? "I was looking for Romona. I'm not exactly sure how to find her. I wish we had cell phones here. Or a sixth sense to know where anyone is at any given moment."

"That would be kind of weird."

"Yeah, I guess so. I wouldn't want to know every time someone went to the bathroom or anything."

He gave me a strange look before continuing. "Well, maybe I can help out. She lives in the same building I do. She might still be there if she hasn't left to get dinner. I could show you where it is."

"That would really be wonderful."

Kevin jogged back to tell his friends he'd be back in a few and returned in no time.

"So where do you guys live anyway? I'm assuming we all don't live in trees."

"You live back in the redwoods?" He seemed genuinely surprised.

"Yeah, is that bad?"

"Oh no, that's pretty cool actually. It's a little further away, but not very many people get assigned out there. You're kind of on the fringe." He didn't have to tell me that. Although beautiful, the giant trees did always feel a little removed. On the fringe—that was a good way to describe how I always felt here.

As Kevin forged ahead, I quickened my pace to keep up with his leggy strides.

"We live over there."

His outstretched finger pointed to a group of shining buildings not far from the training center. I'd taken notice of them several times because of their unique design. The buildings were shaped like an open book, with windows everywhere. It looked like they were floating in the air, but they were actually supported by some sort of clear, crystal-like material. A gigantic escalator brought people up and down from the ground to the first floor, which looked to be over a hundred feet up.

"Do you like it there?" I asked as we approached.

"Sure. It's temporary housing. The same as you're in right now."

"Temporary? What's that mean?"

"It just means we haven't all picked a permanent home yet. That's typical of people who still have family living on Earth."

"Really? Why's that?"

"Because usually you want to wait to settle somewhere near the people you loved when you were alive. A lot of us are just holding tight until that happens, ya know?"

I looked up at Kevin's content face as we approached the bright building.

"May I ask how long you've been there?"

"A while."

"Is it hard to wait?"

He didn't make me clarify. "At times. But I want them to finish out their lives on Earth. If they aren't here, it's because they still have things to accomplish there."

"But even if they have stuff to accomplish, a purpose for still being there, how does that make it easier to not be with them? Just because your head knows something doesn't mean your heart will follow."

Kevin nodded. "That's true—there's a difference when something penetrates your heart as well as your head. I suppose I'm okay because I believe in here," he patted his chest to indicate his heart, "that it's for the best, and I know I'll see them again."

Kevin's comment was surprisingly insightful. I was humbled to think I hadn't considered him very deep. There was more to him than just the sports fanatic I'd seen around the lunch room. I smiled to think I counted him a friend.

"Well, here we are! I hope you don't mind if I head back. I promised the guys a rematch."

I nodded before looking up at the structure before us. The escalator brought people up and down. We were right in front of the building, and I could make out its belly, which was just as see-through as the crystal pillars. People, looking tiny from here, walked back and forth on that first floor. It made my stomach flip simply looking at it.

"I appreciated the company. Do you happen to know which room she's in?"

"Just take the escalator up to the front desk, and they'll direct you the rest of the way. They're really nice."

"Thanks, Kevin!"

I gave him a quick hug for all the kindness he'd shown me. He backed away a few steps after I released him, uncomfortable. "Don't mention it. You're good people, Audrey."

I watched him jog off, then took my time getting to the escalator. Making amends with Romona wasn't going to be as easy as talking to Kevin. Some of my nerve was pinched away when I stepped onto the rising steps.

The escalator was also slightly translucent. Reluctant to look down, I surveyed the view. The city sprawled out before me in brilliant white. It contrasted with the green woods and brilliant sky surrounding it, yet city and nature were each just as beautiful in their own way. Each building had uniqueness about it. Close by, a tall spiral building high enough to pierce the clouds was circled by many shorter square buildings with pointed roofs and etched stones on each corner. The skyscraper beyond plunged and rose in a seemingly random pattern that was still pleasing to the eye. I wasn't thrilled with heights and was relieved to make it to the top without falling over the edge.

I stepped off the escalator and into a world of light. The ground twinkled with inlaid colored diamonds; crystal end tables supported jeweled vases full of vibrant flowers reflecting sparkling light. Even my arms appeared to have picked up a luminescent quality. I looked down to see a distorted landscape below, then jerked my gaze up.

"Is there something I can help you with, Little One?"

The voice had come from behind the large mirrored front desk to my left. The large man standing behind it had a deep voice, filled with warmth. He made me think of Christmas—of Santa Claus, complete with the rosy cheeks and white beard that glowed in the strangely lit room.

"I hope so. I'm looking for a friend. Her name is Romona . . ." How was it possible I didn't know her last name? Come to think of it, I didn't know anyone's last name.

"Romona the hunter?"

"That's the one," I said, relieved.

"She's a very sweet girl, isn't she?"

"Yes sir, she is." It was another reminder of how horrible I'd been to her that day.

He spent a few short moments punching something up on the clear monitor in front of him. "Here we are." The Santa smile lit up his rosy face. "She's up on the fourteenth floor. Room 733."

"Thank you. Is it okay if I just go up?"

"Yes, of course. Have you been here before?"

I shook my head.

"Just take the elevator over there. Straight up to the four-teenth floor and follow the signs in the right direction."

"Thank you, sir."

The elevator, constructed of completely see-through mate-rial, was more than a little unnerving. I squeezed my eyes shut so I didn't have to watch the ground getting further and further away and concentrated instead on the soft harp music. A chime sounded before the doors slid open.

To my immense relief, the floor was not transparent. Shiny as plastic lacquer and illuminated from below, but not translucent.

Squinting against the near blinding whiteness of the ending hallway, I found a plaque opposite me.

Rooms 1–500 to the left, and 501–1000 to the right. A thousand rooms on this floor alone? Romona's room couldn't be larger than a shoebox.

I started off to the right. Sparkling white diamond doors butted up next to each other. Twice I spotted people exit their rooms and tried to get an inconspicuous look as I passed. Were they crammed into a long, narrow corridor of space? Both times I missed a peek as they closed their doors behind them.

When I finally reached room 733, I looked down at a floral mat with the word "Welcome" spelled out. I certainly hope so.

With a deep breath, I lifted my hand and knocked. It was several moments before the door gently opened. When it did, Romona just stood there and stared. I stared back. A few awkward seconds ticked by.

"I didn't realize you knew where I lived." Her tone wasn't harsh, but it was slightly guarded, confirming her hurt.

"I ran into Kevin, and he showed me. Otherwise I would have been aimlessly searching the food district all night."

"Oh."

My uncertainty over coming to see her started to grow. I told myself again this was the right thing to do.

"So, um, would you mind if I come in? I actually wanted to apologize for earlier this evening. You know, after I was leaving the training center. And I was wondering if you wouldn't mind talking a bit. I just have some stuff on my mind I was hoping I could talk about."

I stared down at the mat, feeling rather dejected as she left me hanging outside. And then Romona's hand came to rest on the same shoulder I'd shrugged her off earlier. With relief, I sensed through the empathy link that I was already forgiven. She gave me a reassuring squeeze before letting go.

"Of course. Come on in so we can talk." She held the door open for me.

My jaw dropped as I walked through the door. Romona

lived in a ballroom. Domed ceilings soared at least thirty feet in the air, meeting at a point in the middle where a crystal chandelier dropped down like a pendant to light the room. The walls were draped with rich velvet fabrics and adorned with gilded mirrors. Intricately inlaid wood covered the large square floor from one end to the other. And a wall of glass held a breathtaking view of the distant mountain range.

"What do you think?" she asked

"It's empty," was the first thing out of my mouth. "I mean it's incredibly beautiful, but you don't have any furniture." And then as an afterthought, "And how did this all fit behind your door? There's another door not a foot away from yours!"

She lifted her eyebrows. "I would have thought after we finished your room, you'd realize spatial rules don't really apply anymore." She shook her head, a small smile playing at the corners of her mouth. "And I do have furniture, I just put it away sometimes. I like the peace of the empty room. It keeps me from getting distracted."

She circled the room, pushing points on the velvet walls and inlayed floors. Within a matter of moments, the area was transformed. Thick rugs appeared, expertly placed beneath lounging chairs and couches. A wood-burning fireplace popped out of the far wall opposite a lavish dining room table with eight seats.

"I swap the bed with the table in the evenings," she offered before I even realized it was missing.

"This is so . . ." I couldn't finish. I was entranced.

"It's home for now. But you said you wanted to talk?"

"Yeah, ah, that would be nice."

I took my time getting settled in a peacock-blue wingback chair. Romona sat perpendicular to me on a tufted brown leather couch. She remained silent while I collected my thoughts, but I didn't get the sense that she was angry . . . just waiting.

"I really am sorry for how I acted earlier today."

"Thank you, but it's already forgotten. We all have our bad days."

"But that's just it. You've been nothing but nice to me. I shouldn't have snapped at you. I feel extremely bad for repaying your kindness with sharpness."

"Audrey, none of us are perfect." When I tried to object, she held up a hand to silence me. "We all have our breaking points, and while I was hurt, you've come to make amends, and that's really all that matters. Don't you agree? Our friendship goes deeper than one sharp exchange. We're kindred. There's nothing to have lingering guilt about. But there's more you'd like to discuss, isn't there?"

I nodded. Of course she was wise enough to realize something had set me off. The lightness I'd felt at her declaration of friendship was weighted down by the reminder of my troubles.

"Yeah, that. I had a pretty hard workout today. All the attention we got from being on Earth was awkward. And I met a new hunter today, which threw me for a little bit of a loop." All true.

"Well, the last part at least sounds like good news. You need to meet some more people. It will make you feel more part of the team."

"Yeah, I guess so."

She folded her hands and leaned forward a little. "There's something I'm missing, isn't there? You've had rough training days before. Who exactly did you meet today?"

"I mean, it probably shouldn't matter, but it was another

girl. Her name was Kaitlin. I don't think she's from around here. But she knew Logan pretty well."

Romona looked thoughtful for a moment.

"Kaitlin. Hmmm, yes, I've met her. Logan introduced us a while back. If I'm not mistaken, I think they knew each other back on Earth."

That rocked me. But what did I care if Logan had history with a very blonde and leggy friend? I shouldn't, as long as it didn't interfere with my training. The uncomfortable and confusing knot in my stomach refused to be convinced.

"Oh, well, that explains why they were so friendly." I tried to sound nonchalant instead of unnerved. "I supposed I'm just not used to seeing other girls around the training center. Do you think she'll be around for long?"

Was I really doing this? Pumping a friend for information.

Romona shrugged her shoulders in indifference. "I suppose it depends on what she's doing here in the first place. If it's just for a social visit, then probably not. But she could be here on assignment. In that case, there's no telling how long she's going to be around. She might even have a permanent transfer for all we know."

I tried hard not to show my panic. Seriously, why did I even care? Why were my insides churning? Shouldn't having another girl be around be a good thing? Yes, it was a good thing. I could use another girl to relate to. And why not Kaitlin?

The ugly answer rose in my gut faster than I could ignore. Jealousy. That's why. I was jealous of Kaitlin without knowing much more about her than her perfect ponytail. Disgusted by my own weakness, I sighed heavily.

"What is it?"

"Nothing. It would be good to have another girl around."

"That isn't what that sigh sounded like." Romona eyed me carefully.

I sighed again. "Okay, truthfully I was a little intimidated by her."

Romona only nodded to let me know I could go on, as if she knew there was a deeper core to the matter.

"You're going to make me say it, aren't you?"

She shook her head gently. "Not if you don't want to. But I think you may feel better if you do."

"It's just . . ." I struggled to get the feelings out without betraying any connection to Logan. "She seems to be everything I'm not. I'm not picking this up quickly, Romona. I'm horrible at it. I know I sound like a broken record, but sometimes I think I'm actually getting worse. And if nothing else, Kaitlin seems to fit in so easily. She reminds me of what I'm not. And it puts me on edge."

Romona's brows creased deeper as I spoke. When it was quiet, she spoke up.

"I don't think you're giving yourself enough credit."

"Ha! I don't think Logan would agree with you." I kicked myself as soon as the words were out—I wasn't supposed to be bringing him into this conversation.

"I think he would. That's the impression I got from talking to him about yesterday."

My heart skipped a beat. "You talked to Logan about yesterday?"

"Yes. After you snapped at me, I was worried something worse had happened than what I'd heard. He said it was your quick thinking that got both of you out of the jam. He also mentioned you weren't completely horrible at surfing, which I'm guessing is pretty high praise from him."

A smile played at the corners of her lips. And she was right — "not completely horrible" was just about the highest praise I'd received from him. My heart still beat erratically. I couldn't imagine Logan telling her we'd kissed, but the knowledge that they'd talked about yesterday made me nervous.

"Well, anyway, that's just how I felt today. Kaitlin reminds me of my weaknesses."

"Your differences from the other hunters are not weaknesses, Audrey. You have no idea yet what you are capable of. What special gifts the Lord has given you. You've hardly even begun to figure them out. Kaitlin is absolutely going to excel in some things you don't, but that doesn't mean you are any less important, any less gifted than she is. We're not supposed to be looking to the right or left to see how we measure up."

Even delivered gently, the reproach in her words was loud and clear. I found myself both humbled and hoping it was true. Humbled because of how I'd treated Kaitlin and hoping that I was special—uniquely created for a purpose.

"Do you really believe there's something special about me?" I asked quietly.

"Absolutely! I have no doubt about that at all."

I smiled. "Thanks, Romona. I needed to hear that."

She smiled back and squeezed my hand. This time I didn't even flinch. I welcomed the compassion she always offered so freely.

"Here, let's have something to drink. I think it'll make you feel better."

She reached under the coffee table and pushed a button. A panel slid back, and a polished silver tray holding a teapot, two teacups, cream, sugar, and a few small round cookies rose in the middle of the table. I went for the cookie first as she poured tea.

"So, ah, what's the deal with people falling in love here anyway?" I asked around a mouthful of cookie.

Romona choked on her tea but managed to gracefully regain composure.

"Never mind. Forget I said anything."

Why had I asked that? It had just slipped out. I picked up a delicate cup and took a sip, refusing to look anywhere but out the window. Romona's room faced the outdoor rec area, and a smudge on the glass was suddenly very interesting.

"What made you think of that?" Romona's tone was soothing and nonthreatening, as if she was trying to coax the truth out of me.

I shrugged, still staring intently at the smudge. "Nothing, it just randomly popped into my head. I'm always curious as to what the rules are here. Having missed orientation and all."

Romona stayed quiet just long enough to make me believe she was going to let the topic slide.

"Yes."

"Huh?"

"Yes, you can still fall in love," she answered.

"Oh." I should have left it at that. "So, have you like . . . you know . . . met anyone or anything?" My face warmed as I spoke. I snuck a quick glance at Romona. There was a wistful smile on her face.

"I've already met the love of my life." She took a deep breath and let it out. She was remembering something, perhaps even savoring a memory. She pegged me with clear eyes after the moment passed. "I'm waiting for him here."

"So you mean he hasn't died yet?" I crinkled my nose. "Won't he be kind of old when he gets here?"

Romona burst out laughing even as I literally clamped my hand over my mouth. She laughed so hard she had to put her teacup down to keep from spilling. It took her several minutes to calm down, but she'd started to hiccup. I stared at her with raised eyebrows.

"Well . . . *hiccup* . . . I guess you can just say . . . *hiccup* . . . I like older men."

Ew. I was doubly sorry I'd asked.

13

A SECOND CHANCE

*W*hen I arrived at our training gym the next day, I found a note waiting for me in Logan's distinct handwriting.

There are some things I need to tend to today. You're on your own. You can use our gym or find another to continue training.

Under the brief message was a list of exercises and drills. There was no signature.

Holding the message in my hand, I contemplated the likelihood of being able to blow off training without being caught. As soon as the plot started to form, I dismissed it, sighing heavily. Regardless of whether he'd find out, using his absence to skip didn't sit well with me. And besides, I was unexpectedly enticed by the idea of training for a day without a mentor. It sounded almost peaceful.

I surveyed the familiar gym. No, if today was going to be

different, even special, I needed a change of scenery. Some-place that didn't remind me of Logan so much. Grabbing my bag and shoving Logan's note into one of the side pockets, I set off to find an empty gym.

Craving solitude, I walked to the remote reaches of the training center, assuming a gym this far on the fringe would be vacant. Without thought I shouldered the doors and barged in on someone. Surprising us both.

"Oh, geez, Kaitlin, hey. Sorry, I didn't know you were in here. I'll ah, get going. Good luck." I mumbled the hasty apology while backpedaling out the door.

"Hey Audrey, wait up a second."

I froze with my left leg over the threshold, facing the freedom of the hallway. I'd almost made it out. I let out a quiet breath of frustration before slowly turning, all the while silently reminding myself that she really hadn't done anything to deserve my scorn.

"Sure. What's up?" I plastered what I hoped was a pleasant smile on my face. It might have worked, because she relaxed and smiled back in return.

"You can come back in. I was hoping to find an opportunity to talk to you anyway."

I reluctantly stepped back into the gym. The door swung shut loudly behind me. I wished it stood as a barrier between us rather than confining us together.

Kaitlin brushed a strand of blonde hair out of her eyes. "Listen, I think we may have gotten off on the wrong foot yesterday. I was hoping for a fresh start. I think we could be friends, maybe even good friends. I know yesterday didn't go that wonderfully. I want you to know I really was only trying to be helpful. Well, that and I was trying to be funny, but I see now it fell flat and I just ended up embarrassing you in front of Logan. I really—"

I cut her off. "You didn't embarrass me in front of Logan. I mean, it doesn't make any difference to me what Logan thinks. He's just my mentor. Why would you think I cared?"

I wanted to slap a hand over my mouth again. I could imagine the gears working in Kaitlin's brain to make sense of my outburst. Before she could think about it too much, I continued, "But anyway, yeah, I'm sure we could be friends. Why not, right? And you know, don't worry about yesterday. It was just kind of an off day for me in general."

She twirled a piece of her ponytail as she considered my words. I knew she wasn't buying it.

"Well, I should get going. Lots of fun workout stuff to do today." I took a step backward and searched blindly for the door with my hand.

"Are you sure, Audrey? You seemed a little upset with me yesterday. I would really like to make amends."

My fingers found the door handle. "Yeah, I'm sure. It wasn't you. Like I said, it was just an off day."

"I guess I can understand that. Especially considering what had happened on Earth the day before. Logan seemed a little off as well," Kaitlin said, still twirling her hair and scrunching her perfectly shaped brows together thoughtfully.

It took an extreme effort to keep my features schooled. "Yeah? Not so sure about that. I'll let you get back to it. Have a good workout."

With a quick turn of the handle and a step backward, I was breathing in the free air of the hallway. I took off to the left but slowed to a stop after a few hurried steps. Touching my forehead to the wall, I sucked in a huge breath. What was wrong with me? Was I just a naturally nasty and distrustful person? Is that what I had to look forward to when I reclaimed my memories? Kaitlin had been perfectly nice, and I basically ran out of the room in a panic. Why did I have to react negatively to everything? Why was I incapable of giving Kaitlin a fair chance?

I knew the answers to all my questions. It was because I felt threatened by her. Her very existence made me insecure. It didn't have anything to do with Logan—or at least it didn't *need* to have anything to do with him. I needed to get over this. And quickly.

Before I could consider what I was about to do, I marched a few purposeful steps back to Kaitlin's gym and pushed open the door again. She was in the middle of a series of kicks on the punching bag. She stopped and gave me a quizzical look.

"Hey, I'm sorry to bother you again. I wanted to let you know I really do want to try to be friends. I'm just in kind of a weird place here. This," I used my hand to indicate the gym we were in, "is a little more difficult for me than I think for everyone else. A little less . . . natural. I'm still getting my footing. For some reason, seeing you yesterday threw me off. If you really meant it, and if you can get over my weirdness from yesterday and today, I would like to try again."

Yikes! It wasn't my intention to share that much, but there it was. I was taking a leap of faith that Kaitlin was sincere. I hoped I hadn't made a mistake.

Kaitlin's eyes softened considerably. "Thank you," she finally said. "Thanks for trusting me with all of that."

It was a relief that she understood the risk I'd just taken. "I didn't give you a fair chance. And I'm trying to be . . . better, I guess."

"I understand."

"I hope you aren't offended that I find that hard to believe." My words were free of their usual acid this time—I was being sincere.

She nodded. "I know what it's like to feel like you are alone in all of this."

"Really?"

"Yes . . . I didn't settle into all of this as easily as you might think. I had a learning curve too. And there were lots of things I needed to come to terms with as well. I figured there might be some things you wanted to talk about. I know you have Romona, but I hope you know I'm here as well if you ever need another ear. The guys here are all great, but well, there are just some things they won't get." She finished with a lopsided smile.

"Ha, that's for sure." My barriers were starting to crumble and with it the tightness I carried around inside, loosen a notch.

"Anyway, I know the chance you were taking by coming back in here, and I want you to know I don't take that lightly. And I've got a good feeling about you."

I wasn't sure what that meant. I gave her a look that said as much.

She laughed. "Don't look so scared! It's a good thing. I'm just saying I think you have some amazing things ahead of you. I'd like to do what I can to help you reach them."

Now she was confusing me. "But why would you do that?"

"Why wouldn't I? There's great joy in being able to be a part of each other's victories. And in caring for one another."

"I'm embarrassed to say I haven't given that much thought since I arrived."

She smiled. "Don't be. I know it might not seem like it, but the time you have now, before your memories come back, can be a gift. You have the opportunity to take an unencumbered view of everything. Decide who you want to be, then make it so."

"That easy, huh?"

"No . . . that hard."

I nodded and smiled back, happy she got it too. I'd simply wanted to make amends for my bad behavior—I didn't really expect Kaitlin to turn into a friend. Today was full of surprises.

"So that's about as deep as I can get for one day. Want to train in here with me for the rest of the afternoon?" she asked.

"That's really nice of you to offer, but . . ."

"You like the solitude, right?"

"Yes, I do."

She nodded knowingly. "I get it. It helps me get things sorted out myself sometimes. There's another gym at the end of the hall that's probably available. This far from the center, most of these gyms are probably covered in cobwebs."

"As long as the spiders are long gone, I can handle that. Thanks again."

"Anytime."

The sky was already changing color when I left the training center, which surprised me. It didn't feel like I'd been there all day. Between running drills, I'd been going over all that had happened in the last few days. Calculating moves, distances, and speed while processing conversations, body language, and motives. But instead of being exhausted, I was rejuvenated. I didn't have anything figured out per se, but the freedom to soak everything in on my own seemed to have helped. And something about the actual workout was encouraging as well. For the first time, I felt in sync. Without the pressure of being critiqued, I fell into a rhythm, and my usual awkwardness and clumsiness melted away.

It was quiet on my walk back. The sky was a kaleidoscope —breathtakingly beautiful. I had an overwhelming sense that it was a gift just for me, but of course that was a silly thought.

On impulse I stopped and closed my eyes, taking a deep breath of fresh air, and wished I could freeze the moment to enjoy later. When I opened them, a blur of movement to my left distracted me.

I turned my head in time to see Logan disappear into the forest. In the low light, he vanished so quickly he appeared to be swallowed by the darkness. My curiosity took control, and I jogged to the edge of the tree line. I could just make out his silhouette moving further away. Maybe if I was very careful, I could follow him without being detected. There was so much about Logan I didn't know, I couldn't seem to help myself.

When I stepped under the cover of the trees, I too was instantly swallowed by darkness. The thick forest canopy completely blocked out the vibrant colors of the dying day. I didn't wait for my eyes to adjust to the low light. I had to start moving now or I'd lose sight of Logan completely.

It was a mixed blessing that I was so far behind him. Despite my best effort, I still made a lot of noise as I picked my way through the foliage. Eventually, my eyes adjusted and I started to see more details in the early night.

I didn't wonder if Logan would be mad at me for following him. Instead, I forced myself to concentrate on keeping up. A breeze picked up and tossed my hair behind me. The cool nip to the air sent a chill down my spine. Logan's form was barely discernible—despite his unhurried gait, he was getting further away from me at every step—I could lose him at any moment. A bolt of fear shot though my body. I was suddenly desperate to get closer. The idea of losing him in the dense darkness scared me.

Another gust of night air blew, and mist coiled around my feet with a strong chill. I yelped despite myself and took off in a run. My heart beat violently, and I looked back to see the mist hugging the ground, spreading toward me. I had the wild thought that it was chasing me and picked up my speed, surprising myself by dodging roots and low-growing plants with relative ease. There seemed to be light coming through a break in the trees ahead. If I could just get there, I'd be safe.

I came to a halt a few trees short of the break.

Logan was kneeling on the ground in what might be called a clearing. It was closer to a crack in the canopy that allowed a wide beam of silvery light to break through and illuminate a patch of grass.

His back was to me, his head bent, shoulders slumped, like they carried the weight of the world. The odd silvery light created a glow all around him. With his head bowed and hunched over his knees, the deep rumblings of his baritone voice filtered to my ears. His words weren't loud enough for me to discern, but they were filled with emotion. And something about what I was seeing, even if I didn't understand it, moved me. I stared at Logan with an equal mix of awe and wonder, the mist all but forgotten.

After a time, he heaved a big sigh and said, "You can come out now. I know you're there."

There was no use pretending. This close, knowing Logan,

he could probably hear me breathe. I stepped out from behind the trees at the same time Logan stood and turned.

"Well, I suppose it would be you." He tilted his head back with a humorless laugh. "Thanks."

"You're welcome?" I said.

He gave me a look I couldn't interpret. "I wasn't talking to you, but never mind. What are you doing out here anyway?"

"I saw you walk into the forest on my way back from training and wanted to make sure you were okay."

"And what exactly did you think would happen to me out here?" He sounded amused.

I wracked my brain for an answer that didn't seem incredibly lame. Then something close to the truth hit me.

"That weird mist stuff?"

Logan's brows knit. "Say what?"

"That creepy mist. You didn't see it?" I took a quick look at my feet to make sure none of it was hiding under my shoes.

Logan shook his head and continued to regard me with a look that said he didn't believe a word coming out of my mouth.

"Well, whatever." I shrugged. "Now that I see you're fine, I guess I'll just get going."

I glanced around the forest and realized I had no idea where we were. I chewed on my lower lip while I considered which direction to go. How large could the woods be, anyway? Maybe if I wandered in them long enough, I'd end up in another part of the realm around people I didn't constantly embarrass myself in front of. I was just about to take a step forward when Logan spoke up.

"You know, I think the *truly* implausible thing is that you expect me to believe you spent the entire day training without me there to make you."

I whirled around to face him. "Hey," was as far as I got in my defense. Logan had taken a few steps closer to me, and when I turned we were practically on top of each other. The silvery light had disappeared, so we stood together in relative darkness. The look on Logan's face was obscured by shadows as he peered down on me. I grasped to remember what we were talking about. It was floating close enough to the fringe of my thoughts that it came back to me.

"I really did train all day. You can check the log if you don't believe me." My words sounded breathless. The fire I'd intended to put into them was nowhere to be found.

"Well, that's surprising." Logan sounded annoyingly thoughtful—and not the least bit affected by me as I was by him. That bruised my ego enough to give me the frame of mind to step back and rekindle the fire.

"Well, it shouldn't be. If you'd try to focus on some of my more attractive qualities you might learn to develop a measure of faith in me." I spun in the other direction, determined to get away from him.

Logan huffed out a breath behind me and mumbled something that sounded like, "I'm trying quite hard to do the exact opposite."

I didn't have time to ponder that. He grabbed my arm, halting my retreat. I turned only my head in his direction. "It's this way," he said, nodding to the left.

"Oh."

"Mind if I walk back with you? You know, just in case the mist comes back. I'll need someone to protect me."

I rolled my eyes and grunted in response. Truce, then. We

fell in step with each other and walked in silence for a while before Logan said anything.

"Audrey . . ." He paused a moment before going on. I looked over to see him staring straight ahead with a serious look on his face. I had an intuition that I wasn't going to like whatever was going to come out of his mouth next. "I think we should talk about what happened."

My stomach instantly knotted up, and my heart started to beat wildly. Why was he bringing this up now? Hadn't we already agreed it wasn't something we were going to talk about, ever?

"Audrey, did you hear me? I think it's important that we at least talk about what happened."

My feet propelled me forward even as I felt paralyzed on the inside. It was eerily quiet as Logan waited for me to say something. Where was that creepy mist when I needed it?

Logan sighed after a few long moments. "Listen, I know this isn't something you *want* to discuss, but as much as we would like to, I don't think we can just pretend it didn't happen. There are things . . . rules . . . you don't know about that you should."

He sounded tired. I didn't dare try to read his face. Instead, I busied myself with taking extra care to pick my way along the nonexistent path through the trees.

"I would like to have more than a one-way conversation."

"Well, that's a first."

I could practically feel Logan's walls go up. I'd hit my mark. Rather than being happy he'd stopped talking, I regretted my words. I snuck a look at Logan out of the corner of my eye. His profile was as hard as stone. I'd done that.

It occurred to me only then that Logan was trying to be

vulnerable with me, and I'd just thrown it back in his face. I couldn't think of a way to make it right again. Maybe if I swallowed my fear and just talked about the stupid kiss, it would right things between us.

I'd almost worked up the courage to do so when we broke through the trees.

"I'll see you tomorrow," Logan said before turning in the opposite direction.

"Logan, wait!" I yelled after him. I jogged to catch back up. It was only when I did that he stopped to face me again, the wintry look still on his face.

"It's just that, I don't really know . . ." I wasn't exactly sure what I was going to say, but it didn't matter because that's all I got out before we were interrupted.

"Did you guys just come out of there?" Romona stood a few feet away, looking confused. Her eyes darted back and forth between Logan and me. "It's kind of late to be training out in the woods, don't you think?"

I wasn't sure if she was asking me or Logan. He saved me by replying, but his eyes remained glued to me. "We weren't training. I found Audrey roaming around and helped her find her way back."

It was the one version of the truth that made me appear incredibly incompetent. Between his comment and the intense way he was still staring at me, my emotions teetered between aggravated and uncomfortable.

"Audrey, what were you doing wandering out in the woods by yourself?"

I broke the stare-down. "I thought I saw something out there, and then I got turned around. I kind of stumbled across Logan."

Romona turned everything over in her head. She was clearly having a hard time adding it up.

"I'm going to get going," Logan said. "It's been a long day. I'll see you tomorrow." His voice was less harsh than before, but he didn't wait for us to reply before taking off. By the time I could open my mouth to answer, he was already jogging off.

I stared after his retreating form with a frown, trying to make sense of everything that had happened that evening. What exactly was Logan doing out in the woods? And what was up with that silver light and mist? And perhaps the question I was most curious about—What would have happened if we'd had the talk he wanted? A small part of me was disappointed that I'd missed the opportunity to talk with him.

I almost forgot Romona was there until she laid a soft hand on my shoulder.

"Everything okay?" she gently asked.

"Oh, yeah, sure." I chewed my lower lip in concern. Romona was kind enough to change the subject. "How'd your day go? Did you get the chance to talk to Kaitlin?"

I gave her a genuine smile. "Yes, we did actually get to talk. It went okay. She was nice."

"See!" Romona's smile was from ear to ear. "I told you it wouldn't be that bad!"

"You were right. I'm glad we got the opportunity to clear the air. We decided to try to start over."

"That's really great, Audrey. I'm glad that isn't weighing on you anymore." She linked her arm through mine and propelled me in the direction of my tree. "Now, on to more important things! Let's get you cleaned up. I was hoping you'd want to hit the town with me tonight."

A few hours later, pampered and beautified, we looked at

our made-up, nail-polished, and blow-dried reflections in a salon mirror. She looked beautiful. So did I. It was the last thing I'd expected to do that evening, but I couldn't believe how much it lifted my spirits. And the night was still young—Romona had plans to hit a restaurant afterward. She stood behind me with a soft smile on her face as she looked at my reflection. I took in hers in return.

Romona's hair looked awesome. Her hair was a bit darker than mine and free of my unexpected highlights, but the texture was the same silky thickness. Her skin, slightly darker than mine, held a hint of the same olive shade. Our eyes matched perfectly. It was weird that I hadn't noticed that before. I suppose I wasn't familiar enough with my own reflection to notice the resemblance. Brown seemed like such a boring color I hadn't thought there was much variation. But our eyes were a rich warm mahogany color, not light enough to be considered hazel but not too dark to hide the variety of brown hues.

"Look, we have the same eyes."

Romona's face in the mirror reflected surprise. "Really, you think so?" She took a tentative step toward the mirror to verify my statement.

"Yeah, definitely! I mean, brown is brown, but if they weren't on your face I would swear they were mine."

Romona smiled at that. "Well, that's funny. I guess we're eye twins, then."

"Ha! Yeah, I guess so. Who knew?"

The smile remained on Romona's face even if it didn't quite reach her eyes.

"Feel any better?" she asked.

"Actually, I do."

"Thought so. You looked like you needed some serious pampering."

"In that case, I'm glad you can read me so well, because I would never have guessed this was what I needed."

"Well, it always made you feel better before, so I just figured."

"Huh? What do you mean by that?"

Romona's face fell. "I only meant that you seem more relaxed with some girlie stuff every now and then. Like your room, right?"

I was still frowning. "Yeah, I guess you're right."

By the time I made it back to my bed, I was tired but happy, and I fell asleep instantly. The good of the day far outweighed the bad.

Even so, that night I dreamt dark dreams of running from mist.

14

FIGHT

*L*oud crashes and the sound of colliding metal assaulted my ears. I picked up the pace and rushed down the hallway, bursting through our gym doors with a loud bang. The room was in shambles. Weapons lay strewn throughout the gym. Practice dummies were destroyed, various equipment was overturned, and in the middle of the room two fighters were locked in furious battle.

Even covered from head to toe in body armor, Logan couldn't be mistaken. Kaitlin's long, lean body and ash-blonde ponytail made her hard to mistake as well. I stood in awe of what I was seeing. Blades crashed in blurred movements. Attacks were diverted and sidestepped with unbelievable precision. It was like watching two powerful animals fight, each matched with speed and agility. It was both beautiful and intimidating.

Watching the two of them spar made me realize how lightly Logan was going on me during training. A bit of familiar jealously towards Kaitlin rose to my throat. Even though Logan outmatched her in weight, her movements looked effortless in their quickness and balance. I swallowed down the envy.

In a blur of movement Logan managed to disarm Kaitlin. She quickly threw her body to the side and rolled out of the way, putting herself within arm's reach of the weapons wall. She grabbed a weapon and immediately threw a fighting star at Logan. I gasped. Logan just used the side of his blade to deflect the metal, as if swatting a fly away. But Kaitlin had used the attack to divert Logan's attention and get into a stance to disarm him. The ploy worked, and within seconds Logan's weapon was also lying on the ground. With a warrior's cry Kaitlin launched herself at Logan, taking them both to the ground.

"Yeah, Kaitlin! Kick his butt!" someone yelled behind me. Another voice gave an encouraging hoot to the fighters. I turned my head to see that a small crowd had formed.

Logan and Kaitlin ignored the ruckus. With a series of roundhouse kicks Kaitlin pushed Logan back toward the corner. It was a smart move, leaving Logan with fewer options to retaliate.

Just as it seemed Kaitlin had Logan where she wanted, he quickly turned and ran straight at the wall that was boxing him in. Without hesitation he ran a few steps up the wall, pushed off, and flipped backwards over Kaitlin's head, landing safely on the other side of her. That garnered a round of cheers and shouts from the crowd. Logan swept Kaitlin's feet out from under her. She landed hard on her back with the wind knocked out of her. Logan was over Kaitlin immediately with his recovered blade, and with a blink it was all over.

Logan's facemask melted away to reveal a huge grin as he

leaned over to give Kaitlin a hand up. When she took his hand she made a great show of trying to take him down with her. Logan laughed and effortlessly hauled Kaitlin to her feet. Her mask disappeared to reveal a matching grin.

Alrik stepped forward to give Logan a hug-slap on the back. His voice boomed loudly. "Well, Logan, you need to stay a little sharper. She almost had you there."

"I would have had him if he played by the rules. He didn't get the memo to go easy on girls." And then she spotted me. "Right, Audrey?"

"I don't know about that one. I hate to admit it, but after watching the two of you it's obvious Logan's been giving me more slack than I realized."

"Oh come on, Audrey, I don't believe that. I've heard that you've disarmed him before."

My cheeks warmed. That was *not* my favorite memory. Sure, it was probably the best I'd ever fought, but I hadn't been able to duplicate it with controlled emotions.

"Well, anyway," I said, "from the looks of it I don't think he should be cutting you much of anything. That was really impressive." I was proud of myself for being objective. Her fighting did kick some butt, and it wasn't my place to withhold praise when it was due.

Kaitlin's face lit up, and her grin widened. "No need to worry, then. With my help you'll have him flat on his back in no time."

The unintended double meaning in her phrase drained the color and smile from my face. There was an awkward moment when people expected me to say something back. My tongue was frozen in my mouth. I looked at Logan to see his reaction. His eyes snapped up and found mine in an instant. He looked stricken as well. A breath caught in my throat.

He recovered quicker than I. "If that's the case, maybe I shouldn't encourage you guys to train together." He broke our stare and smiled lightly at the group. A few people around the room chuckled. My eyes swept the crowd. I caught Alrik suspiciously eyeing us, his gaze switching between Logan and me.

"Okay, guys, the free show is over. You'll have to catch the next one." People started to file out around me. A few here and there stopped to praise both Logan and Kaitlin.

Before he left, Alrik bent down to say something to Logan. Logan shook his head once and wouldn't look at him, and a muscle in his jaw jumped. Alrik gave a hearty chuckle and slapped Logan on the back before heading toward the door. He winked and smiled at me before leaving. I was dying to know what he'd said.

When the last person left, Kaitlin slid to the mat with her feet planted, knees up, and arms stretched out on either side of her. The rest of her armor melted away.

"Sheesh, I thought they'd never leave."

Even Logan sat on the floor. He nodded his head in agreement as his armor dissolved. "Yeah, that was a pretty intense sparring session. I didn't realize we'd attracted so much attention."

They seemed to have forgotten me again, which was an annoying habit of theirs. I cleared my throat. Kaitlin's head came slightly off the mat.

"Hey Aud, I'd forgotten you were there." Typical.

Logan just gave me his usual soulful stare. The intensity made me want to fidget. I shifted my weight from one leg to the other. It was my training time, but they looked pretty comfortable together. How did I become the intruder? I began to backpedal slowly towards the door.

"I guess I'll just be going then and let you guys, do, ah, whatever it is you need to do."

My face was on fire. I couldn't make my escape fast enough. Unfortunately, the sole of my shoe caught the mat and I lost my footing. There was a mortified moment of clarity when I knew I was going down. I squeezed my eyes shut and waited for the familiar impact of back and butt on mat, but it never came. Instead, my fall was cushioned by gentle hands. They braced my back so that the whole upper half of my body was lying horizontal to the floor. I slowly cracked open one of my eyes.

Logan's face was a breath away. He'd somehow managed to get from his spot on the floor to me before I hit the ground. How could he have moved that fast? And more importantly, why? He'd never tried to stop one of my falls before. In fact, most of the times my back or butt had collided with the mat were pointedly because of him. I opened the other eye.

Logan searched my face like he was trying to figure something out. His brows were drawn together in what might have been concentration. I didn't dare move a muscle. Logan leaned in further, and his bare arm brushed mine. An electric zing shot through my body, and something intense rushed at me. Before I could gasp, I slammed into the mat. The wind was knocked from my lungs. I shook my head to clear it and looked up at Logan. He'd straightened again and was staring down at me.

"What the . . ." I started, but the look on his face brought me up short. Was he upset?

I looked at Kaitlin. She was staring at us with her eyebrows lifted. "Wow, Logan. That was really an ungallant rescue there."

Logan's stone face returned, and he shrugged. Kaitlin seemed like she wanted to say more, but didn't. Instead, she turned her head to where I was sprawled.

"All right, Audrey, time to get up. You're mine today." She gave me a wicked grin as she rubbed her hands together.

"What do you mean I'm yours?" I asked suspiciously.

"We're going to train together today. I'm going to share some of the super-secret tricks reserved for only the coolest hunters."

She glanced over at Logan when she said the last part, intending to bait him, but he acted like he hadn't even heard her. A shadow of concern crossed Kaitlin's face before it turned to a look of excitement—one that looked forced to me.

"So what do you say? Are you in?"

I appreciated that she was making it seem like I had a choice, even though I knew I didn't. Maybe Kaitlin would have some advice that would step up my game. I forced my own chipper smile as I pushed myself to my feet.

"A day away from the boys? I'm always in."

"Great! Let's get started. We just need to get rid of Logan." Her voice trailed off at the end because Logan had already left. The gym doors were swinging shut behind him.

"Wow, someone's a little moody today," Kaitlin said.

I didn't respond, just stared at the door Logan had pushed through with vexation. Between yesterday and today, I agreed that something was definitely up with him, and I had a bad feeling I knew exactly what it was. I changed the subject.

"Okay, Super-Cool Hunter, where do we start?"

Training with Kaitlin was a lot more fun than I expected. Getting a girl's perspective was insightful. She showed me new kickboxing moves that used my lower body rather than my arms and shoulders. She explained that most of a girl's strength was in our legs, where guys relied more on their upper body. It was important to learn to utilize the whole body for fighting, but learning to channel extra energy to our strongest areas was a big advantage in a pinch.

She also showed me how to use my size to my advantage. Since Kaitlin was almost as tall as most of the guys, I was impressed that she knew some tricks for the vertically challenged. The more I trained with her, the more I found myself wanting to like her, even though there was still a part of me that insisted on keeping her at arm's length. I didn't think I'd ever feel as close to her as Romona, but a genuine friendship was blooming. The training flew by quickly. It almost felt too soon when Kaitlin called it quits.

"That was really great, Audrey. I think you're going to make an amazing hunter."

I felt a measure of pride at the compliment. Kaitlin pulled off a boxing glove before extending a hand. I hesitated before clasping it. I wasn't as wary as some of the empathy link, but I still hadn't gotten used to being so exposed to people. Kaitlin waited patiently. I took a silent breath before extending my hand and steeled myself against her emotions.

Kaitlin's smile widened. I'd always gotten the impression that she was silently laughing at me, but the emotions I absorbed through the link surprised to me. Amusement was definitely present, but respect and acceptance were the stronger sentiments.

It was as if Kaitlin had developed a sisterly affection for me despite my behavior. I think all she was getting from me was shock and perhaps a small dose of distrust, but she didn't seem to mind.

After helping me to my feet, she let my hand drop with an ever-wider smile. Delight danced behind her eyes, as if she knew something I didn't that allowed her to overlook my distrust.

"So, are you excited about the celebration?"

"The what?"

"You know, the celebration!"

Her tone left no question as to whether she was excited. I still didn't have the faintest idea what she was talking about.

"What celebration? What are we celebrating?"

"Oh, Audrey, you are in for a treat! It's basically the biggest and coolest party you've ever been to."

"Who will be there?"

"Everybody!" she answered.

"As in all the hunters?"

"No, as in everybody, everybody. Everybody from the realm is going to be there."

My brain couldn't wrap itself around those numbers.

"But what are we all celebrating?"

I mentally ran through some of the holidays we might be celebrating. But since I didn't remember when I had died, I didn't even know what time of year it was. I was guessing it wasn't something lame like Columbus Day, though.

"We celebrate everything."

"Such as . . .?" I prompted.

"We celebrate everything that has to do with being here. That we are here, how we got here, what we're doing now. It's just a big celebration where everyone can get together and, well, celebrate."

"Okay then, so I guess this is something I should be looking forward to."

She laughed. "Definitely!"

"Well then yes, I guess I am excited." I answered with a laugh even though I wasn't sure I really meant it. Something twisted within the familiar pit at the bottom of my stomach. It signaled my growing anxiety. If I could, I would punt that emotion right out of me.

It was then that Logan decided to grace us with his presence. "So, have you turned her into a fighting machine?"

Kaitlin gave me a quick wink before turning to answer him. "You bet! You'd better watch your back. I've given her all my super-secret tricks."

Logan's face split into a grin that held a playful glint. "Is that so?"

"Yep! Just you wait, you're going to be sparring one of these days and BAM," she clapped her hands loudly, "you're not even going to know what hit you."

Kaitlin was talking me up a little too much, but Logan wasn't taking her seriously. I half listened to their banter while the rest of my mind strayed. It was hard to ignore my jealousy at the effortless way they conversed. If only Logan and I had had that ease in the beginning, we wouldn't be struggling right now. I couldn't deny the part I'd played in building the wall between us. I'd done a good job putting it together brick by brick, but for his part, I'd rarely seen Logan let down his guard. There were only rare moments here and there when I saw through the façade. But his stoic mask always slammed back on eventually. I sighed when I thought of the opportunity I'd missed the night before.

With Kaitlin and Logan still talking, I decided to slip away. There was a twinge of sadness at how easily it was done without notice, but hunching my shoulders, I headed away from them with a heart torn in two.

15

THE
CELEBRATION

*A*fter so many days of wearing workout gear or T-shirts and jeans, it felt good to get all done up for the celebration. I twisted in front of the mirror in my cobalt blue dress. It looked really nice against my olive skin and dark hair. The bodice of the dress was fitted, ruched, and cinched low on the waist. There was a piece of braided material that went over one shoulder to create an asymmetrical neckline. The skirt dropped from my waist to a few inches above my knees. It was a soft silk that looked and felt almost liquid when I moved.

The closet had stubbornly spit out a handful of awful dresses before finally relinquishing this one, but it was worth the wait. I felt absolutely myself when I put it on, both feminine and confident. Some anxiety about the celebration disappeared because I just knew that the dress was me. It was the first time I knew with absolute certainty that I would have liked this dress in life.

Romona had performed true magic on my hair. She curled

the straight locks and pulled up the front in an intricate weave of braids and twists. The light caught highlights I didn't know existed. The curls she'd manipulated fell in soft waves down my back. Besides being a genius with my hair, Romona helped materialize some makeup for me as well. I used a touch of eye shadow, black eyeliner, and mascara to give my eyes a slight smoky effect. I was surprised at how rich my eyes appeared with just a bit of work. I brushed on some blush and shine to my cheekbones. When I looked in the mirror, I finally saw someone familiar looking back at me. Someone not as painfully average as I had been feeling these past weeks.

A small smile touched my lips, and I released a breath I didn't realize I had been holding. This was the girl I was comfortable in.

Romona came up in the mirror next to me. She looked lovely. She'd picked a knee-length dress as well, but that was the only similarity. It was delicate and vintage, lacy and frilly and a perfect fit for both her body and her personality.

Romona had managed to make a masterpiece of her hair as well. She had piled it all on the top of her head with a few tendrils hanging loose here and there. And even though her makeup was lighter to match her soft pink dress, there was no mistaking that we had the same eyes.

"All right, I think we're ready. Want to get going?" she asked.

I took a final look at myself. Something seemed to be missing. What could it be? A wild thought appeared in my head. Was it even something I could do? I wasn't sure, but I wanted to try.

I closed my eyes and concentrated very hard. When Romona gasped a moment later, I knew something had happened. I opened my eyes to watch a thick lock of my dark hair turning from brown to purple. Romona's eyes widened beside me as color slowly spread from root to tip. I beamed triumphantly at my success and had the urge to do a short victory dance. Instead, I turned my head to the side to get a better look at my work in the mirror. *Ha!* I might not be able to master the art of making something from nothing just yet, but this new trick was pretty cool. How many people could turn their hair colors with their mind? Actually, I had no idea.

Romona tentatively picked up the end of my purple lock. "Wow, that is neat!" She looked meticulously through the strands of hair, but then she brought a hand to her mouth and sucked in a quick breath of air. "Oh no, do you think it's permanent?"

I laughed at the stricken look on her face. I could think of a few more horrifying things than having a chunk of my hair a different color for eternity. Still laughing, I shrugged a shoulder.

"Let's hope it wasn't a single flash of genius so I can get it back to brown later." A wave of giddiness started to bubble up inside. "But you're right, let's go. We can worry about this later."

I grabbed Romona's hand to pull her out the door. When our hands connected, I stifled another laugh at how genuinely worried she was. What a silly thing to be concerned about. I wondered what I'd look like with a head full of fuchsia hair?

Outside the celebration tent, people were dressed in almost anything and everything imaginable. Multiple decades and even centuries of formal and casual wear were represented.

"Hey guys!" Kaitlin weaved her way through the crowd. She was stunning. Her hair was pulled back in an elegant French twist. She wore a simple, but chic, pale yellow dress that accentuated her tanned skin and flowed to the ground. She must have had some serious heels on underneath that thing, because she was at least four inches taller than usual. She towered over me now.

"Kaitlin, you have to show me what shoes you're wearing."

She smiled knowingly and lifted the hem of her skirt. The thin spikes she was standing on were nothing short of scary. At least six inches high with an extra inch of platform.

"I know, they're crazy, right?" She hunched down to my level and lowered her voice. "Super high shoes are my guilty pleasure." She wore a sheepish expression. There was nothing to do but laugh.

"Don't worry, there's no judging here. I think they're fabulous!"

"What's fabulous?" came a deep voice from behind.

My body flushed involuntarily as I turned toward the voice. Logan stood casually a few feet away. His blue eyes were electric and his hair expertly styled to look unstyled. His laidback attire for the evening was a white linen shirt rolled partway up his arms and light khakis with brown sandals. He looked every bit the California beach boy he'd once been. I couldn't imagine anything else looking as good on him.

"Oh, um, Kaitlin's shoes. I think they could double as weapons." I answered hurriedly.

"Oh really?" Logan's easy smile was surprisingly soothing.

"Okay, Kaitlin, let's see these things." He indicated with a hand that she pull up her hem.

Kaitlin appeared slightly embarrassed as she lifted the bottom of her dress again. Logan barked out a laugh. It was a rich sound. "Well, that explains why I suddenly feel as if I've shrunk a few inches."

Kaitlin dropped her skirt and laughed back. She was almost as tall as Logan now. I stepped back and noticed what a handsome pair the two of them made. Unwanted sadness seeped through the cracks in my heart as the two of them shared a moment. Turning my head away, I caught Romona staring at me with what may have been a concerned look.

Out of the corner of my eye, I recognized a familiar face and gestured to Romona to say I would be right back. I didn't wait to see if she understood before fleeing. It was cowardly, but I wanted to be someplace else at that moment.

I quickly dipped into the throng. Swiveling my head, I caught another glimpse of Kevin in front of me and to the left and set out in that direction. The thickening mass forced me to maneuver carefully so not to brush up against anyone. I wasn't used to having this much of my skin exposed.

Between chasing Kevin and artfully weaving through the masses, I almost missed the large white tent until it was practically upon me. It stood shiny white, with poles like a circus tent stretching high into the sky. I stopped and gawked.

The trance was broken when someone bumped into me, forcing me to take a shaky step forward. I quickly scanned for Kevin, worried I'd lost him in the horde. Moving in the direction I'd last seen him, I glimpsed his back just as he rounded a corner of the tent. I broke free of the denser crowd to follow, half-jogging, half-speed-walking to catch up.

When I rounded the corner, I smashed right into someone and stumbled. Warm hands shot out to steady me. With a rush, I was ambushed by foreign emotions and sucked in a harsh breath. Surprise, followed by curiosity and a measure of concern. Then the arms dropped away, leaving me alone with my own emotions.

"Hey there! Sorry about that—I just wanted to make sure you didn't fall."

I gave myself a mental shake and glanced up. My near collision was with a handsome prince. Literally, the stranger was dressed like a prince. He caught me staring at his outfit and shifted uncomfortably.

"Oh yeah, this, it's actually kind of a joke."

When my eyes reached his face, I found my voice. "So you're saying you don't dress up like royalty on a regular basis?"

I cocked an eyebrow, a small smile forming.

When he realized I was poking fun at him, he seemed more at ease and matched my smile.

"Only for very special occasions."

"Oh, I see. Well, at least your friends will be able to find you in a crowd." I turned my head and did a quick scan of all the crazy get-ups. "On second thought, maybe not."

He laughed along with me.

"Seriously though, sorry about running into you. I thought I saw a friend head this way." I peeked my head around his side, but no Kevin. *That's so bizarre. How could I have lost him?*

"Yeah, no problem, it was an interesting way to meet. And speaking of . . . Hello, new friend, my name's Jonathon."

"I'm Audrey."

"It's nice to meet you, Audrey. And may I say that color of blue looks very lovely on you."

I willed my cheeks not to change color and smiled politely. With sandy brown hair and eyes to match, he was certainly nice looking. It didn't hurt that he was playing the role of Prince Charming.

"Yes, it does." Logan's deep voice was unmistakable.

He placed a hand possessively on the small of my back. I failed at keeping my cheeks from coloring this time. Jonathon's eyebrows shot up a fraction as he regarded Logan, a sociable smile still in place. Logan wore his usual stoic mask, neither angry nor happy.

"So this must be who you were trying to find?" Jonathon asked.

"Oh no, it was someone else. Jonathon, this is Logan. Logan, Jonathon."

Jonathon immediately extended his hand toward Logan in the traditional greeting. Logan, however, just nodded his head. Jonathon let his hand drop.

I was acutely aware that Logan's hand hadn't left my back and that he stood much closer than necessary. I didn't want Jonathon to get the wrong idea. Heck, *I* was starting to get the wrong idea.

"Jonathon, Logan's my mentor."

Jonathon's eyebrows shot up. "Whoa, so that means you're a huntress? Wow, you are an extremely rare creature. I haven't met a female hunter before." The typical response. His smile broadened. "I guess that means I may be seeing more of you in the future."

"What do you mean?"

"I'm a healer." My blank stare prompted him to continue.

"Almost like a doctor. You guys come to us to get patched up. Most of our patients are hunters. They seem to get themselves banged up on a regular basis."

"Oh." I gestured back to his outfit to change the subject. "So are you going to tell me what the joke is?"

He dipped his head, and his voice dropped in volume. His nearness felt somewhat intimate to me, but I didn't have anywhere to go with Logan's hand boxing me in on the back and Jonathon's broad frame on the front.

"I'll have to tell you about that another time. I think Cinderella is late for the ball and has a few of her mice waiting for her." He shifted his eyes to the side conspiratorially. Following his gaze, I found Romona, Kaitlin, and Kevin all staring at us. How in the world did Kevin get over there?

Jonathon stepped back, took my hand and brought it to his lips for a chaste kiss. There was more heat in that kiss than he showed on his face, and I blushed when he released my hand. Logan moved a bit closer and tensed up.

"Now that I know where to find you, I'm sure we'll bump into each other again. It was very nice to meet you, Audrey." And then, as an afterthought, he included a nod of his head. "Logan."

With a wave, he stepped around us and disappeared into the multitude. Logan's hand dropped from my back the instant the crowd swallowed Jonathon. I found Romona looking between Logan and me thoughtfully, Kaitlin literally doubled over in laughter, and Kevin's eyes as big as saucers. I felt extremely exposed and kind of upset about inadvertently being made a spectacle. Regrettably, I did next what came most naturally. I turned on Logan.

"What was that all about?"

After removing his hand from my back, he'd taken a few steps away. The look on his face was detached.

"What do you mean?"

My eyes narrowed. "You know what I mean. What was up with the possessive act?" I gestured with my chin toward the bulky mass of people.

He shrugged carelessly. "I really don't know what you're talking about." Was that really how he was going to play this?

A strange sound caught my attention. Kaitlin had finally straightened and was wiping tears between giggles and hiccups with a yellow handkerchief that matched her dress perfectly.

"Oh, never mind." I rejoined our friends, giving Kaitlin a scolding glare for good measure.

"Oh, Audrey, I'm really sorry, that was just too much!"

I rolled my eyes and pretended to ignore her, for once not regretting the dark thoughts directed at her. Kevin looked like he'd swallowed his tongue, so I turned to Romona. Her eyes were still thoughtful.

"Well, now that we've found you again, should we go inside?"

No longer in the mood to celebrate anything, I shrugged. The excitement of the night had waned with the weirdness that had just ensued. Was the whole evening going to feel like an emotional roller coaster? Following behind my friends I huffed. It better not.

My jaw literally dropped when I stepped into the tent. I'd been distracted by the emotions of others as we bumped and jostled our way through the sea of people around us, but just one step inside, everything else was shoved from my mind.

The first thing that registered was the magnitude of the interior of the tent. From the outside it appeared to be approximately the diameter of a city block and the height of a ten-story building. By contrast, the inside space had been stretched and pulled to accommodate a city rather than a mere building. It was as if we'd been transported to a whole new world.

Just as I was about to swim against the crowd to double-check the exterior size of the tent, someone interpreted my bewilderment.

"Gateways to all the other parts of the realm have been opened so we can celebrate together. Most of the realm is here right now, so it needs to be big enough to fit everyone," Kaitlin informed me as she searched the crowd. "I may be able to track down some of my friends from home."

I nodded even as my eyes flew over the flocks of people. The music that drifted to my ears was like nothing I had ever heard. The perfect melody was created, sounding as if the wind was playing woodwinds and running water the strings. It was peaceful, exhilarating, and mesmerizing all at the same time. And it was also oddly fast-paced, with a catchy beat. Something you could really dance to.

As we made our way deeper into the tent, the sights took my breath away. Lights hung suspended in the air and twinkled like stars. Colors more numerous than I could count emanated from the crowd and wafted upward, mingling with a multitude of shimmering angels flying gracefully above. I realized with a start that the colors were somehow coming from the people dancing.

My eyes scanned for my friends, who had started to blend

into the crowds. I spotted Kaitlin dancing first. Shimmering golden yellow dust floated around her like a halo before being sent up as she twirled with her hands in the air. Romona smiled at me wildly and grabbed my arm to join the group. A pale blue hue illuminated her and pulsed like a heartbeat. Kevin was dancing out of sync with Kaitlin, but she didn't seem to mind. A bright sunset-orange aura surrounded him, and he sent up sparks every time his feet stomped the ground. I laughed in spite of myself. The atmosphere was infectious.

"It's the colors," Romona was saying in my ear.

"What?" I yelled back above the noise.

"It's the colors," she repeated. "It's like the empathy link, but you don't have to be touching. In here, everything good gets mixed together and shared with each other."

My eyes widened. "Really? That's so . . . so strange."

Romona laughed. "I know! But isn't it amazing too?"

And it was. How was it possible to be so happy, peaceful, and excited all at the same time? It made everything bad go away and just made me, well, want to dance.

And so I did. I closed my eyes and danced like I never knew I could, free of insecurities, and it was amazing.

Time ceased to matter anymore, and when I finally opened my eyes it was to discover that the world was bathed in purple. I caught my breath. My arms and legs were covered in a lattice of glowing lavender. I ran a hand down my arm, and the markings swirled like mist before slowly settling again on my skin like a blanket of intricate snowflakes. It was mesmerizing.

"We were wondering when we might see you again."

It was only after their cloud of mixed teals and greys thinned that I recognized Deborah and LD. Their arms were linked. Deborah's lustrous hair was piled on top of her head in an expertly styled tangle of braids. Her regal, one-shouldered emerald green gown with gold embellishments had an empire waist and flowed to the ground, allowing the tips of her golden Roman sandals to peak out. LD was dressed in a black tux complete with vest and tie. He reminded me of a wiser and more mature version of James Bond.

"It's you!" I exclaimed, slightly breathless. Even though Deborah's strange parting words at Celestial Heights had left me equal parts anxious and eager to meet again, I now felt only excitement from the infectious atmosphere.

"It's us!" Deborah laughed. "We saw you from afar and wanted to see what you thought of the celebration."

"It's kind of unreal." I admitted. "No one really warned me it would be like this."

"It's one of those things that's easier experienced than explained, isn't it?" LD asked.

"I was told that several times over the last week. I can see their point, but I would have preferred to be a little more prepared"

"Well we can't always be one hundred percent prepared for every situation." Deborah pointedly said. Before she'd spoken to me of purpose, plans, and wise decision-making. She now spoke of preparedness.

"Agreed. I'm continually being challenged by that truth." I laughed. "Some days more than others."

"Life, and even the afterlife, is a dance between being prepared and letting go. The wisdom is in knowing how to prepare and when it's time to let go."

She'd lost me again. Was this another riddle of wisdom or a fortune-cookie insight?

LD laid a hand on his wife's shoulder. With an affectionate look and a small nod, she turned her ageless eyes toward me.

"We're sure you are well on your way to figuring out these things on your own."

"You have our every confidence, Audrey," LD chimed in. "Now, what *I* want to know is have you had your first adventure as a huntress yet?" There was mischief in his eyes.

"Oh, I suppose you could say that I have," I hedged.

"That's grand! See, you've already broken the ice!"

"And are things going well with Logan?" Deborah asked.

"Some days are smoother than others," I answered honestly, if vaguely.

"I see." A small smile played at the corners of her lips.

"Romona is here somewhere." I did a half-turn to look for her. "I'll bet she'd like to say hello as well."

"We will keep a lookout for her."

LD shook my hand warmly and then looked at Deborah with playfulness in his eyes. "Audrey, it was such a pleasure to see you again, but I need to steal my beloved away for another dance."

"How could anyone refuse such a man?" she replied.

"My point exactly! Audrey, we are waiting in anticipation for your adventures to play out."

Ha! More like misfortunes. "I'll make the effort to search you out when I have a story worth telling."

"Excellent! Now enjoy the rest of your evening."

As they walked away, still linked arm in arm, their cloud of colors began to grow again, so tangled they existed as one instead of two.

"Wild, isn't it?" Kaitlin had twirled her way over. Her

golden yellow haze sparkled, making her hair and skin shimmer.

"You're telling me! This really is unbelievable. Why didn't you guys warn me about this?" I poked at one of Kaitlin's sparkles before it disappeared.

"You have to admit this is kind of hard to explain. How would you have taken it if we told you space would bend over on itself to create more space and that when you danced you would change colors?" She shrugged. "We couldn't have told you what your color would look like anyway, and that's the best part."

"Do the colors mean anything?"

"Of course they do! They're a reflection of who we are. Everyone's is different because we're all unique. It's a manifestation of your spirit. Now that you've seen yours, there is something you know about yourself that you didn't before."

"That my spirit is purple?"

"Haha, exactly! And look!" She pointed her finger and lifted her face upward. Above us, all the different colors and textures were mingling. Beautiful was too mild a word to describe it. It was like a fireworks display, a sunset, and a rainbow all at once.

Despite the brilliance of the sight above, something vivid from the corner of my eye stole my attention. My eyes followed and settled on Logan.

Through the crowd, I caught glimpses of him dancing with Romona. He was laughing as he spun her around. His light was an intense silver that shone brightly as if a spotlight were on him. He was too far away to detect any details in the color, but even from where I was standing, he was spellbinding.

I yelped at a sudden hand on my back. "I did say I'd see you again." Jonathon's voice was close enough to my ear that he didn't have to yell.

Kaitlin quickly covered the startled look on her face with an easy smile. "Aren't you going to introduce me to your new friend, Audrey?"

Jonathon stepped to my side but didn't drop the hand on my back. That was a little forward, and since Logan wasn't around to box me in this time, I took a casual step to my left, allowing Kaitlin into a circle.

"This is Jonathon. I just met him." And to Jonathon I said, "Kaitlin's a huntress."

"Really! Another female hunter?"

"We like to roam in packs."

Jonathon flashed Kaitlin a smile. "Kaitlin, it's a pleasure to meet you as well." He extended a hand.

Kaitlin lifted an eyebrow before taking it. "Should I perhaps be giving you a curtsy instead?"

Jonathon seemed uncomfortable with the comment. "Oh, this." He looked down at his outfit. "It's kind of a joke with the people I work with."

The smile Kaitlin gave Jonathon could only be described as conspiratorial. "That wasn't what I was referring to."

The side of Jonathon's mouth quirked up. "Oh, please. You know that doesn't mean anything here. Besides, that was a life-time ago."

"And modest at that. Hmmm, interesting."

Jonathon just shook his head.

I glanced back and forth between the two of them. They continued their conversation almost as if I wasn't there. That habit of Kaitlin's was getting old fast.

Finally Jonathon said, "Well, I was hoping to borrow my new friend here if you didn't mind."

"Oh, *I* don't mind." The way she stressed the "I" made it obvious she thought someone else would.

"Oh yeah," Jonathon turned his head to look toward the crowd. "Do you think your boyfriend would mind?"

"Huh?" I started to choke on nothing. Kaitlin gave my back a few hard hits before I got my breath back. "I don't have a boyfriend!"

Jonathon smiled broadly enough to show most of his white teeth. "Perfect! Then let's go!"

Without waiting for an answer, he grabbed my hand and pulled me in the opposite direction. I could barely wave "good-bye" to Kaitlin. The last I saw of her, she winked and turned to weave back through the crowd.

Jonathon pulled me through the crowd. "Hey, I can't feel anything." I lifted our joined hands to demonstrate, slowing our progression.

He smiled patiently at me. "It's because we're all sharing emotions in here, so the link doesn't work the same way. Too much stuff floating around to pick up on just one person."

"That's interesting."

"Let's keep going. I want to show you something."

I didn't resist as he pulled me forward and we dodged through the sea of bodies. Before I knew it I was outside, fresh air filing my lungs. But a sense of disappointment left me bereft, and I tugged my hand free of his, whirling around to return to my friends.

"Hey, wait a second!" he called.

Confused, I turned to glance at him, my hand on the flap of the tent.

"Will you trust me?"

Though friendly, Jonathon's smile made my stomach knot. I'd just met this guy, why should I trust him? And I really did want to get back to the celebration.

As if reading my mind, Jonathon continued. "I'll have you back in plenty of time to enjoy the rest of the celebration. I promise no one will even miss you."

With that comment, something ached in my chest. I thought about my friends having fun and enjoying themselves without me. I imagined Kaitlin and Logan's laughing faces as they danced. He was right, no one would miss me.

I gave Jonathon what I hoped was a normal smile and dropped the piece of tent.

"All right then, what's this amazing thing I just have to see?"

Jonathon's grin widened, making him look younger. There was a twinkle in his eye that seemed almost childlike, making my unease from a moment ago disappear.

We walked away from the tented celebration and toward the darkened forest. While we talked the music faded, and the sounds of the evening became the louder melody. Crickets sang a sweet lullaby that made me want to feel the tickle of the grass on my feet. I resisted the temptation and continued to follow Jonathon as he picked a path into the forest where the trees remained sparse. The denser woods could be easily seen through the foliage.

"Okay, so it's not far from here. He should be around here somewhere."

"He?"

"Yep!"

What "he" was he talking about? Was it possible he could mean the big "He?"

Jonathon grabbed my hand and swiftly placed me in front of him. He settled a hand on my bare shoulder and used the other to direct my line of site. The abruptness of the empathy link startled me. Jonathon was all excitement, and it was hard not to get swept away in his feelings.

"Do you see it? He's right there."

When I detangled my emotions from the ones being thrust upon me, I focused in the direction Jonathon was pointing. My breath caught.

There, through the trees, was a fairy tale come to life. His front legs bent in a low bow as he faced our direction. His eyes closed as if savoring the faint music emanating from the tent. His coat was the purest white, and my hands itched to stroke his flanks. I imagined it would feel like the smoothest velvet. Touching the ground was his shimmering pearlescent horn.

I'd forgotten Jonathon was there, let alone still attached to my shoulder. His words whispered in my ear. "They come out when we are all preoccupied during the celebration to pay their homage."

"He's magnificent," I whispered breathlessly.

"Yes. That's why they weren't around Earth for very long."

Sensing my confusion in the empathy link, Jonathon supplied additional information. "People had started to revere them as gods because of their beauty, so they were destroyed in the flood so we wouldn't confuse the creature with the Creator."

Standing there watching the magnificent being, I could understand how people might have been misled.

The sight of him urged me closer. Making a small movement forward, I accidentally stepped on a dry stick, which cracked loudly. I glanced down at the offensive stick, then up, but all I caught was a blur of silvery white disappearing into the forest.

"Oh, I'm so sorry. I just wanted a closer look."

Jonathon's hand had slid off my shoulder, but I was taken aback by how close he was.

"Don't worry about it. They spook really easily. That's why they're so hard to spot."

"Why did you bring me to see this?"

Jonathon's eyebrows shot up. He looked over my head and shrugged.

"I don't know. I guess I just figured this was probably something you hadn't seen before, you know, being new and all. And when you ran right into me," he gave me a wicked smile, which dropped off his face after only a moment, "I don't know, I guess I felt there was just something . . ." He let the rest of his sentence drop.

The moment hung in the air.

"Audrey, do you know how beautiful your eyes are?"

My mind startled at the abrupt change of subject. "But they're just brown."

"A rich brown."

He was leaning in, and I just froze. In another moment his lips would be close enough to touch mine. An alarm was going off in my head that shouted *too soon, too soon, too soon* over and over again, but my body stayed immobile, unable to obey.

16

BY THE LAKE

"What are you guys doing out here?"

Romona's voice broke my paralysis so suddenly that I jumped away from Jonathon. "Ouch!" Bark bit into my bare back.

"I was showing Audrey the unicorns." Jonathon responded without a hint of defensiveness in his voice. I, on the other hand, immediately felt guilty, so I started to ramble.

"Oh, Romona, it was amazing. I never knew there were animals so beautiful. And it was here one second, then I stepped on a stupid branch and scared it away. But I think it would have stayed if it didn't know we were here, so I'm pretty bummed I stepped on the branch, but I just wanted to get a closer look because it's not like you see one of those every day or anything."

I was out of breath by the time I finished my wordy account. Romona frowned.

"You shouldn't have left the celebration."

"That was my fault. I wanted her to have this experience. I'm sure you know how hard they are to spot."

Romona glared at him with a look I'd never seen cross her face. It appeared to be a mixture of disappointment and annoyance, with a solid measure of anger. Those weren't emotions she usually gave in to.

"Yes, I know they are rare, but showing her a unicorn didn't appear to be the *only* reason you brought her out here," she said with a sharp edge to her voice.

Jonathon held his hands up. "Okay okay, I get the picture. Not the smartest thing to do. I was just a little caught up in the moment. But everybody is okay; nothing happened."

Romona plopped her hands on her hips. "And what if the damage had already been done?"

Her accusing tone seemed to bounce off Jonathon as he flashed a dazzling smile. "Well, we've already established that's not something we have to worry about, now is it?"

"No thanks to you."

I gaped at how rude she was being. Yes, parts of their conversation were going over my head, but what could he have possibly done to make her this upset in just the short time we were away? Especially since, as far as I knew, Romona didn't know Jonathon from Adam. The way she behaved was practically parental.

"Romona!"

Jonathon's tone grew more sincere. "No, don't worry, Audrey, she's just being a good friend. I was out of line. I'll go and let the two of you walk back together."

Before I could argue, he'd picked my hand up and gently kissed the back. He was feeling a little wistful. His level of comfort with physical contact with me was just plain unnerving.

"I'm sure I'll see you around again." Without waiting for my good-bye, he walked away.

I turned on Romona with astonishment.

"What was that all about?"

Romona watched Jonathon's retreating form with eyes slightly narrowed. "I just thought he was taking advantage of the situation."

"Well yeah, I could have guessed that, but care to explain to me how?"

"Specifically regarding your lack of knowledge about some things here."

"What, you mean with the unicorn? How is that harmful?"

With a deep sigh, she angled her face toward me. And skirted the question. "You just have to trust me on this one. Some things mean more than you think."

"Like what things?"

She took a deep breath and deflected my question once again. "I'm not saying that Jonathon is a bad guy, Audrey."

"Well, why don't you explain to me exactly what you are saying so I can make my own assessment?" I shot back.

"Well, for one thing, he would be a big distraction right now."

I lifted an eyebrow as if to say "so what?"

"I think he might take your mind off what's really important."

Something I would consider a plus. Romona was trying to be helpful, but what was the harm she was alluding to? Jonathon seemed to be a decent guy. Not to mention pretty cute and paying some serious attention to me. And who was she to police who I could or couldn't hang out with?

"What are you, like my mom or something?"

The question gave her a visible start. "Hardly. But there are things I know more about than you do right now. It's up to you to trust that I'm telling you the truth. Even in this realm, there are consequences to your actions."

More riddles. I was suddenly very tired. What had promised to be an enchanted night had turned ugly fast. Sad to have lost the joy for the evening, my gut instinct was to pull away. I was inclined to give in.

"I think I'd like to be alone right now, if you don't mind."

"I'm not sure—" Romona started and then stopped herself, giving me a quick nod. "Okay, I understand."

She turned to follow the path Jonathon had taken. Part of me ached to follow her and rejoin the celebration, but I squashed that feeling and headed in the opposite direction.

I walked lost in my own thoughts for a while before stumbling through a break in the trees that opened to a small, pebbly beach on the shore of a still lake. The lake was embraced by forest on all sides and offered a view of the mountains in the distance. Water soundlessly licked the pebbles on the shoreline. This small oasis in the middle of the trees was calming. My heels sank into the stones as I walked clumsily closer to the water's edge. I closed my eyes and took a deep breath of the fresh air. On exhale, it felt as if I had released some of the ugliness toward my friend. The simple act was refreshing to my soul.

"I hear you want to be alone."

I opened my eyes to Logan sitting on a large rock a few feet away. I was certain he hadn't been there a moment before. His forearms rested on his knees as he stared across the lake.

The mountain peaks glowed in the odd night lighting and the lake shimmered and sparkled like millions of faraway stars. The air stirred lazily, causing strands of my hair to float over my shoulder and the hem of my dress to tickle my legs. The slight breeze was refreshing without being cold.

"I just needed to think."

Logan nodded in understanding.

"Mind if I sit down?" I asked.

Logan moved down the rock to make room. There was plenty of space for us both to sit without being in any danger of touching. I stretched my legs in front of me and crossed my ankles. From this position, I had a view of both Logan and the scenery. I took a few moments to study him in silence.

Being with Logan when we weren't at each other's throats was turning out to be oddly soothing. I was reminded of the other beach we'd sat on when I'd thought things were finally getting better between us. I stared out across the water and faintly heard the sweet music coming from the celebration. It was a while before either of us said anything.

"What did you think of tonight?" The soft timber of Logan's voice blended well with the night.

"It was incredible. I never would have imagined something could be so . . ." I struggled for a word to describe it . . . "magical."

Logan softly chuckled.

"I can see why you would describe it that way. There's something quite magical about it. Except the ironic thing is that's what life was supposed to be like. This is really what we were created for, what we'd been missing all along. When we were walking around on Earth, we had a veil covering our eyes, and now that veil has been lifted. If people just understood . . ." He didn't finish his thought, but his voice had turned passionate.

I turned my head. Logan was staring at me intently. I was a prisoner to those intense eyes.

"What is it you are trying to tell me, Logan?" Unconsciously, I moved forward a fraction, lessening the space between us.

Logan released a deep breath and pulled back, breaking eye contact. He ran a hand through his hair, a move I was quite familiar with. He did it frequently when annoyed.

"Nothing you won't learn soon enough."

I let out a small breath of frustration. We were back to that again.

"But not something you will explain to me."

I leaned away, tired of everyone edging around topics and treating me like a child. I just wanted someone to be completely honest with me. I didn't want to have to find everything out on my own. It was like trying to navigate without a map or even a final destination. Completely and utterly impossible.

"I'm sorry, Audrey, I'm sure this is wearisome. When you get your memories back, more things are going to fall into place. Unfortunately, some things can't be explained. There are choices you have to make."

His words rubbed a sore that was already sensitive. I pushed off the rock to walk the few feet to the water's edge. The slight tide rolled up mere inches from my toes, only to recede back a moment later. If I moved forward even a little, I would be able to feel the coolness myself. I remained rooted in place.

"Yes, those elusive memories I don't have anymore. You mean once I remember who I once was, everything will make sense? Ha! But what if it's the opposite, Logan? What if I remember who I was and all of this makes even less sense? What then?"

"It's not who you *were*, Audrey, it's who you *are*, who you've always been all along. You are still you, even though you don't remember the details."

I stared at the water, watching my reflection ripple in the shoreline. I ran a hand down the side of my dress and clasped some of the material in my fingers, feeling its softness.

"Then how does it make sense that I feel more myself in a dress than training gear? How is that supposed to make sense with what I am now? I don't see the two reconciling."

Logan pushed off from the rock, and his reflection in the water appeared behind me. When he finally spoke, his warm breath fanned my shoulder.

"I have to admit, you did seem more comfortable in your own skin tonight. Perhaps you were a pageant girl?"

I heard the smile in his voice as he said it. That idea was absurd for a number of reasons. I had a sudden image of me wearing my fighting armor with a tiara and doing a pageant wave down a runway. It was ridiculous enough to force a smile and a rebellious laugh to escape.

"I don't want to take credit for changing your mood, so can I ask what's so funny?"

I explained the mental picture I'd just had. The corner of his mouth turned up in my peripheral vision as well as in the hazy water reflection below. He took a step forward.

"That may be more of an accurate description of yourself then you realize."

"Ha! Yeah, right!" I scoffed.

Logan's distorted reflection in the water turned ever so slightly toward me. Just as I was studying him in the water, he was studying me. I couldn't make out the look on his face through the clouded image.

"So, is purple hair the new thing?"

I smiled. "Something I was trying out. I didn't think you'd noticed."

"Hmmm," Logan said thoughtfully but didn't expound. My breath caught when he reached a hand up toward my hair, only to drop it to his side a moment later.

"I'll let you be alone now." His voice was still soft but hollow.

I tried not to let myself feel disappointed. I nodded. Logan left as soundlessly as he had appeared.

My reflection mocked me. Each gentle wave distorted the image just as it was beginning to settle. The image of a girl I still didn't know. Who was she? I could count everything I knew about her on my two small hands.

I let out a harsh breath in exasperation and used the toe of my shoe to kick a pebble into the water. The stone slapped the face of the girl looking back at me and sent wild ripples out into the placid lake. Each ripple produced a sweet note of song, eventually fading into the stillness. I didn't want to feel so alone anymore.

As if the wind knew my thoughts, a soft breeze blew from behind, bringing with it the faint sounds of celebration. Involuntarily, something inside me responded yet again. A nudge told me I wasn't alone, I hadn't been forgotten, I did have people who cared about me.

In my mind's eye, I saw friends. Romona with her peaceful and gentle spirit, Kevin with his good and kind heart, joyous Alrik, patient and beautiful Kaitlin, and Logan with his steadfastness.

My heart's desire was to soften, but a ball of bitterness tightened around it instead. Wouldn't a God who truly loved me want to comfort me Himself? Why would He make me go through this alone? Why would He give me a task that was so obviously beyond my skills?

The sweet music from the dance still tugged at my soul, but I turned instead and walked the other direction, away from my friends, away from the comfort, and headed back to my empty tree to be alone.

17

ROMONA'S APOLOGY

"*H*i, can we talk?"

I rubbed my eyes to wipe the sleep from them, leaving a black smear across the back of my hand. *Shoot, I must have smudged mascara all over my face.*

My hazy brain took a moment to register that Romona was standing in my open doorway.

"Oh, ah, yeah, come on in."

She looked at me strangely.

It took me a second to realize how awful I must look in the crumpled dress with my hair all over the place, and a mess of black mascara and eye shadow smeared across my face. "Oh right, give me a second to get this off, will you?"

Romona sat gingerly on a sofa chair and patiently waited for me to pull myself together. Although silent, her face still projected that strange look. *I must look really bad.*

Standing in front of the mirror, I splashed water on my face. My reflection shocked me fully awake. It wasn't just the makeup smear or the disheveled clothes that had Romona transfixed—it was my hair. The wavy mass that wildly protruded from my head had been transformed to jet black and fire-engine red.

I looked like a madwoman.

I started taking in and expelling air at an ever-quickening pace. Each breath in and out was shorter than the last until I was panting like a dog on a hot day.

"Did you do that on purpose?" came a gentle voice.

I shook my head. There was a soft rustle as Romona joined me.

"Here, let's get you cleaned up first, and then we can deal with the hair."

She handed me a bar of soap. I bent to scrub the makeup from my face. Once I didn't look quite as frightening, Romona was waiting with a handful of bedclothes.

"Here you go."

I quickly changed and faced the mirror again to deal with my hair. I concentrated on relaxing and returning it to a normal shade of chocolate brown. Once my breathing was controlled, the black and red started to bleed from my hair. I sighed in relief. "That was really weird." Romona nodded in agreement.

"So what are you doing here so late?"

She took a deep, steadying breath before speaking.

"I wanted to apologize for what happened in the woods tonight. I overreacted, and also . . . I'd like to explain a little more. I think there's something you should know, even if it's intended for you to find out on your own." Sincerity shone in her eyes.

I'd never had reason to doubt Romona's motives. Yet I'd

distrusted her this evening and lashed out in anger. The weight of the injustices I'd committed against her was heavy.

"Oh, Romona, no. It's really not your fault. I keep getting frustrated because there's so much I still don't know. You were only worried because I was out there alone with Jonathon. I see how that could be a little sketchy. Especially since I'd just met him. I should never have left the celebration to begin with."

Feeling my cheeks redden, I looked away. Going off with him was a stupid move.

She was shaking her head. "But, Audrey, that's what I want to explain. It's not only that. I don't care how it looked. Remember tonight when I was talking about consequences for your actions?"

"Yeah."

"Well, there are consequences in this realm for things you might not consider a big deal. We saw the way Jonathon looked at you tonight." I wanted to ask who the "we" was, but she rushed forward. "I was worried you might do something you couldn't take back later."

"Geez, Romona, what do you think we would have done? I just meet the guy! The worse that could have happened was a kiss. You don't honestly think I'd have gone further than that?"

Her eyes grew unnaturally large. "See, that's just it—a kiss is so much more than you think it is."

My heart skipped a beat. Thoughts of Jonathon slid from my mind, replaced by someone else.

"What do you mean?" My voice was flat.

"A kiss is more than a kiss now . . . here." She looked up at the ceiling to piece together words. I got the distinct impression she was getting ready to launch into a lecture on the birds and the bees. "A kiss here is more like a promise. It creates a bond. I was worried that Jonathon might take advantage of you not knowing that."

I only nodded for her to go on. I had to know what type of mess I'd gotten myself into.

"At the risk of sounding melodramatic, I didn't want you to get stuck with the wrong person for all of eternity just because you didn't know any better."

"What! If I kiss him, I would have to be with him *forever?"*

Romona held up her hands for me to slow down. "No, sorry, that's not exactly what I meant. When the bond is created, it intensifies any feelings you have for that person. It draws you to them and them to you. We weren't intended to have more than one soul mate, so when you pick your mate here, it's for keeps. Jonathon could have started that bond with you tonight without your consent, so to speak."

"So the first person I kiss here I'm picking as my soul mate? The person I have to spend the rest of eternity with?"

"No."

"No?"

"No, you still have a choice. What you are doing, though, is taking a step in that direction. You're making a decision to be pulled closer to that person on a soul level. And breaking the bond you create can be very difficult."

My heart beat so loud I wondered if she heard. The blood rushing through my head made it hard for me to concentrate. *My gosh, why in the world didn't I get the instruction manual on this stuff when I arrived?*

"Was this something I would have learned in orientation?"

"Probably."

"Why didn't anyone tell me then?"

"Skipping orientation is very rare, so we don't really know how much to tell you or what you're supposed to discover on your own."

I went to my bed, landed face first, and groaned.

"There are some things that seriously need to be told sooner rather than later."

"This wasn't really something I thought about telling you until this evening."

With the risk of giving myself away, I had to ask: "So when you're talking about all this kissing and bonding and junk, do you mean here in this realm or now that we've passed on in general?"

Romona stared at me quizzically. "I'm not following."

I had to know if I'd accidentally done something to Logan and me without meaning to. I chewed my lip in indecision.

"I mean, is this something that happens now because we are dead or is it just *here?*" I paused before completely spelling it out. "Does it like, count the same if it happens on Earth?"

As expected, Romona sucked in a quick breath. Of course she was smart enough to know something was up. It was visible on her face when all the pieces clicked together. Neither one of us spoke for a full sixty-five seconds.

I counted.

Then Romona asked me the question I'd dreaded and dodged for days. "Audrey, what really happened with you and Logan when you went to Earth?"

The question came out as a whisper. Almost as if she didn't dare ask it for fear she already knew. I chewed on my lower lip some more, my brows furrowed.

When I didn't answer, she asked the more direct version of the question. "Did he kiss you?"

"No."

Romona let out a deep breath, and her whole body relaxed. "Oh good, because . . ."

"I kissed him." I admitted hurriedly. It felt like ripping off a stubborn Band-Aid. Extremely painful.

Romona gasped, and she brought a hand up to her mouth. "I thought you guys could hardly stand each other!"

"Well, that's true most days."

"Then how did this happen?"

"It was an accident. Remember how we said we escaped the demon by blending into the crowd that day?"

She nodded.

"Well, that was true, but we never told you guys *exactly how* we blended in. I basically attacked Logan and made him kiss me so it didn't look like we were running from the demon."

"Oh, Audrey, you didn't!" The horrified look on her face said everything she didn't.

I slowly nodded my head in shame.

"The boardwalk was so busy, and the crowd was parting for us, which was a complete giveaway, and it was all I could come up with to get us away from the crowd and still make it look like we belonged there. I didn't think it through as well as I should have." I looked down at my hands.

With her hand to her mouth, Romona let out a small giggle.

"This is *not* funny, Romona."

"Oh, I know, but it's so unbelievable. And poor Logan, I'll bet he didn't even know what hit him."

I remembered Logan's reaction. If you excluded my complete mortification both then and now, it was kind of funny. I fought the lifting of the corners of my mouth.

"Yeah, he never saw it coming. He just stood there like a statue. I had to step on his foot to get him to snap out of it."

Romona let out a real laugh. "Oh my goodness, seriously?"

I nodded solemnly, but I hoped Romona's laugh and lightened attitude meant I wasn't in any real trouble.

"Okay, so how bad is it? It wasn't even a real kiss, so it shouldn't count. Is there a free pass or something since we were on Earth? Not to mention I was *completely* unaware of that rule!"

Romona sobered a bit.

"I'm afraid that little technicality doesn't matter. You know, now that I think about it, things make so much more sense. There's been something off between the two of you. And especially the way he acted tonight. He must really be fighting it."

I found that to be a little insulting. But Romona didn't mean anything by it.

"Okay, you need to tell me what sort of trouble I've gotten myself into. Am I stuck with Logan forever now?" The idea of being stuck with someone who aggravated me so much was suddenly very serious and a touch scary.

She was thoughtful a moment before answering. "Well, one big problem is that Logan's not really available right now."

Then it was as I expected. There *was* something going on with Kaitlin. I just knew it. Despite having always suspected it, the confirmation still pierced me.

"I see."

"No, I don't think you do, but it's not my place to tell you, it's Logan's. You guys are just going to have to work through this one. To be blunt, you inadvertently tied yourself to Logan whether you meant to," she lifted an eyebrow at me, "or wanted to. Whatever your emotions toward each other might have been, you just prematurely turned it all up a notch."

"Why didn't Logan tell me any of this?"

She shrugged her shoulders. "Can't say for sure. Maybe so he wouldn't freak you out. Maybe he thought it was too much for you to handle. Or maybe he doesn't want to admit it himself."

"So what you are saying is that anything . . . romantic I feel for Logan right now is just because I kissed him?"

"Oh no, that's not what I'm saying. The kiss doesn't fabricate feelings for someone else. It intensifies them. You're really only supposed to kiss the person you stay with, you know, forever. Imagine a seal on an envelope. The kiss is supposed to seal those emotions. That's why it's so important to be careful."

"Great, so I've doomed both of us?" My shoulders slumped in defeat.

"No, not necessarily. I didn't say it couldn't be broken, just that it was difficult. Or, if there really weren't any feelings between the two of you to begin with, then nothing should come of it." She watched my reaction closely.

"Really? So it could possibly mean nothing?" I bounced happily to my knees.

"Yes, but that's only if you can honestly say you don't feel anything romantic toward Logan and he the same." She arched an eyebrow at me that said she had my number. "Are you really going to try to tell me that's the case?"

I huffed. "Okay, then tell me what else I need to do to break the stupid bond!"

She nodded. "You need to let him go."

"Great, done." I brushed my hands together like I was brushing off the whole thing. "That sounds easy."

"It may sound that way, but it won't be."

Determined to hear only what I wanted to hear, I plowed on. "Okay, let's do this thing. Do I need to say some magic words? Burn a picture of him with some incense?"

"Audrey." Romona's look and tone said she didn't think I was taking this seriously.

"No really, let's get this over with. I want to get back to the way it used to be. Or at least should have been. I don't really want to go back to getting thrown into the water, but I'm sure there's got to be something better than this. What we have going on now is . . . distracting. So what should I do?"

"I'm sorry, I can't tell you that."

"What?"

"I can't tell you because I don't know. You have to figure out how to let go of him in your heart. There are no magic words or any rituals to fix this."

"Can't I simply choose to let him go?"

"Sure, in your head you can, but your heart's a little trickier. You've got him hidden in there somewhere."

"Oh come on, it's Logan we're talking about here. Hidden in my heart somewhere? Pa-leeeasse!" I rolled my eyes.

Romona shook her head. "You can deny it all you want, Audrey, but he's there. The faster you come to terms with that, the quicker you can work through it."

She gave me a sad look. One that said she understood how hard this was going to be much better than I did. It concerned me.

"I wonder . . ." She started but stopped with a shake of her head. "You know, a good place to start is to have an honest conversation with Logan."

I looked at her like she was crazy and told her as much. "I

never want to discuss this with Logan, ever. It's bad enough talking about it at all, but talking to him would be sheer torture. Embarrassment taken to a new level."

"I see. Well, it's something I hope you'll think about."

Like there was anything else I would be thinking about now. My only promise was a nod.

She sighed. "All right, I should get going. It's extremely late, and tomorrow brings its own worries."

"What does that mean?"

"You'll see in the morning."

"Romona!" I groaned.

She laughed lightly. "Don't worry, this isn't a secret. Logan will explain tomorrow."

Romona gracefully rose from the sofa chair. I followed her to the door to say good night. Before leaving, she gave me a hug that folded me in a cushion of love. I hoped some of my gratitude made it back to her.

With all the thoughts swirling in my head, I assumed it would take me a while to settle down, but when my head hit my pillow, I was already half-asleep.

18

MEETING THE
ARCHANGEL

I kept expecting something important to happen the next day at training, but it turned out to be an unexpectedly normal day. Logan was neither more nor less talkative than he had been of late. We ran through the usual training drills and sparring lessons. We started and finished the day at roughly the same time as had become customary. There was no talk about whatever Romona had hinted at the night before. All things considered, the day was anticlimactic at best.

I pushed through the locker room doors in a restless haze. Kaitlin was finishing getting dressed, her hair still wet from the shower. The sight of her sent a sharp stabbing pain into my chest. Romona's words from the night before replayed in my head. *Logan's not really available right now.*

"Hey." I nodded in her direction, not allowing our eyes to connect.

It was difficult. On the one hand I was starting to like

Kaitlin. She was confident, friendly, and nice with a sharp sense of humor and a wicked roundhouse kick. There was something magnetic about her. As if she were a bright light we were all drawn to like flies. And that was exactly what kept me wary of her. It was too easy, too effortless for her.

"So I didn't see you again last night after you took off with Jonathon." She purposefully let the statement float in the air.

I shrugged.

"Did you ever make it back to the celebration? I was hoping to introduce you to a few friends."

"No, I took the opportunity to spend some time on my own. It was really peaceful."

"I see." She nodded. "Did Logan ever find you then?"

"What do you mean?" I asked.

"Last night. When I told him you'd left, he took off after you. I just wanted to know if he ever found you."

"Yes, he did . . . eventually."

"That's good. He seemed rather . . . um . . . agitated."

Had Kaitlin told him in order to point out I was preoccupied with someone else? And if so, shouldn't she be upset that he'd gone to look for me? Nothing was making sense right now.

The doors behind me swooshed open and Romona came in, mopping her brow with a small towel.

"Hey girls," she said breathlessly.

"Let me guess," Kaitlin said, "the gauntlet?"

"You got it! Man, it really kicked my butt!"

"What's a gauntlet?" I asked.

"It's a training exercise. It's an obstacle course, but after every obstacle you have to defeat an opponent and then move on to the next. It's intense!"

"And really long," Kaitlin piped in. "Sometimes it takes hours to get through."

"Eww, I don't want to hear either one of you mentioning it to Logan."

"Ha," Kaitlin laughed, "too late; he already ran it this morning before he started training with you."

I shook my head in awe. And I thought *I* needed to get out more. He must have been at the training center for sixteen hours already.

"So why haven't I heard of this thing before?" I asked.

"Probably because they only break it out before big missions, when they are planning on sending a larger group of hunters down to Earth. It's like a qualifier to make sure everyone is still on their game."

"Oh." I looked at Romona. "So you're headed down for a mission soon?"

She looked perplexed. "Um yeah, but . . ."

"What?"

"Nothing, I guess." She turned to Kaitlin, who simply shrugged, before changing the subject. "Let's have a girls' night tonight!"

Their misdirection came to light as we were all leaving the locker room.

"So, Aud, you ready for tomorrow?" Alrik's voiced boomed from down the hallway.

I frowned at him. "What's so special about tomorrow?"

"What? Don't tell me they haven't told you yet," he continued after a moment of silence from me. "Well, that's a surprise. Tomorrow's your first mission."

I glanced at Logan who was in conversation with Kevin a little further down the hall.

If what Alrik said was true, why hadn't Logan said something to me? You don't spring this on someone last minute! I looked at Alrik in disbelief. He must have it wrong. I told him as much.

"I don't know, Aud, I heard it from up the chain. You've created quite a stir. A number of people are interested to see how your first official mission goes considering the adventure from your last trip to Earth."

I still blushed every time someone brought that up. This time especially since Alrik might know more about that fateful day than he let on. The twinkle in his eye whenever he brought it up said as much. Rather than stand there and argue with him, it was better to go to the source and get some answers. I brushed past him to get to Logan, who was still in conversation with Kevin.

The casual and friendly air Logan had with Kevin vanished when I faced them. I watched him slip on his mask of indifference. I sighed internally. Was it always going to be this way?

"What's this about my first mission being tomorrow?" I pointed a thumb behind me toward Alrik. "He's got it wrong, right?"

"Aren't you hanging out with the girls tonight?"

"Logan, come on, is there something you're not telling me? If it's true, I would have appreciated a little more heads-up, and to have heard it from you."

"There's nothing to give you the heads-up about. You're not going."

He actually had the nerve to turn back to Kevin as if I wasn't even there. Did he think I was a child he could dismiss with a wave of a hand?

Peeved, I did the unthinkable and grabbed Logan's forearm

to get his attention. It was barely a fraction of a second before he snatched his arm away from me, but it did the trick. I had his full attention. It only took that moment of contact to realize the indifference he'd tightly cloaked himself in was far from genuine. I was taken aback at the strong emotions churning inside him. He was more worked up about this than I had perceived. There was some satisfaction in that.

Logan glared back as if I'd committed some giant violation of his privacy. Which I guess I had—he was the most anti-empathy link person I knew—but I was beyond caring.

"What do you mean I'm not going?" I asked.

He stepped out of my reach, making it abundantly clear that he didn't want me to touch him again. *Pfft.* As if I'd even want to. "I contested the decision. You're not ready." He said it matter-of-factly.

"Excuse me! You contested the decision? What gave you the right?" Unlike Logan, my emotions were on display for everyone to see.

"The fact that I'm your mentor and I don't think you're ready."

I flinched as if I had been slapped. I knew Logan wasn't one hundred percent pleased with my progress so far, but I'd thought I was getting better. To contest an order meant he really doubted my abilities. When I recoiled I might have seen something soften in his eyes, but it was gone in an instant.

"Hey man, that was kind of harsh." It was Alrik who spoken up in my defense.

The way Logan's eyes never left mine you'd think he hadn't heard him, but a moment later he addressed Alrik in a way I'd never heard him speak to his friend. "This isn't your business."

"Maybe not, but you know you're not playing by the rules.

She's right, you don't have the authority to make that decision even if you are her mentor. If it was a direct order, only Audrey can contest it."

I turned my head to gawk at Alrik. Could he be right? When Logan didn't respond, it verified that Alrik spoke true.

Man, I could have kissed Alrik! Figuratively speaking, of course. Victory was within my grasp! I smiled brightly back at Logan, ready to end the issue right there and enjoy the rest of my evening. But Logan wasn't ready to concede defeat. He stared coolly at Alrik.

"You don't know what you're talking about. You weren't there the first time we went down. It was almost a catastrophe."

"Hey, I'd hardly call that fair!" I clenched my teeth. "If you remember, I was the one who finally got us out of trouble."

Logan's eyes widened and then narrowed again as if he were picking up the unspoken gauntlet I'd just thrown down.

"I had everything under control," he said. "Besides, it's not as if your *methods* would really come in handy in another situation."

"At least I know how to think on my feet," I shot back.

I was extremely glad we were in a poorly lit section of hallway, because I was certain both our faces were on fire. Luckily, no one except Romona really knew what we were talking about.

I was so wound up I almost jumped out of my skin when Alrik laid a steady hand between my shoulder blades.

"Listen, you two, let's just bring it down a notch. Logan can contest, but I've never heard of the council changing a decision because of a mentor's suggestion. Aud, if you want to go tomorrow, you should be able to."

Logan shot Alrik another annoyed look. When in the world had Alrik become the levelheaded one? I knew I was being handled, but considering Logan and I had publicly stumbled upon a very personal topic, it was probably best to listen. Suddenly I didn't feel like a girl's night anymore.

When I opened my eyes in the stillness of my room the next morning, I was assaulted by the nervousness I'd held at bay last night. I'd worn a brave face in front of my friends, but now, listening to the rapid beating of my heart, I was a bundle of doubts.

I closed my eyes and remembered what it felt like being stalked by an unseen demon. A shudder ran through my body. I had been so scared, desperate even.

Sitting up, I threw off my comforter, hoping to also throw off the apprehension that had my insides twisted. It didn't work, and although the temperature in the room was perfect as usual, an uncontrollable shiver ran through my body. I walked to the sink and surveyed myself in the mirror. My hair stuck up at weird angles and tangled its way down my back. My eyes looked darker than usual and my skin paler. *Am I crazy or just plain stupid?*

Perhaps I should have swallowed my pride and listened to Logan. If he didn't think I was ready, what chance did I really have?

I brought my hands to my face and rubbed the sleep from my eyes, taking a deep breath to steady myself. I wished for the hundredth time that I knew a little more about my life. Maybe there was a past experience I could draw on to gain confidence. Instead, all I had was a short history of poor performance and rash decisions.

"Come on, God, if you're out there, I could use a bit of encouragement and reassurance right about now."

I held my breath and waited in silence. For what, I wasn't sure, but I hoped for something.

Exhaling harshly, I shook my head. *What was I expecting to happen, anyway?*

A loud knock sounded at my door and I almost jumped out of my skin. Frozen in place, my heart raced fast and loud. Was there a chance God had actually heard me and was literally knocking on my door?

Another loud rap was followed by a voice. "Audrey, are you in there? It's me, Kaitlin."

My heart deflated. I took a quick moment to compose myself, then grabbed an elastic to wrap my hair in a bun. Kaitlin always looked so perfect. *Oh well.*

I opened the door. She stood with a big, if somewhat strained, smile on her face.

"Hey," I said.

"Hi! Romona told me where you lived."

Awkward silence followed. What was she doing here, anyway?

"Oh."

"I, ah, could we talk for a sec?"

It was bizarre to see Kaitlin so unsure of herself. She fidgeted with some bracelets on her right hand and shifted her weight. I was equally curious and cautious.

I invited her in. Relieved, she gave me a smile that lit up her whole face. She studied my room with interest.

"Cool chairs," she finally said.

"Thanks."

"So would you like to sit down?"

"Yeah, that would be great, thanks."

We settled into the overstuffed chairs. The strained smile on Kaitlin's face faltered.

"I know you aren't ready to start confiding in me like you do Romona, but I wanted to let you know I'm supporting your decision to go on this mission today."

Kaitlin's arrival had temporarily pushed that from my thoughts. But the cool fingers of trepidation crept back up my spine.

"Logan wouldn't agree with you."

She smiled sympathetically. "You know, Logan does have his reasons for not wanting you to go, but you shouldn't think they all have to do with your ability. I've seen you fight, remember—I've trained with you. You're going to be fine."

I sat back. "You really think so? Logan was pretty specific about his reasons last night."

"Yeah, well, sometimes we don't always say what we know to be true. And Logan has some fears of his own he's still working through. Scars that have absolutely nothing to do with you. I think they have more to do with his reaction to your mission than you realize."

"What scars?"

Kaitlin had the sense to squirm uncomfortably. When she answered, it was apologetically.

"It's not really my place to say. You'll have to take it up with Logan. But I do want you to know that I think you're ready. And I'm not the only one, or else they wouldn't have assigned you."

It was disappointing to have hit another wall where Logan

was concerned. Kaitlin had dangled a piece of the puzzle in front of my face only to snatch it away again.

She took my silence as an invitation to continue. "And besides, you'll have a lot of people with you."

I gave myself a mental shake to get back on topic. "Really? Do you know who will be there? Are you going?"

"No, I won't be there. This is something for your region only. But Romona should be there. Maybe even Kevin or Alrik."

Kaitlin's support was a balm for my raw emotions. Despite myself, I was getting closer to her.

"Thanks, Kaitlin. You've actually made me feel a lot better."

She smiled knowingly. "I thought you might be a little anxious about today. I didn't think the bravado from last night was one hundred percent genuine."

Her words left me feeling exposed, but I didn't mind. I found myself wanting to open up to her.

"Yeah, I guess you're right about that. I think the adrenaline was talking last night. And there's another reason I'm glad that you came this morning."

"Really, what's that?"

"Well, Kevin mentioned we weren't supposed to wear our armor today, and I think you are the perfect person to help me figure out what to wear instead!"

Kaitlin gave me one of her megawatt movie-star smiles.

"You've got that right! Time to check out your closet." She jumped up and faced my closet. "Hey there, Hot Stuff," she said to the door, "it's time to see what you've really got."

Not only was Kaitlin the ideal person to help me figure out what to wear, but she also had me ready in record time, which was why I found myself waiting alone in the training gym before anyone else arrived. As I sat in silence, my mind drifted to my first day of training. I was almost as nervous and unsure now as I had been then.

I glanced at the weapons wall and pushed off the mat to browse the now familiar objects, silently reciting the names and uses of each. My slow progression stopped when I reached the broad-bladed sword I'd first picked up. I grabbed it with confidence this time and brought the blade up to inspect, catching my reflection in it once more. This time the girl staring back was more familiar. Still mysterious, but certainly recognizable.

"You shouldn't be touching those. You could hurt yourself."

There was no bang of the door to announce Logan's entrance this time, and I kept a firm grasp on the hilt. Rather than chilling flatness, there was a warmth in Logan's voice that made me smile despite myself. I wasn't the only one being nostalgic this morning.

I carefully returned the blade to its spot. Logan was standing on the opposite side of the room, the doors still softly swinging shut behind him. I had expected round two of our argument from last night.

"You think so? Or are you worried I could hurt *you* with it this time?"

Logan smiled. "Part of me is always worried you could hurt me."

So rarely were his smiles directed at me that I mentally saved this one. It made him appear younger. I appreciated the softness I wasn't often privy to but purposefully ignored the slight hitch to my breathing that it caused.

It seemed silly to be talking across the expanse of the room, so I forced myself to confidently stride toward him. When I was halfway there Logan made the decision to meet me in the middle. We stopped our customary distance from each other. Neither one of us invading the other's bubble.

"How are you feeling today?"

I shrugged. "Fine, I guess."

He nodded as if I had said something more important. "That's good."

But I couldn't leave well enough alone. "So how'd your appeal go?"

"I decided to retract it." Logan studied my face.

I was stunned. "Why?"

Logan smiled. "I was given some good advice that I finally listened to."

Huh? Advice? Was Kaitlin the one who had changed his mind? Despite her encouraging words this morning, I realized how desperately I needed to hear some from Logan as well.

I knew how vulnerable I sounded, but I had to ask. "So does that mean you think I'm ready for this?"

Logan blew out a quick breath and ran a hand through his unruly locks before answering me, not quite meeting my gaze. "Oh, Audrey, I'm not sure I'm the best person to be assessing that anymore."

He said it with a half-laugh as if he considered himself the butt of a joke. Unexpectedly, he took a few steps closer, breaking the invisible barrier we'd been keeping. Something on the inside heated up as I looked up into Logan's deep blue eyes.

He was as serious as I'd ever seen. "But Audrey, I promise, I'll be there the whole time. Nothing is going to happen to you."

His gaze intensified. "Nothing."

His voice wasn't loud, but it vibrated in my head as if shouted. My heart thudded inside my chest loud enough to be heard. Any words I might have spoken died in my throat. My only response was to nod and hope he knew I understood.

The door flew open with a bang as a joking, laughing group of others arrived. I jumped away from Logan guiltily. I hadn't thought my heart could beat any louder than before, but I was wrong. It took a moment for the erratic beating to subside, and that was only after I realized no one was giving us much notice.

I glanced at Logan, but he didn't appear concerned. He strode over to the group to say hello. Man, he could change gears fast enough to give a girl whiplash.

Romona broke free of the small group. As always, I was grateful for her support. I wondered if I'd had friends as loyal and supportive as her when I was alive. I hoped so. She met me with her familiar friendly smile and a tight hug. I didn't need to feel her encouragement through the empathy link because her face revealed it clearly enough.

"Hey, so how are you feeling about this?" Direct and to the point. I both liked and disliked that about her.

"Good, I think."

"Don't worry, we'll all be there with you."

The group atmosphere was unexpectedly chill and relaxed. Any nervous energy in the room was mine alone. The others chatted lightly. Even Logan appeared at ease, trading jokes about demons with Kevin.

There were fifteen of us total. All of the hunters were familiar, even if I didn't remember their names.

"No, I've got a better one," I caught Kevin saying. "What do you call a demon that's having a bad hair day?"

He didn't get to finish because Shannon walked in just then, and all chatter ceased. Taking time to scan our faces, her gaze stopped on mine for an extended moment before traveling on to the next.

"Thanks for being on time. As you know, I'm here to give you a further rundown of your assignment. I expect you all know at least the preliminary details."

I inconspicuously scanned the other hunters. Their faces only showed focused attention. No one betrayed any inclination of confusion. Logan had done a poor job of preparing me —again. I heaved a sigh of frustration.

"You have something to say, Audrey?"

"What? No, thanks. I mean, sorry, I'm good."

The look on Shannon's face wasn't exactly disapproving, but I wouldn't call it benevolent either. After a pregnant pause, she nodded and resumed her speech.

"Your primary objective today is simple. You are going to be doing some reconnaissance work."

Some muffled groans wafted up from the group.

"I know this is a little basic for most of you. But it's still necessary. It will also be good for those of you without much ground experience to cut your teeth on something more supervised."

I knew whom she was talking about.

"There has been some out-of-the-ordinary demon activity in the section we are sending you today. You are to split into groups and check out the area, then report back on any findings. You are intended to blend in today, which is why you aren't in your body armor for this trip."

She gave us all a hard stare. "Under no circumstances are you to engage a demon. We have angels standing by to provide extractions should anything dangerous arise, but they are positioned far enough away not to raise suspicion. I need to make sure this point is clear and understood."

We nodded obediently.

Shannon was quick to dismiss us and make her exit. That's when Logan took over, making quick work of giving us a few basic details.

We arrived in an abandoned warehouse on Earth with as little fanfare as possible. I was in the first group to be sent down and watched the other hunters arrive, shimmering into being. One moment there was empty air, the next a twinkling, and then a person appearing. I giggled. It looked remarkably like the grainy TV image of Star Trek characters being beamed all over the galaxy—so much so that it hardly seemed coincidental. But how could the creators of a TV show know anything about the afterlife?

Romona lifted her eyebrows questioningly. I shook my head, not sure she would share my amusement.

The warehouse was large, poorly lit through a few dirty windows, musty and damp. I didn't like it. Too many dark places.

Logan's small group of hunters was the last to arrive. When he solidified, he immediately scanned the area until his eyes found mine. They only held for a few seconds before he turned businesslike.

"All right, we'll split into a few groups of two to do surveillance."

I did the quick math—our group of fifteen didn't split evenly. Logan quickly rattled off the names of people who were to form groups. There was no discussion or disagreement; people just moved around to stand with their partners. That just left Logan, myself, and an extra-large hunter named Dean. Dean was easily the largest guy there. Figures; Logan didn't consider me as a real hunter yet and as such had assigned an extra babysitter. The familiar twinge of annoyance prickled inside my chest.

Romona was paired with Kevin. She looked over and offered an apologetic smile as if she knew exactly how the extra person in my group made me feel. Subpar. I schooled my features so it wasn't so obvious.

I was about to move toward Logan when an impossibly bright light appeared directly behind him. I wondered later why it didn't frighten me. Instead, my eyes remained fixed on Logan, silhouetted by the light with his hair lit up like a halo. The brightness forced my eyes shut and seared the inside of my eyelids. Then, as suddenly as the brightness appeared, it disappeared, leaving me blinking rapidly to adjust to the low light in the warehouse. Splotches danced in my vision. I pressed the heel of my palms to my eyes and rubbed to relieve the sting.

Whatever that was had been beyond conspicuous. What had happened to lying low and staying out of site?

I looked up, and standing behind Logan was the largest and most intimidating angel I'd ever seen. My eyes grew larger.

"Who is that?" I whispered in Romona's ear. I'd subconsciously moved behind her, putting a physical barrier between myself and the majestic being. I had a hard time imagining how he could ever be mistaken for a human.

The angel had the form of a man but stood at least eight feet tall. He was dressed in white linen, with a thick belt of what might have been solid gold around his waist. His body looked as hard and smooth as a yellow gem, his face glowed like lightning, his eyes were like flaming torches, and his arms and legs gleamed like polished bronze. A sword hung loosely in a scabbard attached to his belt, easily twice the length of the ones I was used to wielding. Looking at him directly caused my knees to weaken.

Romona bent her head to whisper, "He's one of the combat angels. He fights the *really* bad guys."

I shivered. "What do you mean? Aren't they all bad?"

"Some are worse than others." As we spoke in hushed tones, Logan turned to address the angel with a surprising amount of ease. I couldn't quiet the tremor running throughout my body, but Logan looked like he was chatting with an old friend. My mind buzzed with fresh questions.

"Wait, so you're telling me there are different types of demons?"

"Of course there are. Demons were angels who turned against God and were cast out of their home and down to Earth. Since there are different levels of angels, there are different types of demons as well."

"Do demons look like angels then?"

"No."

"Why not?"

"It's because of the curse. When they were thrown out of

our realm and led man astray, God put a curse on them. The weight of the curse has misshapen their bodies into a reflection of their innermost being—all twisted, black, and unrecognizable. When they lost their glory and splendor, their bodies became a reminder of how far from grace they had fallen."

Romona inclined her chin toward the angel Logan was speaking to.

"He's an archangel, and he fights the warrior angels who were hurled to Earth. The ones trained in battle strategy, with the strength of numerous men. We're not equipped to take on that type of force. At least not alone. I, for one, am thankful he's around. The fallen archangels are really nasty."

"Archangels. That sounds familiar." I searched my mind. "Do you mean like Michael and stuff?"

She nodded. "But don't forget, Audrey, every demon is dangerous in its own right. Don't be deceived into thinking that one demon is more dangerous than another just because of his size. A seed of jealousy, lust, or greed planted by a sly demon can be as destructive as a tornado."

Logan called my name. I looked up sharply. He was motioning me over. I swallowed. Even with my eyes averted, I felt the heat of the mighty angel's gaze boring into me. Romona gave my arm a slight squeeze and a subtle push forward. For once, I wished the empathy link still worked on Earth. Her emotions were always encouraging.

Squaring my shoulders, I walked toward them. My mistake was letting my eyes drift to the angel's face. I had the wild urge to fall to my face before him, and I faltered a step and diverted my eyes. The warehouse had become conspicuously quiet.

Logan made the introduction. "Audrey, this is Gabriel."

I choked on nothing. My eyes widened. The angel, Gabriel,

bowed deeply.

"Gabriel. Like the Gabriel who helped Daniel with his visions in the Bible?" I blurted out before I could filter myself. How in the world did I know that?

Logan appeared surprised as well. Out of the corner of my eye I caught the barely susceptible lift of his eyebrows.

The angel simply bowed again. "My lady."

My head was spinning. "Huh?"

"Audrey, Gabriel is simply showing you the respect your position warrants."

"My position?"

Logan's voice was crisp with frustration. "Yes, as a human. As a child of God."

How did that make any sense? Gabriel was a majestic creature. Who was I to be given the respect?

"Oh, well, that's not really necessary. I'm not really that important."

Logan looked upward and took a deep breath. Yep, I was definitely testing his patience. The mighty angel managed to look both dismayed and understanding at the same time.

"My lady, that is not true. You were fearfully and wonderfully made at the hand of the Creator. It is my honor to show you respect."

Even the angel's voice was imposing. When he spoke, it was as if the rush of many voices escaped his lips, each harmonizing with the next to create one perfect and powerful sound.

I was at a loss. What was so fearful or wonderful about *me?* Certainly *he* was the one that was wonderfully made. I tried to look him in the face but shied away again—it was like staring at the sun in the middle of an eclipse. Possible, but still too bright for human eyes.

"Audrey, Gabriel is here as your personal escort. You're not to go anywhere without him while we are all here."

"Are you kidding? They sent me a celestial babysitter?" I realized how insulting that sounded only after it escaped my lips. I hastily addressed the angel. "I'm really sorry, I didn't mean it that way. It's just, you know," I lowered my voice, "kind of embarrassing."

"Not at all, Little One. I assure you it is a great honor. And I'm not only here for your protection, but also to deliver a message."

"Really?"

"Yes." Gabriel looked at Logan and the rest of our group. "I ask that you go ahead of us. We will catch up shortly. I have some things that need to be said to young Audrey here. Alone."

Logan looked like he might argue, but he gave a quick nod and led everyone from the warehouse, saying they'd wait down the block. Romona was the last to exit. She gave me a warm smile over her shoulder before disappearing with the rest.

"Is it hard for you to look upon me?" the angel asked.

The question startled me. "Yes, in a way. I guess I just don't see how I can be more special than you. I'm just so . . . ordinary."

"You do not yet understand because you do not yet believe. Your faith is surely small."

Ouch. "Maybe it's small because no one has ever explained to me why any of this has happened to me," I shot back.

"Do you really think you are in a position to question God?" He said it matter-of-factly, yet his statement humbled me to my core. I hung my head.

"There is much, Little One, that God has concealed of His own wisdom and understanding and power and might. He has even hidden secrets of the universe. It is said that it is the glory of God to conceal a thing, yet to search out a matter is the glory of kings. Perhaps you are searching for the wrong thing. Perhaps you are searching for answers rather than searching for the One who has concealed the matter?"

I didn't know what to say to that. The only consistent things I'd done since the day my existence changed forever was question, demand, doubt, and deny God, but had I ever searched for him? Would that have made a difference?

The angel waited patiently for me. When I turned my face toward him again, he smiled back for a moment before going suddenly as still as a statue.

A sudden yet familiar fear knotted my stomach, and the stench branded my brain a split second before the angel pulled his sword from the scabbard and charged me. I blinked, and he leapt over my head, collided with something invisible midair, and came crashing down in a heap behind me. I spun around. The angel kicked at something solid to free himself and stood like a barrier of bronze before me. His body coiled, ready for another attack.

Darker than midnight, with burnt, blackened flesh, I had mistaken the demon for shadows, but next to the shining radiance of the angel I now distinguished its features. It snarled and snapped at the angel with a misshapen mouth full of jagged teeth. Its hands, if you could even call them that anymore, were elongated by sharp talons on the end of each fingertip. It crouched low to the ground like a rabid animal, shuffling back and forth as it panted. Dark spittle dripped from its jowls and smoked like acid as it hit the dust-covered ground.

I screamed.

19

THE FIERY SWORD

Gabriel's head snapped toward me at the sound of my scream, and with a sickening shriek the demon plowed into the angel, catching him off guard. The sword flew out of his hand and went soaring in an arch off to the left. Angel and demon went down hard. The warehouse shook. Brittle pieces of the building's frame snapped off and fell to the floor.

Paralyzed by fear, I hadn't moved an inch. Where were Logan and the others? They had to have heard the commotion! The mighty angel needed help, and there wasn't much of that I could give.

The demon bore down on Gabriel even as he was trying to get to his feet. A swipe of the beast's tail sent them both down and rolling across the cement floor. The glow of the angel was slowly being swallowed by the shadows of the demon.

The glint of Gabriel's sword caught the corner of my eye. It lay on the ground several feet from where the supernatural forces tangled, far from where my own feet remained glued to the floor. The demon fought with its fanged teeth and jagged claws. There was little Gabriel could do without his weapon but stay on the defense. The demon knew this and was keeping its body positioned in front of the large blade.

Gabriel leapt high to overcome the mangled beast and reach his sword but was once again smashed by darkness. I yelped, eyes riveted to the scene.

My gosh, where's Logan?

Battling against my own fear, I forced my body to move, scrambling up some boxes to skirt the fight. One was viciously knocked to the floor, and the world shook beneath me. I silently thanked Logan for all the emphasis on balance during training. Otherwise, I was sure to be lying in a broken mess on the floor.

Another box was knocked away, and again I kept my balance. It was slow going, but I finally managed to place myself on the other side of the warehouse. The huge sword was almost within reach. Was I even strong enough to carry it? I forced thoughts of failure from my mind. I had to try.

The demon and angel grappled with each other on the floor, but the instant I lunged for the weapon, the demon's head snaked up and spotted me. My movements had given away my intent, and with a horrible shriek, the beast dislodged himself from the fight to advance on me.

Without a moment to think, I reached my hand out to the sword.

The creature was mere strides away, but when my hand closed around the hilt, it was as if a hundred watts of energy shot through me. The weight of the sword melted away, and it blazed like the sun. The demon cried out in shock as I arced the blade though the air with an instinct I wasn't aware I had. I smelled the demon's dark flesh burning as the fire from the sword sliced into its shoulder. It roared in anger and lunged for me again.

I fell to a knee and rolled to the left to avoid the collision. The demon crashed into some boxes but quickly regained its footing, nails scraping against the concrete before it charged me again. I was barely on my feet but still managed to slash the sword up with strength I knew I didn't possess.

The severed head of the demon rolled back and fell to the ground before its body smashed into me, knocking me to the floor. My head snapped back and cracked on hard cement. I was smothered under the creature's weight before its flesh dissolved into smoke and ash. The sword remained clutched in my hand.

The building was eerily quiet except for the buzzing in my ears. I took a long, steadying breath before pushing myself up on an elbow. There was a small audience standing in a semi-circle around me. Gabriel stood on the left next to Romona, then a few of the fighters I didn't take the time to recognize as I scanned for Logan, all the way on the right. Every single one of them wore the same stunned look. My rapid breathing was loud, even to my own ears. I didn't know what to say—I could barely believe what had just happened myself. And they were all staring at me so strangely.

Finally Romona took the first steps toward me—approaching me like someone would a feral animal.

"Audrey, are you okay?"

"I think so."

I took a quick survey of my body. Everything seemed to be all right. No blood, and nothing was throbbing besides my head. The sword in my hand, still blazing with its strange fire, had shrunk to a more manageable size.

I gasped, quickly releasing the weapon. It clanged to the ground and extinguished itself. The warehouse dimmed considerably.

Romona set a comforting and gentle hand on my shoulder. "Do you think you can get up?

"Yeah, I think so."

She extended a hand and helped me to my feet. My head pounded furiously with the movement. Romona threw her arms around me and hugged tightly. "I've never seen anything like that."

She pulled back to look into my eyes. "Are you sure you're all right? I've never seen anyone go up against a greater demon on their own. It was . . ." her voice trailed off. I got the feeling she was more horrified than impressed. The events of the last few minutes started to sink in, and a slight tremor shook my body.

"I wasn't trying to be brave or anything. I was just trying to get the sword back to Gabriel. When that thing came at me I reacted out of self-defense."

Behind Romona, Gabriel and the other hunters stayed where they were. I don't think I fully understood the implications of my actions. Killing a demon was obviously hard, especially a greater demon, but there was a serious amount of tension in the room. Only Romona seemed impervious to it.

"I knew you were special!" she said, squeezing my shoulders.

I backed up a step and out of her grasp. "Wh-what? I was just trying to protect my butt. I didn't do anything special."

"No . . . it was the *sword*, Audrey."

"Oh, right!" I reached down to grab the Gabriel's weapon, hoping it would grow in size again once returned to the warrior. "Gabriel, I'm sorry. I know this belongs to you."

As soon as my hand closed around the hilt, it flamed back to life. I immediately dropped it again. "Sheesh! That's distracting." I looked at Gabriel for an explanation. "Does it do that a lot?"

The angel met my gaze with awe, seemingly incapable of words. This was really starting to freak me out.

"What? What's going on, guys?"

No one made a move. I looked to Logan for help. His usual stoic mask was firmly back in place. At least something was normal.

"Logan, what's going on?"

His eyes connected with mine, and although he appeared to have his feelings in check, there was emotion swirling in his eyes. Even he hesitated before speaking.

"The sword's never done that before, Audrey."

I just stared at him for a minute. "O-kay, well, sorry, I didn't do anything on purpose. What's the big deal?"

"It *is* a big deal."

"Why?" I looked around at all of them.

I didn't want it to be a big deal. I was tired of everything being a big deal!

There was another long pause before Logan continued. "Because the only other swords like that were given to the Cherubim who are guarding the gates of the Garden of Eden. God's never given a blazing sword to anyone else."

"Well, he didn't give it to me either. It's Gabriel's sword."

I bent to pick it up, and again the fire took over the instant I touched it. As I turned to Gabriel, he began to back up.

"Here, it's yours." I stretched out my arm and took another step forward.

Gabriel shook his head. "No, Little One, that weapon was obviously meant for you. It is no longer mine."

My heart in my throat, I burst out, "Well, I don't want it! You have to take it back!"

The angel bowed low.

"That sword is now yours. It is a gift from the Father. You'll gain understanding of its importance in time."

He wouldn't take it back. What was I supposed to do with it? I didn't want the thing! I stood lamely with the sword still in my outstretched hand.

Romona gently rested a hand on my shoulder.

"Come on, Audrey, we've got to get back now. We have to report what happened."

She looked up at Gabriel. "Can you take a few of us back? The rest can stay and finish."

"Of course."

He spread his wings so we had a spot to grasp. Romona was the only one who would come within a three-foot radius of me. I felt a little silly with the fiery sword in my hand, but I didn't know what other choice I had. After touching the soft angel wing, we were back in an instant.

Word spread just as quickly as it had when Logan and I escaped the demon. Except this time, rather than mobbing me, no one wanted to talk to me. Hunters gave me a wide berth and avoided my eyes as I trekked through the training center. It was bizarre.

The sword's fire had blessedly gone out the moment we returned to our realm. And it was a good thing, too, because I may have singed some of Gabriel's wing on the way back. If he noticed he didn't say, and I was too embarrassed to ask.

I'd left the sword in my room this morning in hopes the atmosphere would return to normal. Seeing the averted glances and whispers that trailed me, I knew it had not.

It was actually Logan's reaction the night before that was the most worrisome. Both of my trips to Earth thus far had been eventful. But this second trip had Logan more shaken up than the first, and that was saying something.

At dinner with Romona and a few of our friends, I spent most of the time pushing food around my plate and sneaking glances at Logan as if he were a barometer. I was around him so much I was beginning to pick up subtle changes in his guarded expression. And he looked worried—so that made me worry.

This morning I'd woken up with another stomach full of knots. As reluctant as I was, I needed to know more about that sword.

I pushed open the gym doors to find Logan staring at the weapons wall. Everything about his stance was rigid. He was running his hands over the hilts of different swords and didn't acknowledge my presence. Heading to the bench, I dropped my bag.

"You know we're going to have to step up your sword training now."

I figured that.

"At least it's not my worst skill. Fiery nunchakus would have been a problem."

He half-turned with a slight smile on his face. Fencing and

swordplay did come somewhat easier to me than some of the other weapons. Unfortunately, that wasn't saying much.

"Logan, we need to talk."

"Is that so?" One eyebrow rose. The rest of his face was the same as always. Emotionless.

I crossed the distance to him in a few purposeful steps, for once able to match his serious expression. I made sure to keep our customary distance. After discovering the potential damage from our shared kiss, I was only too happy to keep the tradition going.

"You need to tell me what's going on."

His eyes roamed my face without settling. Worry crept into his eyes before he captured my own with his steely gaze.

"Would you believe me if I told you I wasn't sure?"

There was a time I wouldn't have, but now I did. "Yes."

He quietly released the air from his lungs.

"But that doesn't mean you can't tell me what you do know, or at least what you think you might know."

Logan regarded me before answering. "I suppose that's only fair."

I was slightly taken aback at the ease with which he acquiesced. I had been prepared for another battle.

He turned from me to grab a sword from the wall. It was a large, sturdy blade, probably twice the girth and length of the Cherubim sword safely tucked in my room. Studying it, he continued, "I think we should take this lesson out of the training center today. A little bit of fresh air might be good."

He turned his gaze back to me. "Let's pick that sword of yours up on the way."

Thirty minutes later I was using the already infamous sword to cut a path through the forest. Logan had picked a trail where the foliage was so incredibly dense I could hardly take a step without getting tangled. The topography resembled a jungle more than forest.

Logan navigated with ease. He only had to slash with his sword every now and then to maneuver forward, where I had to hack everything in my way to do the same. Glaring at his back, I'd just begun to grumble when I tripped on a vine. I yelped and threw my free arm out to try to catch myself. Logan did a quick turn, and I fell face-first into his chest. He tried to steady me, but instead we both went crashing into the underbrush.

I landed square on top of Logan and heard the air whoosh out of his chest when he absorbed the impact of both the ground and me. We were a tangle of arms and legs. I squirmed to get off of him and realized the offensive vine was still securely wrapped around my ankle.

Logan was a statue beneath me. My face was squished into his chest. He smelled like fresh laundry and wooded pine. I tried to roll off, but we were wedged rather tightly between thick thorny vines, roots, and underbrush. My movement only managed to get us more snared.

"Will you just give me a second?" Logan's voice rumbled in his chest.

"My gosh, Logan, I'm so sorry. I think I tripped on a vine or something, and I'm still caught. Oh no . . . I dropped the sword." I tried to swivel my head even though it was still squished to his chest. "It has to be around here somewhere."

I took my hand off his chest to brace myself on the ground

and push off him. As soon as my hand connected to the ground, pain shot into my palm.

"Ouch!" I quickly yanked it back to discover I'd impaled it on a thorn. A small droplet of blood was starting to form.

"How bad is it?"

I glanced up from my hand to see Logan mere inches from my face. Or rather, I was mere inches from him. He was staring at my hand.

When I didn't answer, his eyes made their way back to my face. A physical awareness skated down my spine when our eyes locked. Despite the low light, the blue in his eyes was electrifyingly bright. My pulse picked up speed. Neither of us said anything. I licked my lips and inadvertently drew Logan's attention from my eyes. My forearms were being used to prop myself only slightly off his chest.

Logan's arms moved gently to my lower back. Then one slid up to apply the faintest amount of pressure, bringing me ever so slightly closer to him. My eyes started to slide shut as Logan's breath tickled my cheeks. I smelled peppermint, just as I remembered. Without a coherent thought in my head I leaned in closer, and then . . .

"Audrey, you need to get off of me now."

It was like being doused with a bucket full of ice water. My eyes snapped open. Logan wasn't looking at me any longer. Instead, his eyes were staring at the canopy above my head. His arms had melted from my back, or had never been there at all, and were instead pressed firmly against the forest floor. His face was hidden in the shadows.

I sucked in a quick breath of air and frantically searched for the fastest way to get off him. I pulled again at my leg and found that the vine had magically unwrapped itself from my ankle. "I just, uh, need to figure out where to put my foot." The urge to ramble bore down on me.

Please let my hair be a normal shade.

"You should be able to put one on either side of my left leg and use the saplings around us to pull yourself up." He was still staring straight up, and his voice was succinct and to the point.

"Oh right, yeah." I struggled to rock back on my feet with the least amount of physical contact possible, taking care not to knee him anywhere important. When I steadied myself on my knees, Logan wasted no time scooting out from underneath me and righting himself. In fact, he was so fast about it he was standing before I straightened myself. Taking a cue from Logan, I looked anywhere but at him.

"My sword has to be around here somewhere. I dropped it when I tripped." Something reflected the sun to my left. I took a few careful steps and located the weapon lying in a small patch of sunlight among some mushrooms.

"Whoops!" Picking it up I brushed off dirt and mushroom grime, being careful not to cut myself. "Doesn't look too much worse for the wear."

"Okay then, let's get going. We're almost there."

Logan had retrieved his sword as well and was waiting for me, facing the other direction. His pace was slower than before, and he took more care to clear a path for me.

I tried to concentrate on the cleared path rather than what had just happened, but it was difficult. What *had* just happened? Had Logan almost kissed me? Had I almost kissed him? Did I have a hallucination and then Logan got too uncomfortable with me invading his personal space? I almost wished I had brushed some of his skin to get a read on what he was thinking. Then I cringed at the thought, because it meant Logan would have picked up on my emotions as well.

I was so absorbed in my own thoughts that the break in the forest took me by surprise. I stumbled into a clearing. Everything was bathed in gold. I put my hand up to my brow and opened my eyes further, looking first at my feet. I was standing on something soft. The breath in my throat caught as I extended my gaze from the ground up.

The clearing, although not large, was covered in hundreds —perhaps thousands—of small golden flowers. They were so densely grown that it looked like a carpet of gold had been laid out for us. I inhaled the sweetest smell imaginable, the essence of everything sugary, warm, and cozy. I don't know how a smell can be cozy, but this one was. The scent filled my lungs.

I lowered my hand and took in the beauty before us. I had the urge to run into the middle and create a snow angel in the flowers. A soft breeze blew my ponytail over my shoulder, and a soothing wave of calm enveloped me.

I had a vague recollection that Logan was here somewhere, but it was barely a concern. Inexplicably, in that moment I felt loved, cherished, and protected. All feelings I craved.

Logan wasn't looking at me. He had closed his eyes and was breathing in the same air I was. "This is the place I come when I want to be alone with God." *What, God's around here somewhere?* I quickly looked around, but it was just the two of us in the field of gold. I was inexplicitly disappointed.

"Does it only work if you are by yourself? You know, being alone with God." I blushed. *Stupid question. Of course you can only be alone with God if you are actually alone.*

But Logan just smiled. "It's not like that. It's more like a still, small voice right here." He laid his hand on his chest. "And a feeling of well-being despite whatever else is happening. Getting alone and away from everything is important. Sometimes He speaks in the silence."

I let Logan's words sink in. "I think I might know what you mean."

Logan was describing what was happening to me, minus the voice in his head, or chest, or whatever. An overwhelming sense of peace settled on me even as I continued to breathe the sweet air. I wondered if it was specific to this exact place. Was there a part of God manifested in this field? Was that even possible? Was this what Gabriel meant when he talked about seeking out God?

"I think it's time we talk more about this sword." Logan broke my train of thought. I'd almost forgotten about the heavy weight in my hand. "Come on, let's sit down over here."

He walked to a small knoll and sat. He looked relaxed. It reminded me of when we were on the beach. He spread his legs out in front of him and leaned back against his arms, bending his head back to soak in the warmth. I came to a seat a few feet away and carefully laid the sword between the two of us.

Logan seemed content to sit in silence. Perhaps having a silent conversation with himself. A pleasant one, because with his eyes closed and his face raised, he smiled. Time stretched on.

I waited until I couldn't wait anymore and cleared my throat. The sense that he was having a conversation was so intense that I felt awkward barging into his thoughts.

"Okay, Audrey, I know you're still there." He languidly opened his eyes and took another deep breath before adjusting his body so that he faced me.

"So, the sword. What questions do you have?"

I almost didn't know where to start. *Why are people treating me differently now? What does the sword do? What does it mean about me? Why me?* I had to start somewhere. "Tell me more about the Cherubim."

Logan appeared relieved that I'd started with something so easy.

"Cherubim are a type of angel. Like most angels, they have wings, but they aren't as humanoid as most angels. They have many eyes and many wings. There aren't very many of them, and they protect things that are very important."

"You mentioned something about the garden of Eden before."

"Right. God placed Cherubim at the entrance of the Garden of Eden to make sure no man could enter it again while the curse was still on the world."

He'd lost me. "Huh?"

"Okay, let's start a little further back. Do you know about Adam and Eve?"

I remembered that Adam and Eve were the first man and woman and had been tempted by a serpent to eat fruit from a tree that God told them not to. Then they were thrown out of Eden, and something about being naked. I relayed as much to Logan, who laughed lightly.

"So you seem to have the nuts and bolts down. God created man to have fellowship with him. When Adam and Eve willingly disobeyed God, they allowed sin into the world. The Garden of Eden was a place where we could be in perfect communication and live with God. Since Adam and Eve opened Pandora's box, so to speak, and let sin into their lives, they weren't able to live in the garden anymore. Since we are all sons and daughters of Adam and Eve we all inherited that sin nature, so we also can't be let into the garden." He looked over at me to make sure I was following. "You still with me?"

I nodded.

"So God put his most trusted protectors, the Cherubim, at the entrance of the garden of Eden to make sure no one could enter. Cherubim also guarded the ark of the covenant." I must have had a blank look on my face then, because Logan rushed to explain. "The ark was where the Law, also called the Ten Commandments, were held. For centuries, the Lord only manifested himself to men above the ark. So it needed to be heavily protected as well. God even told the people making the ark to include Cherubim into the design so they would remember how important it was."

"Okay, so Cherubim are like God's secret service."

He chuckled. "I guess you can look at it that way."

"Okay, but what does that have to do with the sword catching fire when I touch it?"

"That takes us back to the garden of Eden. That was the only time we know of when God gave anyone a flaming sword. It was the weapon the Cherubim were given to protect the entrance to the garden."

"So what does that have to do with me?"

Logan paused for a moment before answering.

"To be honest Audrey, I'm not sure. The only thing we know for sure is that the only other flaming swords in the universe are guarding the Garden of Eden. And they are wielded by some pretty powerful angels."

"So why in the world would it start on fire when *I* touch it? I'm not an angel."

He looked at me with sadness in his eyes, this time clearly

wishing he had an answer for me. "I'm really not sure, but I know it must be something important. These things don't just happen by chance. There is a purpose."

"But you're telling me you don't know what that purpose is?"

Logan shook his head.

"I'm willing to bet you have a guess."

"A guess, a theory, is not an answer."

I scooted just a tad closer, still keeping the sword between us. "I'd like to hear what you think."

"I'm not sure that would be very beneficial to you."

"Why don't you let me be the judge of that for once?"

I could see that Logan was fighting an internal battle. His jaw set when he'd made up his mind. "No. There are too many options. Too many possibilities. I can't pretend to know the heart of God. You are meant to figure this out on your own."

I wanted to explode. More riddles. More things to figure out. More things to wait on. When was I going to get any answers around here? "Seriously? You're not even going to *try* to help me figure it out? We're just going to add it to my growing pile of mysteries? One more thing that doesn't make sense in my life anymore. Or death, or whatever."

"Audrey, you know it's not like that. I am helping you. I'm giving you the knowledge you don't have. I can't tell you what it means because I don't know, but I'm trying to tell you as much as I know for sure. You need to look to God for the answers, not me, not Romona, not anyone else." Logan's voice held an exasperated edge.

He had a point, one that echoed Gabriel's sentiments as well, but I wasn't in the mood to be reasonable. It felt like another blow. Like someone was playing a game with my life and having a grand old time doing it.

I stubbornly refused to look at Logan. Part of me wanted him to be as miserable as I was at the moment. I closed my eyes and leaned back into the blanket of flowers. They tickled my forehead as they swayed in the breeze. Fabric rustled and shifted as Logan moved. A soft ringing echoed from the blade as he touched it, followed by a series of scraping sounds as he pulled the blade toward him. I honestly didn't care. He could have the thing if he wanted it.

He continued talking even though it was obvious I was trying to ignore him. "Audrey, you need to look at this like a gift rather than a curse."

I snorted. If you counted suffering, confusion, anger, and misery a gift, then sure, it was a gift.

But then some things rebelliously leaked into my consciousness. My friendship with Romona, the joy of the celebration, naming new creatures, the beauty all around me, even the sword saving me from the demon.

Neither of us spoke for several minutes. With eyes shut, I imagined Logan inspecting the weapon like he had a hundred different swords before, with great precision and care. It got me thinking about something.

"Logan?"

"Yes."

"Why do we do this?"

He paused for a few heartbeats. His voice was unexpectedly quiet. "What do you mean?"

My heart was heavy. I needed to know that we had a clear purpose. Not a hidden one we didn't know about, but a real, solid, concrete reason for what we were training to do. And I needed to know that it was good.

"Why are we called to protect people, to fight off demons, to fight off evil? What is it about us that got us chosen for this job? Why does God need us at all?"

I opened my eyes and propped myself up on an elbow to watch him. His face was a bit melancholy. Again with the weight of the world on his shoulders.

Logan put the sword carefully back down before speaking. "I think," he began, and then paused to inhale and exhale, "I think for each of us the answer to that question is different."

Too vague. I was looking for someone to make sense of things. Of at least *one* thing. I needed to be assured there was a reason we were all here.

"Do you know what the answer is for you?"

Logan closed his eyes and took a deep breath. I thought for a moment he wouldn't answer. "I assumed there would come a day when you asked me that." When he opened his eyes, he turned his head to look at me. There was a storm brewing in his blue depths. "For me, I believe it is about redemption."

What did that mean? Logan continued without my prodding, but he turned his head away to surveying the clearing as he spoke.

"I lived my life like I was out of control. There was always something new to chase. A new sensation, a new high. And I was very creative at finding new experiences. My life was lived without regard for others. It was only at the end that I realized the damage I'd caused to those who loved me and how little I'd actually given to anyone."

Logan's face, even though I was only privy to his profile,

was as closed off as I'd ever seen it. His expression was a blatant contradiction to the vulnerability of his words.

I wondered if he thought revealing some of the more unsavory details of his life would make me think differently of him . . . less of him. I wondered if regret over the way he'd lived his life was what caused his pendulum to swing so far in the other direction. He was so disciplined, even rigid at times. It made sense that he might believe one extreme would balance out his sins. But there had to be another reason for the distance he kept—the wall he erected to shield himself. I was getting a glimpse, but not the full picture.

"So you're trying to work off the deeds of your life?"

"No. I know it might sound like that. Real redemption, salvation, is a gift, not a penance to be worked off. There's no way for any of us to work off our regrets. No amount of good deeds could cover the bad ones in our lives, in any of our lives. There's only one way to cover those sins, and it has nothing to do with what works we do here in eternity. But even so, my spoiled life did have an effect on me after death. I believe I was chosen for this job, this duty, because of what I was supposed to have accomplished on Earth. I believe the plan for my life was greater than what I lived out. I think I've been given the second chance to live that purpose. And to realize that no matter how many good things I do, there is only one covering for my sin."

I turned Logan's words over in my head. They forced me to look introspectively. Did my afterlife fit into any plan? Could I expect to have a great purpose? I secretly feared waking one day to be reacquainted with a person I wished had stayed forgotten. A person full of hate and ugliness. What if that reality became true? It sounded like for Logan, it had. How would that change me now?

"Logan, how long did it take you to remember?"

"Not long. I remembered my life almost right away. It was important that I remembered so soon."

"Why was that?"

"Before I died, my heart had started to change. Things were different, but by then it was too late to make a real difference. When I woke up here, I needed to remember what had happened for the change to be complete. It only furthered my desire to serve the living, to help protect them. But it's been a journey to realize where true redemption comes from. I'm still making the journey. I understand here," he pointed to his head, "but I'm still working on believing it here." He pointed to his heart.

I couldn't stop the questions from falling out of my mouth. "What changed you then?"

Logan reached down and plucked one of the small golden flowers from the ground. He brought it closer to his face to inspect it with a small smile on his lips.

"I met someone."

Something in my stomach dropped. I didn't want to hear anything about Logan's romantic relationships on Earth. Seeing him with Kaitlin was hard enough. To break the bond I needed to let go of him, but that was getting harder as we grew closer.

"It was the most important, life-altering relationship I've ever had," Logan continued, oblivious to my inner turmoil. "I was loved for being me and accepted unconditionally, even with all the black marks in my past. When I started to truly see the mess I'd made of my life, it was hard to think that anyone could love me like that. Realizing someone would accept me in that state, well, that will change a person. I only wish I'd discovered it sooner."

My heart continued to drop. How do you compete with something like that? And did I even want to? There was a physical ache in my chest I wanted to ignore.

"It was a relationship that convinced me I was worth something. That my life was worth something. That everything ugly I'd done would be forgotten and it was possible to leave my old life in the past."

A stillness hung in the air, and Logan's next words were very gentle, almost a whisper.

"Audrey, I think you know this person as well."

And that's when I knew he'd really lost it. I sharply swiveled my head to find him staring back. There was a depth to his eyes that I couldn't begin to understand.

He might have gone on, and I might have questioned him further, but instead something came crashing through the trees.

20

ANGELIC
ENCOUNTERS

I was on my feet an instant after Kevin loudly stumbled into our clearing. He was out of breath and a bit scratched up.

"You guys gotta come quick." He paused to swallow another gulp of air. "We've been called in for duty." He looked at Logan. "Level One combat."

Logan's jaw set, and he nodded once before scooping up both our weapons. He handed me the sword. I caught Kevin taking an apprehensive look at the weapon before I sheathed it.

Logan headed for the trees without a word, and I took after him at a jog. The idea of another mission so soon sent a bolt of something through me—whether fear, apprehension, or even excitement, I wasn't sure.

"Kevin, what's going on?" I asked.

"Some sort of crisis. They called a bunch of us in to help.

Some hunters have already headed down to start the attack. Or perhaps prevent one."

Logan's head swung around. "Who's down already?"

Kevin looked nervous. "Alrik and Romona. And some of the hunters from the northern region, including Kaitlin. I would have gone too, but they wanted me to find you guys first. They want us to meet up with them at the safe house as soon as possible."

"This is something we're working on with another region?"

Kevin nodded once.

At that, Logan faced forward and continued his fast trek through the foliage.

"Kevin," I tried not to let my voice carry too far, "is there something wrong with that? What's the big deal with working with another region?"

Kevin dipped his voice as well.

"It's just unusual. We have enough hunters here that we don't usually need to work together. It only happens when something big is going on."

We were through the trees and walking into the training center in record time. I bent over with my hands on my knees to catch my breath, and pinched my side where a stitch had formed. Logan went to get the details of our mission and returned almost immediately. "Kevin was right; a group of hunters has already been dispatched. We're to meet up with them on Earth to get the full rundown. We need to get into our gear and leave immediately."

He looked at me pointedly. "Make sure to bring that sword of yours."

I nodded once as my stomach flopped. He thought we were going to be in a situation where I would need it. Since one touch of the sword seemed to slice through demons like a knife through warm butter, they most likely hoped I would be an asset.

"Audrey, do you have body armor here?"

My heart dropped. "It's in my bedroom."

"Use this, then."

Logan closed his eyes in concentration, and a moment later a puddle of liquid material formed in his upturned hands. He tossed the fabric to me. I caught it midair and shook my head.

"How do you even know my size?"

Logan simply lifted his eyebrows, looked me up and down quickly, and gave me a wicked smile. After that, he turned on his heel and headed down the hallway, his own armor quickly melding to his body. I was left staring after him, speechless and flushed. If I didn't know better, I would say that had been rather flirty.

Halfway down the hall, he threw an order over his shoulder. "We'll meet you in five minutes in the gym. Get that sword strapped to your back so you don't accidentally set someone on fire."

Kevin jogged down the hall after Logan with a small smile for me. I hurried to the girl's locker room. This time I didn't stop to admire myself in front of the mirror. I only spared a moment to make sure I'd put the armor on correctly before shoving through the doors to meet Logan and Kevin.

Minutes later we were standing in an alley on Earth. I was so jumpy that my hand itched to grab the sword from its sheath on my back. I willed it to stay. I'd draw attention the moment it roared to life. Attention we were looking to avoid.

"Audrey, stay here." Logan's voice made me jump from the tension, though I wasn't tense enough to instantly comply.

"What do you mean? Why can't I go with you guys?"

"We're going to make sure the coast is clear and figure out where we're meeting the other hunters. It must be somewhere close by. You'll be safer here."

The alley dead-ended not far to the right.

"Oh come on! You've got to be kidding!"

The look he shot me said he wasn't. I changed tactics and appealed to the easier target.

"Kevin, come on, this is silly."

Kevin shifted nervously from one foot to the other, his eyes moving between the two of us. "Sorry, Audrey. Logan's your mentor, it's up to him."

I leaned against the wall. "Fine, go off and do your thing. I'll just follow after you've rounded the corner. I'm getting a little tired of the overprotective act."

Part of me meant that. Another part was scared out of my mind and secretly fearful of being left alone. I firmly put a lid on the latter emotion and concentrated on the annoyance.

Logan forced my attention. "Audrey, you know I'm not asking for permission." His voice sounded menacing. He was trying to further intimidate me by trapping me against the brick wall. I stiffened my neck. "Kevin, would you mind giving Audrey and me a minute? I'll catch up with you in a moment." He didn't take his eyes off me when he spoke.

Kevin's footsteps retreated. Logan was using his eyes to their full advantage. I was reasonably certain that this time he knew exactly what he was doing.

"Audrey, we've talked about this before, and you need to promise to do everything I say today. I can't have you challenging every order, not here, not with the reality of these stakes. We're not in the training center anymore. This isn't a game or a joke or even a battle of wills."

My throat was so dry I couldn't find my voice. Logan took a half-step forward to take hold of my shoulders. I sucked in a quick breath. He was always so careful not to touch me, so when he did, even without the empathy link, it was a shock to my system. Standing here like this in the dimly lit alley, it was very hard not to remember the last time the two of us had been in a similar location.

Logan's mind wasn't in the same place as mine.

"Audrey, do you understand what I'm saying? I need to know that you'll listen to me. That you'll get yourself to safety if I tell you to." There was an edge of desperation in Logan's voice. It was his vulnerability that finally broke through my pride.

I was only able to nod once as Logan's eyes searched my face. When they lingered on my lips a moment longer than they should have, I flushed. Perhaps he *was* remembering the same thing.

He dropped his hands. Still standing close, it seemed he wanted to say more, but with only a nod, he abruptly turned and followed Kevin out of the alley. I couldn't move until Logan had disappeared around the side of the building. I kicked an empty can out of frustration, and it ricocheted off the opposite wall loudly before bouncing to rest not far from where it had first been. Why were things with Logan always so confusing? I had an answer for that almost as quickly as I thought it. That stupid kiss. And I had a suspicion that Logan had just effectively used it to manipulate me.

When this was over, I was really going to have to figure out what to do about the bond. In the meantime, the innocent Coke can received another kick for good measure.

I wasn't sure if it bounced back to the same spot because what happened next blasted me off my feet.

The powerful bright light sent me sailing, ending with a bone-shattering butt landing. For a few horrible moments, the world was nothing more than a burst of red and yellow behind closed lids. And then with a blink, the world returned to normal, and I was on the pavement with a very sore backside. My body armor had saved me from scrapes along my hands and arms. I shook my head once to clear the fuzz.

"I seem to have startled you." The strong voice echoed off the walls of the alley and again through my head, rattling painfully even after he stopped speaking.

I put a hand to my ear before looking up to see who had spoken. My eyes widened.

Lounging against a brick wall in the single ray of sunlight that had defiantly snuck between the buildings was the most beautiful angel I'd ever seen. In fact, the most beautiful *being* I'd ever seen.

His skin, smooth like polished stone, sparkled in the light, reflecting a myriad of colors. He wasn't looking at me, but was instead inspecting a speck on the knife he held. He turned it this way and that, letting the sunlight glance off the weapon as he moved it, blinding me occasionally. I was truly stunned speechless.

Without looking up, he addressed me again.

"You seem to have lost your way." It was an observation, not a question.

"Ah, not exactly."

"Is that so?" Still looking at the knife, he arched a brow.

"I was just waiting. Is there something I can do for you?"

That seemed to amuse the angel. He smiled.

"Perhaps. But it's a little too soon for that."

His words befuddled me. Something in his voice caused the thoughts in my head to jumble whenever he spoke—like talking in a dream, where things made sense without making sense. Something inside nagged at me that I should do something, but I only sat and stared.

The angel continued, almost as if he was speaking to himself.

"It is strange he would pick one such as yourself. Burdened by weakness and easily controlled by your passions. I would have thought a bigger challenge was in store, but it appears that is not the case. Disappointing even."

His words cut sharp and deep. Just like the knife in his hand was capable of doing.

"I suppose if he really cared, he'd have picked a more worthy opponent—but then again, he has always enjoyed sending a sheep to the slaughter."

The words became like ice in my gut as I struggled to understand the angel's strange musings. Struggled to do anything but sit there and stare.

"Nevertheless, it is what it is, so I suppose we shall play another round."

The angel heaved a sigh. Was he bored? Frustrated?

"So what is it exactly that you have there?"

Without my permission, my hand inched toward my sword. My fingers were just about to wrap around the hilt when a flash of white and gold landed in front of me, shaking the ground.

Gabriel.

His appearance halted my hand. He stood between me and the other angel, who hadn't even looked up at the intrusion.

"What do you want?" Gabriel's words, booming in my ears, were surprisingly harsh.

"Nothing, dear *brother*. It was just a bout of curiosity. It appears to have been a waste of my time."

"I doubt it was only that."

The angel shrugged—he didn't care what Gabriel thought. He was still fixated on that knife, casually turning it over in his hands again and again.

"This one is under my protection for now." Gabriel took another step to shield me with his body.

"Hmmm, for *now*, you say. I was once a guardian myself. I wonder how long you will be in the position."

Gabriel began to glow. His hands clenched into fists and heat radiated off him, growing hotter every moment. Sweat started to trickle down the back of my neck.

"It would be good of you to remember whose domain you are in now, brother," the angel said.

"It would be good of you to remember how long that will remain true," Gabriel retorted.

A small clench of the jaw was the only thing that gave away the mysterious angel's anger. He covered it quickly with a slow smile as he shrugged again. "Perhaps."

Finally sheathing the knife in a holster on his belt, he turned in my direction. I gasped. Where his eyes should have been, there were none. Instead was just blackness, a fathomless abyss. Even with no eyes, I knew he was staring straight at me, perhaps straight into my soul—the real me who I didn't even know. Enthralled as well as repulsed, I had the sensation of falling into empty space before he broke eye contact to stretch his arms above his head. A pair of wings, made of shadows that spanned the height of a man in either direction, unfurled from behind him.

"There are more pressing matters to attend. Enjoy your babysitting while it lasts."

With a fluid motion, he coiled his body and leapt into the sky, dark wings barely flapping as he shot straight into the air. A strange, faded shadow trailed behind him as if tethering him to the earth. I craned my neck, watching him until he was barely a speck.

I was still sitting on the ground when the archangel turned to me.

"Who was that?" I asked, finally able to find my voice.

"He goes by several names," he replied wearily.

"Care to try one out on me?"

"He comes as the angel of light he once was, but now he is Abaddon."

"Huh?"

"Destruction."

I lifted my eyebrows. Scary, but I'd never heard that name before. "How about if you try out a few more on me?"

Gabriel said them like curses. "Accuser, Adversary, Deceiver, Leviathan, King of Babylon."

I swallowed. "Those all sound pretty bad. How is he still an angel then?"

"I said that he *comes* as an angel of light, not that he is one."

"I'm missing something ridiculously obvious, aren't I?"

The angel nodded his head.

"I think the name she knows him by is Satan."

I jerked my body around to see Logan walking briskly up the alley.

"Did you just say what I think you did?"

"Yes."

"Oh my gosh! Oh my gosh!" I started to hyperventilate, "You guys left me alone in an alley with the devil! Are you insane?" I stumble-crawled to my feet. "And what the heck is he doing looking all angelic? Well, except for his crazy wings and missing eyes. Shouldn't he be all shriveled and black with red pointy horns or something?" I used my hands atop my head to demonstrate the horn and skewed my face into a snarl. I was all over the place.

"Well that's obviously a misguided stereotype," Logan answered.

I stared at him incredulously. "You left me alone . . . in an alley . . . with the devil!" I punched his arm for emphasis. He only gave the spot a passing glance, but hurt flashed across his face and I knew it wasn't from the punch. It was gone when he looked up.

"Yes, and now you've lived to tell another tale."

"You're making a joke out of this?"

"No."

I let out a perturbed huff.

"Listen, I know we're supposed to be getting along better and that I should be following your lead, but I hope you realize the next time you try to leave me alone in a dark alley, or dark warehouse, or—"

"Gabriel was with you in the warehouse," Logan interrupted.

"Or dark wherever," I continued, "I'm *so* not having it!"

Gabriel interrupted our argument as if we hadn't had it at all.

"Satan is the great deceiver. He can appear in a number of

different forms. For whatever reason, that was the form he wanted you to see. Do not be tricked into thinking his true form is anything more beautiful than any other demon. His is the most misshaped and deformed of all. He simply does a better job of covering that up."

"Have you ever seen him before?" I addressed Logan after the span of a few heartbeats.

A muscle in his jaw moved. "Yes."

"Is that normal? Do all new hunters get a special visit from him? Like a 'welcome to the club, lookin' forward to sending my evil minions after you' type of thing?" I was more than half-serious.

There was a long pause before Logan continued. "No. Unlike God, he is not omnipresent. Meaning he can only be in one place at a time. He has a lot of ground to cover, which means he's generally not concerned with a few hunters here and there. He usually leaves us to his demons."

"So what does it mean that he sought me out?" There was a touch of desperation in my voice.

"Perhaps nothing to be concerned about, but regardless, we'll have to deal with this particular issue later. You're going to have to try to put it out of your mind for now. We have a job to do today," Logan answered.

"Right, like this is going to be an easy thing to forget."

Logan rolled his eyes. I looked back at the spot the fallen angel had been only moments before and shivered when I considered what might have happened if Gabriel hadn't appeared. I shared as much.

"He could not have touched you." Gabriel answered, his voice booming with authority. "He uses words and manipulation to lead people astray. He personally could not have physically harmed you. Not without permission. That is part of his sentence."

"Permission? Permission from whom?" I asked.

"God."

Permission from God to hurt me? What?

"What was his interaction with you before I arrived?" Gabriel inquired.

I explained as much of the conversation as I remembered. Already some of the details were muddled. When I finished, the looks on their faces weren't comforting. To someone who didn't know him better, Logan's expression might have passed for indifferent, but there was a hardness in his eyes that scared me. The silence stretched.

"Will somebody please say something?"

Gabriel's attitude changed immediately. "Let's get you to the safe house, Little One. Logan's right, we'll have to deal with this later."

Logan's posture hadn't changed, and that had me profoundly concerned. He turned his face toward the spot where the dark angel had stood. I took a step closer and laid a hand on his forearm. He looked down at my touch and then up at me. I willed myself not to be intimidated.

"Logan, what is it?" Something very real, very strange, was going on with Logan. As if he was drowning in his own mind. What was happening?

The angel looked on in silence.

I slowly moved my hand down his arm and twined my fingers with his stiff ones, all the while returning his stare, and gave his hand a squeeze, hoping to give him something substantial to grasp, even if it was physical rather than mental. His gloved hand was warm and his pulse pounded rapidly.

"Logan," I whispered.

A barely discernable shudder ran through Logan's body, and when it reached our joined hands, it was as if a bolt of electricity burned through me. It was so sudden and sharp that I gasped and jumped back, releasing Logan's hand. Logan remained rooted in place, but the look on his face confirmed that he'd felt the electricity too. His eyes were wide with surprise.

"Did I hurt you?" He took a step forward, and out of reflex I flinched away, holding my hand protectively against my chest.

"What was that?" I accused.

The steel flooded back into Logan's schooled features.

"What was what?"

"You've got to be kidding me, right?"

"I just squeezed your hand too tight. I'd forgotten you were holding it." It was a lie—we both knew it.

"We need to leave now." Gabriel's commanding voice ended our standoff. Logan's attention jerked toward the angel. He probably welcomed the interruption.

Did he truly think that would be the end of it? Whatever had happened in that moment was not normal, and in the aftermath, Logan's unveiled expression had proven he knew that as well. I wasn't about to pretend nothing had happened. But I did agree with Gabriel: we needed to get going. Being out in the open gave me the willies.

I paused beside Logan. "We *will* talk about this later," I said. There were a lot of other things we should have talked about that we'd buried instead. I was finally ready to get my big-girl panties on and dive into everything, no matter how uncomfortable.

I let Gabriel and Logan usher me out of the alley, Gabriel in the lead and Logan protecting my back. We met up with Kevin at the mouth of the alley.

"Man, what was keeping you guys?"

He didn't look mad, only jumpy—probably anxious to meet up with the other hunters. The only reason he wasn't already with them was that he'd been sent to find us first. What plans were moving forward without us?

Kevin absorbed the serious looks on our faces but didn't press for an answer. I didn't relish the notion of rehashing the past thirty minutes with anyone. Too much had happened. And it would only give people another reason to stare at the strange girl hunter.

We started forward in silence.

21

THE GAME PLAN

Getting to the safe house was taking a lot longer than I expected. Without another option, we set off on foot. Our drop-in point had been on the opposite side of town. Kevin explained that everyone dropped in at different sites around town so we wouldn't give away the location of the safe house. Hunters were arriving in intervals so as not to be overtly obvious that we were traveling to the same place. We were taking a roundabout way to be extra careful not to be followed.

After meeting the devil, that last point only made me more paranoid. Convinced there were hidden eyes tracking our progress, I twisted my head side to side, sure I would see a shape stalking us from the shadows, only to end up searching the darkness in vain. There was a solid chance it was only nerves, but something felt off.

No one spoke as we walked through mostly deserted streets and alleys. Logan's shoulders were tense as he carried his sword free of the scabbard. Kevin and Gabriel followed behind Logan and on either side of me. A nervous giggle threatened to bubble up at the thought of having two dead and one celestial bodyguard. This was silly because sometime today we were going to be in a battle. A battle where I was going to be a fighter, not a ward.

While I was busy searching every shadow, I somehow missed the turn we took to the residential part of town. We passed modest but well-kept homes with green lawns and flowerboxes. We passed groups of kids coloring with chalk on driveways or playing in sprinklers on the front lawn, laughing and squealing. Even though leaves were beginning to turn red and gold, people were taking advantage of the warm day.

Something about the neighborhood felt inviting and slowly began to soothe my anxiety. A quick look at my companions showed I was the only one affected by the ambiance. Gabriel, Logan, and Kevin were all still on high alert. Muscles tense, eyes surveying the area with single-minded focus.

Growing more relaxed, I slipped into daydreaming. Popsicles and bike rides . . . the feeling of jumping into cool water on a hot, humid day and warm breezes ruffling my hair. With a start I realized these were memories and tried to hold on to them, but they were elusive. I groaned quietly. Logan cocked his head slightly to address me. "We're almost there now. The safe house is just up ahead."

"Oh, that's not what I . . ."

The explanation died on my lips. The house we were headed toward looked like it was hosting a party and had invited every demon hunter in the region. A two-story white house at the end of a cul-de-sac, it had blue shutters and a plantation-style wraparound porch. The sun, which was high in the sky by now, gleamed off the metallic body armor of the hunters and bronzed bodies of angels.

"Try not to stare," Kevin whispered. "If anything's following us, you don't want it to guess where we're going."

"Are you kidding? How could I not?" I hissed back at him. "Besides, they're just hanging out there in broad daylight."

"Demons can't see them. It's a safe house, remember? Once we walk over the border of the property, we'll be invisible to them as well."

"You think we're being followed?" I scanned the area frantically, my fear renewed.

"No, but we want to be careful."

"Why is it that they can't see us when we cross the border?"

Kevin, focused on the territory behind us, barely registered my question. "It's because the house and its property are cloaked in the prayers of the residents."

"I'm not following you."

"Shhhhh." A sharp command from Logan.

I scowled at his back. We *were* being quiet. I shot Kevin an apologetic look. He looked slightly dejected and moved far enough away that I couldn't rope him into another conversation.

Logan wasn't leading us directly to the house. Instead he guided us to a neighbor's backyard, and we weaved our way under the cover of the trees. A few houses away, he stopped.

"You think we're clear?" he asked Gabriel.

Gabriel nodded solemnly. "Okay, you two," speaking to Kevin and me, "we're going to take it at a run from here. Try to keep yourselves hidden in the tree cover. Got it?"

He looked at Kevin, who gave a short nod, before turning his blue stare on me. We were so close to the safe house that the high drama for these last few feet seemed seriously over-played. Logan knew me well enough to interpret the look on my face.

"I'm serious, Audrey. If we *are* being followed, it's in this last leg that they'll attack."

"If everyone is invisible, then a demon doesn't know where the last few feet *are.*" Pleased with my logic, I gave Logan a self-satisfied smile.

"That's assuming they haven't already figured out where we are congregating. They could have spotted another group entering and are waiting for the next one."

"Oh." I sighed. "I'll follow your lead."

Logan pressed his lips together, then turned and took off in a dead run.

Unable to keep a short exclamation from escaping my lips at his sudden departure, I scrambled to follow. Kevin and Gabriel, acting as guards, matched my pace.

The backyard was even more packed than the front. No one seemed particularly concerned about three hunters and an angel sprinting toward them. In a matter of moments we were there. Logan stopped short just past the boundary line. I collided with him.

"Oof!" The wind knocked out of me, and I landed on the soft grass. Logan merely took a step forward to steady himself.

"Oh jeez." I lay there for a moment while the world came back into focus. "You gotta warn a girl if you're going to put the brakes on that quickly."

Logan looked down on me. I spied the amused glint in his eye.

"You need to be more aware of your surroundings. A demon won't give you the heads-up."

"Thank you, Obi-Wan Kenobi, for another enlightening Jedi pep talk."

"You're comparing me to a Jedi master?" He appeared to like that idea.

I pushed myself to my elbows and then to my feet. "Boys."

"There you guys are."

The look on Romona's face was serious.

"Yeah, sorry," Logan answered cautiously. "We had a little incident that held us up."

Romona looked troubled, glancing between the two of us. Logan wasn't aware that Romona knew about our little bonding issue, so he couldn't read her face correctly, but I did. I needed to stop her line of questioning. We didn't need any more spikes in the awkward factor.

"Romona, can we chat for a minute . . . like alone?"

"Sure." She gave me a puzzled look, then turned toward the guys. "They're meeting about strategy in the front yard. Once you're briefed you can fill in Audrey after we, ah, chat."

We waited for the guys to leave. "So, out with it," Romona said with her hands planted on her hips. "What was the *distraction* Logan was talking about?"

"Not what you think it is."

She raised her eyebrows in interest.

"We kind of got interrupted when we arrived."

She nodded for me to go on. I worried the truth would freak her out. Besides, how exactly do you tell someone you met the prince of darkness himself and for reasons unknown, he's taken a personal interest in you? I tried to stop, but the words popped out anyway.

"Logan left me alone in an alley with the devil." I clapped my hands to my mouth.

As soon as "devil" left my mouth, Romona's features blanked. I expected gasps or a female overreaction. But nothing. When she spoke, it was as if to herself.

"I suppose I should have expected something like this to happen. I don't know why I didn't. What have I done?" The last question was barely a whisper. Her eyes stared through me. Instead of freaking out, she was freaking me out.

"Romona, what are you talking about?"

"Nothing, I'm sorry, just forget it. Are you okay? What'd he want?" Her face transformed into that of a concerned friend. Why was everyone reacting so peculiarly? First Logan, now Romona.

Before I could answer, someone hollered my name. "Yo, Audrey!"

I turned my head. "Kevin, I'm right here."

He jogged over to us. "Hey, hate to interrupt, but Logan needs to talk to you."

I sighed. "Okay then, well I'd better find him." Before I turned to leave, Romona gently caught me by the arm.

"You will tell me about it later though, right?" There was genuine concern in her eyes.

"Sure. How about after we get this craziness settled?"

She nodded and released my arm.

I shoved my way through the multitude in search of my mentor before spotting him in a corner of the yard by himself. When I reached him, there was a serious intensity to his stare. His casual stance against the tree was at odds with his face. His eyes held strange fire in them. Logan regarded me silently for a few more seconds than necessary. I wondered what was turning through his brain. He shoved away from the tree, eyes never leaving mine.

"What we're dealing with today is serious."

I fought the desire to roll my eyes and say, "No duh!"

"A boy has brought a gun into his school. There's already a battle going on between the angels and demons, but the angels have been unable to get into the school. The angels don't want any more demons in the school to feed the panic or hysteria, and the demons don't want any angels around to stop the massacre. We're going to distract the demons so we can infiltrate the school. The hunters will be able to slip into the school easier than the angels. We don't have the same power, so the hope is the demons will stay occupied with battling the angels. We're assigned to find and fight the demon that's influencing the boy. The hunters stationed outside the school will be acting to divert the demons' attention so the angels can fight them more effectively. Hopefully a few angels will be able to slip in with us. With their addiction to hunters' emotions, we'll be very distracting to the demons."

The magnitude of the situation pressed heavily on my chest. I couldn't begin to imagine the horror that awaited us. Logan took my silence as a cue to continue.

"The demon's been influencing the boy for a long time. Years perhaps. Our goal is to free the boy of the demon and to protect as many of the students and teachers in the school as possible. And if the boy is resolute about his path after the demon's detached, then we're going to try to minimize the damage until the authorities can take over."

"What do you mean if the boy is resolute? Won't the crisis be over after we get the demon? Won't the boy just stop? Surely it's the demon making him do this."

Logan shook his head. "That's not how it works. The demon can't make him do anything. He's been guiding the boy with lies and deceit, but the boy made a choice. He chose to bring a gun into school with him with his own free will. We're just hoping that if we can stop the influence of the demon, the boy's mind will be clear enough to make the right choice in the end. The demons have surrounded the school to keep us away from him. They know that free of the demon's influence, there's a chance a major tragedy can be stopped."

This was a lot to wrap my brain around. "But why weren't we just sent to the boy sooner? Why wait until it's escalated this much?"

"I can't answer that for you, Audrey. I don't know the answers to everything; I'm not God. Perhaps the boy never asked for help, perhaps we tried and he turned it down."

"But if God knew this would happen, why would He let it?"

"He's sending us now. Without us it would be a massacre."

I wasn't convinced. "Even if no one is hurt, this kid's life is going to be over after today. The minute he whips out that gun, his life is never going to be normal again."

"You don't know that."

"What do you mean I don't know that? Of course I do! Do you know how serious it is to bring a gun into school? Without even causing a single injury, that kid is never going to have a normal life. How could God turn a blind eye to that?"

"Audrey, you're not listening to me. God's not turning a blind eye. He knows the full picture. We don't. Yes, we have to live with the consequences of our decisions, but there's always hope. There is always the chance to turn things around. I can attest to that as well as any of us."

That shut me up. Our conversation in the meadow flashed through my mind. I think Logan was talking just as much about his life on Earth as his new beginning in the afterlife.

Logan took advantage of my silence, getting more heated himself.

"Life is so much bigger than what we see of it. And yeah, bad stuff does happen here, and that's because people aren't perfect. That kid is making a choice today. That is what we've always had—free will. God uses all situations for good in the end, but we have the freedom to royally screw up. In fact, sometimes it's those screw-ups that lead us back to God. So no, I can't explain to you the whys of today. I can only say that I trust that God's got a much better handle on this situation than you are giving Him credit for."

The last comment felt like a slap on the face, and I flinched when he said it. His words definitely left a mark, but on my heart, not my cheek. It all came down to trust. Why was I having such a hard time trusting God? The answer came to me quickly. Because it was a hard thing to do. It was hard to trust a God when I didn't have any proof of His trustworthiness. I stared at Logan in silence, not sure if he was aware of the battle raging inside of me.

"Okay, it sounds like we should get going then." I started to turn when Logan grabbed my arm, halting my movement.

"That's not all I wanted to talk to you about."

I averted my eyes.

"I want your word that you won't do anything without asking me first, and when I say something, you'll do it immediately and without question."

"Haven't we already had this conversation?" I asked in defeat.

"Audrey, I am beyond serious about this. The moment I have an inkling you aren't going to listen to me, I'll pull you out, do you understand me? I'll personally drag you out by your purple hair if I have to. Because if you can't agree to these terms, we can end this right now. I'll leave you tied to this tree."

His words were firm and harsh, but his eyes pleaded, almost as if he was scared . . . scared for me. This wasn't serious Logan who always had to get his way—this was another Logan all together. What I read in his eyes that hadn't passed his lips was that he would do anything to keep me safe. This was a Logan I couldn't refuse.

"Yes. I understand. You have my word."

"Thank you."

I nodded my head, eyes still averted. I was suddenly ashamed that he had to work so hard to garner my cooperation. Was I being difficult just for the sake of being difficult? If that were true, the frustration and fatigue in Logan's eyes made that much more sense. I was going to do better, to be better!

I took a deep breath and told myself to hold it together. I just needed to get through this day. One step at a time. There was a boy and a school full of kids that needed our help. Everything else could be dealt with later.

22

TO BATTLE

As we approached the school, what at first appeared to be a low-hanging lightning cloud quickly proved to be something else. A myriad of angels and demons flew through the air, locked in combat. The enormous swarm of bodies was so dense that not even a ray of sunlight penetrated. The mass moved as if a single being rather than a mixture of opposing forces. Its energy was palpable, pulsating and wafting over the school campus.

Yet the creepiest part wasn't what my eyes were seeing, but rather what my ears *weren't* hearing. It was as if someone had pushed a cosmic mute button on the battle raging in the sky. Noisy cars drove on the road, students laughed and chatted in between periods, and even the wind rushed by my ears, but not a single sound from the conflict above. It made everything that much more surreal.

I looked to the hunters on my left and right to gauge their

reactions. Determination was etched on each of their faces. Romona's face, usually soft and kind, was hard with concentration. Logan's customary stoic mask was sterner. Even Alrik, whom I'd yet to see attack any situation without an air of humor, looked resolute. Only I broke form—less stern and more bewildered.

"They're keeping each other out." Romona reiterated what Logan had told me.

"Why can we see the fight but not hear it?"

"We're being protected. The sound of that battle is more horrific than you can imagine. An angel is casting a protective shield. Once a demon breaks the barrier, we'll be able to hear plenty."

If the sound I'd heard coming from that one demon in the warehouse with Gabriel could be multiplied by a hundred or a thousand, my guess was we'd all be incapacitated in a very short time by the sound.

"So what are we waiting for?" I asked.

"Them to attack us," she answered.

I remembered the part about the demon's addiction to emotions. The thought that demons would attack us to get a fix was just plain scary. Some of us were essentially going to be demon bait.

"Why? Why don't we just slip into the school now while they aren't looking?"

"We need a few angels to be freed up first to help with transporting us back." She seemed reluctant to go on but did after a short pause. "For those of us who get seriously hurt and need to get back for medical attention quickly. We can't move forward until we know there are at least a few angels on hand for our wounded."

Romona turned to face me fully. Her eyes remained hard and serious.

"Audrey, please do your best to stay with Logan. You need to do exactly what he says. I can't stress how important that is." She was pleading with me, much like Logan had.

"Romona, is there something specific I should know about this mission?"

Her stillness confirmed my suspicions.

"What is it? Why am I here?"

"This is a serious fight, and they wouldn't usually allow someone as new as you to be here. But for some reason they have. I don't like it. I do know that . . ."

She was cut off by an unwelcome sound. The high-pitched shrill of a demon. I looked up as the "unsmell" burrowed into my brain. One of the beasts had broken away from the pack and was diving at an angle straight for us.

Before I knew what was happening, Logan had shoved me behind him. I was about to object when I remembered my promise. Even with the demon coming straight at us, the horde of hunters surrounding me made me feel safe.

The closer the demon got, the larger it appeared to be. Its wingspan alone must have been the length of two humans, its body the width of a large tree. Its flesh was the consistency of blackened bark.

The hunters around me held their ground, eyes glued to the shrieking beast. In mere seconds the demon would be on top of us. I started to shout a warning when a sharp command came from the ranks, and quicker than I could process, a line of hunters pulled bows from their backs, aimed, and fired arrows that crackled like fireworks as they sailed through the air.

The demon tried in vain to change its course, its wings flapping furiously as the first volley of arrows connected with their target. I covered my ears against its scream. Black ooze poured from the wounds and melted into shadows, but even so it still came at us. A second command was yelled, and another round of arrows shot into the free-falling beast.

Spurred by a sudden bad feeling in my gut, I glanced behind us. The other hunters' attention was so drawn to the injured demon that they had missed the silent approach of one from behind.

Instinctively, I grabbed the knife from the sheath at my thigh and threw it at the demon, yelling a warning to the hunters around me. The blade connected with the target, imbedding itself in the creature's blackened flesh. A number of quickly drawn arrows swiftly joined my knife. The crowd of hunters parted where the demon crashed to the ground.

On the other side, the first demon was still fighting a group of hunters on the ground. Even wounded, it was far from defeated. The creature had two tails of reflecting scales that went invisible at times, wreaking havoc on the hunters working to take it down. My body was moving even before I'd made up my mind to help. On the third step, someone jerked me off my feet.

"NO!"

I went limp. Fighting off Logan wasn't going to leave me much energy for much else. And again, there was that promise. Logan released his hold.

"We're headed over there." He pointed to the side of the school. "We're going around the building to slip in the side door. There's still time to catch the boy before he does something stupid."

I didn't bother with words, just nodded my understanding. Logan took off without looking back, trusting for once that I would follow.

I made the mistake of looking up as we made our break for the side entrance. More demons had broken off from the cluster and were headed toward the group of hunters we'd just broken away from. Including Romona. A few angels swooped down in a failed attempt to intercept them.

The pressure in my head built with every demon that broke through the barrier. I stumbled but caught myself before I fell. Logan disappeared around the corner. Focused on catching up, I sprinted to the point where he'd vanished.

I rounded the corner without any intention of slowing down, and the next thing I knew my stomach collided with a metal bat—or at least, that's how it felt when the tail of a demon swatted me in the midsection and threw me into the air. I landed on a soft patch of grass. I blinked to clear the stars and gasped for breath. My fear compounded as the demon approached, reaching near-hysteria levels as I coughed and hacked and struggled to get to my feet. Just behind the demon, I caught sight of Logan's shocked face as he ran back toward us. The demon must have dropped between us when we separated.

It felt as if I was drowning with air all around me. I still couldn't get in a breath, and my vision was starting to blur. I got to one knee and willed myself to get up. Logan wasn't going to get here in time. I was going to have to fight off the demon myself, and I could barely even get to my feet.

The demon shrieked and jumped for me. I dropped back to the ground and freed my blazing sword to defend myself. It was going to take me down with a fiery sword in its gut.

I could almost feel the tearing of the creature's claws when a blur of light slammed into it from behind and sent it sailing over me. Finally able to take in a breath, I scrambled to my feet to see Gabriel take down the demon with one mighty blow, severing its body with a downward sweep of his sword.

Someone grabbed my shoulders and roughly turned me around.

"Are you okay?" Logan's face was strained.

"Yeah," I croaked, and then bent over to cough before going on, "I'm okay. I just got the wind knocked out of me."

"Logan, get her out of here."

We turned our heads toward Gabriel, who gave Logan a stern look and waited for him to nod back before shooting into the air.

"You need to stay closer to me."

"No kidding."

"Audrey, I'm not joking."

"Neither am I."

It must have been the scared-to-death look in my eyes that convinced him. He nodded once. "Okay. Are you sure you can keep going?"

I wanted to say yes, but I had a suspicion if I opened my mouth that's not what would have come out. I just nodded. This time when he turned toward the school, he kept my hand firmly in his.

I was breathless with exertion and adrenaline when we burst through the side doors. A half-dozen other hunters were already there, scanning the empty hallways. It must have been in the middle of a period.

Logan dropped my hand the moment we crossed over the threshold. "How much time do we have?"

A large guy with fire-red hair and a full red beard answered him back. "Not much. We're running on borrowed time. If we don't find the boy soon, there'll be a riot on our hands." Logan's mouth was pressed into a straight line. "We have a scout team already moving through the school. We were getting ready to sweep this wing." The red-headed guy paused for a moment and looked straight at me.

"Is this the new one? The one we've heard about?"

"Yes," Logan answered.

Big Red nodded back, eyes burning a hole in my forehead.

"You can come with us. But put out that fire for now. I don't want any of my team singed."

The sword.

I'd almost forgotten it was still blazing. I sheathed it quickly as Big Red waved his team forward. The sounds from outside were getting louder. We jogged past classrooms full of people completely ignorant of the commotion outside. Angels, demons, and hunters battled outside the windows of the class-rooms, yet the students inside were completely unaware—taking notes, whispering when they didn't think the teacher was looking, even cheating on tests. One part of my mind was focused on keeping up with the other hunters, but there was another detached half that was with the students of this school.

I wondered if this was what my life had been like. What did it feel like to sit in a classroom? To have friends to pass notes to? What subjects had I liked and disliked? Did I have many friends—a boyfriend? Did I play sports? An instrument? As inopportune a moment as it was, I couldn't stop question after question from assaulting my brain.

I didn't realize how unfocused I'd become until Logan had to call my name twice to get my attention.

My face must have reflected my guilt. There were more important things going on right now. Logan narrowed his eyes, suspicion forming. He opened his mouth to say something when the first gunshot rang out.

23

A SINGLE JAR
OF PICKLES

An eerie silence followed that first shot. The noise ricocheted off the locker-lined halls as all eight of us stood still. On the second shot, all hell broke loose.

Screams started from down the hall—human screams and the pounding of footsteps as a stampede headed our way. Within moments, we were mobbed by a sea of bodies that divided like the Red Sea when it hit our knot of hunters. The hysterics caused people to push into us, but most ended up falling, which caused others to stumble on their fellow class-mates and teachers.

"Split up!" shouted Big Red. And we did.

Hunters dispersed into the crowd and worked their way against the current. Most stayed toward the sides to help the flow and prevent any further accidents. But I was still frozen in the middle of the hallway with people funneling around and right into me. My brain told my feet to move. But the shock that we'd been too late, that a shot had been fired, that this was actually happening, was too much.

It was the quietest of whimpers that broke my daze. A girl huddled on the linoleum floor to my right. She lay on her side with knees drawn to her chest and her arms wrapped around her head.

And she was being trampled. Someone stepped on her leg in their haste. She screamed out in fear or pain, maybe both. My feet finally in action, I ran the short distance, determined to throw myself on top of her if necessary to keep her safe.

I was only a half-step away when I was pulled off my feet from behind.

"Let me go! She's hurt!"

"No, Audrey, that's not why we're here."

I struggled futilely against Logan. "But she's hurt. They're *stepping* on her!"

As I said it, another person tripped on her, this time kicking her in the head. I heard her muffled sobs. She was too scared or too hurt to get up and move on. I understood. I struggled more furiously against Logan.

"Let me go!"

Logan only tightened his hold, restraining me within arms of steel. I struck out blindly and scratched his cheek with my nails, drawing blood.

"Audrey, stop, look!" He shook me once, hard. Down the hallway, an angel soared above the crowd toward us.

"We're not here to protect them, but *they* are. She'll be fine." I stopped struggling even as the angel settled over the girl, spreading its wings above her.

"If we want to stay in this fight, we've got to go." Logan's voice was even, but there was urgency beneath the calm.

Logan was difficult to keep up with. Even though theoretically I could have run forward unhindered, I couldn't stop the reflex to dodge people, and I kept ramming myself into the walls to avoid them. Whenever I glanced forward, Logan seemed further away. I rushed to catch up, but it was slow going.

An all-too-familiar screech rang out, higher-pitched and louder than what was coming from the scared kids around us. And then, in front of us, a hunter was thrown through the air and collided with a locker. He hit it with a dull thud and slumped to the ground. A few more hunters rushed to his aid. Logan stopped to assess the scene. My heart rate picked up. The boy and his demon were just around the corner.

"Get out of here, Lyons!" a strained voice shouted.

"Man, you don't have to do this."

Someone was trying to reason with the shooter. Someone young.

The only people around me were hunters. I hoped that was because all the teachers and students had made it out of the school unharmed. That is, except for the two boys around the corner. The two I could hear but not yet see.

"I mean it, you're not like them, but I'm warning you, that doesn't mean I won't do it," the shooter's voice said.

It was silent for a moment. The tension froze my forward momentum.

A loud bang reverberated down the passage, filling my ears and searing into my heart.

I started violently at the sound of the shot.

"I said get out of here!" screamed the shooter.

My heart beat wildly. Was there going to be a dead boy around the next turn? Would I be able to deal with that?

Not waiting any longer, Logan rounded the corner not more than twenty feet in front of me. I started to follow but heard the skidding footsteps too late and collided with someone at the bend in the hallway. I stumbled back at the force. A boy lay at my feet, knocked on his back by the collision.

He cast hasty looks around as he frantically scrambled back up, and for a split second, he glanced up and looked right at me. I blinked and the moment passed—and so did he. The boy who had been talking to the shooter. He was okay.

But on the heels of that thought, I fell straight to my knees in the middle of the hall, in the middle of the chase. It was all there in an instant.

Every memory from my life, back where it always should have been.

I remembered my parents, Judy and Dean. I remembered my siblings. My sisters Jessica and Lainie, and my little brother, James. James Lyons.

The same little brother who had just rushed by to get away from the gunfire I was running toward.

The same precious little brother I'd stepped in front of and pushed out of the way of the car.

I put my hands on my ears and pressed down, hoping to block out some of the memories that were flashing through my mind.

It was too painful, too hurtful to remember now.

I wasn't ready, wasn't prepared to deal with them.

This timing was all wrong.

I cried out in anguish, and it sounded as if my voice came from somewhere far away.

I had something to do, I knew I did, but my mind couldn't push past the memories of all I'd lost.

I may have heard my name being shouted, but it barely registered.

I remembered the pickles again.

Those stupid pickles.

They were the last thing I'd fought with my brother about. I'd found them left out in the morning and thrown the whole jar away. He said it was fine to leave them out, and I said that once they'd been in the refrigerator they had to stay there.

I didn't even *like* pickles, but I was still lecturing him for leaving them on the counter all night when the car came screeching around the corner—headed right for James, who was frozen in shock in the middle of the crosswalk.

It was as if I was there again. I felt my body start into motion with the ball of fear in my chest. I screamed at him to get out of the way, but he wouldn't move.

Why wouldn't he move?

I made it there in time to give him a shove strong enough to push him out of the way but ended up smashing into the vehicle myself.

In my mind I felt bones breaking, my body scraping across the ground after I'd been flipped over the car, and finally the blinding pain before the complete blackness as my head smashed into the pavement.

With a gasp I opened my eyes and was back in the school hallway. My heart would surely beat out of my chest as I gasped for air. I was having a panic attack, or else I was in shock.

My name was being yelled and I found the strength to lift

my head. Logan, shouting for me to get up. I caught his blue eyes, the urgency in them. He needed me. They all did.

Down the hall, a demon's claws were deeply imbedded in a boy no older than my brother.

A sophomore at most.

I didn't remember his name—he would have been two grades below me—but I remembered his face. I'd seen him sitting alone in the lunchroom and walking through the halls with his head down, hood up, shoulders hunched.

He was small for his age. I didn't remember having ever talked with him, but I also didn't remember him looking this bad. His hair was matted and disheveled. His clothes were hanging loosely off his boney frame, and his eyes were glazed and vacant.

The demon snapped at the dozen or so fighters closing in but refused to relinquish its hold on the child. Logan and I stood several feet outside the shrinking circle of hunters. I had to do this. No matter what was going on in my head right now, I had to push it aside and get up.

I mentally shouted at my body to obey me, and for once it actually listened. A tear slipped down my cheek as I took a step toward the fight. I was ripping pieces of my heart out with every step, ordering myself not to turn around and look for James. I caught up to Logan, who grabbed my shoulders and gave me a shake.

"Audrey, what's going on? Are you all right?"

He looked rattled, torn between the demon and making sure I was okay. Although my mind was full, I suddenly felt very hollow. I didn't know how to answer him. I looked him straight in the eyes, which was probably a mistake because it showed what a mess I was.

He nodded once, his lips drawn into a straight line. "Okay, we have to get you out of here. You're not ready for this."

I shook my head—I couldn't leave now.

Another shot rang out. An angel appeared from who knows where and deflected the bullet intended for the fleeing students who had just burst out of a classroom. The chem lab, if I remembered correctly. Mr. Elliott's class.

I flinched. There were more screams, but they seemed very far away. I looked frantically around to see if anyone had been injured. It didn't appear that anyone was hit. I think the bullet had slammed into a locker.

Impulse took over. I shoved Logan's hands off my shoulders and hurled myself toward the boy and the demon attached to his body.

The demon wasn't the largest one I'd seen by far, but it was doing an effective job of keeping the other hunters at bay with its long, scaled tail, whipping it back and forth so quickly that no one could get close enough to pry the monster off the boy's back. At this point the boy's eyes were glassy. The demon had taken so much of his essence that he was barely a shell now.

I willed the boy to hang on.

Not stopping when I reached the other hunters, I pulled my sword from its sheath, and it instantly blazed to life. The demon shrieked at me. With a clean swipe, I severed its tail from its body. The tail turned to shadow, then disappeared.

I advanced on the beast. Its talons dug deeper into the boy, and the child's arm rose one more time, although this time he bent his wrist toward himself.

We were almost out of time.

Without a thought I brought my arm up and threw the blazing sword right at the demon's head.

The sword missed its intended target but sank deeply into the creature's shoulder. With an agonized scream, it finally pulled its claws from the boy and fell to the ground.

The demon pawed at the sword, trying to dislodge it.

The sword held its mark.

The flesh around the wound started to char and crumble away like overused coal.

I jerked my head up to locate Logan when the warning was shouted but couldn't react fast enough. The demon coiled its decaying body and sprang at me, bringing us both to the ground.

We slid across the floor until I slammed into a row of lockers. The air was violently expelled from my lungs. I was suffocating with the demon right on top of me.

It gave a horrid scream, then sank its three rows of teeth into my right shoulder.

After that, I may have screamed myself.

The beast was tearing at the very fabric of my soul as well as the soft shoulder flesh. With the empathy connection made, I knew exactly what it wanted to do—what it craved doing. To rip my body to shreds and feast on my soul.

It hated me. Hated me with the purest hatred there was.

It lived only to see my destruction.

It was all rot and death and evil. And in that moment, it was all I felt and what I had become as well.

It offered a black hole to swallow me whole. Soon I was unable to feel fear because the creature's vile blackness was consuming everything.

And then the hatred was ripped off of me.

I gasped for air, and my back arched off the ground. My

vision was still black as I swam in the vile sensations and passions of the beast.

Someone put pressure on my shoulder, and I screamed in pain, my whole body arching away.

"Hold still!" someone yelled in my ear.

Out of instinct, I obeyed. It was Logan.

He knelt on my left, his shirt pressed against my shoulder. Naked from the waist up, he must have stripped off the top half of his body armor in order to use his shirt as a pressure bandage.

I would have made a joke if I didn't hurt so badly and if my mind didn't feel so fractured and violated.

The waves of pain were relentless. I held still out of sheer willpower to obey. Logan's cheek and one of his arms were stained, or rather coated, with fresh blood. I panicked.

"Oh my gosh, you're bleeding!"

I tried to sit up, but he pushed me roughly back.

"Don't move. That's your blood, not mine. Except for that scratch you gave me earlier."

Oh. An angry ocean churned in blue eyes that wouldn't meet my own.

A voice behind my head said, "It's taken care of. The hunters are tending to the boy until an angel can arrive."

Without turning from me, Logan nodded once. "I'm going to get her out of here. She needs to be treated. Send word that I'm taking her to the extraction point outside."

"Yes, sir."

And with that, Logan lifted my right hand and pressed it against the shirt covering my wound. He finally looked me in the eye. "I don't care how much it hurts, press down on this hard."

I'd seen Logan mad before, but I wasn't sure I'd ever seen him this worked up. Blackness still tinged the edges of my consciousness, but at this moment he scared me more. I nodded in agreement. The pain was truly dizzying, but I managed to keep pressure where he instructed.

He slid an arm underneath my knees and another under my back and lifted me from the ground. I bit my cheek to keep from crying out and tasted blood from biting down too hard.

Logan's long strides took us to a courtyard in the middle of the school in a matter of moments. There were still some hysterics going on outside, but through the hurt it all seemed far away. I grasped at anything to take my mind off my injury.

"You know, Logan, if you wanted to get me in your arms again, all you had to do was ask."

My lame attempt at a joke fell very flat. A muscle in Logan's jaw twitched as if he was gritting his teeth, and he didn't look down on me. A small knot of panic formed in my gut. Had I finally pushed him too far?

After a few long, silent moments, an angel appeared. He enveloped us in his wings, and in an instant we were gone.

We were taken straight to the healing center, the afterlife's equivalent of a hospital. Logan pushed through a set of doors that led to what looked like an operating room. He briskly but gently set me on the flat bed and put his hand over mine to add pressure to my wound.

The empathy link between us sprang to life, and I was assaulted by Logan's anger. I gasped at its intensity. He was furious.

He must have thought I gasped at the pressure, because he immediately let up a little, and in that moment I detected something hidden under the thick layer of anger. Logan was deeply concerned. So much so that he was trying to bury it under his anger. This was the first time Logan had ever purposefully touched me in this realm, and despite the pain, I found myself desperate to understand what he was feeling.

My eyes widened as I searched deeper, unable to get as far as I wanted. If I could have reached for his feelings with my fingers, I would have just grazed what he felt for me. I wanted to snatch it and bring it closer to get a better look, but it was buried too deep. But what I *could* brush felt strong and pure and had me panting for breath.

Was this what it meant to be bonded?

Logan stared down at me with one hand still applying pressure to my wound and the other pressed to the bed adjacent to my shoulder. His head blocked the light in the room, and his face was partly shadowed by his hair as he leaned over me. It reminded me of the first time I had fainted shortly after meeting him. Perhaps he was searching as deeply into my feelings now as I was into his.

The tricky thing about the empathy link was that if you weren't completely sure of your feelings, they could easily get confused with those of the person you were touching. When I looked up at Logan, I wasn't entirely sure whose emotions I felt. Something was blossoming in my chest, and I sucked in a quick breath.

"Why didn't you wait?" he asked.

"What?" I couldn't piece together what he wanted.

"What happened to you out there? Why didn't you wait for us? Why didn't you listen to me like you promised? Do you have any idea what could have actually happened to you?"

His voice wasn't harsh, but it wasn't gentle either.

"You mean something worse than this?"

Logan pressed his lips together in a thin line. "Yes, something worse than this."

"It's not like I could have been killed. I'm already dead."

I let out a humorless laugh, but it caused my shoulder to move, and another bolt of pain shot through my body. I bit my lip to keep from gasping.

So quietly I almost couldn't hear, Logan answered, eyes averted once again. "There are some things worse than death."

I felt a bolt of dread shoot through Logan's anger. He had a point. What in the world had I been thinking, attacking the demon like that? It was stupid and reckless, and I'd suffered because of it.

With a start, it all came crashing back. The memories. The pain, the sadness, the loss. Logan felt the moment it happened with the same intensity as I. He sucked in a breath of air so quickly it sounded like a hiss. He cradled my cheek with his free hand, capturing my eyes with his own.

My eyes pooled with tears, and the breath escaped my mouth in short gasps. Logan's face began to blur, but I heard his voice and felt his gentle touch.

"Audrey, what's going on here? What's happening to you?"

I couldn't get the words out. The anger in Logan's core evaporated and was replaced with deep concern that bordered on panic. Closing my eyes, I blocked out the world. I didn't even want Logan's touch right now, and I struggled to get out of his grasp.

"Audrey, stop, stay with me. What's going on?"

In that instant, the doors of the room flung open. The sound of people arguing filtered through to me, but I was in too much physical and emotional pain to comprehend. After a moment Logan's hands left my body, and I was left to deal with only my own pain. Then, a soft familiar voice spoke in my ear, telling me to relax, and the next moment it was black.

24
GOD

Golden warmth pressed itself against my closed eyelids. I floated on a cloud, every part of my body perfectly relaxed and tranquil. I breathed in air so fresh I could have sworn it had begun to circulate through my body, energizing everything from fingertips to toes.

I brought my arms above my head and stretched languidly. I'd never felt so alive yet so peaceful. I could rest here forever. Wherever I was, it felt like heaven.

I pressed my fingers to the cloud beneath me and was startled by the frosty bite of cold. I sucked in a crisp breath of air, and my eyelids fluttered against the brightness.

The world slowly began to take shape. The golden glow suspended above me morphed into blue skies. A brisk gust of wind forced my eyelids shut once again and blew strands of hair across my face, tickling my cheeks.

It didn't take long for the cold beneath my fingers to seep in, causing a chill to run up my arms and down my back to my feet. I opened my eyes with more clarity this time. I had been wrong. I wasn't resting in a cloud but was instead sprawled face-up on a brittle bed of snow. I pushed the weight of my half-frozen body to a sitting position and then to a stand, crystallized snow crunching underneath as I moved.

Hand to brow, I surveyed the world around me. I stood on the summit of a snow-covered peak, high up and looking down at the sparkling city beneath. Buildings and structures I'd first considered cold, sterile, and untouchable, I now knew pulsated with life. I imagined a warm glow palpitating from the white marble. Another gust of wind, noticeably colder than the last, added ice to my blood, reminding me just how far away I was from the sanctuary below.

I took a more discerning look at my immediate surroundings. The area was completely covered in a blanket of pristine white snow. It was flat for a twenty-foot radius around me, but beyond that was a straight drop. I was as trapped as if I'd been buried in the ground.

How had I been plucked from the valley and set up here? The mountain was far too steep to hike. My last recollection was of lying on a stiff bed with a bloody wound, Logan's concerned face floating above me. And me, a bundle of emotions too painful to explore. But that wasn't where I was anymore, and the pain, both physical and emotional, was absent.

I jerked my head to the left to check my injured shoulder, but I couldn't inspect the gash because I was covered from neck to wrist in white. The unfamiliar dress was tightened at my waist and flowed down to my feet. A few of my toes, still painted bright pink from my salon day with Romona, poked out the bottom. I took the material just above my knee and rubbed it between my fingers. It felt like soft linen. Lifting the hem, I found I was wearing white leather sandals, the style at odds with the cold snap of the snow at my feet.

Still bewildered, I had a sudden urge to look straight up and saw a small, dense cloud descending. Strange because it was the only cloud in a cloudless sky. Strange because it was moving vertically instead of horizontally. Strange because it was changing altitude at a rapid pace. I stood with eyes transfixed on the mass above until its white brightness enveloped me.

The first few moments in the midst of the cloud were eerily quiet. I held my breath in anticipation, realizing something was coming but not knowing what. I may have been standing on the edge of the cliff, only a small nudge from plummeting into the nothing.

A crack of thunder directly on the heels of a blinding lightning bolt broke the tension in a terrifying way. I jerked and gasped in shock, breathing rapidly. The wind picked up, and a tiny piece of hail, no larger than a mustard seed, hit my hand. I was pelted on my left shoulder by two more, this time the size of small pebbles. The hail increased, mixed with snow in an aggressive wind.

With another flash of lightning, a violent storm erupted, and the force of it sent me to my knees. My very breath was pulled from my lungs as wind, hail, and snow whipped, wailed, and whirled around me in an angry tornado. Fear, as icy as my surroundings, gripped my insides.

Thunder vibrated deep in my chest until my entire being trembled with aftershocks. I was in the presence of a power so enormous I could do nothing but cower before it.

I buried my head and clasped my arms around my knees,

pulling myself into as small a ball as possible. This was more frightening than looking into a swarm of battling demons. In desperation, I cried out for help to the only being I was certain could hear. The one I'd been running from since the beginning. The torrent raging around me instantly swallowed my voice.

And then the thunder formed words that spoke to the very core of me. "Audrey, do not be afraid. I have redeemed you. I have called you by name; you are mine."

Despite my turmoil, my trembling stopped, and I lifted my eyes in search of the one who had spoken my name.

He was walking toward me. My lips formed words that were stolen by the wind. This was the Lord. This was my God.

He appeared brighter than the whiteness all around, His features obscured by the light emitting from Him. The closer He got the brighter He became, until the brightness was so intense that I could no longer look at Him and was forced to shade my eyes.

When I looked away, the world was silenced. The only sound was the hitch in my breath. The wind evaporated, leaving only the cold in its place. I shivered.

A hand settled on my shoulder, and liquid warmth spread from the spot outward, replacing the icy bite of the snow and air. It wasn't a moment before I was encased in a heated bubble even as I remained crouched on the frozen precipice.

It was then that I became ashamed to look up at the God I'd forgotten along with the rest of my life. What could I possibly say or offer to Him that would be good enough? I bowed my head low to the ground, pressing my forehead to the snow. I had nothing more than humility to offer.

The snow crunched beneath Him as He stepped even

closer. His hand had left my shoulder, but the warmth He'd given remained.

"Why do you hide yourself from me?" His voice was now a whisper in my ear. A loving caress to my soul. But despite the affection in His voice, I remained bowed at His feet. Like a servant to her master.

I forced my mouth to move, the words barely a breath from my lips. "You are El Shaddai—God Almighty." I spoke it as if it were an answer to His question.

"But am I not also Abba Father? You did not receive a spirit that makes you a fearful slave, but rather you received My Spirit and have been adopted as My own. You sought me in life and so have been given the right to be a child of Mine."

He paused while I remained paralyzed at His feet.

"I created your inmost being and knit you together in your mother's womb. My eyes saw your unformed body, and all your days have been written in My book before even one of them came to be. Shall I continue, dear Audrey, to tell you how great My love is for you? Shall I tell you how I have always known the plans I have for you, plans to prosper and not harm you, plans to give you a hope and a future? Shall I remind you how you came and prayed to Me and how I listened? How you found Me because you sought Me with your whole heart?"

Words I had once known came up from a deep place within my heart: *How great the love the Father has lavished upon us, that we should be called children of God.*

With those words, I knew that what He said was truth. I knew that He was love and that He loved me. And His love had been made complete in me so that I could approach Him with confidence.

My face lifted. Unshed tears blurred His image hovering above, with arms open wide, waiting . . . waiting for me.

With a cry, I half-stood, half-stumbled toward Him and was caught in His embrace. He lovingly wiped the tears from my eyes, and I took refuge in the shelter of His arms, awed that the Creator of the universe truly cared for me.

Eventually my tears dissipated enough for me to absorb the suspended world around me. Intricate ice crystals and water particles hung in the air as if attached by string to the sky itself. Twisters of snow stood frozen mid-turn. An encircling mist so thick it was tangible shielded us from whatever reality lay beyond. I held my breath in wonder.

"Are you feeling better, Dear One?" He asked.

"What's happened?" I whispered.

"I have stopped everything to show you how important you are to Me."

"I didn't even know that was possible."

He smiled. "But of course. For Me a day is like a thousand years, and a thousand years are like a day."

"So nothing else is moving forward in time except us?"

"You need only know that I'm here to be with you. And to answer a few of those questions you've been throwing at Me like darts these past few weeks."

With those words, I hung my head and stepped out of His embrace.

A soft sigh emanated from Him. "Always pulling away from me." In my mind's eye, I saw Him shaking His head sadly. "When will you learn to stop hiding behind fears and realize the depth of My care for you? It is not your questions I'm disappointed in, but rather the doubt of Me reflected in them. I cherish a heart bent toward understanding. But you must learn to stand firm on the truth as well."

"But I forgot the truth with the rest of my life," I protested.

"No, it was always there with you. More a part of you than those memories you missed so much. There was nothing in the Heavens or on Earth that could separate you from the truth. Nothing that could separate you from Me."

"I don't know what you mean," I sobbed, despair and shame leaking into my heart.

"Audrey, what is the first truth you learned about Me?"

I experienced a moment of panic before I realized I knew exactly what it was. *God is love.* That was the first verse I'd ever memorized. The first memory I had of my Creator.

Without me having uttered a word, He knew I'd captured the memory.

"And what has happened to make you doubt that?" He asked simply.

My head lifted even as my eyes struggled to remain down-turned. Some hesitancy lingered in my soul up until the moment I looked at His face.

His eyes, set in a wrinkle-free face, spoke love. From forehead to chin, He radiated strength but also compassion. It was an ageless face full of grace and mercy. A human face, but somehow different, eternal, powerful. Beauty personified.

"This is what you look like?" My voice was hardly above a whisper. I'd surprised myself by getting anything out at all.

"This is how I choose to appear to you. This isn't the time to reveal My full glory to you. It's safe to say that would be a little overwhelming right now."

"So you look different? I mean on a normal day or whatever?"

He smiled down at me. A smile that spoke of both amusement and patience.

"I have as many different faces and shapes as are possible to imagine. Each one reflects a different part of who I am. I can manifest for you in whatever way I want, yet My form in its true glory is not able to be looked upon. For now, this is how I choose to appear. In time you'll learn to recognize My other faces as well."

That sounded like more riddles to me.

He chuckled warmly.

"They are not riddles, Dear One, meant to confuse or deceive you, but rather mysteries that are best unraveled over time. Discoveries are intended to be searched for. It makes the prize that much more precious. But I am here now to set some things straight and ease your mind. Come sit with me by the fire so we can talk."

I didn't have a chance to ask what fire before I spotted the flames to my left. The burning wood crackled and popped loudly as if carrying on its own conversation. The air twinkled with frozen water still suspended in place. Snowflakes felt like butterfly wings brushing my cheeks as I moved through them. We settled on white pillows positioned on the snow. The snow no longer held the chill it had before He arrived. He wore a robe much like my dress, but with a golden sash tied around his middle. His sandaled feet stuck out as he sat cross-legged facing me. The experience was normal and surreal at the same time.

"Is this real?" I asked.

"More real than anything you have ever experienced" was His answer. I believed him.

"Shall we finally talk about some of the things that have been on your mind?"

I teared up at the question, and my mouth spoke the words my heart had been crying. "Where have you been?"

He leaned closer yet made no move to touch me. "I've been here all along. Here with you from the moment you arrived. I never once left you. You have been too blind to see."

I was taken aback. Yet, I thought I understood. I remembered the moment by the lake when I'd felt His tug on my heart yet had denied it. I thought of the time I lay crying into my pillow and was comforted. And then I realized that if He'd been there all along, He knew all the times I had lashed out in anger.

Once again knowing my mind, He spoke. "As I said before, you were wrong to doubt Me, Audrey, but not to question. I want you to question things, to find deeper meaning in circumstances. To seek My will with all your heart. But through ups or downs, you should never doubt who I am. You should never doubt that I'm going to do what I say I will do."

I chewed on that a moment, debating whether to speak. But when I considered who He was, and that He already knew what I was thinking, I didn't see a point in holding back.

"I'm so sorry," I began, "but how am I to know that? How am I to believe that? I just feel so much fear sometimes, and I don't understand what You're doing."

"Believing those things is a choice, not a feeling. True faith is believing in Me even when you don't understand. Believing in Me even when you can't see the evidence with your own eyes. For there are times when your eyes will be deceived, and you will need to rely on the truth buried in your heart to overcome."

I was both overwhelmed and unsure.

He gestured toward the fire. "I have some things to show you. For us to watch together."

The crackling had subsided, and embers started to swirl at the base. I squinted and cocked my head. If I looked just right, it almost appeared as if I could see something other than the fire-eaten wood within its depths. And then, like a movie screen brought to life, the flames snapped into a flat line, and images sprang from the embers.

We sat together and watched moments of my life. Moments I had lived on Earth but now saw with the veil removed. He showed me the times in my life I had cried out for Him, and that He was there. He showed me the places I was too weak to go and He had carried me. He showed me the protection given to me by a multitude of angels and hunters. He showed me the things He'd protected me from. I was ashamed when time and time again that He went unthanked—that the blessings He gave me went unappreciated and the opportunities I had to love others passed me by.

When it felt like I was in the pit of self-loathing, He stopped the images, His attention fully on me.

"Audrey, I'm not here to bury you in guilt, but rather to set you free. You cannot do a single thing to make Me love you more or less than I do. My love for you is unconditional and everlasting. Its depth surpasses knowledge. It is not based on anything you may or may not accomplish."

I tried to grasp what He was saying, but it was simply too big, too overwhelming for me to process. I had a family on Earth, and I knew they loved me. In fact, they loved me a great deal, but the love He described was altogether different.

"I know this is something you will grapple with, but

remember the words I just spoke to you. My love is not given by the measure of works you complete. In truth, you could never do anything good enough to earn it. It's given without regard to accomplishments when you became a child of mine."

Dare I believe something so radical, something so unbalanced as that? A part of my heart clung to the old feeling that I needed to do something to be good enough for Him despite what He said.

He sighed and shook his head, assuredly knowing what thoughts were bouncing around in my brain. "Just remember My words. There will inevitably be times you will be challenged and need them. Now, let me show you a few more of My favorites."

The images in the fire blazed back to life.

I didn't know how long we stayed together like that, watching the moments of my life in the burning fire. I was mesmerized. He'd lifted the veil and opened my eyes to what my life on Earth had really been like.

"You have got to be kidding!" I burst out as one of my chubby toddler moments appeared in the flames. We were having a family picnic, and I'd followed a butter-colored butterfly into the woods until it flitted over a stream. Wanting to follow it yet scared of the water, I danced a foot in and out of the riverbank. To my shock, I now saw that a sinister demon lurked in the water, silently teasing me forward.

A flash of light blinded me, and the demon was gone. An angel disguised as a human appeared on the path behind me. He explained to my toddler self how badly my family was missing me, and we agreed that a pretty butterfly was less important that my loving family. He pointed me in the right direction, then was gone.

It was my grandmother on my mother's side who found me as I waddled down the path the angel set me on. Her long hair, twisted into a braid, was dark mahogany with only a few grey streaks running through it. Even in her elder years she had remained beautiful. She picked me up and squeezed me tight, then pulled back to look me in the eye.

I gasped. The slight wrinkles and sags were not what I was most familiar with now, but her youthfulness shone through them anyway.

"You have mighty deeds to do in the future, little girl," she told me. "Things the Lord has prepared for you. I don't believe getting lost and scaring your family half to death is one of them. Let's get you back where you belong."

I'd grabbed her braid with my chubby hand and tried to tell her about the shiny man who'd said to return to them. She smiled and whispered in my ear that I must have a guardian angel watching over me. I giggled and squealed when she tickled a rib. But no one else believed me about the man. It was our secret forever after that. Whenever I was scared or discouraged, my grandmother would remind me that my angel was there looking out for me.

But I was trying to process what I now knew. "Romona's my grandmother!"

He chuckled at my reaction. "Yes. So much of who you are is because of her. She asked for you, you know."

"What do you mean?"

"She asked for a legacy, that a great warrior would be placed in her family. A person of integrity who would be used as a light in My kingdom. Her prayers for you and for the generations to come were frequent and heartfelt. It was because of her faithfulness to Me that you were placed in her family. You, my dear one, are the fulfillment of a promise I made to her."

Fulfillment of a promise? That sounded serious. The magnitude hit me hard.

"But how can that be true?"

"Just like all my creations, you have a great destiny."

I had a hard time swallowing that, and I told Him as much. "But what of real value did I ever do in life? I didn't live long enough to fulfill any type of great destiny!"

"Your destiny is far greater than what you accomplish on Earth. You forget there's an eternity to think of."

"But . . . look at me." I waved a hand to indicate my whole 5'3" frame. "What great feat could someone like me possibly accomplish?"

His eyes softened, and His voice took on a gentler note. "I am looking, Audrey, but I don't see as man sees. Man looks at the outward appearance, but I look at the heart. I've chosen you to carry my light. You were created with a specific mission in mind, on Earth as well as throughout eternity. You have the passion, truth of spirit, and character to be the one person to take on this task. You have my noble strength."

The words were inspiring, but something about them still bothered me. "Are you saying I'm just a robot created as a means to an end?"

I worried for a moment that I'd overstepped, but instead laughter rolled up from his gut. It shook the ground beneath us as well.

"Oh Audrey, so blunt, so perfectly you. Yes, you were created with a purpose in mind, but the decision has always been up to you. Just as you decided to give your life for your little brother. You have always had free will—the freedom to make up your own mind. You can choose what I have to offer or you can reject it. Just the same as when you lived on Earth."

I chewed my lip nervously. "So will I get kicked out of here or something if I don't want to be a hunter?"

His smile was gentle. "No, you won't get kicked out. You are here to stay as long as you want. You'll just be reassigned somewhere else. You'll simply be choosing a different path for yourself."

"But won't you need someone to do what I'm doing here?"

"You won't need to worry about that. The ends will be the same, but the means may be different. I've got a pretty good handle on things." He surprised me with a wink.

I chewed on my fingernail absently as familiar doubts rose to the surface.

"Tell me your fears."

"Don't you already know them?" I asked.

He smiled warmly at me. "I'd like to hear them from you, if you don't mind."

I bit my lip, embarrassed by the truth. "Well, what if I can't do this? What if I fail at it? What if someone gets hurt because of me? It's not like my first couple of missions have gone well."

"On your own, you will fail, My precious child."

My heart sank. That wasn't what I wanted to hear.

"This task isn't meant to fall on your shoulders. This isn't something you do yourself. Instead, you will need to rely on Me, and I will give you what you need to accomplish it. It's not by might or power you will prevail, but by My Spirit. My light will go with you and give you victory."

"There just seem to be so many people more capable than I am. My own *grandmother* is better at this than me. I'm nothing special. It doesn't make sense that you would choose me."

"Do you know how many miracles I've carried out through those you would consider ordinary? The people you read about in My Word, the saints living on Earth, they are all just ordinary people. But they are ordinary people with an extraordinary God. They are people who have given up on trying to live an extraordinary life on their own merits. They are people who understand that the only way to do great things is to rest on their faith and believe I am who I say I am and I can do what I say I can do. I will be the One who goes with you to fight against the enemy and give you victory. That's the confidence you should have moving forward."

"Confidence?"

"Yes, confidence in Me, in my power through you. Not confidence in yourself. That will always fail you."

"And you think I have the ability to do that?"

"Not think, I know. Did you just see the moments we watched? The girl you are?"

It was hard to argue with that. Despite the failures, in life I had been fearless. Perfect, no, but confident in my God and His plan for me.

The trouble was, I hadn't been that girl since getting hit by that car. I was someone different. Someone with doubts, with insecurities. Someone who'd crumbled and been crippled by the hit she'd taken.

"Am I still her anymore? I feel . . ." I had to pause before going on. "I feel broken." I cast my eyes down in shame. I had always thought I would handle the hard times with strength through my faith, yet I had not.

His hand settled gently on mine. "Everyone falls. You have the opportunity to be built up even stronger than before. I'd like to show you one more thing. Look over there."

I turned my head where he pointed and found myself in a familiar place. It was my family's lake house. I stood and turned in a circle to get my bearings.

I was in the living room. The sun pouring into the western windows indicated it was late in the day. There was a commotion outside, and the front door was thrown open. I nearly cried out when my dad step into the room followed by a miniature version of myself. I remembered this day.

Little Me squealed in delight and clapped her hands together as she followed Dad into the kitchen. I followed not far from their heels.

"Yay, Daddy!" Little Me cheered and did a happy dance, one that suspiciously resembled the pee-pee dance. "We did it! You said that we could, and we did."

"That's right, Audrey." My dad bent down to Little Me's level and tweaked her nose.

"And I was so brave, Daddy, wasn't I?"

"You most certainly were! The bravest little girl ever."

"Did that fishy almost get away?" Little Me's face changed from delight to little-girl seriousness.

My dad's face attempted to mirror the same, but he didn't quite manage it. "Yes, he almost got away, but we didn't let him, did we?"

Little Me shook her head fiercely. "No, Daddy, I wouldn't let it get away. It was caught fair and square. I helped get the fishy."

"Of course you did, Audrey. Remember, you're Daddy's little helper. I wouldn't have wanted to catch that fishy for dinner any other way."

Little Me's face brightened with Dad's praises. Her smile got impossibly larger, and she threw herself in Dad's arms. He scooped her up in a hug and rocked her back and forth as he planted kisses on the top of her head.

A tear slid down my cheek, but before it could land on the ground, I was looking into the smoke around our fire.

"That was one of my favorite days."

"Yes, I know."

"Thank you."

"I didn't just show you that for nostalgia's sake. I wanted to remind you of that day for a reason."

I brought my hand to my face to wipe the wetness away.

"Do you think your earthly father needed you in order to catch those fish?"

I shook my head. "Of course not." Looking back now, if anything, I must have been a hindrance.

"But at the time, what did you think?"

I took a moment to bring back the memory. It was one of my first, so if it hadn't been shown to me, I wasn't sure I could have recalled the details. I was only four at the time.

"I really thought I was my dad's helper that day. I thought we'd brought those fish in together. I remember thinking he probably couldn't have gotten as many without me. I was even a little smug about it." I chuckled a little at the thought.

"But what was the truth about that day?"

"That Dad would have done just fine without me. That he let me help him because it was fun for me and he could teach me how to fish, not because he needed me there. He wanted me there for companionship . . . because he loved me."

"Exactly, Audrey. Things are not so different today."

He gave me long moments for the implications to sink in, for the knowledge and the assurance to reach my head and heart. I was still meditating on it when He spoke again.

"You and Logan are not bonded like you believe."

It was said bluntly and so off topic I was shocked into continued silence.

"I know you were wondering about that but wouldn't ask."

I suppose my reaction was silly, but I couldn't help but be embarrassed. Embarrassed about the situation, embarrassed that He knew all about it, and embarrassed that I was really curious about what that meant for Logan and me.

"How is that possible?" I asked. "I mean, we did that thing that I didn't know we weren't supposed to do that makes you bonded." Oh gosh, I couldn't even say "kiss." There was a decent chance I was now sporting a head full of pink hair.

"It's still a choice, my dear Audrey. A conscious decision. A covenant, if you will, that you have to make with a person. One kiss was never meant to unknowingly seal you for eternity. It is not the kiss that does it, it's the covenant—the promise to one another. That is something you and Logan have not given to one another. But I'd be careful about the next time."

"Oh." I frankly couldn't think of what else to say. This whole time it had never seriously occurred to me that it wouldn't count. I was perplexed as to whether or not I thought it was good news. And what did that mean for how I felt about Logan? I knew I felt *something*. I'd just never taken the time to figure out what that something was. In all honesty, I'd always been scared to search too deeply.

"Wait, what? Next time?" My voice had a super attractive shriek-squeak thing going on. "There's going to be a next time?"

He only smiled broadly and shrugged.

"But what am I supposed to do now . . . about Logan?" I

gazed at Him with wide eyes. Desperately hoping He would just tell me what to do but fearing He wouldn't.

"You know, Audrey, I created you with both a heart and a head. And the reason for that was for you to use both. When you try to follow one without considering the other, you will make bad decisions. This especially pertains to relationships. You need to evaluate where you are with Logan by using both of those important parts. I think once you do, the answer will be fairly clear."

I blew out an exasperated breath, not trying to hide my frustration; He already knew how I was feeling, so there wasn't a point to that.

"Audrey, what do you think your life would be like if I took away all your decisions? Took away your ability to decide what was right and wrong. Just marched you forward with a personalized life map, something you knew from birth that said 'You will like these subjects and dislike these. You will have this job, and on this day you will marry this person.'"

I took a moment to really think about that. On the one hand, it would mean I would never make any mistakes, never run into any problems. My map would force me to steer clear of them. On the other hand, there would never be any adventures or mysteries. Never any excitement or real need to use my brain. That didn't seem very fun either.

Still, there were some things I'd rather have an answer about right away. The messiness with Logan was one of those things. I looked at Him hopefully.

He shook His head. "You have a journey to discover. One that I've planned with infinite care and consideration. As my beloved child, I won't take that away from you."

"But I don't know what to do." There was a hint of whine in my voice.

"You will need to figure it out."

I chewed on the tip of another finger. The manicure I'd gotten with Romona was long past saving.

"But what if I do something wrong? What if I make the wrong decision?"

"If you trust in Me, I'll give you a gentle nudge back in the right direction."

"But you know who I will be with someday?"

"Yes."

"And you won't tell me if it's Logan or not."

Another smile. "No, I won't take your love story away from you by revealing its end."

"Love story?"

"I am the Creator of love in each of its forms. Learn what pure love should be, and it will lead you to the love of your life. Be watchful of what love is not, and discernment will steer you away from what is false."

"That easy, huh?"

"It is for those who earnestly seek Me."

"Ha. Okay, so I'll give up the life map, but I think the after-death orientation would have helped me out a bit these last few weeks. Why didn't I get that like everybody else?"

He smiled. "Let's just say you are more of a 'learn through experience' type of girl."

I wrinkled my nose. There were more than a few situations that would have gone down differently had I attended orientation. Namely kissing Logan. Was that the point? Was I supposed to kiss Logan—so that I would think we were bonded, or just as a way to escape the demon? Or did that situation have no bearing on missing orientation one way or another? I looked to Him for an answer.

"Not telling." He seemed immensely amused by this situation.

I buried my face in my hands.

"Audrey, I have one more thing for you before you go."

I uncovered my face and was pushed over by a very large, very warm, and very furry body. His laughter vibrated over the mountainside as my face was covered in slobbery dog kisses. I could actually feel the emotions rolling off the animal as he tried to reach over my head to chew my ponytail—all love and joy and excitement and happiness. It almost sounded like the animal was saying *I missed you* over and over again in my head. My eyes started to fill instantly.

"Bear! I missed you so much, boy!"

The slobbering continued as I struggled to get to a sitting position. My 110-pound golden retriever wasn't done saying hello. I grabbed the dog's head to look into his eyes.

"He's been waiting for you for some time."

I hugged Bear tightly and looked past his head to see Him beaming down at the two of us.

"I thought I'd never see him again. He died a few years ago. It was so sad. We'd gotten him as a puppy, and he slept in my room every day of his life. I didn't even know he *could* be here."

"Yes, the bond between some animals and humans is very strong. They were created with a purpose as well."

"Does that mean I get to keep him?" I asked.

He only smiled and said, "I think you'll find your old friend here will be a great help to you."

My eyes welled up with tears once again. I buried my face in the soft coat of my precious friend and let it dry some of the wetness from my face. What thanks could I offer? What payment could I give?

When I looked up to attempt to give thanks, Bear and I were alone. The cloud had dissipated, and the air was clear. It was as if He'd never been there at all.

"Thank You," I whispered into the breeze. I knew He heard and was glad.

25

AWAKE

When I woke, the world was no longer bathed in gold. Instead, I was indoors and staring at a white ceiling. It was a moment before I realized I wasn't in my room in the tree, reverted back to a blank slate. I tilted my head to the side and looked through an open window to the mountains in the distance. The white peaks glistened.

I sucked in a deep breath of the fresh air that had drifted in from the opening. Windows were hard to come by when you lived underground in a tree, but not in the city. It was clear I was tucked safely in a bed in the healing center.

I was taking my change in location rather well until I spotted the figure asleep in a chair at the end of my bed. Logan was stretched out with eyes closed in a sofa chair. Hospital chairs didn't look any more comfortable here than back on Earth—the barely padded seat looked as if it would squeak and squeal with even the smallest of movements.

With his long legs extended and arms folded across his

chest, his only movements were the barely perceptible rise and fall of his chest. Logan looked as relaxed and peaceful as ever.

I took the moment to secretly soak in the sight of him, memorizing everything from head to toe. When my gaze had traveled the length of him and then back up to his face, striking blue eyes stared straight back at me. My breath caught.

He hadn't moved a muscle, but sometime during my unabashed ogle of his sleeping form he'd woken up. I blushed, seeing a piece of my hair slowly turn a rose color as well. Who knew how much of my appraisal he'd observed? It was difficult to pretend I was doing anything other than checking him out.

I tried a lame cover-up as I struggled into a sitting position and willed my hair to turn brown. A dull ache from my injured shoulder protested the movement. "I was just, ah, wondering if you were dead."

His mouth quirked up in a half-smile. "So who's this guy anyway? He just showed up sometime last night. Trotted right in here as if he owned the place, actually. I wasn't about to argue with him."

Logan pointed to something on the floor. I followed his finger to a pile of fluff on the ground. Bear was fast asleep on the cool tile floor, sprawled out on his back, tummy up, back legs spread, front legs bent and crossed as if praying, mouth open. There was a small pool of drool where his tongue lolled from his jowls.

I smiled broadly and ignored Logan for a moment to savor the simple act of remembering. My memories had been missing for so long it was now a precious gift to be able to search them, even the painful ones.

I had numerous such presents still waiting to be

unwrapped, but now was not the time to relish them. I gave silent thanks to my Creator for the return of my companion as well as the other gifts He'd bestowed on me on that mountaintop. Perhaps to others it looked as if I hadn't left this bed, but I knew better.

Logan's eyes watched me, patiently waiting for an answer.

"This is Bear."

"He certainly could be one," Logan commented.

I smiled at that. The dog was huge. "He was a Christmas gift when I was four. He stayed smaller than me for about four months, and then I never caught back up. He died a few years back. Didn't think I'd ever see him again. I'm glad I was wrong."

The memory of losing him, even knowing that he was there with me now, caused my throat to constrict. I coughed to hide the sudden emotional rush. I was going to be having a lot of those in the coming days.

"So what happened at the school?" I asked.

I glanced at Logan. Concern wrinkled his brow.

"You mean you don't remember anything?"

"I meant what happened after this?" I gingerly touched a hand to my sore shoulder, avoiding his eyes as I did so.

"Oh." It was a heartbeat before he continued. "No one was hurt, including the shooter. He's in police custody now. We'll be sending groups down to keep an eye on him to make sure the demon can't reattach itself, but considering everything—"

"Wait," I interrupted, "you mean the demon got away? Even after I cut up half its body?"

"Yes." Logan's voice turned to ice. "After I pulled it off you, it barreled through the other hunters and got away."

I was suddenly unsure whether the hardness in his voice

was directed at me or the demon, and I was too cowardly to meet his eyes and see. Silence stretched between us.

As if on cue, someone knocked on the frame of the open door. I looked up to see Romona standing outside the room, looking unsure. Nervous even. I absorbed the sight of her. How could I have spent so much time with her and not put together the pieces?

As she stood before me now, her face aged in my mind's eye. Wrinkles were added, extra laugh lines. Her hair turned grey but still remained vibrant. She'd had a scar on her left eyebrow where her sunglasses had cut her when she was playing catch with my younger brother and one of his throws went a little wild. I remembered how bad James had felt, but she'd just told him it would make her look more distinguished and get her some much-deserved respect.

And then I took in her eyes. They were always the same. Timeless. Beautiful, soulful, and rich. *My eyes,* I finally remembered. Everyone had always said I'd gotten my eyes from her. It was one feature I'd always been proud of. How amazing that now she stood before me, her body transformed back to youthfulness. Somehow she was still as much the Grandma, and the Romona, I knew and loved.

Logan cleared his throat stood. I had no idea if he knew who Romona really was, but he knew enough to know that we needed a few minutes alone. He didn't say anything when he left, just nodded to Romona on the way out. She took hold of his arm to stop him from brushing by and whispered something to him. My eyes widened because she'd grasped his bare arm just underneath the edge of his sleeve. Logan stiffened a little but didn't pull away.

"I mean it," she said softly, but with authority.

He gave a small, tight smile and another nod of his head. Romona released his arm, and he disappeared through the door and out into the hallway.

I couldn't hold back my curiosity when she turned to face me.

"What was that all about?"

"I was just thanking him. He has a hard time taking gratitude." Her eyes looked worried. "Are you okay? You've been out of it for a while."

I now understood just how deep her concern for me went. Man, how could I have missed it for so long?

A tear leaked from my right eye and clung its way down my cheek. It held onto my chin for a few stubborn moments before relinquishing its hold and plummeting to the blanket below.

"I missed you." My voice was barely a whisper, small and childlike, but I knew she heard me.

She made a noise that sounded like a half-sob and brought a hand up to cover her mouth. Matching wet trails ran down both her cheeks.

When she finally spoke, her words were as soft as my own. "You aren't upset with me?" she asked hesitantly.

At first all I could do was shake my head. When I found my voice it still shook a bit.

"No. If you had told me before I remembered myself, it probably would have weirded me out." I took a big breath to steady myself. Then suddenly another connection clicked into place, and I slapped a hand to my forehead. "Of course! Grandpa's the old guy!"

Her face split into a grin. "Oh, how I wish you could have

seen your face! You were so appalled at the idea of me being with an elderly man. I almost completely lost it that day."

I was laughing so hard my eyes started to tear up again. I only got out a few words between laughs. "That makes," I paused while I tried to suck in some air, "so much sense now!"

It took effort, but I eventually gained control of my giggles. "But wait, how is it you aren't old anymore? There are people of all different ages here. Why aren't you the age you were when you died?"

"That's mostly thanks to the job. I needed a body that was a little more nimble. Age isn't really an issue here, so a lot of people look different than when they died. Your body is a reflection of the perfect age that you need to be."

I silently sent up a prayer of gratitude that I hadn't known that before. I would have made myself crazy simply wondering how old I was when I died. But as soon as I thought it, my mind went into overdrive trying to guess how old everyone else was when they died. There was just no way to tell. Besides a few very subtle tips, I would never in a million years have guessed Romona had been well into her eighties.

With all the noise we were making, we finally managed to disturb the other resident of my room. Bear's head poked up unexpectedly, and he rested his chin on the side of my bed, seemingly waiting for something.

"Hey there, buddy, are you confused too?"

"Is that Bear?" Romona had been standing in the threshold this entire time, but she finally entered the room to greet the dog. His tail wagged so hard his backside moved back and forth with the motion. Romona dropped to her knees to take the furry dog's face in her hands and look in his eyes.

"Well I'll be. It *is* Bear. It's good to see you, old boy."

Bear answered by breaking free from her grasp and planting a sloppy kiss on her left cheek and eye.

"Oh yuck. I'd forgotten about that. He's a chronic kisser."

Romona gave the dog another affectionate scratch behind the ear, expertly dodging his second attempt at a kiss before straightening and coming to sit on the edge of my bed.

Unable to hold back any longer, I launched myself at her for a hug, just like I used to. She absorbed my weight with a grunt, but her arms tightened around me. I closed my eyes and remembered the last time I'd given her a hug like this. It had been too many years ago. I'd been only in middle school. Her death was the first I'd ever had to deal with, and it felt as if she'd taken a big chunk of me with her. I sobered when I imagined how my family was dealing with losing me right now.

Giving her a final squeeze, I pulled back to sit cross-legged, facing her. Bear's head appeared on the side of the bed between the two of us.

"I miss them already."

Romona didn't pretend to misunderstand me. She put a comforting hand on my shoulder.

"I know."

"Do you know how they're doing?"

She paused before answering. I watched her face. The maturity in her gaze now made sense. "They are . . ." she took another short break to find the right word, "coping right now."

"Is there anything we can do to help?" I expected what came next, but my heart still sank.

"No, I'm afraid not. We all have to deal with loss at one point or another. They have to learn to cling to the truths they know. We're not the ones intended to offer comfort right now."

"But if they just knew that I was okay, that I was safe, I'm sure that would—"

Romona cut me off with a look and a hand in the air.

"That's not how it works. They need to learn to move on, on their own. It's a test of their faith, and they need to push through it without us."

"But if . . ."

"I promise you, Audrey." She took my cheeks in her hands and forced me to look her in the eyes. "They have everything they need to make it through right now. No one is ever promised a life free of pain. Far from it, in fact, but they have all the comfort and support they will ever need. That and more. Your parents and siblings are well looked after right now. It's going to test your faith to believe that as well."

My heart was breaking into a million pieces, but deep down, I knew her words were true. The moisture had returned to my eyes and was spilling over before I had the opportunity to stop it. Romona pulled me toward her, and I buried my face in her shoulder and sobbed. She rubbed my back and murmured in my ears.

I don't know how long we stayed like that, but finally my sobs subsided into small hiccups. There was still an ache in my chest, but I could manage it. Something about a good cry seemed to wash my insides clean.

A wet nose pushed between us. I looked with puffy eyes to see Bear's front paws on the side of the bed. Through his heavy pants, he was letting slobber from the tip of his tongue drop to the bedding below.

We always did have trouble keeping him off the furniture. "Bear!" I gave him a halfhearted and ineffective shove. Instead of budging, he gave my cheek a lick and discovered he liked the taste of my salty tears. He attacked me to lap up the remains. With a squeal, I tried to escape by burying my head under my pillow and yelling for help. Romona laughed.

"Looks like I picked the right time to make my rounds. Damsels in distress happen to be my specialty."

Surprised to hear Jonathan's voice, I made the mistake of lifting my pillow-slash-shield and was promptly slimed by a hot wet tongue.

"Oh yuck! Bear, down!"

Having completed his mission, Bear happily planted himself back on the ground and padded over to the now unoc-cupied chair, made a short jump up, turned in two circles, and settled into a comfortable position. I shook my head at him as I wiped the saliva from my face.

With a friendly smile on his face, Jonathan watched Bear make himself at home. Jonathon wore a long white coat that made him look very much like a doctor. It came back to me in a flash that he'd told me he worked as a healer of some sort. I had a vague remembrance of hearing Logan argue with someone in the operating room before I'd passed out, but couldn't be sure if that had been him or not.

"So how's my new patient doing?" Jonathan was all smiles and confidence. Romona had quietly relinquished her spot on the bed for a seat across the room.

"Oh, hi. I mean, I'm good I guess."

I was suddenly embarrassed by the state he'd discovered me in. I was sure my hair was standing up at funny angles. My face still felt puffy, and I thought with a sudden horror that I hadn't even taken note of what I was wearing. I quickly looked down to see I was in a white tank top and hot pink scrub bottoms.

Kinda cute actually.

I self-consciously attempted to smooth my hair and snuck a peak at a few strands to make sure it was still brown. I breathed easier when I found that it was.

Jonathan's smile didn't change, and he went on unfazed by my disheveled appearance.

"Great. I came by to see if you'd woken up yet. Mind if I take a look at your shoulder while I'm here?"

Suddenly mute, I shook my head. Jonathon took a seat on my bed and moved the strap of my tank top slightly toward my neck to fully expose the bandage beneath. His expert hands found the edges and slowly peeled it away.

"You doing okay?" he asked without checking my face.

I nodded before realizing he wasn't looking and let a quiet "yes" squeak out. His fingers probed different spots on my shoulder, some more sensitive than others.

"Can you move it all right?"

Without thinking I shrugged as if to say "I guess so."

"That's good. Any residual soreness?"

"Some, but it isn't that bad."

His smile returned, and his fingers left my arm. It wasn't until they'd left that I realized I didn't feel anything from the empathy link. I remarked as much.

He nodded in confirmation. "Yes, our empathy link is kind of in the 'off' position here so we don't upset the patients."

"That makes sense."

I snuck a glance at my shoulder and sucked in a breath when I saw what was peeking out from either side of my strap. The skin had been knitted back together expertly, but there was still visible evidence of my attack.

"You okay, Audrey?" Jonathan laid his hand on my good shoulder.

"I just wasn't expecting to have scars."

Jonathan nodded, as if understanding my confusion. "Demon scars are like emotional scars you can see. They'll disappear when you've worked through the emotion. Until then, they'll stay on your skin as a reminder of what you still need to address."

The deep scars that latticed Logan's back sprang to mind. So that's most likely where he'd gotten them. There must be something he was hanging on to as well.

Jonathan was still talking with his hand familiarly on my shoulder, and he leaned in close, but I wasn't really hearing the words he was saying as I thought about Logan.

"Hmm, I'm surprised Logan hasn't come back." Romona mused loudly.

Jonathan moved back to a safe distance in response to her words.

That *was* strange. Had Logan not come back because of Jonathan? That didn't sound like something he'd do—if anything, Jonathan's presence seemed to make him overly protective, borderline possessive. Maybe since I was okay he didn't want to stick around anymore?

Jonathon cleared his throat, pulling me out of my musing. His demeanor had changed. He seemed a little nervous and unsure of himself, which weren't traits that I'd picked up on before. His eyes wouldn't meet mine and he was fidgety. It was curious behavior for him.

"Audrey, there was something else I wanted to talk to you about. I realize that I came on a little strong at first, but I truly would like the opportunity to get to know you better." His eyes shifted to Romona for a moment before finally landing on me. "I'd like to take you out sometime, if that's something you might be open to." There was a hint of hopefulness in his voice.

It took me a moment to comprehend what was going on. Jonathan was asking me out. Here, in front of my grandma-slash-best friend.

I snuck a desperate look at Romona, who was staring wide eyed at Jonathan as if she hadn't seen this one coming either. She glanced at me and offered a small shrug as if to say, "you're on your own with this one."

"Ah, well, yeah, I guess that would be okay." I fumbled through my response.

Heat was coming off of my face in massive waves. Pink hair for sure.

Jonathon smiled broadly, looking as if he'd just won the lottery. That was kind of sweet, but the sentiment was over-shadowed by my embarrassment.

"That's great! I already have something special in mind. I know you'll love it."

"Ah, okay." I sat on my hands to keep from chewing a fingernail. These types of interactions always made me uncomfortable. Unsure if he was waiting for me to say something else, I just stared at him. He stared back.

It was a few more awkward heartbeats before Jonathan broke the silence. "Looks like you'll probably get out of here today now that you're awake." He smiled and winked. "But don't worry, I know where to find you." He bent down to kiss my cheek and then turned to leave. I was left gaping in his wake.

It was only a fraction of a moment longer before I remembered Romona was still there, watching me with wise and thoughtful eyes.

"What color's my hair?"

"Do you really want to know?"

I groaned loudly. Maybe I should just turn my hair pink permanently and then no one would know when I was really humiliated. I closed my eyes for a moment to change it back.

"So have you decided what you are going to do?" Romona asked.

"About what?"

Romona wore a sly smile. "I remember when you were 8 years old and two little boys from your class had a crush on you. You got so freaked out you punched one in the nose and were so mean to the other you made him cry. I wonder how much you've matured since then?"

I'd completely forgotten about poor Rob and Peter. There were a few more details to that story, but she'd gotten the basic structure of it right. I'd gotten in a heap of trouble for punching Rob, even though I told my parents he was trying to give me cooties. Totally valid reason to defend myself. The poor kid went home with a shiner that day, but to his credit he didn't cry. Peter, on the other hand, was reduced to a pile of tears with only a few choice words. He never did look me in the eye again after that, even when we entered high school.

"Oh whatever," I batted my hand in the air as if I was brushing the whole thing away, "I was just doing my part to harden both of them up a bit. I was probably instrumental in helping them deal with an inevitable future heartbreak. Any boy who cried just because someone called him a booger-eater needs a little toughening up anyway." Seriously, who didn't eat their boogers at that age?

"Hmm, I wonder if they would look at it the same way?"

I had no idea what either of them thought about it. Rob had

moved away the next year and I never talked to Peter again. I shrugged as if I didn't care, but something about her insinuating that there was a comparison to my present day events bothered me. Maybe it was being likened to an eight year old me that irked me. Maybe it was something else. Either way, I found myself squirming uncomfortably in my bed. Desperate to change the subject, I cleared my throat then moved on.

"So, I'm a little unsure what I should call you now. 'Grandma' sounds a little funny to me. What do you think?"

Romona just shook her head with a soft smile that told me she knew exactly why I'd changed the subject, but she obliged me anyway. "I see the dilemma. I'm honestly happy with whatever you feel most comfortable calling me now. What do you think that is?"

Looking at her sitting there, I could once again see my grandmother. But in the short time I'd been here I'd gotten to know a completely new dimension of her that was fully Romona, my good friend. My head was starting to hurt as I tried to reconcile the two.

"Maybe we should stick with Romona since that's what I've been calling you since I got here. Besides, it might be strange to other people if I start calling you Grandma now."

Romona smiled and nodded in agreement.

Romona stayed with me throughout the afternoon. We shared some of our favorite memories. Sometimes laughing with each other, sometimes letting some tears fall freely. But it was a good time of remembrance. Cleansing even. And I was thankful to have someone to share it with.

Bear never left the chair he'd taken over after Logan left, and Logan never returned to reclaim it. Neither of us brought him up again, but he was never far from my thoughts. A decision was forming in my head that I wasn't ready to talk over with her.

If Romona had an inkling of what was on my mind, she never let on. For that, I was thankful. I had an overwhelming number of things to chew over, and now wasn't the time to talk them all out. I had a feeling she understood that.

Before night had a chance to fall, a pretty brunette entered the room. Glowing slightly in the familiar way I'd come to expect of angels, she cheerfully informed me that I was free to return to all my normal activities. Within a matter of minutes I was up and changed into clothes, which, after a good amount of concentrated effort, I was able to materialize all on my own. There were no discharge papers like there would have been on Earth, no pushing me out in a wheelchair or hoopla of any sort. I left as if I had been a visitor rather than a patient.

Romona started to head in the direction of my tree when I stopped her. I explained in as few words as possible that I needed to do something first. The corners of her mouth tweaked ever-so-slightly downward, but with a hug and a quick scratch for Bear she let me go, promising she'd meet me at the training center for breakfast the next day.

After watching her leave, I let out a low whistle for Bear to follow and headed in the opposite direction, knowing I'd made the right decision but already slightly regretting it. But I knew the regrets were for the wrong reasons, so I picked up my step and walked resolutely toward my fate.

26

GOOD-BYE

"*Y*ou know he was there the whole time?"

Early the next morning I stood in the hallway outside our training gym—Logan's and mine . . . ours—silently watching Logan train. The voice behind me was so soft I wasn't startled.

Lost in his routine, Logan wasn't aware I was there. It felt voyeuristic, but I figured it was only fair. Who knew how long he'd watched me in the healing center before I woke up?

"What do you mean?" My eyes stayed on Logan when I answered. I was determined to drink in as much of him as possible while it lasted.

"He was there when you were recovering. Practically every minute. I think he even slept in the chair a few nights."

I let the implications sink in. Romona, my grandmother, wouldn't be telling me this without a reason. I shook my head lightly. In the end, what did it matter? I'd already made my decision, and a few minor details weren't going to change my mind. There was a saying for that. Too little too late.

"Doesn't matter anyway," I replied.

"Do you truly mean that?"

I nodded because the words were caught in my throat. I hoped she didn't notice.

"This will change things, you know."

Another nod. Of that I was sure.

I didn't understand how she knew what was going on, but I took her continued silence as acceptance. Perhaps she'd already been notified through the chain of command. Or perhaps she just knew me that well.

She crouched down to run her hand over Bear's back. He was spread on the ground like a bearskin rug, limbs out in each direction. He closed his eyes and purred like a cat as she continued her strokes. What a weirdo. What dog actually purred? I smiled at the thought.

Her next words were laced with love and support.

"Whatever you want to do, I'm behind you. And I'm always here to talk." She stood back up and gave my shoulder a gentle squeeze.

From behind my eyes, tears threatened to break free. She reminded me so much of my mom at that moment. My constant support and sounding board. The wisdom of the generations had certainly passed through Romona to her daughter. I silently prayed some of it had also trickled down to me.

As quietly as she had appeared, she left. I stole a few more greedy moments alone before making my presence known.

Logan was really working something out on that practice dummy, delivering a series of blows so strong it rocked back on its stand again and again. I expected its head or an appendage to come flying off at any moment.

He stopped and placed his forearms on the mannequin, limply draping a hand over each shoulder as if he were fatigued and needed the support. His head hung forward, causing the longer hair to fall forward.

It was only then that I spoke up.

"Gym was my least favorite class." It wasn't what I'd intended to say, but it was what came out.

The only acknowledgement that my presence surprised him was a sudden tenseness in his shoulders, which relaxed a moment later.

As usual, Logan didn't miss a beat. "I think I could have guessed that." I heard the smile in his voice even though he was facing the opposite direction.

"I needed four gym credits to graduate, and I put them all off until the last semester. I would have had two hours of gym classes every day if I'd lived long enough. Do you have any idea how wonderful just two hours of gym sounds these days?"

He chuckled. The richness of the sound comforted my frayed emotions. "Knowing you, yes."

"I suppose someone else is getting the last laugh now."

"Well, now you know there's truth to that saying."

"Which one?"

"About God having a sense of humor."

The corners of my mouth snuck up. He did have a point. "Yes, I suppose so."

This whole time he'd remained facing his practice dummy. When he finally turned, he lifted an arm to wipe the sweat from his forehead. He'd really been going at it hard today.

Despite all the training I'd done with Logan, I'd rarely seen him sweat.

"So what was your favorite then?" he asked.

"What?" Embarrassingly enough, I'd completely forgotten what we were talking about the instant he turned and captured my gaze. His blue eyes were as mesmerizing as ever.

"Classes . . . which one was your favorite?"

"Oh." I thought about it for a second. Although everything was safely back in my brain where it belonged, there were still things I had to search through the memory catalog to find. I smiled when I found the answer I was looking for.

"Art."

"Mine too," he answered without pause.

I lifted my eyebrows in slight disbelief. Not only was I skeptical that we had something in common, but art wasn't a subject I could easily imagine Logan enjoying, let alone taking at all. But then I remembered thinking that his hands were those of an artist when we were on the beach. It was the first time he'd ever touched my skin. I was so caught off guard by the contact that I'd missed the point he was trying to make completely. The memory warmed my cheeks.

"Really?"

He nodded his head. "I liked to draw. I thought one day I might be an architect."

Now that was something I could believe. I imagined you'd have to be very precise and have a lot of patience for a career like that. As much patience as it had taken to train me.

I smiled. "I liked to draw as well, but I always imagined myself growing into a profession less practical and more whimsical. Maybe a fashion designer or makeup artist." The smile widened on my face. The irony of where I'd ended up was too thick to ignore.

Logan smiled back and shook his head as if he were thinking the same thing. After a moment his face turned more serious.

"So is everything back then?"

I sobered as well. "Yes."

"How are you doing?" he asked gently.

I shrugged and finally looked away. How should I answer that? Everything was . . . different now.

"Okay, I guess."

"That's not a real answer."

I huffed.

What was he looking for? I looked at my existence here in a whole new light now. How was I supposed to explain that to him? That no matter how much he thought I was the same, no matter how often he'd told me I would be, I wasn't.

I saw the ugliness in me so much more clearly now in light of who I was and who I wanted to be. And even though I had friends and Romona here, I grieved for a lost family. A family I was sick to think was also hurting because of me.

And it was painful.

On top of all that, I was also grieving the loss of my own life. Yes, I had an eternal life, but my plans, hopes, and dreams for the future on Earth had died with me that day. And now new ones needed to be born. It wasn't something I was going to come to terms with in a single day.

"What do you want me to say, Logan?"

He remained silent, staring at me so intently I fought the familiar urge to squirm. I wasn't sure if he was waiting for me to give him a better answer or trying to determine what to say next. It seemed as if he was working something out in his head, but I never was completely sure with him. Eventually his mouth turned down.

"I had hoped it would be better for you once you remembered. Is that not the case?"

His words surprised me. They shouldn't have. Logan was always one to cut through the layers of superficiality. Oddly enough, despite the contention it had caused between us in the past, it was one of the things I appreciated the most about him.

I answered as honestly as I dared. "Better, but different."

He nodded slowly as if he understood.

"But I'm thankful to at least have my grandma back now," I added, trying to lighten the mood.

Logan tilted his head and lifted an eyebrow in a silent question.

"You do know that Romona is my grandmother?" I asked. His eyebrows jumped up in another rare moment of being caught unawares.

"No, I can't actually say I saw that one coming," he said thoughtfully. As he began to put the pieces together, his face changed to a look of chagrin. "I suppose if I'd been paying better attention, I might have caught on. She did a good job of keeping the secret."

"Yes, from even me," I said.

"Well, I'm happy for you. To have someone here to help bridge the gap. That has to be a comfort."

I detected a hint of sadness in him. I longed to know the cause and absently took a few steps closer to him. He remained rooted in front of the practice dummy, and I was just barely over the threshold. The physical distance between us was vast considering the intimacy of our conversation, and as if pulled by a cord, I shortened the distance.

I came to my senses when I reached our customary distance and Logan hadn't made an attempt to meet me half-way. It was like hitting an invisible force field that stopped me short.

Logan regarded me with hooded eyes. I had no idea what he was thinking, but that was true of most of the time. I should have left it alone, but Romona's words swam in my head. *You know he was there the whole time.* Was it possible that meant more than I'd given it credit for? Before moving forward, I needed to know. I needed to hear it from him. No more guessing.

"Romona said you stayed at the healing center with me until I woke up. She said you even slept there."

Logan's eyes remained veiled, his gaze not quite meeting mine.

"I wanted to make sure you were all right. When I brought you back and they started to heal you, I felt . . . " He paused as if searching for the words. I held my breath, anticipating what he would say next.

". . . responsible for what happened to you out there. If I'd trained you better it wouldn't have gone down like that. You would never have rushed into the fight like that."

His hands fisted at his sides. My heart deflated along with my lungs. I wasn't sure exactly what I'd been secretly hoping he would say, but that wasn't it. Not only that, but the way he said it made me feel bad about everything, like I'd done some-thing wrong. Like I'd failed. Failed *him*.

I now knew I'd been mistaken about what I had sensed through the empathy link before I passed out in the healing center. The strong emotion had only been something fleeting after all.

"So that's why you left when I woke up. Because you were disappointed that I didn't follow directions better." It was more of a statement than a question. I already had as much of an answer as my heart could take.

Rather than replying, Logan took a step toward me, and I took one back. Confusion flickered in his eyes and perhaps hurt as well. The look was unfamiliar to me. I steeled my resolve. He was about to say something, but I went on quickly before he had a chance.

"I've asked for a different mentor."

I'd shocked him twice today. His eyebrows shot up, his eyes grew larger, and his whole body froze as if he'd been hit by a stun gun. We stood in silence for several heartbeats.

"Why?"

The one question I knew he would ask—the one I'd been dreading. He deserved an honest answer, but I wasn't ready to be that vulnerable with him.

"I don't think this," I broke eye contact, "whatever it is that we are doing, is healthy for either of us."

"Audrey, I know there are times when we frustrate each other, but I don't think—"

He wasn't getting the right idea, so I blurted the one thing I didn't want to talk about the most. "And we're not bonded."

One, two, three . . . was that Logan's heart I heard jump into his throat, or my own?

I could have once again slapped a hand right over my mouth. My whole body flushed from the tips of my toes up to the roots of my hair. I caught something out of the corner of my eye that I was fairly certain was the beginning of hot pink highlights. I couldn't worry about that now.

"What are you talking about?"

Was he seriously going to make me spell it out? That was so not fair. Sometimes things with Logan were so difficult.

I forced myself to look straight at him when I spoke. As uncomfortable as it was, this conversation was long overdue.

"When we kissed, when we were hiding from the demon, it didn't count. We didn't accidentally bond to each other."

The room was once again silent while what I'd said sunk in. An eternity seemed to pass as Logan's eyes sought to determine my truthfulness.

"Are you sure?" His voice had gone flat again. Emotionless.

I nodded my head. "Yes, we got a 'get out of jail free' card. I didn't know any better because I missed that part in orientation." And because I couldn't say the next thing while still looking at him, I dropped my gaze and stared at an invisible spot on the ground, my voice a notch softer than before. "And you, of course, didn't know I was going to attack you like that. We didn't *mean* to form a bond, so no bond was formed."

"That's not a loophole I've heard of before. Who told you that?"

"Who do you think?" I started a little at the slight note of bitterness in my own voice. The pit of embarrassment I was wallowing in was deep. I tried not to, but I snuck a peek at Logan to study his reaction. I knew it was going to be bad, but I couldn't look away.

After a moment, the implications of my words finally penetrated. I told myself the emotion I read on him shouldn't surprise me, but it did. The tension that always seemed bundled tightly around him slowly dissipated. His body relaxed as if a heavy weight had been lifted. His eyes widened slightly in awe, and his facial features softened. His lips moved in soundless words as if he was sending up a prayer. He closed his eyes for a quick moment and let out a breath of air.

His whole persona radiated relief.

That was what he felt about us not being bonded.

Relieved.

More than anything else that had happened between us, this moment hurt the worst.

When he caught me watching him, he quickly changed his expression to indifference. He waved a hand in the air as if brushing the whole thing off as no big deal. "Well, if that's the case, then I don't see the complication with us continuing to train."

The pieces snapped together for me. He'd probably never told me about being bonded because he couldn't figure out why he felt nothing for me. Now he could move forward without that enigma nagging at him.

You stupid head, I wanted to shout. *Just because you weren't affected by that kiss doesn't mean I wasn't!*

I marveled for a moment at my ability to tuck the hurt into a hardened corner of my heart. Hurt that was teetering on the edge of anger and weariness. Uncharacteristically, the scales were tipping to the latter. I didn't want to obsess over what I thought of Logan anymore.

I was tired of it.

I didn't want to spend eternity next to someone who didn't want me back. I was fatigued from wondering what he thought of me and who else he was spending his time with, and always making sure I knew where he was in a crowd. Our relationship might just be peachy for him, but it was unhealthy for me.

I needed to move on. *I* needed to deal with mourning the loss of my family and working on who I was created to be.

I'd done what God said to do and tried to think about our relationship with my head and my heart, and this was what I now realized. I was finally able to be honest enough with myself to realize Logan was occupying way too much of my brain power. And I wanted it back for more important things.

Gosh, I could have hit him right then and there for his self-centeredness.

My next words escaped a few degrees colder than I had intended. "You don't need to understand, just to accept. The decision's already been made. I talked with administration yesterday after leaving the healing center. They're going to assign someone else to continue training me right away."

I turned to leave. I wanted to be anywhere but there right now.

I hadn't gotten two steps before Logan stopped me. He grabbed my bare arm and turned me to face him. His emotions slammed into me hard. I sucked in a breath of air. He was angry, and confused, and above all, very hurt. Some of those emotions mirrored my own at the moment, but surely for different reasons.

He released my arm as suddenly as he'd taken it. I looked up to see a blue fire blazing in his eyes. His stoic mask had melted completely, and I was reminded of how he'd looked at me after I'd been wounded by the demon. I couldn't understand how this situation was similar.

"Do you not care what I think about this?" In contrast to his face, his words were spoken softly and without emotion.

"Logan, I'm just . . ." I didn't know what to say to him to

make him understand. "Tired. I'm just tired." It was the closest to the truth I could bear to admit.

He went on as if I hadn't spoken. "Because this doesn't make sense to me. I can't understand why this won't work. We had already started to make it work. Why can't we just be friends and move forward?"

I shook my head sadly. I couldn't make myself meet his eyes anymore. "I'm sorry, Logan, I'm not going to be able to do that."

"Why not?" The words were spoken as chillingly softly as before, but with a tinge of vulnerability that coaxed my eyes to his face. There, I discovered a question. A need for understanding that I couldn't, wouldn't, fully give him.

I thought back to the moments of jealousy I'd felt around Kaitlin and the times we'd fought over nothing. I thought back to all the moments of longing and the confusion they brought with them. I wasn't going to sentence myself to an eternity of that.

With a sudden clarity, I realized that Logan and I had never been friends, and even if feigning friendship were a way to keep him close, we would never be that to each other. And that was something he needed to hear.

"We were never friends, Logan. We can't go back to something we never were."

"I don't believe that. I don't accept that." His voice was beginning to take on an intensity that matched his face.

I shook my head. I wasn't going to bare my heart fully to him. I took a step back to create more physical distance between us. A move I'd learned from him. I needed that space to stand my ground.

"You're going to have to accept that. I'm not willing to do

this anymore." This wasn't some battle of wills we were going to have to fight out. He needed to realize that.

Logan was tense all over. "I'm not going to pretend to know exactly how you got to this point, but it seems to me you are running away, and that can't be the answer. Why aren't you willing to fight through this, whatever it is? Because that's what I'm willing to do."

The blaze in his eyes smoldered. Anger still shimmered there, but also a bit of desperation. I stood firm and tried to hold the pieces of my heart together. I wasn't about to share my feelings for him when it wasn't something he was capable of returning. I knew that something better was intended, and that this, whatever it was, had to change. We were meant for so much more, and if that couldn't be realized between us, then we weren't meant to be anything to each other.

"I'm not running away. I'm running to something. Something new."

Logan turned into a block of cold steel. His posture went from intense and focused to distant and guarded, and the life in his eyes dulled.

"Something new," he repeated. "And you're telling me I'd just be in the way?"

Well no, that was not exactly what I meant. I mean, yes it was, but an uneasiness coiled in my gut, as if he was going down the wrong rabbit hole. Something I'd said had stung him on a personal level, and he'd retreated behind his mask. The one he put on to protect himself. My heart wanted to reach out and rip the disguise off. My resolve was shaken.

But all I had to say was *yes*, and it would be done. I'd be free. Logan would let me go without grilling me for more information, without trying to force my hand.

"Maybe." I stopped.

What was I going to say? Maybe it would be okay if he remained my mentor? Maybe in time we could be friends? Maybe someday things would all work out and we'd be able to laugh at how messed up I'd thought this was?

But I couldn't say that. I wasn't willing to take a chance on those maybes.

"Maybe I'll see you around."

Turning my back on him, I headed for the exit with a heavy heart, no longer sure I'd done the right thing. I walked briskly out of the training gym, forcing my legs to move at an even pace, hearing Bear's feet padding along behind me after I crossed the threshold.

I counted the steps as I moved away from Logan. Ten, then fifteen, then thirty-five. How many more steps would I have to hold off the tide before I got back to the safety of my room? Before I could tend to the internal wounds that had just been inflicted?

Too many was the answer, and I ducked inside the girls locker room before I completely lost it. I ran to the first steam shower and turned it on full blast, stepping in with my clothes fully on and letting the hot water wash away the tears already running down my face.

27
MENTORS

"Oh, sorry. I thought this was my new training gym."

The man in the middle of the room was so frail I had no idea what he could be doing in the training center, let alone my gym. He leaned heavily on a cane as he slowly turned toward me, his back bent at the shoulders.

"I'm sorry, but can I help you find something? Are you lost or anything?"

Clear grey eyes stared back at me before crinkling heavily at the corners when he smiled. He nodded his head, and I was momentarily distracted by the poof of white poodle-like hair that bobbed along with it.

"Why, yes you can. I'm looking for Audrey Lyons."

"That's me, actually." But I was drawing a blank as to why this old man was looking for me.

"Why, so it is. Audrey, it's nice to finally meet you. I'm your new mentor."

My eyes widened, and my mouth fell open.

"You're a hunter?" I bluntly asked.

Would there ever be a time I handled the unexpected gracefully?

The smile on the old man's face widened, creating even more wrinkles and divots. "I'm actually more of a jack of all trades. We thought you could use me during your next phase of training."

So now my new trainer wasn't even a real hunter. What was going on?

"I don't mean to be rude, sir, but what does that mean? New phase?"

"I'm sure you'll see soon enough. But let me at least properly introduce myself." He took a few moments to shuffle over to me and held out his gnarled hand, which looked as if it had been ravaged not only by time but also by arthritis. "You can call me Hugo. I believe we are going to make a great team."

My mind was a skeptical mess as I reached for his feeble hand. But when my palm connected with his, a blast of power shot through his surprisingly sturdy handshake. My head jerked up, and I fastened on his sharp eyes. Whoever this man was, what he appeared to be on the outside wasn't all there was to him.

A genuine smile grew on my face. Maybe one day people would say the same about me?

I had the sudden premonition that the future was going to take some interesting turns, starting with this one. Anticipation bloomed in my chest. The afterlife had proven to be a bucket full of the unexpected, so why should Hugo be any different? I was no longer certain about my happily-ever-after ending, but if this was my journey, it was about time I started looking forward to the ride.

"Where do we begin?"

EPILOGUE

"She is the one!" the creature hissed. It was curled in on itself in the corner, writhing and barely able to speak. Its barbed tail had been sliced off, along with a good portion of its left front flank. The hunk of charred meat, for that was all he considered the creature to be, still lived only for verification. Verification of what he already knew to be true, for he'd seen it for himself.

He smiled. She was vulnerable. Throwing herself into a fight she wasn't ready for. Whether from pride or sheer ignorance he didn't know, nor did he care. Either weakness was as deadly as the other, exploitable and leading easily to ruin. He'd been using them for as long as the feeble humans had roamed the Earth.

She was the key to his freedom. By her hand he would be freed to finish the task he'd set out to accomplish so many millennia ago. He'd reign over the Heavens and the Earth and any other realms there were to be ruled.

A pain-filled screech from the thrashing beast in the corner only stirred annoyance in him. With eyes narrowed in irritation, he turned to it. His jaws opened and disjointed like a snake's.

"No!" the creature screamed its plea right before the liquid fire burst from his open mouth, engulfing it. It took longer than he liked for the shrieks to subside and the beast's body to crumble completely. He didn't bother giving the remains another look as he walked into the adjoining room, slipping on his human skin as he did.

When the door clicked shut behind him, the human seated carelessly in front of the fire looked up with one dark brow cocked.

"A mercy, I assure you." He smoothly answered the unasked question.

"Of course." The human replied with a half-smile on his face, seemingly unconvinced.

"I have the confirmation I need. What else do we know?"

The human stood as he answered. "We received a report that she's not training with Logan anymore."

He raised an eyebrow of his own, feeling the fake flesh stretch and bunch on his face. That was interesting. He'd seen the result of Logan's training firsthand—they both had. The boy had worked miracles in a short time. Losing Logan as a trainer was most likely to their benefit. But that depended entirely on the replacement.

"Do you know who has been reassigned to her?"

"Our sources weren't sure but said that would be confirmed on the next report." As if knowing the significance of his next words, the human paused. An arrogant smile played across his features. "The reassignment was at her request."

Another surprise, but this time it didn't show on his face. Letting her decide to leave Logan was a bold move.

He dismissed the human with a flick of his hand, resisting the familiar urge to swat. This one, in particular, was useful. Misguided to think they would ever truly be allies, but useful nonetheless.

The manipulation was already forming in his head as the fallen human bowed and exited the room. He was too close to what he wanted for anything to stand in his way.

PLEASE WRITE A REVIEW

Reviews are the lifeblood of authors and your opinion will help others decide to read my books. If you want to see more from me, please leave a review.

Will you please write a review?
http://review.HuntressBook.com

Thank you for your help!

~ Julie

JOIN THE NEWSLETTER
GET FREE UPDATES & PRIZES

Please consider joining my exclusive email newsletter. You'll be notified as new books are available, get exclusive bonus scenes, previews, ridiculous videos, and you'll be eligible for special giveaways. Occasionally, you will see puppies. 🐶

Sign up for snarky funsies:
JulieHallAuthor.com/newsletter

I respect your privacy. No spam.
Unsubscribe anytime. 🩶

JOIN THE FAN CLUB
ON FACEBOOK

If you love my books, get involved and get exclusive sneak peeks before anyone else. Sometimes I even give out free puppies (#jokingnotjoking).

You'll get to know other passionate readers like you, and you'll get to know me better too! It'll be fun!

Join the Fan Club on Facebook:
facebook.com/groups/juliehall

See you in there!
~ Julie

ABOUT THE AUTHOR
JULIE HALL

My name is Julie Hall and I'm a USA TODAY bestselling, multiple award-winning author. I read and write YA para-normal / fantasy novels, love doodle dogs and drink Red Bull, but not necessarily in that order.

My daughter says my super power is sleeping all day and writing all night . . . and well, she wouldn't be wrong.

I believe novels are best enjoyed in community. As such, I want to hear from you! Please connect with me as I regularly give out sneak peeks, deleted scenes, prizes, and other freebies to my friends and newsletter subscribers.

Visit my website:
JulieHallAuthor.com

Get my other books:
amazon.com/author/julieghall

Join the Fan Club:
facebook.com/groups/juliehall

Get exclusive updates by email:
JulieHallAuthor.com/newsletter

Find me on:

a amazon.com/author/julieghall
f facebook.com/JulieHallAuthor
BB bookbub.com/authors/julie-hall-7c80af95-5dda-449a-8130-3e219d5b00ee
g goodreads.com/JulieHallAuthor
O instagram.com/Julie.Hall.Author
▶ youtube.com/JulieHallAuthor

ACKNOWLEDGMENTS

A special thanks goes out to everyone who worked directly with me and behind the scenes to make sure the best possible version of *Huntress*, from cover to cover, was presented to the world. A lot of blood, sweat, and tears (okay, really it was mostly tears) went into the publication of this novel and there are a few individuals I need to take a moment to thank personally.

A huge thanks to my three Rachels! Each of these ladies, instrumental to the editing of *Huntress*, is forever special to me. Rachel #1 was never afraid to tell me when something was super cheesy and always came through in a pinch. Rachel #2 was my very first beta reader and would-be editor. She suffered through my terrible first version and offered encouragement when it was so desperately needed. My newest Rachel, beloved editor Rachel Starr Thomas, is now forever and henceforth (in my mind) dubbed Rachel #3. She not only taught me to be a better writer through her patience and edits, but also picked through my manuscript with a fine-toothed comb.

Thanks to my dear friends and first writing group, Carrie and Stephen Robertson. Without their help, my meager writings would never have spring-boarded into something more. Both are phenomenal writers. I look forward to reading their completed work someday soon.

My biggest cheerleader (although he'd prefer not to be labeled that way) is the love of my life, my husband, Lucas. He encouraged, loved, and sometimes even pushed and prodded me along the way. Without him, my dream of writing a novel would not have been accomplished. To all the single ladies out there, never sell yourself short. Although the man that holds my heart is truly one of a kind, there are men equally fabulous out there.

My family, in-laws and otherwise, also deserve a good, old-fashioned shout out. Even though I quit my job to chase what probably looked like a pipe dream, every single one of them lent me their support.

A very important thanks to all my other beta readers and life encouragers, Tracy, Joy, Bri, Kim, Rebecca, Laurie, and all "my girls" over the last few years who served as inspiration for me. If you look hard enough, you may find parts of yourself in one of my characters!

And thanks to my God, who has been with me every step of the way. If nothing else ever came of *Huntress* but the time I spent writing with Him, it still would have been worthwhile.

BOOKS BY JULIE HALL

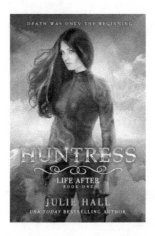

Huntress (Life After Book 1)

www.HuntressBook.com

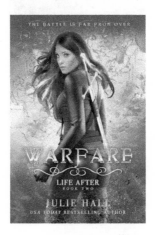

Warfare (Life After Book 2)

www.WarfareBook.com

Dominion (Life After Book 3)

www.DominionBook.com

Logan (A Life After Companion Story)

www.LoganBook.com

Life After - The Complete Series (Books 1-4)

www.LifeAfterSet.com

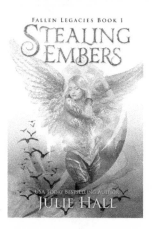

Stealing Embers (Fallen Legacies Book 1)

www.StealingEmbers.com

Forging Darkness (Fallen Legacies Book 2)

www.ForgingDarkness.com

AUDIOBOOKS BY JULIE HALL

My books are also available on Audible!

http://Audio.JulieHallAuthor.com

CPSIA information can be obtained
at www.ICGtesting.com
Printed in the USA
LVHW091534130421
684378LV00019B/571/J